HEART STOPPER

SPECIAL EDITION

MICHELLE HERCULES

INFINITE SKY PUBLISHING

Heart Stopper © 2020 by Michelle Hercules

This book is a work of fiction. Names, characters, places, and incidents either are products of the author's imagination or are used fictitiously. Any resemblance to actual persons, living or dead, events, or locales is entirely coincidental.

Editor: Hot Tree Editing
Illustration: Seaj Art

Paperback ISBN: 978-1-950991-73-0

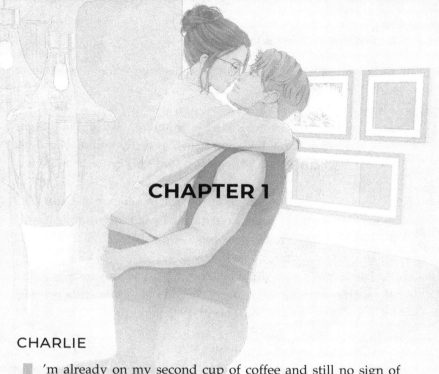

CHAPTER 1

CHARLIE

'm already on my second cup of coffee and still no sign of Troy Alexander, the star of the Rushmore Rebels football team, who I have to interview for the school newspaper. I almost strangled Blake when he gave me the last-minute assignment. It was only his promise to be my bitch in next week's LARP event that convinced me to step in for Ludwig, the dude who usually covers the sports section of the paper.

Football and jocks are not in my orbit, so I spent the last twenty minutes learning as much as I could about the Rushmore Rebels' quarterback. People seem to regard him like a god, and honestly, no one deserves to be treated as such. He has an okay average, winning more games than losing them. This year is different though. He's a senior, and most of the time, that's when the players really try to give their all. But Troy seems to have lost his steam, not really going the extra mile when he should. That's according to the notes I got from Ludwig, of course. I wouldn't be able to tell the difference if I watched a game, which I haven't.

Since the jerkface is late, I snoop his social media profiles. I can't gather much from Facebook unless I'm friends with him, and there's no chance I'll send a request, not when his Instagram feed has plenty of photos that paint a picture of who Troy Alexander is. It's clear the guy has acquired a taste for high-adrenaline sports, from skydiving to mountain climbing. Some are quite intense and dangerous, such as extreme snowboarding. I wonder what his coach has to say about his quarterback's new hobby.

I swallow the last drops of my coffee, already debating if I should go for a third cup, but when I can't stop bouncing my legs up and down, I have my answer. I'm already jittery as hell; inhaling more caffeine is definitely a bad idea.

The coffee shop's doorbell chimes, earning my attention. But it's not Troy coming in, only a couple of sorority girls wearing their matching pink hoodies with their house's emblem embroidered on them.

Clenching my teeth, I check the time. *Fuck.* He's forty minutes late. It's safe to assume he stood me up. I lost track of time, or I wouldn't have waited so long. *Great.*

I'm busy texting Blake, telling him he owes me big time, when someone drops onto the chair opposite mine. It's Troy, looking hotter than Hades in casual jeans and a T-shirt. Golden hair, golden skin, and a face that belongs on the cover of a magazine. He's sex on a stick, something I wasn't prepared for. His Instagram pictures don't really do him justice.

"Hi, you must be Ludwig's replacement. Have you been waiting long?" He smiles as if he didn't already know the answer to that.

I pick my jaw up from the floor, hoping he didn't catch me drooling, and frown. "How did you know who I was?"

"You look like the type who works for the paper." He shrugs, then eyes the two girls who entered the coffee shop earlier, giving them a wolfish grin. They were already ogling him, but Troy's attention sends them into a fit of giggles.

Really?

"What's that supposed to mean?" I snap.

Troy faces me again, sporting an innocent expression. "Are you that unaware of the vibe you give off?"

I lean back, crossing my arms over my chest. "Enlighten me."

His lips curl into a smirk while his eyes dance with glee. "Your T-shirt with the paper's logo. That's how I knew."

Heat rushes to my cheeks. I had completely forgotten I was wearing it.

"But you also have the nerd look about you," he continues, renewing my irritation with him.

"Nerd look, huh? Could it be my glasses?" I push the frames back up my nose using my middle finger.

Troy quirks an eyebrow. "Probably. Can we please make this a quickie? I have places to be."

I scoff. "You have some nerve. You're the one who was forty minutes late!"

He flinches as if my outburst surprised him. "Gee, I'm sorry, okay? I had to deal with a situation. I'm here now, so fire away."

Flaring my nostrils, I grab my phone. "Is it okay if I record this?"

"Sure. Go ahead."

"So, Troy, when did you decide not to give a fuck about football anymore?"

He doesn't answer for a couple of beats, narrowing his eyes. "Excuse me?"

"I mean, your performance in the last game was half-assed at best, and you only won because the other team was awful."

A humorless laugh escapes his lips. "So, this is how it's going to be, huh? I'm late a few minutes, and you're going to pull the heinous bitch card."

I try not to wince at his name-calling, but if I'm going to succeed in this profession, I can't let assholes get under my skin. "Oh, sweetie. It's cute that you think I'm asking tough questions because I'm mad at you. But we both know the truth. You messed up royally in the previous game. What was your excuse? Did you also have to deal with a *situation* then?"

Troy's face turns ashen, and his jaw clenches tight as he shoots daggers from his eyes. I notice his balled fists on the table and how his breathing is shallow now. Boy, I got to him good. I feel kind of guilty. You never know what issues people are dealing with.

He stands up suddenly, almost toppling his chair over. "We're done."

Shit. Maybe I went too far.

TROY

Fuck. I knew today was going to be hell. I can always count on everything going wrong whenever I have to meet my mother. Sometimes I suspect she's a witch because she sure as shit can hex my life. We had our monthly lunch at an upscale private club, during which she spent the hour downing martinis and picking on my sister, Jane, and me. Well, she mostly enjoys criticizing Jane. It's her feeble attempt to act motherly.

I can handle Mommy Dearest's harsh words, but poor Jane takes everything to heart. The more Mom talks, the more my sister shrinks into herself. It pisses me off. I was late for my interview with that shrew from the paper because I'd had to undo all the damage Mom had done to Jane.

I can't believe I let that Lois Lane wannabe get under my skin. To be fair, I had already been on edge. I should have just rescheduled the damn meeting. What I shouldn't have done is storm out of the coffee shop like a coward. No wonder my blood is still boiling.

Who does she think she is to judge me like that? I doubt she knows anything about football or even attended the last game. She'd have been with Ludwig, and I'd have remembered a face like hers. Too fucking pretty and doesn't even know it. *Damn it.* She had to go and be a bitch.

Coach Clarkson already gave me a tongue-lashing for sucking last Saturday. I had fucked up. My head wasn't in the game, but explaining why wasn't an option. Sure, if the coach knew the truth, he wouldn't have given me such a hard time. Only I'd rather people believe I slacked off for no good reason than them know it was the anniversary of Robbie's death. No one knows, not even my closest friends. What would they think if they knew I'd let my brother die?

I can't go back to the mausoleum I call home in this state. I don't want to be alone right now, and I have too much pent-up aggression that needs to go somewhere, so I shoot a quick text to Andreas, telling him I'm headed to the gym. He's always game for a workout. The guy has an infinite supply of energy. He's like the Energizer Bunny, a comparison that suits him well in more ways than one. The fucker is a damn Casanova and has probably banged his way to New Zealand and back.

When I park in front of the upscale warehouse-style gym, my anger has decreased by half. I spot Andreas's Bronco two spots to my left. No surprise he's already here. He, unlike me, lives right on campus in a shared apartment with Danny Hudson, a freshman who will probably take my place as the new QB next year.

I grab my duffel bag from the trunk and head inside the building. It's the middle of the afternoon, and the place is pretty packed. It annoys me to work out in a full house, but beggars can't be choosers.

I quickly change and then head to the gym's main room. Andreas is spotting Danny at the bench press when I find them.

"Dude, who stole your cookie?" he asks.

I roll my eyes. Everything out of the guy's mouth is related to food or girls. "It's one of those days. I had lunch with my mother and Jane earlier. You know how those events usually go."

"Like eating sawdust?" Danny chimes in.

"Pretty much."

"How is Jane doing? I haven't seen her in months," Andreas asks casually, not even glancing in my direction.

He knows he's not allowed to get near my sister or entertain any ideas about her. She's still in high school, for starters. Also, she doesn't need to get her heart broken by the most notorious manwhore on campus.

"Jane is fine," I reply through clenched teeth.

"Whoa. You don't need to bite my head off. I was just asking."

"You look pissed," Danny pipes up. "Are you still sour about your talk with the coach?"

"Nah. I'm over that," I lie. I hate that I screwed up, but wallowing in it won't help either. "He had the right to chew my ass. My current mood is in part to blame on a fucking nosy reporter from the school paper."

"Wait. I thought Ludwig was a buddy of yours." Andreas arches his eyebrows.

"He couldn't make it, and his replacement was a fucking bitch. She dared to ask when I stopped giving a fuck about football."

"Wow. That's savage." Danny chuckles. "Your charming skills didn't work on her?"

"I wasn't myself."

"Please tell me you put the bitch back in her place," Andreas retorts angrily.

I take Danny's spot on the bench. "That's what I should have done. Instead, I left."

Andreas whistles. "Troy Alexander avoiding a confrontation. That's new. Are you sure you didn't sleep with her and forget to call the next day?"

"Unlike yours, my bedroom doesn't have a revolving door. I remember my hookups."

He shrugs. "If you say so."

"Can we drop the subject? I didn't come here to gossip like a fucking sorority girl."

A wicked grin appears on Andreas's face. "Speaking of sorority girls...."

He proceeds to tell us about his latest sexual escapade, not sparing us any details, but I tune him out. No matter how much I want to forget what happened in the coffee shop, I can't get the Lois Lane wannabe out of my head.

Damn it.

CHAPTER 2

CHARLIE

'm in the zone, my fingers flying over the keyboard, when Blake sits on the edge of my desk. I ignore him. It took forever for me to get a good flow going, and he's not going to mess it up.

Wishful thinking.

Blake is a pest and clears his throat, as if his butt occupying precious space on my workstation wasn't obvious enough.

With a sigh, I lean back in my chair and glance at him. "What?"

"What the hell did you just send me?"

I fake an air of innocence. "You have to be more specific than that."

"Cut the bullshit, Charlie. You know I can't publish that article about Troy. You destroyed him. Shit, I've seen movie critics be kinder to *The Phantom Menace*."

"I only wrote what was presented to me. It's not my fault Troy bailed from the interview when I asked the tough questions."

"Come on, Charlie. I know you. You can't fool me with your

angelic face. I've seen your dark side, and it's mean as fuck. You got mad at Troy because he was late, and you decided to get revenge. You can do that on your own time, not in my paper." He jumps off the desk, fixing his tweed jacket in the process.

Blake is the poster child for the dress-for-the-job-you-want mentality, hence the stupid jacket and slacks. His dark hair is combed back, highlighting his widow's peak and pale complexion. It's not by chance that he plays a vampire in our ongoing LARP game.

We've known each other since kindergarten, and we dated in high school. Most exes can't remain friends, but Blake and I had a solid friendship before, which helped. And the decision to break up was mutual.

"Whatever. I'm not rewriting it." I turn to my screen.

"We can't simply not run the interview!"

I shrug. "Get Ludwig to write one for you. He's buddies with Troy. I'm sure he can come up with a bullshit article that highlights all of Troy's assets."

"You can be such a bitch sometimes," he mumbles.

"Heinous bitch. That's what Troy said." I smirk.

"Did he really call you that?"

I look at Blake, noticing the deep frown. He can call me names—*sometimes*, when I deserve it—but we have the relationship for that. He won't tolerate any jerk disrespecting me.

"Chill, okay? Technically, he said I was pulling the heinous bitch card, which, to be fair, I was. You can put away your knight in shining armor outfit for now."

He clamps his jaw shut, but he'll ruminate on that for hours. "If you were trying to get me to publish your interview, it won't work. I'll think of something to fill that spot."

"Whatever."

I don't care one way or another. I wrote the article, which served as a way to get rid of the anger. I might also have tweeted about it, but no one in Troy's circle follows me, so the chances he'll read it are slim.

I'm fine if my article never gets published. I have bigger fish to fry. I'm writing the storyline for next weekend's LARP event, and it needs to be finished today. Most of the time I don't mind this side job. It's fun to come up with crazy stories that will be acted out, but I've had to work on several assignments for school as well, which has made my schedule this week hell.

A text message pops on my screen. It's from Ben, my baby brother. I see it's a picture, so I click on it. A smile blossoms on my lips. Ben finally finished his costume for this weekend. His character is a troll hunter and, as such, needs several props. He's been working on that project for months. I reply with a heart emoji.

Growing up, Ben and I shared our love for fantasy worlds and grand quest stories, so it's not a surprise we both got into LARPing. He found it first, a suggestion from the school counselor to help him with his social anxiety.

"Wow, did you see that? Ben is looking badass," Blake says from across the room.

No surprise Ben also texted Blake. They're close.

"Yeah. I can't wait for this weekend."

"Me neither. How is that storyline coming along?"

"I'm almost done."

"If you make me look good, I'll forgive you for the Troy mishap." He winks at me.

"You're out of your mind. You've already agreed to be my bitch. No backsies."

"Ugh. You're the worst."

"I'm going to ask again. Why aren't you two dating?" Angelica, the newest member of the *Rushmore Gazette*, asks.

"Been there, done that, bought the T-shirt," I reply with a shake of my head.

"But you have great chemistry."

Blake and I trade glances, then burst out laughing.

"What's so funny?" The poor girl alternates looking between us.

"Maybe one day we'll tell you," I say.

Unlikely.

Blake and I are the perfect match on paper. We like the same movies, the same books, are into similar hobbies, and mesh really well intellectually. But chemistry, the stuff that makes my knees go weak and my stomach turn into knots, is what we never had or will.

"Are you going to the Pike party tonight?" She changes the subject, thankfully.

Blake snorts. "Not in this lifetime."

Angelica gets the dumbfounded look again, so I'm quick to explain, "Blake doesn't do Greek Row."

"Why not?"

"Because they're all fucking assholes," he replies angrily.

She glances at me for further explanation, but I just shrug. That's Blake's issue. It's up to him to elaborate.

"We also have a LARP meeting tonight," I add.

"Oh, that's the Live Action Role Playing thingy, right?"

"Yep."

"I've always thought people who were into those things were a bunch of weirdos, but you guys aren't."

My spine goes taut, and I see Blake has a similar reaction to mine. Angelica's comment wasn't malicious, but it's hard not to get defensive.

"How do you know we aren't weirdos?" Blake raises an eyebrow.

Angelica's cheeks turn bright pink, and she drops her gaze to her laptop, avoiding eye contact. "I have to finish this article before my English Lit class."

Blake and I share a what-can-you-do glance. A second later, he sends me a message through Facebook.

"I'm kind of tired of people's bullshit. Aren't you?"

"Since when do you care about what people think?"

"I don't."

"Hmm. It sounds like you do, or is it Angelica's opinion that you care about?"

"Ha-ha. She's too vapid for my taste."

"Oh, look who's judging now."

"Shut up. What time are you picking me up?"

"Excuse me? Why do I have to drive?"

"Because my car is being serviced."

"What about Fred?"

"He's going straight from the store. He said he has a surprise for us."

"Oh, I love Fred's surprises."

"Samesies."

I chuckle out loud. *"Samesies?* What are you now, a thirteen-year-old girl?"

"I'm practicing being your bitch for this weekend. LOL."

"Right. I'll pick you up at five."

"Sounds good."

Fred is one of my best friends, but he's also a lunatic with mad convincing skills. If the guy wasn't an artist, he'd be a fantastic salesman. It's the only explanation for what's happening just outside of Zuko's Diner in the pouring rain.

The California sky decided to drop on us with all its fury as we were taking pictures, wearing Fred's surprise. His father owns one of the biggest movie prop companies in LA, and he scored us some sick postapocalyptic costumes. It won't work for our current LARP theme since we're not doing the *Mad Max* thing, but it was too badass to resist trying them on.

"I think we're ruining the pictures with our umbrellas," I joke.

"I'm not getting this baby wet," Blake replies.

"Just take the damn picture already," Fred shouts at Sylvana, the coordinator of our LARP group, who also happens to be his cousin.

"Stop talking and strike a pose, dumbasses," she fires back.

We have fun for about ten seconds until Sylvana demands to be in the pictures too. I remove my headgear and then trade places with her. Despite the rain, the sun hasn't set yet, and the clouds are scattered, so it's not as dark as it could be. I wait for them to get in position, aiming the phone in their direction. I only manage to take one photo before a splash of cold water drenches the back of my pants.

I yell and then turn around to curse at the driver who sped over the puddle near the curb. The four-wheel-drive truck stops not too far from us at a red light. I can't see his face, but the license plate says it all—ALXNDR7. It's Troy's fucking truck.

Son of a bitch.

He lowers his window and waves at me before speeding off as the light turns green.

"Who was that?" Sylvana asks.

"Troy Alexander, Rushmore Rebels' quarterback," I reply.

"Did he run over that puddle on purpose?" Fred asks.

"Sure looks like it." I pat my butt, confirming that it's soaking wet, underwear included.

Shit. I have to go home.

"What an ass," Fred replies.

"You know what?" Blake chimes in. "Fuck him and the football team. I'm running the article you wrote."

"What about not using the paper for revenge?"

He looks straight into my eyes. "That fucker just made it personal. No one messes with my staff."

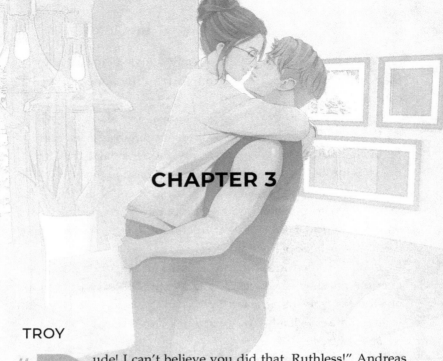

CHAPTER 3

TROY

"Dude! I can't believe you did that. Ruthless!" Andreas laughs from shotgun.

"Shit, man. Remind me never to get on your bad side," Danny pipes up from the back.

I tighten my hold on the steering wheel while I wrestle with the immediate guilt that followed my impulsive act. I'm not an asshole, and I usually don't hold on to grudges. I thought I was past my anger with the little reporter until I found her tweet about me. She called the experience of meeting me akin to attempting a conversation with a Neanderthal and said she'd have more luck with the caveman from the Geico commercial.

Once again, I let her get under my skin, and the result was me acting exactly like she'd said I did. It's my fault for cyberstalking her. I learned her full name from the email Ludwig had sent me. Charlie Fontaine. I was quick to find all her social media profiles, and that included her tweet about me. She didn't mention me again, but that one judgmental paragraph was enough to set me on edge.

"Accidents happen. It's her fault for standing near a puddle."

"Sure, like you didn't accelerate on purpose." Andreas chuckles.

"Can we drop this? Charlie is taking too much airtime."

"Charlie? So, you learned her name finally?" Danny makes that annoying remark.

"You'd better shut your piehole before I make you walk back to campus."

"Gee, relax."

"Are you coming to the Pike party?" Andreas finally changes the subject.

"A frat party? Not in the mood to hang out with that crowd. Besides, I have plans."

"Oh yeah? A hot date, or are you back to eating old porridge?"

"Man, you have to stop with the bad food analogies," Danny retorts.

"I couldn't agree more," I grumble. "And no, I don't have a date."

"It's old porridge. I knew it. You have to stop sleeping with your ex, man. It's not healthy."

"For the thousandth time, I'm not sleeping with Brooke," I grit out. "We just chatted after that one game when she came to visit—that's all. Besides, she lives in New York, remember?"

"Okay then. If you say so," Andreas replies sarcastically.

"Whatever. Believe what you want. I promised Grandma I'd have dinner with her. That's my hot date."

"Ah, cool. Is Jane going too?" Andreas looks out the window casually, but his left leg begins to bounce nervously.

What's up with him?

"Yeah. I have to pick her up in thirty."

"Where are you heading for dinner? I could eat."

I peel my gaze from the road for a second to glower at him. "Did you just ask to tag along to a family dinner? Are you for real?"

He shrugs. "What? We're friends, and your grandma loves me."

"Sorry, buddy, but I have to get back home," Danny interjects. "I have a major test tomorrow that I have to study for."

"No worries. I'm dropping *both* of you off first."

"Wow, really? You're terrified that your grandma loves me more than you, huh?"

I roll my eyes. "Yeah, that's it."

I wouldn't mind Andreas tagging along if it was only me. But Jane is in the mix, and I really don't want him near her. My sister is shy and completely different than the girls Andreas goes for, but she's a knockout, and bro code or not, I won't risk getting her on his radar.

CHARLIE

Things couldn't get any worse. On my way back to the house I share with three other girls, I receive a text from Vivian, one of my roommates, telling me there's been a fire at our place. When I get there, the firemen have already put it out—it was concentrated in the kitchen, thankfully—but we can't stay there. They discovered what we'd already known all along—the house is a freaking hazard and in violation of several housing codes. Long story short, I'm homeless.

"Shit. Where are we going to live?" I ask Vivian while we wait outside for the firemen to allow us in to collect our things.

"My boyfriend said I can move in with him, so this has turned out great for me." She smiles from ear to ear.

"Wasn't he totally against commitment?"

"Yeah. This fire was divine intervention."

"More like cheapskate-landlord neglect." I pull up my phone to text my parents. They'll tell me to stay with them until I find a new place, but they live an hour from campus. The commute will kill me.

"What are you wearing anyway? I thought your LARP deal was this weekend," Vivian asks.

"Oh, this was a gift from Fred."

She gives me an elevator glance, arching her eyebrows. "Interesting gift. It'd be great for Halloween, although it's not very sexy."

"Hmm, I don't know. I guess if I forgo the pants, I can be a slutty Imperator Furiosa."

"Who?"

"*Mad Max: Fury Road*?" I reply. Vivian gives me a blank stare, earning a shake of the head from me. "Never mind."

I also text Blake and Fred.

Almost immediately, Blake calls me back. "Please tell me you were joking about your place."

"I wish I were. At least it's stopped raining."

"What happened?"

"Who knows? No one was home, so we're assuming a fuse blew. That house was a disaster waiting to happen."

"When can you go back?"

"It's going to be months."

"Do you need a place to stay?"

I knew he was going to offer, but Blake lives with two other guys, and their place isn't that big. I'd have to sleep on the couch for sure.

"Thanks, but I'll just head to my parents' tonight and then start looking for another room to rent ASAP."

"It's going to be brutal finding something now that school has already started."

I pinch the bridge of my nose. "I know, but I can't worry about that now. I just need to get out of these damn wet clothes."

My fury with Troy returns, and I don't think it will go away that easily. Even knowing my article will be published isn't helping me feel better. Why am I allowing that smug bastard to control my emotions? I'm better than this.

"Are you still up for LARPing this weekend?" Blake asks.

"Yeah, Ben will be disappointed if I don't go. Besides, I'm in dire need of some fun."

One of the firemen approaches us, so I end the call quickly.

"You can go in to pack up your personal belongings now," he says.

"Thank you, sir," I reply.

"Nice outfit, by the way. Very authentic."

Heat creeps up my cheeks. "Uh, thanks."

I quicken my steps, trying to hide my embarrassment.

Vivian catches up with me, and once we're inside, she asks, "Why did you run away? He was cute."

"I didn't run away." I make a beeline to my room. What's up with all the girls I know trying to set me up with random guys? Do I look desperate to them?

I pack a duffel bag with clothes that will last me a week, and also my costume and props for the weekend. Then comes the difficult decision to select only a few beloved books to bring with me. I'm not against e-books, but there's something to be said about holding a real book in your hands. Plus, you don't own e-books; you just buy the license to view the content. It can be erased from your digital library without warning. No, thank you.

In the end, I choose my Tolkien collection. I have to come back here Sunday to pack the rest of my stuff. I'll do that after my volunteering job. As busy as I am, I can't miss it. It's Gladys's ninetieth birthday party, and I have to be there.

I'm heading out the door when text messages and notifications start to blow up my phone.

What the hell? This can't be about the fire.

I click on a random message, which turns out to be hate mail.

Shit on toast. The article about Troy is out.

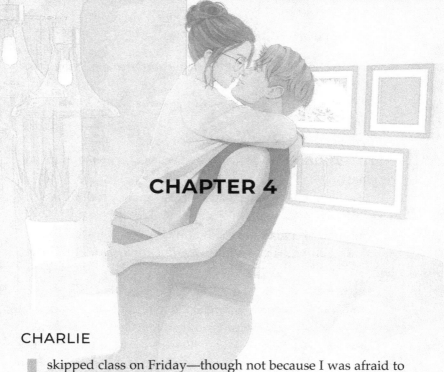

CHAPTER 4

CHARLIE

I skipped class on Friday—though not because I was afraid to deal with my article's repercussion. I don't give a flying fuck about Troy's fan club outrage. No, thanks to that idiot, I caught a cold—one more item for my list of grievances against him. I was still all sniffles and coughs during LARP, which made for a rough event. Thankfully, I'm feeling better today, so it didn't completely ruin my weekend, only half of it.

It's 9:00 a.m., and the parking lot at Golden Oaks is still relatively empty. Sunday is prime visitation day for the assisted living part of the complex, and I'm glad I got here before the crowd. Gladys's party is not until noon, but I promised the administrator I'd help set it up.

It was sheer luck that I kept the décor for the party in my trunk. I'd have stored it near the kitchen if I had unloaded it last week. I hoist the two extra-large bags over my shoulders and then head inside the building. Cheyenne Benson, the administrator, is behind the reception desk today. Her face splits into a wide grin when she sees me coming through the door.

"Charlie! You're here early. Nice dress." Her smile broadens.

"Thanks. I wanted to beat the traffic. I'm staying at my folks' in Littleton."

"Oh no. You had to brave the freeway? That beast never slows down."

"Perks of living near LA." I wink at her.

"For sure." She walks around the desk. "Let me help you with that."

I give her one of the bags. "How many people are we expecting today?"

"The usual number for a Sunday. I'm not sure if Gladys's grandkids will be here. I couldn't get a confirmation from her son."

"That's too bad."

"Yeah. Between you and me, I don't think the grandkids want to be here. She doesn't remember them, and it's just hard."

Gladys has Alzheimer's, and the disease is progressing fast now. The birthday party is more for the residents in the independent living wing of Golden Oaks than her.

We head to the entertainment area where tables have already been set up. I'm not surprised when I spot Ophelia Holland, the coolest lady I've ever met, giving orders to Jack Morris and Louis Romano, her boyfriends.

She's already dressed to the nines, wearing a pink Chanel suit and her pearls. Her chin-length hair is curly and currently baby blue. Every week it's a different color. She turns around and smirks when she sees my outfit. I lost a bet last weekend, and this is my penance—I have to wear a Sailor Moon costume today. I'm all for cosplaying, but there's a time and place for it, and it's definitely not at a ninety-year-old's birthday party.

"Looking good, Charlie," Louis says, not hiding his amusement. "Jon-Jon would have loved it."

"Yeah, right. He'd probably think I'd lost my senses completely."

Jon-Jon was my grandpa. He lived here for five years before he passed away last year. It's how I got to know the place and their residents. I became so attached to them that I kept coming back every weekend. Cheyenne was the one who suggested I list my time here as volunteer work to make my résumé look good. But that's not the reason I come. I love everyone.

I set the bag near the table before I hug Ophelia. She won't reveal her age, but even so, I can tell her body is becoming frailer. She looks healthy though, and she's full of energy as usual.

"Why are you here so early, Charlie? Didn't you have your LARP event yesterday?"

"Yeah, but I'm staying at my folks' temporarily, and it's a drive."

She furrows her white eyebrows. "Why are you staying there? Is everything all right?"

"There was a small fire at my place, and now I have to find another room to rent."

"Oh no. That's dreadful. Was there a lot of damage?"

"Mainly in the kitchen. Still, it's going to be a pain in the butt finding a room that's not out of my price range or a complete dump."

A light bulb seems to flash above her blue head as she widens her eyes. "I have the perfect place for you. You can rent a room from me."

"What do you mean?"

"I own a house fairly near your school's campus. My grandson goes to John Rushmore too, and he's currently living there."

"And he won't mind getting a roommate?"

"No, of course not. He's such an angel. You'll love him. Besides, the house is big enough that you won't be in each other's hair."

I begin to feel hopeful. I'd rather rent a room from Ophelia than deal with another sleazeball like my previous landlord.

"What's your grandson's name? Maybe I know him."

"Wolfgang, but I call him Wolfie."

I chuckle. "Love it."

"How about I give him a call and tell him you'll be coming by to check out the house? When can you stop by?"

"I guess as soon as I leave here."

"Sounds good. He should be home later today."

Something heavy crashes on the floor, earning our attention. The bottom of the box Louis and Jack were trying to move gave out, and now the karaoke machine is in two parts.

"What have you done?" Ophelia strides in their direction, ready to give them a good old tongue-lashing.

I shake my head, trying not to laugh at the scene. There's never a dull moment when the trio is involved, that's for sure. I'll have to remind Ophelia to call her grandson later. I've noticed she's become forgetful, and she's also been confusing names.

My chest becomes tight. I don't want to think about losing Ophelia. It was hard enough when Grandpa died. I can't bear the thought of her leaving me too.

TROY

Karma is a bitch. My stunt in front of Zuko's Diner earned me Charlie's prompt retaliation. She published a scathing article about me, but it backfired royally. She was destroyed on social media, #canceled being used everywhere in association with her and the paper. Even the dean got involved and forced the article to be retracted immediately.

I should feel vindicated, but oddly, I don't. I was an ass to her in the coffee shop. I should have apologized for being so late. I also shouldn't have splashed her on purpose. Now all I have is an annoying sense of guilt swirling in my chest.

There's nothing worse nowadays than to become a social

pariah. Keyboard warriors and their digital pitchforks are a bunch of fucking bullies. But man, that article... she didn't hold back. And it was all bullshit. I'm not an entitled rich boy who doesn't respect their teammates. Yes, I do practice extreme sports, but they aren't life-threatening. At least not all of them. Besides, I know what I'm doing.

Damn it. I really shouldn't feel bad about what happened to her. She dug her own grave.

I've just gotten out of the shower when I see there's a missed call from Grandma. She left a voice mail. I listen to it immediately because you never know what kind of shenanigans she's involved in. Mom thought we wouldn't have to worry about Grandma when she decided to move in at Golden Oaks. *Yeah, right.*

There's a lot of noise in the background, so I can barely understand what she's saying. It doesn't help that Thing One and Thing Two—aka her boyfriends—are talking over her. They sound drunk, which means they probably are. What I can make out from their slurred speeches is that Sailor Moon is going to come by the house later to check out a room to rent.

I rub my forehead. Knowing Grandma, I can't simply discard her message as nonsensical. She's probably decided to rent a room to some stranger. But she wouldn't let my friends move in. Typical Ophelia Holland move. I'm not even annoyed. That's how Grandma rolls. I hope the girl isn't a fucking groupie. The last thing I want is to room with a football fan.

I doubt the girl's name is Sailor Moon, but I can't get hold of Grandma to ask for more details, such as when she's coming by.

I glance at the clock. I was planning to head to the grocery store now because I'll be too lazy to go later.

Ah fuck it. I'll just leave a message at the front door in case "Sailor Moon" decides to stop by before I get back.

CHAPTER 5

CHARLIE

I go check out Ophelia's house straight from Golden Oaks, which unfortunately means I'm still wearing my Sailor Moon costume. I wasn't planning on stopping by anywhere after the party, but it would be insane to go home and change considering the drive. I hope her grandson doesn't think I'm a lunatic.

I park in front of the Spanish-style house and stare at the construction for a minute. It's in a nice area, quiet, and the best part, it's only five minutes away from campus. It's closer to school than my old place was. And Ophelia wasn't kidding when she said the house was big. Judging from the outside, it must have at least four bedrooms. I wonder why Wolfie never got any roommates.

Maybe he likes to live alone. *Shit. Am I imposing?* It's Ophelia's house and she can do whatever she wants, but the last thing I want is to feel unwelcome.

I fix the skirt of my dress first to make sure my ass isn't showing and then stride toward the front door. Taking a deep breath, I look for the doorbell. My eyes catch a note taped next to it. It's addressed to Sailor Moon.

What the hell? How does he know? I groan internally. Ophelia must have said something. I don't know if I should be relieved or mortified.

I grab the folded paper and read the note.

H ey, sorry I missed you. I had to run a quick errand. Feel free to go in and check out the house. The key is under the welcome mat. I'll be back shortly.

P.S. In case you're not Sailor Moon but a regular burglar, I have hidden cameras everywhere. Steal from me, and your ass is mine.

A chuckle escapes my lips. I think Wolfie and I will get along fabulously.

I retrieve the key from under the mat and let myself in. A faint old-house smell reaches my nose, and as I walk farther inside, it mixes with a delicious lemony aftershave scent. Goose bumps break out on my arms. I'm a sucker for good smells.

The living room is large, but even so, the L-shaped leather couch almost looks too big for the space. There's also a brand-new flat-screen TV that takes up most of the wall, and tucked neatly in the storage unit below it, I spot several video game consoles. I shake my head. Boys and their toys.

I veer for the kitchen, and my excitement grows by leaps and bounds. It's been remodeled recently with top-of-the-line appliances. I like to bake when I have the time, but my old kitchen offered me zero motivation. It was small and too old. This is heaven.

It's a two-story house, and I quickly head to the second floor. I wish Wolfie had told me which room would be mine if I decide to stay, but he's not here, so that means I can explore the entire house.

I open the first door I come to, which leads to a big, airy room with large windows. It's almost empty except for some boxes that are stacked up in a corner. I walk in, guessing this one would be my room. There's an en suite bathroom, and the walk-in closet would fit all my clothes and costumes. This is a dream-come-true bedroom. I really have to make sure Wolfie likes me because I'm already in love with this place.

I continue my perusal of the second floor. The next door I try opens to a room that's currently being used as a home gym. There's a bench press, several dumbbell weights, elastic bands, and a treadmill. Apparently, Wolfie likes to work out. I wonder if he'll let me use this space too. I have a gym membership, but if I go there twice a week, I consider it a win. Working out from home would be much easier.

There's another door at the end of the hallway. That must be Wolfie's bedroom. I debate opening the door to peer inside, but then I remember his threat on the note to the potential burglar. He said there were several hidden cameras in the house. Was that a bluff or the truth?

The sound of the front door opening makes the decision for me. Curiosity killed the cat, but that won't happen today.

"Hello? Sailor Moon, are you still here?" Wolfie's baritone voice echoes from downstairs.

"Yeah, I'm coming down."

Suddenly, butterflies take residence in my stomach. I'm in love with this house, and I want Ophelia's grandson to like me. When I reach the living room, he's in the kitchen, putting away groceries in the fridge. His back is to me, and he's wearing a hoodie, so I can't really see his face.

"This house is amazing," I say as I approach the kitchen counter.

"Yeah, it's not too bad."

He turns then, and my stomach bottoms out.

Troy fucking Alexander is standing in front of me.

His eyes widen in surprise, and for a moment, neither of us speaks. My brain is going a hundred miles an hour.

This can't be happening. It must be a sick joke. Troy can't possibly be Ophelia's grandson.

"What the hell are you doing here?" he asks finally, narrowing his eyes.

"I came to see about the room," I reply automatically. I'm still in shock at Troy's presence here.

His eyes take in my ensemble. "*You're* Sailor Moon?"

Like an idiot, I drop my chin and look at my clothes for a second. "I guess I am for today. She told me your name was Wolfgang."

"That's my middle name. She never calls me Troy." He threads his fingers through his long bangs, pushing them back. "I can't believe this. How the hell do you know my grandmother?"

"She lives in Golden Oaks. My grandfather was also a resident before he passed. I've known Ophelia since she moved in. I still visit every weekend."

His eyebrows arch. "Why?"

"Why?" My voice rises. "Do I need a reason to visit friends?"

Troy stares at me with his mouth hanging open. He doesn't speak for several beats, but I bet his mind is whirling just like mine is.

"You're friends with my grandmother?"

"Yes. Is that a surprise to you? She's awesome."

His expression softens a tad, and I notice a faint twitch of his lips. "Yeah, she is."

"Well, I guess I should go."

I turn toward the front door. There's no sense in lingering. Troy would never agree to me moving in. I can't even blame the guy, not after the shitty article I wrote about him.

Mom was right. Sometimes it's better to just forget stuff and move on.

"Wait. What did you think?" he asks, making me pause.

Slowly, I turn back and look at him. "Are you asking me about the house?"

"Yeah. Do you like it?"

I don't detect sarcasm in his tone, and his eyes are devoid of deceit.

"I love it."

"Yeah. It's pretty nice. Why do you need to rent a room?"

I let out a heavy sigh. "There was a small fire incident where I used to live. No major damage, but the house was a dump to begin with. Now my landlord has to fix all the problems before we can move back in."

"I'm sorry to hear that. Well, if you like the house, I suppose you can move in. That is, if you don't mind sharing it with me."

My jaw drops to the floor. "Are you serious?"

He shrugs in a boyish way, making my heart skip a beat.

"Sure. I can't simply say no. Grandma likes you. That counts for something. Plus, you're wearing that." He pulls his cell phone from his back pocket and snaps a picture. "I can't send Sailor Moon away."

I cross my arms over my chest, feeling uber self-conscious. "Why did you take my picture?"

"Leverage." He shoves his phone back in his pocket.

I roll my eyes. "Dude, do you think I'm embarrassed to be wearing a costume? I LARP, for crying out loud."

"You what?" His eyebrows shoot to the heavens.

"Never mind." I step closer to the kitchen counter. "Okay, here's the gist. If you're saying I can move in only to get back at me for writing that article, just tell me now. I don't have time to engage in childish games."

"Wait. Do you think this is all part of a retaliation plan?"

"I'm not discounting anything."

He scoffs. "Girl, you're too conceited for your own good. I don't need to retaliate. Besides, your article has already been pulled down, and you're currently the most hated person on campus. I think that's plenty."

I ball my hands into fists, trying to hide how much his offhanded comment aggravates me. Several choice words get lodged in my throat, but I bite my tongue and keep them bottled inside. I need a place to live, and this is the best I'll get.

"Most hated person, huh?"

He shoves his hands into his hoodie pockets. "Do you want the room or not?"

"I'm assuming I'd get the one with the boxes."

"Yep."

"I do want it, but if you're not doing this as some kind of sick joke, then why?"

"Unlike you, I don't opt for below-the-belt retribution."

"Oh my God. You're so full of...." I trail off, almost forgetting that I can't antagonize Troy.

"So full of what?" He quirks an eyebrow, smirking at me.

I purse my lips, hating fate for putting me in this situation. "You know what? Forget it. When can I move in?"

"Whenever you want. We have an away game next weekend, so I'll be gone Friday."

I don't move from my spot as I keep watching Troy through slits, trying to sniff out the lie. But either he has a perfect poker face or he's truly moved on from our feud. If that's the case, he's a better person than I am.

Anger is still simmering in my gut. I don't care about all the bullies who came out to defend his honor. I'm pissed that he got the dean involved, which resulted in my article being removed from the paper's site.

What happened to free fucking speech?

CHAPTER 6

TROY

Coach Clarkson went hard on us during training, so now we're licking our wounds at Tailgaters, a college bar two blocks from my place. I just told Andreas and Danny about my new roommate, and now they're staring at me with matching stunned expressions.

"You're joking, right?" Andreas finally snaps out of his stupor.

I take a sip of my beer before I reply, "Nope. It turns out Charlie is best friends with my grandmother. I didn't think it was worth upsetting her over that girl."

"Yeah, but she was horrible to you," Danny argues. "What if she's a bitch 24-7?"

"Then I'll kick her out, and Grandma won't be able to say a thing. Besides, she needs this room badly. She'll be on her best behavior."

"That doesn't mean *you* have to behave." Andreas raises an eyebrow.

"I'm not going to be an ass on purpose."

He shrugs. "Whatevs. It'd be the easiest way to get rid of her."

"Nah. She'll move back to her old place once the landlord finishes renovations."

I sense the lie as soon as it leaves my mouth. Charlie said her old place was a dump. She'll never move out of her own accord. But I won't resort to douche tactics. Maybe it won't be as bad as everyone thinks.

Or maybe you're just thinking with your dick, Troy. She sure looked hot in that Sailor Moon costume. Fuck.

My cock stirs in my jeans as I remember Charlie's getup. It's not helping my case that I took a picture of her… and I might have jerked off to it as well.

"Uh-oh. Troy has gotten the look," Danny pipes up, bringing me back to the present.

My erection is now straining against my jeans, but if I try to find a better sitting position, the guys will immediately know about my situation.

"What the hell are you talking about?" I take a large gulp of my beer, hoping the alcohol will give me some relief.

"Oh yeah. The look. I think our friend is not telling us the whole story. Come on, Troy. Spill it already. Why did you agree to let Miss Stick Up Her Ass move in with you?"

I shake my head. "There's nothing going on. I'm just helping her out."

Andreas watches me through slits. "Right." He turns his attention to his phone, and after a moment, a victorious grin splits his face. "Aha. Mystery solved."

"What?" Danny leans closer to look at Andreas's screen. "Oh. You didn't say Charlie was hot."

"She's not hot. She photographs well." I chug the rest of my beer, dropping the glass back down with excessive force. "I'm going home."

"We just got here." Danny glances at me.

Andreas elbows his arm. "He has a reason to hurry back. There's a sexy nerd waiting for him."

I get up and throw some money on the table. "You can be a real dick sometimes, Andy."

With a knowing smile, he leans back in the chair, linking his fingers behind his head. "Don't hate me because I'm right."

"Whatever."

I stride out of the bar, ignoring the hungry glances I receive from the girls I pass. If they're looking for cock fun, Andreas and Danny will gladly provide that. I love sports, but banging as many chicks as I can is not one I care for. That's Andreas's department. I'm not a saint, of course. I do hook up; I just don't make a game out of it.

When I turn on my street, I don't see a moving truck. Charlie told me she'd bring all her stuff today. Maybe she's done moving in. We don't have a garage, and to my annoyance, Charlie took my usual spot in front of the house. Grinding my teeth, I drive a little farther until I find another parking space. The walk back to the house serves to turn my irritation down a notch. If I tell her not to park in my usual space, it'd be a dick move. Besides, it's not reserved for me. Any of our neighbors can park there. They simply don't out of courtesy.

I'm looking forward to chilling out and playing a video game, but when I walk into the house, I realize that's not happening tonight. Charlie didn't simply move in. She took over my entire living room. There are a bunch of boxes spread in the area, some still shut but others with spilling contents. Loud music is pouring from her room upstairs.

"Charlie?" I call out.

I hear her hurried footsteps on the wooden floor, and then she appears at the top of the stairs wearing an oversize T-shirt and nothing else that I can see. Her legs are long, tan, and lean, and they're making my life seriously difficult at the moment.

Fuck me.

"Hi, Troy. Sorry about the mess. I didn't know you'd be home early." She runs down the stairs, pulling her hair back in a pony-tail. The action lifts her shirt, revealing tiny jean shorts that barely cover her sweet ass.

"We have a six-hour bus drive tomorrow and a game on Saturday. Can't really stay out late." I stare at all the costumes and props that are covering my couch at the moment. "What happened here?"

She starts to collect the dresses that are draped over the back of the couch. "Oh, since I have so much more space, I decided to bring my stuff out of the storage unit. But I was doing a triage, and things kind of got out of hand."

"No kidding. If you don't mind, I'd like to have my couch back."

Charlie winces, and that's when I realize my words came out a little too harsh.

"Yeah, sure. I'll get this cleaned up right away. I'm not a messy girl, I promise." She quickens her pace, grabbing a load of clothes and tossing them back into boxes.

"Let me help you." I bend over to grab one of the closed boxes to bring up to her room when the bottom gives out. A myriad of clothes and objects falls out but luckily nothing break-able. "Okay, who did the packing?" I stare at the mess at my feet.

"I did, and don't give me that look. Some of those boxes got damp in storage."

I set the damaged box aside and bend over to retrieve one specific item that caught my attention. "What kind of cosplay are you into?" I show her a wooden dildo the size of my forearm.

Her blue eyes widen behind her glasses, and her plump lips make a perfect O. "Oh my God. Give me that." She snatches the dildo from my hand and hides it behind her back.

Her face is now brighter than a tomato, which makes me laugh.

"Hey, I'm not judging. But seriously."

"This wasn't part of a cosplay. This was a gag gift."

"That you decided to keep."

"Of course I did. It's an antique."

"If you say so."

"Oh, shut up and help me clean up this mess."

I arch both eyebrows. I can't believe Charlie just gave me an order. "Excuse me?"

"You're the one who dropped everything on the floor."

"I was just trying to help. It's not my fault you have terrible packing skills."

"I don't have terrible packing skills." She throws her hands up in the air—one still clutching the megalodon of all dildos.

A burst of laughter hits me again.

"What's so funny now?"

I stare at the object in her hand, making her roll her eyes.

"Oh, grow up."

"That's rich coming from the girl who still dresses up as fairies and princesses."

Her eyes narrow as she throws me a death glare. "Are you calling me a child?"

I shrug, shoving my hands in my pockets. "If the shoe fits."

"I knew things were too good to be true."

"What's that supposed to mean?" My good humor vanishes in a flash.

I sense she's about to blow a fuse, but whatever she was planning to blurt out gets stuck in her throat.

She shakes her head and says, "Never mind. Give me ten minutes. I'll get everything packed."

I was still willing to help, which is fucking crazy. But I sense that if I try, it'll only make matters worse.

Damn it. It's our first day as official roommates, and we've already argued over nothing. This will only lead to a bitter coexistence or angry sex.

My cock is totally on board for the latter.

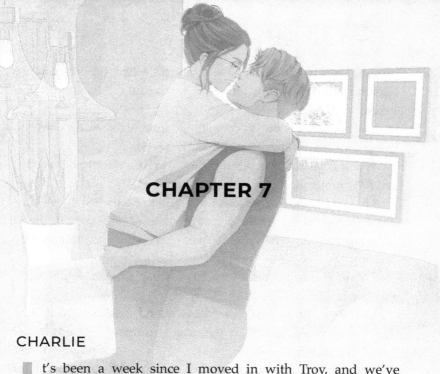

CHAPTER 7

CHARLIE

I t's been a week since I moved in with Troy, and we've managed to avoid each other. Our schedules have been chaotic, and we're barely home. The beginning of our living arrangements was rocky, to say the least. It seems we can't be in the same room for more than five minutes before we start to argue. I've never met anyone who can push my buttons without even trying.

Troy had a game yesterday and didn't come home until the early hours of the morning. I only know the exact time because the jackass made a ruckus when he came in. At least he didn't bring a girl with him. We don't share a wall, but I'm sure I'd hear them getting it on.

I bet he's good in bed.

Whoa. Where did that thought come from?

You probably need to get laid, Charlie. It's been months.

Shut up, whore!

Ugh, my conscience is being such a bitch this morning. I'd better get my mind out of the gutter pronto.

I went to Golden Oaks yesterday, so I have Sunday all to

myself. I hit the gym first—I still haven't asked Troy if I can use his home workout room. Honestly, I don't think I'll ever ask. I'm in total avoidance mode.

The next stop is the grocery store. I load up, so I don't have to make another run in the middle of the week.

When I get home around noon, Troy is still sound asleep. I can hear him snoring from the hallway.

I haven't decided yet what I'm going to do the rest of the day, but a shower is the first order of business. I'm in the middle of washing my hair when the hot jets turn into drips, followed by nothing.

I glare at the showerhead while turning the knobs. "Are you kidding me?"

Cursing, I wrap myself in a towel and test the faucet. Dry. The toilet won't flush. Did the water company cut our water supply on a Sunday? *Fuck*. It can't be for lack of payment, and they warn you when they need to cut supply for maintenance work. I bet they did send a notice, and Troy simply forgot to tell me. *Son of a bitch*. I'm going to kill him.

Still dripping wet, I march to his bedroom. I don't barge in, but I do knock hard on his door.

"Troy! Get up!"

He groans, then says, "Go away!"

"No. Get your ass out here."

I hear the sound of sheets being tossed aside, then heavy steps stomping closer. He opens the door with a yank. "For fuck's sake! Wha—" His eyes widen. "Why are you naked and covered in soap?"

"Because I was taking a shower when suddenly the water cut off," I grit out.

"And how is it my fault that you forgot they were going to turn off the water for a couple hours?"

"I didn't forget! You never told me." I gesture widely with my hands, and the towel almost comes undone.

Troy notices, and his smirk is infuriating. "I attached the

notice on the kitchen board. It's really not my fault you missed it."

"Ugh! You're so annoying." I turn around and stride down the hallway. Instead of returning to my room, I run downstairs.

I have to get the shampoo out of my hair, and the only water we have in the house is Troy's sparkling shit. I grab a few bottles, then lean over the sink to rinse my hair with his fancy bubbly crap.

"What are you doing?" he asks.

Fuck. I didn't know he'd followed me.

"What does it look like?" I pour fizzing, ice-cold water over my head and hair, getting goose bumps immediately. Maybe I should have warmed it up in the microwave first.

"You'd better replace my Perrier," he says.

"Yeah, sure."

A throaty chuckle follows.

"What's so funny?" I ask.

"Do you realize that bent over like that, you're giving me quite a view?"

I snap back into a straight position, wincing as my now cold hair slaps against my back. "Were you ogling me?" I turn to glare at him.

He's not smiling now, and his hungry eyes make my mouth go dry. My pulse skyrockets as I wrestle with feelings of anger and desire. I was too pissed when I banged on his door to notice Troy was only wearing boxer shorts. Now his shredded abs and chest are all I can see.

My eyes have a will of their own. They travel south... and hot tamales. My lady parts turn into flames. Troy is aroused—big time. Emphasis on *big.*

Damn it. I can't fall for the trap that's Troy's godlike body.

"I couldn't help but look. You were flashing your... *goods.*"

Heat creeps up my cheeks as I hug my middle, feeling completely exposed. "Well, don't get any ideas. That's all the view you'll get."

Summoning all the dignity I have left, I walk around him with my chin raised high. I purposely keep my pace normal, fighting the urge to run. Once in my bedroom, I begin to form a plan to protect myself from Troy's charms. I text Vivian, asking if her offer to set me up with one of her friends still stands. It's high time I get back into the dating scene.

TROY

Damn Charlie.

Why does she have to be so fucking hot? Now I'm sporting a raging boner, fantasizing about plunging my cock into her sweet pussy while she's bent over the sink like before. It's a sin for someone who I loathe so much to be that irresistible. And the worst part is that she wants me too. I saw the craving reflected in her blue eyes when she noticed my erection.

I. Cannot. Go. There.

She left a mess on the kitchen counter and on the floor. I focus on that, which helps dissolve any desire I had left. I clean up and then decide to head out for lunch. I didn't sleep nearly enough, but I can't go back to bed now.

After I put some clothes on, I go to one of my favorite joints, Zuko's Diner. It's an automatic decision. I always come here after a night of partying since they serve breakfast all day. But being here reminds me of Charlie again.

Hell. I need to get her out of my head.

I keep my sunglasses on as I stride to my usual booth; my head is pounding, so if I have to look like a douche, so be it.

"Troy?" a familiar voice calls out.

I turn slowly, and then my jaw drops. "Brooke? Holy shit. What are you doing here?" I change direction and stop next to her booth.

"I transferred to Rushmore," she replies excitedly.

"Really? Couldn't handle those New Yorkers, huh?"

She makes a face, furrowing her eyebrows and scrunching her nose as if she smelled something bad. "Ugh, no. They got two years of my life that I'll never get back. I'm a California girl through and through, no matter how much my old man wants me not to be. Are you meeting someone?"

"No. I'm solo today. I have the worst hangover."

She giggles. "I was gonna say, you do look rough. Sit with me. I can't believe I bumped into you here."

I slide into the seat opposite hers. "When did you get back?"

"Last week."

"And you didn't call me? I'm wounded." I press my hand against my chest, pretending to be hurt.

She waves her hand dismissively. "Stop. I was going to. I had to get situated."

"Where are you staying?"

"At a friend's condo for now. It's fifteen minutes from campus, but I'm hoping to find something closer. Is your grandmother still against you having roommates?"

She smiles in a persuasive way, making me uncomfortable. Like I'd ever want to live with my ex. Charlie is bad enough.

"Actually, I just got one."

Her eyebrows shoot up. "Oh, really? Let me guess. Andy?"

I snort. "Yeah, right. Grandma would never allow him to move in. Actually, my new roommate is a girl."

The easygoing smile wilts from her face. "Oh, you have a new girlfriend?"

Brooke seems hurt, which makes me uneasy.

We started dating in high school. She was a junior, and I, a senior. When she went to NYU, we tried the long-distance thing for six months. In the end, we decided to break up and remain friends. I hope she didn't transfer to Rushmore, wanting to rekindle our relationship. The spark is gone. I'm not sure if it was even there to begin with.

I laugh. "No, nothing like that. She's Grandma's friend, and she needed to rent a room last minute."

Brooke leans against the booth, looking relieved. "Oh, so you didn't even know her?"

"Nope. Total stranger."

"Is she nice?" Brooke asks casually, but I hear the double meaning of her question nonetheless.

Alarm bells sound in my head.

"Brooke, please tell me you didn't move back to Cali for me."

Her eyebrows shoot to the heavens. "What? Of course not. Gee, aren't you conceited?"

I shrug. "Just checking. I'm stoked that you're back, but we're just friends."

She narrows her eyes, flattening her lips. "Keep acting like an ass, and that friendship card might be revoked."

"Okay, okay." I flash her a dazzling smile. "Did you order already?"

"Yeah."

I flag the waitress and put my usual order in. She returns a moment later with a big cup of steaming coffee.

Brooke waits until she's gone to speak again. "So, you didn't answer my question. Is your roommate nice?"

I debate telling Brooke the truth about Charlie. The answer that comes out of my mouth surprises me. "Yeah, I think so."

Why did I lie?

"Well, I can't wait to meet her."

CHAPTER 8

TROY

Another week passes, and I barely see Charlie. I should consider myself lucky, but at the same time, I secretly want to bump into her. Each one of our encounters has given me a perverted rush, and the adrenaline junkie in me craves that kind of stuff.

I just got home from the game, which we'd almost lost. If it wasn't for that field goal near the end, we might have. I'm pissed even though I did everything I could. I love football, but lately, extreme sports have been giving me the type of satisfaction I need. I can't stop; I have to keep moving, or bad memories will take over.

Charlie's accusation comes to the forefront of my mind, darkening my mood. If I'm honest with myself, my anger stems from the fact that she guessed about my inner conflict. It's not like I don't care about football anymore; it's just not my favorite pastime. I'd never jeopardize the team on purpose though. For her to assume that based off one game was bullshit.

Distracted, I open the small closet under the stairs to stash my duffel bag when a tower of boxes collapses on top of me.

"What the hell!"

This wasn't here this morning. I don't need to look inside to know this is Charlie's cosplay crap; she's written it neatly in block letters on top. She has a huge closet in her room. Why did she store her shit here?

Son of a bitch. It's bad enough that she's taken over my thoughts—I can't stop thinking about her—but now she's taken over my entire house.

I shove the boxes back into the closet, then go grab a beer from the fridge. I don't want to get into an argument with her now. The boys are coming in a few, so we can chill out and plan our next trip in December when our season is over. I'm jonesing for adventure and also to get Charlie out of my system. Too bad it's only the beginning of October.

The door opens with a bang, and Andreas comes in, carrying a case of beer. Danny follows, holding two bags full of snacks. Andreas wanted to throw a party, but I'm completely destroyed. The idea of cleaning up tomorrow makes the idea even less appealing.

"So, is your roomie home?" He sets the beer on the kitchen counter.

"Her car is parked in front of the house, so I'm assuming yes."

"Excellent. I can't wait to meet her." He rubs his hands together.

"Don't even think about it," I warn him.

He widens his eyes innocently. "Since when can you read my mind?"

"I know you."

"Should we order pizza now? I'm starving." Danny opens a can of potato chips and shoves a handful in his mouth.

"Yeah, go ahead," I tell him.

"Wait. It's your house. Why do I have to order? I got the chips."

Groaning, I reach for my phone. "Fine."

The doorbell rings then, and I glare at Andreas. "You'd better not have invited anyone here."

He raises both hands. "I didn't. I swear."

Suspicious, I jump off the couch and check the door through the window. There's a guy standing outside, and judging by his posture and fidgeting, he seems nervous. He'd better not be a salesman.

I open the door. "Can I help you?"

His eyes snap to mine, and a second later, his jaw drops. "You're Troy Alexander."

"Yes… and you are?"

"Ah, sorry. My name is Jacob Mueller. I'm here to pick up Charlie?"

Ugh, I hate people who end a statement as if they're asking a question. I keep my expression neutral, but my mind is whirling. *Charlie is going on a date with this guy?*

I open the door wider and let him through. "I don't think she's ready yet."

"Oh yeah, I'm a bit early. She didn't mention her roommate was you."

I shut the door hard. I'm aggravated, and I don't know why. Who cares if Charlie is going out on a date?

"Who's the preppy boy?" Andreas asks from the kitchen.

"I'm Jacob Mueller, Charlie's date. You're Andreas Rossi," he says in awe.

"Sure am. Are you a football fan?"

The guy chuckles. "Am I a fan? Yeah, you can say that. Great game today, by the way."

"What the fuck are you talking about? We almost lost," I retort angrily.

The guy's face goes paler. "I mean, yeah, but you didn't."

The sound of Charlie's hurried footsteps down the stairs makes me turn. *Fuck me.* She's wearing a burgundy bodycon dress that leaves nothing to the imagination. It's a dress that screams she wants to get laid. My cock immediately reacts, but it's fury that's coursing through my veins now. She wants to bang a loser like Jacob Mueller?

Why do I care? Damn it!

Andreas wolf-whistles, adding fuel to my anger. I'll never hear the end of it.

"Hi, Jacob." Charlie smiles at the guy, completely ignoring me. "Am I late? I lost track of time."

"You're not late. Romeo was so nervous, he got here early," I reply bitterly.

Charlie throws me a questioning glance, and then I see she's wearing makeup. She went all out for this guy. An ugly emotion swirls in my chest, and it feels like jealousy. I must have suffered a head injury on the field today because that's the only explanation for my reaction.

"He's not lying. I was a bit nervous," Jacob confesses.

Charlie smiles. "That's sweet. Well, we should head out then."

"Hold on." Andreas walks around the kitchen counter. "Introductions are in order."

I suppress a groan, pressing a fist against my forehead. He already knew Charlie was good-looking, but she's fucking gorgeous tonight. He'll be all over her, date or no date. I bet he already forgot we're supposed to dislike her.

"Let me guess. You're on the team," Charlie deadpans.

"Running back, babe. The name is Andreas, but you can call me Andy."

She narrows her eyes. "Right. Well, nice to meet you, *Andreas*." She glances at Danny, who hasn't moved from his spot. "And you too, Pringles Boy."

Danny arches his eyebrows, but since he's chewing, he doesn't reply.

As soon as Charlie and Jacob leave, Andreas whirls on me. "Dude, Charlie is way hotter than I thought."

"Don't let all that makeup fool you." I let the venom drip from my tongue.

Damn it. I am jealous.

"I know a beautiful woman when I see one. Since she's your roommate, I'm going to ask, are you planning to tap that? Because if you aren't, then I'm game."

I glower at him. "Don't even think about it."

His eyes become rounder. He lifts his hands, palms facing me, and steps back. "Okay, okay. Just checking. I won't get in your way."

"That's not why—you know what? Forget it."

"Is it wise to hook up with your roommate though?" Danny asks.

"I'm not going to hook up with her," I grit out.

"Then why were you acting like that Jacob guy stole your candy from under your nose?" Andreas quirks an eyebrow.

"I wasn't." I return to the couch to grab my phone.

"Sorry, bro. Your head might know Charlie is the enemy, but your dick sure doesn't."

"Fuck off, Andy." I keep my attention on the phone.

"Are you finally ordering food?" Danny asks.

"No. Change of plans. We're having a party."

CHARLIE

This has been the worst date of my life. Jacob spent the entire dinner yapping about football and how Troy is a god among us. How could Vivian set me up with a football fanatic? And if he's such a fan, doesn't he know I was the one who wrote the nasty article about Troy?

Jacob seems oblivious that I want to gag him with a chain saw as he drives me back home. I'm ready to bail as soon as he parks the car in front of my house, but it isn't to be. The house is packed with random people. Some are outside, chatting animatedly, and loud music can be heard, even from inside the car.

I can't believe this. Troy decided to throw a party without telling me? That's fucking wrong.

"Whoa. I didn't know you were having a party tonight." Jacob drives past our house instead of stopping, so I can get out.

"Where are you going?"

"Uh, I'm going to look for a place to park."

Shit. Of course he wants to come in.

Angry doesn't begin to cover my feelings right now. I'm going to throttle Troy when I get the chance.

Jacob manages to park his car two blocks away, which means the asshole is forcing me to walk all the way back to the house in high heels. If the date hadn't already been a bust, the lack of gentlemanly conduct would seal his fate.

I stride ahead in silence, not hiding the fact that I'm pissed. On the front porch, a stupid drunk girl almost spills beer all over me as she misses a step. Patience is not a virtue I possess. Troy had better stay the fuck out of my way tonight.

I have every intention to disappear into my room, but the sight I encounter as I walk through the front door raises my blood to the boiling point. Strangers are wearing the cosplay outfits I had separated to donate to my brother's high school. Some of those costumes cost hundreds of dollars and are now being ruined by monster football players who are too big for them. I'm going to lose my shit in front of all these people.

Fuming, I search for Troy in the crowd, finding him in the kitchen, surrounded by his adoring fans. Curling my hands into fists, I march in his direction. He doesn't notice my presence until I push one of the girls to the side.

"Hey!" she complains. "What the hell!"

I ignore her, keeping my murderous stare on Troy.

His lips curl into a lazy, drunken smile. "Hey, roomie. You're home. How was your date?"

"Why are your friends wearing my costumes?"

"Oh, I didn't think you'd mind. They were marked as donation."

"You ass! You had no right to go through my stuff!"

His bloodshot eyes narrow. "If you don't want me to mess with your personal belongings, don't leave them lying everywhere."

"So, the gloves have finally come off."

"Who is this bitch?" a random redhead asks.

I turn my ire on her. "What did you call me?"

Troy suddenly jumps in between his guest and me. "Whoa. Everyone, calm down. Charlie, why don't you grab a beer and chill? This is a party, for fuck's sake. Relax." He reaches for my arm, but I quickly pull away.

"Don't touch me."

I whirl around and make a dramatic exit, stomping with the fury of a stampede. I could call the cops and end the party, but everyone already hates me, and I don't need to give them more reason. Besides, my beef isn't with them; it's with Troy.

But if he thinks I'm going to simply forget his assholery, he's sorely mistaken.

He wants war? I'll give him war.

CHAPTER 9

CHARLIE

Trying to sleep while the party was raging downstairs was pointless. Eventually, the guests left at around four in the morning, but I was too angry to fall asleep. Now it's six o'clock, and I'm out of bed, showered, and ready to go.

The living room and kitchen are completely trashed. There are empty beer bottles, discarded cups, and leftover food everywhere. I wrinkle my nose in disgust. If Ophelia could see the condition of her house, she'd flip out. Troy had better clean this mess by the time I get back.

I search for the costumes I was going to bring to Littleton today. I find none scattered with the trash, and my heart sinks. It's possible Troy's teammates simply went home with them. I open the closet below the stairs, hoping they might have left something untouched. To my surprise, most of the stuff is back in boxes. Unfortunately, they stink of beer and other unsavory smells. And I'm pretty sure most are damaged.

With a sigh, I pull the boxes out of the closet and carry them to my car. I'll sort them out when I get to my parents'. Ben will be so disappointed when he sees what happened to the costumes.

A new surge of anger erupts from the pit of my stomach. I can't let Troy get away with this without retaliation. I'm a fair person, but I won't sit back and let people do bad things without retribution.

The hour drive serves to calm me down, and when I park in my parents' driveway, my anger is almost gone. The garage door is open, but only Mom's car is inside. It's still fairly early. I wonder where Dad is.

I bring all the boxes to the garage, and then I follow the smell of Sunday breakfast—pancakes, eggs, and bacon. Mom is behind the stove, cooking more food, while Ben is sitting at the table in the kitchen nook. Bailey, our golden retriever, is the first to come greet me.

I lean forward to rub behind her ear. "Hey, girl. How are you?"

She wags her tail and then licks my hand, making me laugh. Like a miracle, the dark cloud above my head dissipates. That's the power of Bailey. She's been part of our family for fourteen years. Her muzzle fur has already turned gray. There's no denying her age, and the certainty that she'll be leaving us soon brings a pang to my chest. I hate aging. I wish we were all immortal.

"Hi, Charlie. How was your drive?" Ben asks me.

"Not too bad. It's early."

I step close to Mom to give her a kiss. "Where's Dad?"

Her eyebrows furrow, and her lips become nothing but a thin flat line. "He went to the warehouse before we even woke up."

"On a Sunday?" I wash my hands at the sink, eyeing the rows of bacon. My stomach grumbles.

"Dad has been really busy lately," Ben pipes up. "We barely see him."

I frown. "Really? I thought he was going to slow down."

"Well, that's what we all thought. He put Roger in charge of daily operations, so I really don't know why he spends most of the time in the warehouse now."

Mom's bitterness is clear. I've been so busy lately that our phone conversations have been superficial. I didn't realize this was going on.

Dad has a successful carpentry business. He designs luxurious furniture for the rich and famous in LA and other parts of the country. His beginnings were humble though, working out of the garage at our old house. It wasn't until ten years ago that he sold a piece to a celebrity and his business boomed.

"Oh, before I forget, my boss is throwing a barbeque for his employees and family," my mom says. "It's two weeks from now. I hope you can make it."

"Is it on Saturday or Sunday?" I grab a plate and begin to fill it with delicious food. I didn't realize I was this hungry until I got here.

"It's Saturday, and don't worry, Charlie. We don't have LARP that weekend," Ben chimes in.

I sit across from him at the table, noticing his new hairdo. His blond hair is sticking out at odd angles, but it was done by design.

Pointing with my fork, I ask, "What's up with the porcupine look?"

"Oh, do you like it? This is for when Sir Lorenzo gets hit by lightning and gains new powers."

That's his LARP character, and we usually drop them in conversation as if they were real people.

I furrow my eyebrows. "When does that happen? I didn't write it."

"Oh, Tammara did. I have to show it to you." Ben gets a goofy grin on his face.

"Who is Tammara?"

Redness sneaks up Ben's cheeks, and he lowers his gaze to the plate before answering, "My girlfriend."

I hit the table with an open palm. "Shut up! You have a girl-friend? When did this happen?"

Ben just turned sixteen, so I shouldn't be too surprised by the development. But he's my baby brother, and I'm very protective of him. He was bullied when he was younger on account of his Down syndrome. I got into many fistfights to defend him. It wasn't until we moved and he enrolled in a private school that things improved. Understandably, I really want to know who this Tammara person is.

"Relax, Charlie. Tammara is nice. I've met her," Mom butts in.

"She's like me." Ben smiles from ear to ear.

I glance at Mom, and she confirms with a nod. When Ben says she's like him, he means, she has Down syndrome too.

"All right. Does she want to be a writer then?"

"Well, she likes writing stories for LARP. She's coming to the next event too. Isn't it great?"

"Yeah, that's awesome. Where did you meet?"

"Online."

My jaw drops.

I glance at Mom, and she simply shrugs. "It's how it is these days."

I shake my head and smile. "Man, look at you. All grown up. I can't believe my baby brother has a girlfriend, and I'm still single."

"You're only single by choice, sis."

"You got that right," I reply.

I tell Ben and Mom about my fiasco date, which leads to me also talking about my roommate from hell. Mom pulls up a chair and takes a seat with a cup of coffee in her hand.

"To sum up, most of the costumes are dirty or completely ruined, all thanks to Troy."

"I think you should look for a new place to stay, Charlie. That roommate of yours sounds like an ass."

"Mom! Language." Ben laughs.

She rolls her eyes.

"The house is pretty nice though, and the rent is cheap." I sigh. "I don't know. The problems only arise when we bump into each other, which doesn't happen often."

"I think Charlie should stay, but she can't let him get away with that. Raven the Sorceress would never let that slide."

Ben loves to bring up my LARP character into conversation. To be fair, I do the same to him.

Mom frowns. "Revenge should never be the answer, Ben."

"Okay, maybe not revenge, but a little prank never hurt anyone," he replies.

I sit straighter, resting my forearms on the table. "Oh, I like the sound of that. What do you have in mind?"

Mom stands. "Okay, if you're not going to listen to me, I'm out of here."

We ignore her remark. Mom has her convictions, but she never tries to impose them on us. She believes we're old enough to make our own decisions. But she *will* tell us *I told you so* when we—I—fuck up. Ben never does, so I'm intrigued by his remark.

"I saw on YouTube the other day that some guy pranked his roommate by filling his room with chickens. They shat everywhere. It was hilarious."

"That sounds like a fit punishment, but where am I going to find dozens of chickens?"

Ben's blue eyes light up. "Tammara's parents own a farm. They have a chicken coop. I'm sure we can borrow them."

I nibble on my bottom lip. It's one thing for me to do something outrageous on my own. I can take the repercussions of my actions. I'm not sure if I want to involve Ben in my shenanigans.

"I don't know. Maybe I should come up with something easier."

His shoulders sag in disappointment. "Oh, okay. Let me know if you change your mind."

CHAPTER 10

TROY

My head is pounding when I get up. And don't get me started with my mouth. It tastes like something died in it. I need a shower and a shave, but I only use the bathroom to relieve myself before I drag my feet downstairs for a damage report. I don't know what time everyone finally left, but I'm glad I made it to my room alone. Waking up next to a random girl would have made this hellish morning even worse.

I stop halfway down the stairs and stare at the mess. It looks like a hurricane passed through. This will take hours to clean.

Fuck.

I sit on a step and text Andreas, cursing him for putting the idea of a party in my head. Technically, this isn't his fault—I was the one who changed my mind—but I need a scapegoat, and I'm choosing him.

He asks for a picture of the chaos. Apparently, he left with two girls way before the party was over. Typical. I do as he said, and a minute later, he texts that he'll come over to help. My bullshit alarm immediately rings. Andreas is not one to volunteer to do anything, especially a cleanup, but I'm too tired and hungover to question him.

I get my ass off the stairs and head to the kitchen. Coffee is in order and probably several painkillers. While I wait for it to brew, I investigate my fridge. As suspected, there's nothing appealing inside. Not even Charlie's food. *Damn it.* I text Andreas again, asking him to bring me something greasy.

He takes his sweet time, finally showing up forty minutes later. I've showered and changed already and just finished cleaning the kitchen when he opens the front door, wearing his leather jacket and sunglasses like he's Tom Cruise in *Top Gun*.

"Help has arrived," he announces, removing his glasses in a dramatic fashion.

"I didn't think you'd show up," I grumble.

"I said I'd come." He looks over his shoulder. "Come on, guys. This place won't clean itself."

Five freshmen come through and immediately get to work. They don't even ask where the cleaning supplies are, guessing their location.

"Who the hell are they?"

"New Pike pledges." Andreas grins, taking a seat on a high stool by the kitchen counter. "Am I good or what?"

"How did you get these guys?"

He shrugs. "Unlike you, I cultivate relationships off the football field. I promised Leo tickets to the next game and a date with the head cheerleader."

"You got Heather Castro to go out with him?" I quirk an eyebrow. "The Ice Queen of Rushmore?"

"Let's say, I can be very persuasive." He wiggles his eyebrows up and down.

I narrow my eyes. "You didn't fuck her, did you?"

Andreas looks surprised. "Are you crazy? She's not my type."

"She has a vagina. She *is* your type."

He shakes his head. "No, I draw the line at colder-than-Siberia chicks."

I pinch the bridge of my nose. This conversation is making my headache worse. I need to load up on carbs to soak up all the alcohol that's still in my system.

"Fine. You can tell me the details of your deal later. Where's my food?"

Andreas widens his eyes. "Oops. I forgot."

"Dude! Come on."

He jumps off the chair. "No worries. Let's get some grub while the guys clean."

"I'm not leaving them here alone."

The dude closest to me pipes up, "It's okay, Troy. We won't break anything. Promise."

Clenching my jaw, I debate between taking Andreas up on his offer and staying to supervise these guys. But in the end, the hole in my stomach wins. I need food, pronto.

"Fine. We'll be back soon. Stay off the second floor," I warn them.

CHARLIE

On the way back home, I think about Ben's chicken idea. As complicated as it would be to pull off, that would be an awesome prank. But no, I really need to learn to let go even though, last night, I promised war. Ben and I went through the boxes, and besides the beer stains, the costumes aren't completely ruined. After a wash, they'll be wearable again.

I make a pit stop at the grocery store first because, most likely, the little bit of food I had left in the fridge and pantry are long gone. I know how ravenous drunk people get.

It takes great effort on my part to keep my irritation to a

minimum when I think about last night's party. One of my flaws is the inability to forget and forgive.

I park just behind Troy's car and wonder if he managed to clean up the mess already. Boy, if he didn't, there will be hell to pay.

No, Charlie, you can't get mad all over again.

After a mental pep talk inside the car, I finally get out, bringing all the grocery bags with me in one trip. I prepared myself to deal with Troy, not the four strangers who are currently cleaning the living room, and it takes me by surprise.

"Who the hell are you?"

I would have dropped the bags and reached for the pepper spray can in my purse if it weren't for the fact that these guys are on their hands and knees, scrubbing.

"Uh, we're Pike pledges," one of them answers.

Like that's supposed to make me feel better. Fuckers.

"Okay, *pledge*. Why are you cleaning my house? Where's Troy?"

"He left with Andreas to grab food," a second dude replies.

"Of course he did."

I head for the kitchen, which is spotless. They did a good job here, I'll give them that, but my anger has come back with a vengeance nonetheless. Who leaves four strangers in the house and goes out? Nimrods like Troy. *Damn.* He didn't even stop to consider what I would think. Like that's every girl's dream—to walk into her house and find four strangers in it.

I put away my groceries and then head to my room, locking the door for good measure. I'm seriously considering Ben's chicken idea now. Still obsessing about Troy and my aggravation with him, I begin to take off my clothes. Absentminded, I open the bathroom door, half-dressed, only to find another pledge taking a shit in my toilet.

With a scream, I slam the door shut and quickly put my jeans back on.

"What the hell! Why are you in my fucking bathroom?" I yell.

"Sorry. I didn't want to go downstairs."

Fuming, I storm out of my room, almost colliding with Troy.

"What happened?" He looks at me, worried.

"What happened?" I shriek. "You're a fucking asshole!"

I don't think twice, just lift my knee, hitting Troy's crown jewels with all my might. He groans, folding forward as he covers his crotch with his hands.

"What the fuck? Are you insane?" His face is contorted in agony as he stares at me as if I'm crazy.

Poop Boy comes out of my room, sporting a guilty expression on his pale face. "I'm so, so sorry."

"Get the hell out of my sight," I grit out.

Giving me a wide berth, he hurries down the stairs.

Troy is standing straighter again, but his expression is no longer contorted in pain. Fury flashes from his eyes instead.

"You are one crazy bitch," he says.

"That's typical male behavior. You screw up, and when I retaliate, I'm the bitch."

"How in the world did I screw up this time?"

"Really? You don't know?" I gesture wildly. "How about you throwing a party last night without the courtesy of letting me know first? Never mind letting your friends tear through my things. And now I come home to find a bunch of strangers in my house with you nowhere in sight. But the cherry on top was to walk into my bathroom and find a dude taking a big dump in my toilet."

My breathing is coming out in bursts by the time I'm done with my tirade.

Troy is no longer shooting daggers from his eyes. What I see shining from those hazel depths is much worse than hate. It's desire. The realization that he wants me serves to awaken a fire in the pit of my stomach that quickly travels through my body.

"I'm sorry," he says in a husky voice.

My bones melt, and my pussy throbs as if getting it on with Troy is actually an option. Hell to the fucking no. He's an asshole. I don't fall for those, no matter how good-looking they are. Heart-stopper as he may be, I'm not going to succumb.

"Right," I say, hating how feeble I sound.

My knees are weak, and if he keeps staring at me with that hungry gaze, I might combust on the spot.

I run back to my room and lock the door. I have to do something to make Troy forget any ideas about me. I'm not sleeping with him, and he needs to stop wanting that.

Chickens in his bedroom it is.

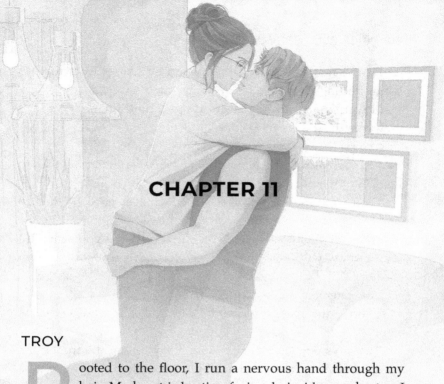

CHAPTER 11

TROY

Rooted to the floor, I run a nervous hand through my hair. My heart is beating furiously inside my chest as I stare at Charlie's closed door. My junk still hurts like a mother, but that didn't stop my cock from standing at attention. I got a hard-on watching Charlie vent her frustrations. I must have gone insane. But her furious red face and wild arm gestures made me want to pin her back to the wall and crush my lips to hers.

"Oi, Troy. Everything okay up there?" Andreas asks from the bottom of the stairs.

His voice brings me back to the situation at hand. And then I get fucking angry. I practically run down the stairs just in time to catch the idiot who used Charlie's bathroom before he can sneak out.

I grab him by the back of his shirt and yank him away from the front door. "What the hell were you doing in my roommate's bedroom?"

His pale face turns ashen, and sweat dots his forehead. "I-I had the shits and didn't want anyone to know."

His friends snicker, but one pissed-off glance from me has them shutting their pieholes in an instant.

"I warned you to stay clear off the second floor, didn't I?" I glower at the guy in my hold.

"Y-yes. I'm so sorry."

"Troy, come on. He didn't do it on purpose." Andreas tries to help, but I'm not having it.

"You shut your mouth too. I should never have listened to you."

"Man, all that fuss because Charlie is pissed at you again. If I didn't know you any better, I'd say you have a major crush on the nerd."

His statement makes me see redder.

I shove the pledge forward. "Get out of my house. All of you!"

The guys don't waste any time, hurrying out the front door. Andreas doesn't move a muscle, just keeps staring at me with a knowing smile on his stupid face.

"You're wrong about me. I don't have a crush on Charlie."

He raises his hands. "Sure you don't. It's cool, man. I'm not judging."

"The hell you aren't."

He holds my stare for a couple more beats before turning his attention to the living room. "At least they finished cleaning the place."

I fleetingly look at the living room before my cell phone pings in my pocket. I welcome the interruption; if I continue the conversation with Andreas, I might use him as a punching bag for my frustrations. It's a text from Jane, asking if I want to hang out this afternoon. Damn, if she'd asked me an hour ago, my answer would have probably been no, but considering my mood and the situation with Charlie, I could use the distraction.

"So, what do you want to do?" Andreas asks.

"I don't know about you, but I have plans." I veer for the door.

"Really? I thought you said you wanted to do nothing but veg out in front of the TV."

"Well, that was before the clusterfuck with the pledges and Charlie."

"Who texted you?" He nods at my phone.

"Jane. She wants to hang out. And no, you can't come."

Andreas flattens his lips. "Charlie was right. You're an ass."

He strides out the front door with his shoulders tense and a storm of bad emotions hanging over his head. I pissed him off—something that's almost impossible to do. Whatever. I'm too wired already; I don't want to worry about Andreas flirting with my sister on top of it. Even if he swears he'd never cross that line, it's in his DNA to chase pretty girls.

After Jane tricked me into going shopping with her, we headed to our favorite restaurant in Manhattan Beach. The sun is shining, and the temperature is mild, so we grab a table outside. Perks of living in California. I'm almost over my hangover, but I still order a beer. I need to take the edge off.

"Are you finally going to tell me what was eating you when you picked me up?" Jane plays with the straw in her drink, watching me closely.

"I already told you. I was hungover. That's all."

Like I'm going to tell her about Charlie. I don't need another busybody on my case about that she-devil.

"All right then. I want to ask you something."

"Shoot." I relax against the back of my chair.

"Mom is on my case about school next year. She doesn't want me to attend Rushmore."

"Why the hell not?" I frown.

Jane twists her face into a grimace. "She wants me to go to an Ivy League school. Barf."

"Hmm, you're smart enough to get into one. What about Stanford? It's not Ivy, but it's a top school, and you'd still be in California."

"I don't want to move to Northern California. I like it here. Besides, John Rushmore is an excellent school. Why aren't you taking my side?"

I pause for a couple seconds. I'm always on my sister's side, especially where our mother is concerned. So why the hell am I not rebelling against the Ivy League idea?

"Because we're talking about your future here, Jane. If you can go to a better school, why not?"

Pursing her lips, she crosses her arms over her chest and glowers at me. "I'm not moving. If you're not going to help me convince Mom, then please don't gang up with her against me. It's bad enough that Dad is with Mom on that front."

He would be, considering he's a Stanford alumnus. Maybe I am being an ass by not supporting Jane with her decision.

"Sorry. I won't join the Stanford team. I'm on your side."

Her serious expression softens. "Thank you."

"You're welcome."

I glance to my right, trying to catch the attention of the waiter, when I spot a familiar face on the other side of the restaurant. *Son of a bitch.*

"Speaking of the devil, Mom is here."

Jane turns to look. Our mother is sitting alone at a table, but then a man approaches her. She glances at the stranger, and her face splits into a radiating smile. The man leans down to kiss her on the lips.

"Whoa. Mom has a new boyfriend?" Jane says in awe.

"It looks like it."

We watch the scene unfold in silence. Mom's new guy sits across from her and then covers her hand with his. The way they keep staring at each other tells me the relationship is new. They're in the honeymoon phase.

"I don't feel comfortable staying here. Should we go?" Jane asks.

"Sure, but not before I introduce myself." I get out of my seat. "Troy...."

Ignoring Jane, I make a beeline toward Mom's table. She doesn't notice me until I'm hovering over them.

Her boyfriend glances at me, frowning. "Can I help you?"

"No, just came by to say hello to my mother."

The guy's face becomes pale in an instant. He looks at Mom, who has a deer-in-headlights gaze. It's clear my interruption is soiling their romantic mood. Ah, something is finally going my way today.

"Troy, what are you doing here?" she asks finally.

"I could ask you the same thing." I turn to her companion, extending my hand. "I'm Troy Alexander. And you are?"

"Bill. My name is Bill."

We shake hands, and then an uncomfortable silence follows. Not for me though. I'm having a great time making Mom squirm for a change. This is too much fun.

"So, how long have you kids been seeing each other?" I ask.

"Uh, your mother and I are just friends."

The lie confuses me. Why would he say that when a second ago, they were gazing at each other like two teenagers in love? They both look extremely uncomfortable now.

"Is everything all right here?" a newcomer asks.

Glancing at his button-down shirt and slacks, I guess him to be the manager. Man, he's good if he noticed the discomfort at this table from afar.

"Everything is peachy. I was just saying hello to my mother." I flash the guy a dazzling smile.

He glances at my mother and her boyfriend as if to get confirmation that I'm truly not bothering them. Mom remains frozen, but her date nods ever so slightly.

I clap my hands together. "Well, I'd better get back to Jane. It was really nice meeting you, Bill."

"Yeah, same," he mumbles, still dazed.

I'm smiling from ear to ear when I return to my table.

Jane's green eyes are as round as saucers. "I can't believe you went there."

"I would never pass up the chance to annoy Mom. You should have come."

"Who is the guy?"

"Some schmuck called Bill. He didn't give me a last name."

"Odd. Maybe he was afraid you'd come after him." She laughs.

"Or he's a gigolo and Bill is his code name."

Jane glances over her shoulder. "Oh look. They're leaving. What did you say to them?"

My eyes are widely innocent when I answer, "Nothing."

CHAPTER 12

CHARLIE

I have to wait until Saturday to exact my revenge since I don't know Troy's schedule. During the week, he tried to apologize again for what had happened, but I really didn't want to hear his excuses. The reason was simple: I didn't want him to convince me to forget about the prank. I can't afford to fall for his charm. A beautiful, cocky football player like him would crush me and obliterate my heart if I let my guard down. Then, I'd have to move out.

My accomplices today are Ben, Tammara, and Fred. Blake vehemently refused to help, citing his aversion to birds as an excuse. I would have preferred to not involve Ben in my schemes, but since he's the one with access to the animals, I couldn't leave him out. He and his girlfriend were like kids on Christmas morning as they helped load the birds in the van Fred had borrowed from work.

Troy left the house before the sun was up, and he won't be back until the end of the day. Enough time for our aviary friends to get comfy in his room. We brought only a dozen chickens with us, which should be plenty to get the job done.

Right before we release the animals in Troy's room, hesitation grips me. Maybe this prank is a little too extreme. But then I remember everything Troy has done to me since we met, the lack of respect and common courtesy, and the guilt takes a back seat.

I've never been in his room before today. He keeps it in immaculate condition. There isn't a thing out of order. No dirty clothes on the floor, no dust covering the furniture.

Man, he's going to blow a fuse when he comes home.

"Wow, look at this room. Who knew homeboy Troy was such an organized freak," Fred pipes up. "Are you sure you want to do this, Charlie?"

"I found a guy taking a shit in my bathroom last weekend. Yeah, I want to do this."

He shrugs. "Okay. You're the boss."

"Too bad we won't see his reaction," Ben says. "We should have bought a hidden camera."

"I thought about it, but I think the chickens are punishment enough. We don't need to add invasion of privacy on top of it," I reply.

"Oh, glad to hear there *is* a line you won't cross." Fred chuckles.

"Ha-ha. Shut up and help me release the birds."

"Release the Kraken!" Ben shouts.

"Make sure Troy doesn't harm the chickens, okay, Charlie?" Tammara glances at me.

"Yeah, of course. Besides, I don't think Troy is the type of person who hurts animals."

Once all the chickens are free, we close the door and head downstairs. We hang out for a little bit before Fred has to return the van and Ben and Tammara go to the movies.

It'll be hours until Troy comes home, and without company, I begin to worry about the birds loose in his room. What if they eat something they shouldn't? *Shit.* Maybe I should have waited longer to let them out of their cages. The lengthy wait makes me paranoid, and during the day, I check on them several times.

I'm in the kitchen making a sandwich when I hear a car door bang shut outside. My heart skips a beat, and then it accelerates to a hundred. I'm suddenly nervous about Troy's reaction. It's one thing to lash out in the heat of the moment; it's quite another to plan retribution. I realize then that serving revenge cold is not my game.

Troy comes in carrying his huge duffel bag over his shoulder. His hair is damp, pushed back off his forehead in a messy way. A wisp of desire curls around the base of my spine, an odd contrast to the twisted ball of nerves in my belly. I wish I weren't attracted to the guy. It would make my life so much easier.

He glances in my direction and hesitates for a second before he says, "Hello."

"Hi," I croak.

Shit. Okay, Charlie, you can still stop this. There's time to avoid Armageddon.

But as much as my conscience urges me to do something, I don't move from my spot. Instead, I watch in frozen terror as Troy heads up the stairs. I'm literally shivering.

Ugh. This is fucking madness, Charlie. Snap out of it. Raven the Sorceress would never second-guess herself.

I turn toward the fridge and pull a bowl of strawberries and a can of whipped cream from it, setting both on the counter.

A moment later, Troy curses so loudly that I'm sure it can be heard from miles away. I wince and then glance at the front door. I can make a run for it.

"Charlie! I'm going to kill you!"

Fuck. I don't think he's joking. But he's already at the stairs, so running now would be pointless. He'd be able to catch me.

"What? Didn't like my surprise?" I ask innocently.

His hazel eyes are dark with fury, and his body is coiled tight with tension. He strides in my direction and then walks around the counter like a lion that's about to attack. I lose my bravado then and stagger backward until my back presses against the fridge.

"My room is a fucking mess! There's shit and feathers every-where," he screams, invading my personal space.

I've never experienced this kind of wrath aimed at me from this close, but all I can think about is how delicious Troy's after-shave smells.

What the hell is wrong with me?

"That's payback for the party, my ruined costumes, and Poop Boy in my bathroom. Now you know how it feels."

"Are you fucking kidding me? I said I was sorry."

"Well, excuse me for not taking your apologies to heart. Now, get out of my way. You're smothering me." I press my palms against his chest and push back. He barely moves. "Troy, I'm fucking serious. Do you want me to crush your balls again?"

He narrows his eyes. "You wouldn't dare. Besides, you won't catch me by surprise this time."

"Try me."

He watches me for a couple more seconds before he finally moves away. I let out a breath of relief when he turns his back to me, but it's too soon. A second later, he whirls around, can of whipped cream in hand, and the next thing I know, I have white foam all over my face.

I let out a shriek and then blindly try to find a towel near the sink to clean my eyes. They burn. Behind me, Troy laughs, making my blood boil. I finally find a dish towel and quickly wipe my face. I still have whipped cream everywhere, but at least now I can open my eyes.

Troy is doubled over, cackling like a madman. Him laughing at my expense snaps something in me. I see he no longer has the can in his hand, so I lunge for it. Before he can stop me, I squirt what's left of the whipped cream on his face.

Take that, sucker!

His amusement ceases immediately. He wipes his face with the back of his forearm, but I don't wait for him to attack again. I bolt for the stairs.

"Oh no. You're not escaping now. It's on."

He tackles me, wrapping his steely arms around my body and keeping me from moving.

"Let go of me." I struggle against his hold, though I know I won't be able to break from his boa constrictor embrace.

"No. I won't let you go until you apologize for all the headaches you've caused me since we met."

"You're crazy! You're the one who's acted like a jackass from the beginning."

I try to stomp on his instep, missing it. However, my effort makes Troy lose his balance, and we both end up on the floor. The fall would have hurt me if Troy hadn't taken the brunt of it.

"Fuck," he grits out.

His hold slackens, allowing me to slide away from him. It's not until I'm on my knees, ready to get back onto my feet, that I see he's clutching his right arm and his face is twisted in agony.

"Are you okay?"

"No. I think I dislocated my shoulder."

Shit. His shoulder does look weird now.

"Can you get up?"

He opens his eyes and peers at me. "Yeah. Can you call Andreas? I probably need to go to the emergency room."

"What? Are you crazy? We're not waiting for your friend to pick you up. I'll take you."

"You?" His surprised tone is obvious.

"I'm not a heartless bitch." I crawl to his left side and help him to a sitting position.

He winces when I move him, making me feel horrible. I'm responsible for his pain. I wanted to make him suffer but not like this.

"I'm so sorry," I say. "How bad does it hurt?"

"Not too bad. It's not the first time it's happened."

Our eyes lock. His are bloodshot thanks to the whipped cream. We don't speak for several beats. The air between us seems to be charged with electricity despite our situation. His gaze drops to my lips, making my breath catch. My heart drums a staccato beat in my chest, the sound so loud, I'm afraid he can hear it.

"We should go. I'll help you up." I clutch his left arm, then drag him up with me as I rise from the messy floor.

He steps closer to me, which sets my face aflame. My entire body is humming thanks to his proximity. He's like a beacon and I'm a moth, drawn to his light. I keep my eyes glued to his chest, but I don't step back.

Good grief. What the hell is happening to me? Troy is the enemy, and our war probably just took him out of commission. If he didn't hate me before, he does now.

"Charlie? You can let go." His voice is low, strained, *sexy.*

Not sexy, you fool. He's in pain.

At once, I let go of him and step back. Still not making eye contact, I return to the kitchen sink to wash my face properly. The small hairs on the back of my neck stand on end when I sense Troy's approach. I reach for a towel, stepping aside to let him use the sink as well.

"Can you help me?"

I freeze mid-motion, then slowly lower the towel from my face. He's watching me expectantly, but I also notice the tension around his mouth. He's trying to hide his discomfort.

"Sure."

I grab a clean towel from the drawer, and after dampening it with lukewarm water, I offer it to him.

He glances at the offering, then back at me. "Do you mind? It hurts when I move."

"Oh, okay. Sure."

I try my best to focus on the task and not on the fact that Troy's eyes are glued to my face. Neither of us speaks as I drag the towel across his cheeks, nose, chin, and forehead. When I'm done, I move away quickly, afraid my body will betray me further and I'll do something stupid, like lick his damn lips. I bet they taste sweet now.

Gee, Charlie, get your mind out of the gutter already.

"I should change," I say.

"Oh no. If I have to wear a whipped-creamed T-shirt to the ER, so do you."

"Really, Troy? Are you that petty?"

"Petty?" He arches both eyebrows. "There are a dozen chickens in my bedroom, and I have a dislocated shoulder."

Remorse sneaks into my chest, making me lose my misplaced annoyance. "I'm sorry. Let's go."

CHAPTER 13

CHARLIE

After three hours in the ER, we're finally home. The doctor gave Troy a strong painkiller, and he's now a little out of it. I have to help him out of the car and hold on to him as we walk into the house for fear he'll stumble and fall again.

I haven't stopped feeling awkward thanks to my proximity to him. My heartbeat is still accelerated, and radioactive butterflies are having a rave in my stomach.

"I'm hungry. Are you hungry?" he asks.

"Yeah, sure. Let's get you to bed, and I'll make us a couple of sandwiches."

"Oh shit. We can't get to bed. My room is now a chicken coop." He chuckles.

Damn it. I had completely forgotten about those stupid birds.

"Ugh. Karma is indeed a bitch," I mumble.

"Sure is. Look at me. Coach is going to skin me alive."

"It was an accident. I'm sure he'll understand that."

"Are you coming to my defense? The journalist who roasted me for not caring about football anymore?"

I sigh. "I thought you were supposed to be loopy."

"I am or I wouldn't be so nice to you."

There's nothing I can say to that. He has every reason to be furious with me.

Clamping my jaw shut, I veer for the stairs, my hand firmly clasped around Troy's bicep.

"Where did you find them?"

"What? The chickens?"

"No, the alien babies doing the cha-cha in my room. Yes, the chickens."

I ignore his remark. "Someone I know owns a farm."

"Man, aren't you resourceful?"

I steer Troy to my bedroom because he needs to lie down and rest. "Okay, it's time for you to take it easy."

He smirks lazily. "Charlie, if you wanted to get me into your bed, you didn't have to go through all that trouble."

"Ha-ha. The doctor said you need to sleep, and thanks to me, you can't use your own bed."

"And where are you going to sleep? With me?" He grins.

"Not in this lifetime, pal. The couch will do."

I let go of him to pull the duvet out of the way. Troy crawls onto the mattress, shoes still on and everything.

"Hold on. Let me take off your dirty sneakers first, dummy." I drop into a crouch to get to them.

He laughs again. "You called me dummy. That's cute."

No, you are. Fucker. Even acting like a moron thanks to the drugs, he manages to be irresistible. Maybe it's because he's not acting like an ass now.

"You should take my jeans off too."

Heat spreads through my cheeks. "Not going to happen."

I unfurl from my crouch, meeting Troy's gaze. He has a lopsided grin on his face, which matches his up-to-no-good stare.

"Are you afraid you won't be able to resist me once you see what I'm packing?"

"Please. You think too much of yourself."

Before he can see the truth in my eyes, I escape to the kitchen. Hopefully, he'll fall asleep after his belly is full and stop tormenting me with his flirtatious comments.

My appetite is gone thanks to the knots of worry in my belly. Troy is acting carefree now because he's as high as a kite, but tomorrow will be another story. Maybe he'll kick me out, and I'll have no one to blame but me.

Knowing I can't eat right this second, I only make one sandwich. When I return to my bedroom, Troy is fast asleep. Okay then. I set the plate on my nightstand, then go take care of the chickens that are still loose in his room.

The place reeks of bird shit, making me wrinkle my nose. I'm definitely not eating anything tonight.

Getting the chickens back into their cages takes forever, but the worst part is definitely the cleanup.

Why did I agree to Ben's idea?

Since I'm not calling Fred to collect the birds now, I bring them all to the living room. We never made arrangements for after the prank, but the chickens have to be returned to the farm, obviously.

I feel disgusting, so I head back to my room to shower. Troy is still out to the world, but I don't want to risk waking him up. I cross my room on my tiptoes and then turn on the bathroom light, keeping the door open only a sliver. In the semidarkness, I quickly grab a change of clothes, then lock myself in the bathroom.

A quick glimpse at the mirror makes me wince. I look dreadful. My hair is hard and matted thanks to the dried whipped cream, and today's stress has given me dark circles under my eyes. I take my time in the shower, washing my hair twice. A sweet strawberry scent wafts from the bottle, and yet I can still smell chicken poop. Yuck.

I've almost reached pruny state when I finally step out of the stall. The bathroom is warm and foggy like a sauna. I brush my hair and teeth first before I put on my clothes.

"Wait. Where are the pajama bottoms?" I glance at the clothes I grabbed.

Crap. I took two T-shirts instead of a T-shirt and a pair of pants. At least I didn't forget my underwear.

The T-shirt is long enough and covers my butt, so I head back into my room like that.

"Charlie?" Troy calls from the bed.

Ugh. Of course he would wake up to witness me prancing around without pants on.

"What are you doing up? Go back to sleep."

He sits up instead, turning on the nightstand light. "What are you doing, skulking in the dark?"

"I wasn't skulking," I grit out.

"I'm really uncomfortable. Can you please help me out of my jeans?"

With a sigh, I head over to the bed. I wouldn't want to sleep wearing jeans either. "Fine. Just promise you won't make stupid comments."

"Cross my heart and hope to die."

I roll my eyes. "Please." Focusing on my irritation and not that I'm about to see Troy in his underwear, I unzip his jeans and try to get them off. "You have to help me. Lift your butt."

He does as I said, but even so, it's hard to remove someone's pants when they're sitting down. I force my gaze away from his crotch, but my eyes have a will of their own. They stray, giving me a glimpse of his package.

Shit. It's as big as I suspected.

"See something you like?" he asks in a dangerous tone.

"You wish."

I finally get his jeans off, but Troy doesn't do anything to cover himself. I fold his pants and set them on the chair by my desk, knowing I have to escape soon.

"Charlie?"

"Yeah?"

"Can you fix my pillow, please?"

With a groan, I glance at the ceiling. "Really, Troy? Now you're just milking it."

"I'm not. I'm in agony, and it's your fault. The least you can do is—"

"Cater to all your whims?" I quirk an eyebrow.

He smirks. "I wouldn't call them whims."

"Fine." I stomp back to his side.

As I lean closer to adjust the pillows behind his back, Troy's good arm snakes around me, pulling me in bed with him.

"What the hell, Troy? What do you think you're doing?"

He reaches for the back of my head, tangling his fingers in my hair. Damn, it feels good.

Too good.

"You smell like strawberries, Charlie. Do you taste sweet too?"

Grabbing a fistful of my hair, he pulls me to him and covers my lips with his. I should resist, but the moment we touch, a current of electricity spreads through my veins, sending tingles down my spine. His tongue teases my lips, prying them open. I don't fight, just completely surrender to the moment, to the fire that ignites in the pit of my stomach. I'm kissing the enemy, the bane of my existence, and it feels fucking amazing. It's a toe-curling, knee-buckling, panty-melting kind of kiss, and it's short-circuiting my brain.

A needy moan escapes my mouth, eliciting a throaty chuckle from Troy. My mind finally snaps into action, reminding me that this is a mistake of epic proportions. I pull back, ending the kiss abruptly, and jump off the bed as if I'd been electrocuted. My lips tingle, and my entire body is humming with desire.

Damn everything to hell. I can't believe I let this happen.

"You taste delicious, Charlie," he says lazily, right before he lies back down and closes his eyes.

I don't move from my spot, too stunned about what just happened. Troy kissed me, and I let him. Even though the kiss was a product of his medication, I still loved it. What does that say about my sanity? We don't like each other, we don't get along, and worse, we're roommates. That's a recipe for disaster.

He's high on drugs, but what was my excuse?

You have none, Charlie.

All I can do now is pray he doesn't remember a thing about tonight.

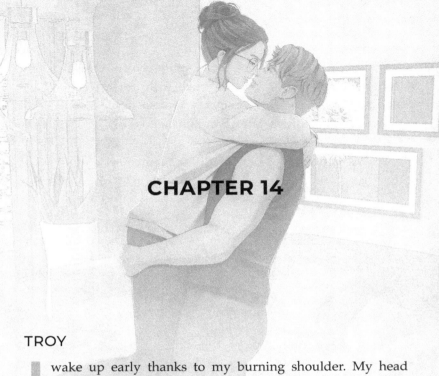

CHAPTER 14

TROY

I wake up early thanks to my burning shoulder. My head feels like it's filled with cotton candy though, and I don't recognize where I am right away. This is definitely not my bedroom. When my nose catches the faint scent of strawberries, I remember that I slept in Charlie's room. Then the memories begin to trickle down.

Son of a bitch. I kissed Charlie last night.

Groaning, I press a closed fist to my forehead. I had to go and do something stupid besides getting my shoulder dislocated. I can't believe she let me get near her. Maybe she doesn't hate me as much as I thought.

A plate on the nightstand catches my attention. Instead of finding the sandwich I didn't eat last night, there are pieces of oranges and grapes on it. My prescribed painkillers and a bottle of water are next to it. A strange warmness spreads through my chest. It seems I like the fact that Charlie is taking care of me. I must be the stupidest moron on campus.

The ping of an incoming text sounds in the quiet room. I try to pinpoint its location, but it's only after a second text comes in that I discover where it's coming from. My phone is on Charlie's desk. I'm not sure how it ended up there. It's not until I get out of bed and come closer that I see it's connected to a charger. She must have done that since I have zero recollection of doing it last night.

The texts are from Andreas and Danny, asking if I'm meeting them at the gym. I said I would yesterday, but that was before my accident. I have to call the coach and tell him what happened. He's not going to be happy about it, but Danny is ready to take my place. I won't be letting the team down, only myself. I can't go back in time and not dislocate my shoulder though, so there's no sense in worrying about it now.

I take another pill and then eat a couple grapes before I head to my room. Bracing for the stench of chicken poop, I'm surprised when I smell vanilla instead. There's a scented candle burning on my dresser. Charlie cleaned the whole place, and she opened the windows to let fresh air in as well. Once again, a fuzzy feeling spreads through my chest, though I'm not sure why I'm so pleased that she cleaned her own mess.

I put on a pair of sweatpants and then head downstairs. The couch is empty, and the only signs that she slept there last night are the pillow and folded blanket.

Sitting on a stool, I bite the bullet and call Coach Clarkson.

He answers on the second ring in his usual grumpy voice. "Troy, if you're calling me this early, it means you have bad news for me."

"You know me too well, Coach."

"Out with it already."

"I dislocated my shoulder last night."

"What the hell did you do, son?"

"I fell in my living room."

"You fell, huh? That's it?"

"Yep."

"You expect me to believe that an elite athlete like yourself simply lost his balance over nothing?"

Ah shit. Yeah, that'd be pretty hard to believe.

"Actually, my roommate was mopping the floor, and I didn't notice. It was one of those stupid moments of distraction."

I pinch the bridge of my nose, realizing too late that I should have thought of a better story before I called the coach.

"Right. There's nothing for it now. I want you to come in and see the team's physician anyway."

"Sure thing. I'll drop by later."

Coach ends the call without another word. I should be glad he didn't chew me out over the phone, but that didn't make me feel any better.

It's my fucking fault that I got hurt. I should have never tackled Charlie. It wasn't only anger that propelled me to do so. I wanted to touch her, to wrap my arms around her body. If I hadn't lost my balance, I might have kissed her right then and there. Though she probably would have ripped my nut sack off in that moment.

But later, on her bed, she kissed me back. I'm sure of it.

I text Andreas and Danny, telling them I'll be out of commission for a while. I should have known Andreas would want an explanation in person. Ten minutes later, he and Danny are knocking on my door and calling my name.

With a sigh, I let them in, then veer back to the kitchen. I need coffee, stat.

"Dude, how the fuck did you dislocate your shoulder?" Andreas asks as he follows me.

"I told you, I fell." I reach for the coffee jar, but opening it with one hand is a struggle.

"Jesus, give me that." He pries the jar from my hand and then proceeds to fill the coffeemaker.

"That must have been a pretty epic fall. What did you do?" Danny asks.

"I tackled the wrong person," I mumble, immediately regretting my slipup.

Andreas whips his face to mine. "Come again?"

I walk around the counter, turning my back to him on purpose. "Nothing."

"Bullshit. I knew your accident had something to do with your roommate. Was it another prank?" Andreas is angry, which is never a good thing. I definitely don't want him gunning for Charlie when she's not at fault.

"Relax. She didn't do this. If she had, she wouldn't still be living here." I sit down on the high stool, facing him again.

He's staring at me through slits, trying to sniff out a lie. There isn't one though.

"Okay, fine. Charlie didn't do this, but I don't get your comment. Who did you tackle if not her?" Danny pipes up.

I pinch the bridge of my nose. "I *did* tackle her. We got into a whipped-cream fight, and things got out of hand."

Andreas's jaw drops, and he's looking at me with a goofy expression now. I stunned him into silence.

"A whipped-cream fight? That sounds like foreplay, buddy." Danny chuckles.

Hell, I don't want them to know how close his comment is to the truth. It would have been foreplay if I hadn't gotten hurt.

"Trust me, it wasn't."

Andreas crosses his arms and continues to scrutinize me. "Whatever. If you're not going to fuck her, then why keep her around? Even if she didn't plan what happened to you, she's still partially responsible. Please tell me you're going to retaliate."

"What the fuck are you talking about? I'm not going to punish Charlie because of this."

The sound of a key turning interrupts our conversation. Charlie comes in wearing skintight gym clothes that serve as a shot of desire straight down my crotch.

Shit. Why does she have to be so stunning?

She glances apprehensively at Danny and Andreas, maybe catching the tense vibe in the air, and then looks at me. "Oh, hey. You're up."

"Yeah. Where did you go so early?"

From the corner of my eye, I see Andreas shaking his head.

"I had to return the chickens."

"Uh, what?" Danny looks at me.

Ah fuck. I had forgotten about them. If I tell the guys what Charlie did to my room, Andreas will have my balls for not doing something about it.

The thing is, I'm tired of this bullshit war between Charlie and me. I'm more interested in getting to know her than getting revenge.

"Troy didn't tell you?" she asks.

"No, Troy seems to be tight-lipped these days when it comes to you," Andreas retorts angrily.

Charlie's eyes widen a bit, but that's the only sign that Andreas's comment caught her by surprise.

"Oh, well, never mind then." She veers for the stairs but stops before she takes the first step and glances at me. "I don't have class until later, but I can drive you to school if you need a ride."

"Uh…." I turn to Andreas, who is watching everything with rapt attention. "I'll let you know."

"Okay. I'm headed for the shower."

Why is she telling me that? Does she want me to imagine her naked? My cock twitches in my pants. *Son of a bitch. I have a hard-on. What am I, fifteen?*

She goes up the stairs two steps at a time, almost as if she's running away from me. I don't blame her. This was an awkward conversation. It would probably have gone better if we didn't have an audience.

"Okay, what was that?" Andreas asks.

"What was what?" I look at him innocently.

"Something happened between you and that girl." He points accusingly.

"Nothing happened," I grit out.

"Bullshit," Danny replies. "Even I noticed."

"You fucked her, didn't you?" Andreas says.

"No, I didn't. And since when are you a gossipy old fart?"

"Since that girl just cost us our QB!" He throws his hands up in the air.

"Danny is more than capable of holding down the fort until I'm better."

"That's not the point, Troy. Yeah, I know Danny will do an amazing job, but this is your senior year. It's the last time we're going to play together."

Ah hell. Now I get why Andreas is upset.

"What do you want me to do? I fucked up. Don't go blaming Charlie for something that was totally my fault. Besides, the doctor said I could be back in four weeks."

"Okay, that's not too bad," Danny chimes in, trying to defuse the tension. "That means our ski trip isn't canceled."

"Yeah, thank fuck for that." Andrea snorts. "Seriously, Troy, you have to get your head straight. Fine, I get it. Charlie is a hot piece of ass. But she's also a fucking menace. If you need to screw her to get over whatever it is you have going on, do it. And then kick her to the curb and out of your life."

Danny whistles. "Things escalated fast."

I curl my left hand into a fist, fighting the sudden anger that's bubbled up my throat. "You'd better watch your tongue, Andy. I'm not a fucking pussy who needs to be rescued by his friends."

His face remains closed off, but the storm has vanished from his green eyes. He knows he went too far. "Good. I'm glad you're not completely whipped."

"Don't worry, man. There's zero chance of that happening."

The biggest fucking lie I ever told.

CHAPTER 15

CHARLIE

Maybe Troy doesn't remember our kiss. Yesterday, when I came home from the gym and found him with his teammates in the kitchen, he sure acted like he'd forgotten. I didn't want to linger to find out, especially when Andreas kept glowering at me. Troy must have told him that I was to blame for his accident. I'd be pretty pissed at me too if I were him. Their quarterback won't return to the game for a month.

Damn. I wonder if Troy is angry with me. He didn't show any indication, but he also didn't take me up on my offer to drive him to class yesterday or today. I only offered because it was the right thing to do.

You live in a house of lies, Charlie.

Ugh. Shut up, conscience!

It doesn't matter. My schedule is already busy enough as it is. I'm low on cash, so I decided to take more editing jobs. I have a two-hundred-page novel to start tonight. I'm glad I stopped by my favorite Tex-Mex restaurant and grabbed dinner. I was running all day and barely had time to eat a handful of nuts.

Troy is watching TV when I come home. He glances over his shoulder, and his eyes give me a quick once-over before he says, "Hi."

"Hey," I croak.

What the hell? Where is my damn voice? Oh yeah, it's being squeezed by the tightness in my throat. One single glance from him makes me as nervous as a schoolgirl in front of her first crush.

What was that look all about anyway? Was he checking me out?

Oh God. Maybe he didn't forget about the kiss after all.

I veer for the kitchen, angling my face in a way so my hair covers half of it. I'm acting like an idiot, but it seems that kiss shattered my protective shield, revealing the bumbling mess that I am. It was so much easier to pretend I wasn't attracted to him when I had all that hate going on.

"What you got there? It smells good."

"Tex-Mex. I got plenty if you're hungry."

He jumps from the couch. "Yeah, I'm starving."

Great. There goes my plan to make a plate and eat in my room. If I do so now, he'll know I'm avoiding him. I can't give Troy that kind of leverage. *Never show weakness.*

"All right then." I grab plates and utensils. While I'm unpacking all the food, I feel his gaze staring a hole through my face. "What's up, Troy? Got something on your mind?"

"You've been living here for three weeks, and this is the first time we're going to sit down to have a meal together."

"We have busy schedules. And there's also the fact that we don't like each other very much." I give him a lunatic grin, but Troy's face remains serious.

"Yeah, I don't think that's the case anymore," he says casually as if his words don't make my heart skip a beat.

"You can't possibly tell me that after everything I've done, you like me now. Come on. You had a chicken run in your room all thanks to me."

He finally cracks a smile, making my erratic heart go

haywire. It doesn't know if it should speed up or stop beating altogether.

"The room looks perfect though. I think you've made up for your mistakes."

"Well, you sure haven't made up for yours. I can't open my bathroom door anymore without a slight degree of apprehension."

He twists his face into something like remorse. "I'm truly sorry about that. I specifically told those pledges to stay clear off the second floor."

"You can't trust frat boys, that's for sure."

"Where is that comment coming from? Do you have a feud with someone from Greek Row as well?" He quirks an eyebrow.

"Not me per se. A friend of mine does."

He narrows his eyes. "Hmm. And you're the type of person who lets others' opinions sway yours?"

"If you're implying that I'm a sheep without a mind of my own, you're mistaken," I snap.

"Ah, there's the Charlie I know. I was beginning to worry you'd left me for good."

That makes me pause a beat. "What? You like when I'm mean to you?"

"Oh yeah, I live for your testy barks." He chuckles.

"You're crazy."

I pull up a chair, making sure I skip one so there's plenty of space between Troy and me. We eat in silence for a moment, and I begin to relax. He doesn't remember the kiss, or if he does, he wants to forget it happened too.

"This is pretty good," he says.

"Yep."

"Not as good as your kiss though."

I choke on my food as it goes down the wrong pipe.

"Are you okay there?" Troy glances at me, half-amused, half-worried.

Lost in a fit of coughing, I reach for the glass of water. When the danger of suffocating on fajitas is gone, I dare to look at him. "You remember we kissed?"

He turns in his chair, leaning his good elbow on the counter. "Charlie, no drug on earth would make me forget that."

Oh my God. What the hell does he mean?

"Is this a joke?" I ask.

He sits straighter, furrowing his eyebrows. "What?"

The doorbell rings, interrupting our conversation. Damn it, I wanted him to answer that. The butterflies in my stomach are wide awake now and wreaking havoc in my belly.

"Don't go anywhere," he tells me.

I stare at my plate, suddenly no longer hungry. My mind is spinning like a top. What the hell is going on here? Troy must be concocting something. It's the only explanation for why he would say he would never forget our kiss.

I mean, I know he's attracted to me. I've seen plenty evidence of that. That must be it then. He just wants to get me to sleep with him before he gives me the boot.

A female voice jars me from my inner thoughts. I turn in my seat to find a beautiful Barbie in our home. Her attention is one hundred percent on Troy, but I don't need to have a good look at her face to recognize her. She was in a few photos with Troy on his Instagram account. They seemed close in them.

"I can't believe the Pied Piper of all daredevils got injured at home. Are you sure you weren't doing tricks with your skateboard?" she asks.

Troy chuckles. "No. I wish that were the case."

He glances in my direction, catching me staring at the duo like an idiot. The girl follows his line of sight, and for a couple beats, her expression darkens.

"You must be Troy's new roommate," she says with a tight smile. "I'm Brooke."

"Nice to meet you." I get up from my seat with my plate in hand.

Troy arches his eyebrows. "Where are you going?"

"Now that you have company, I won't feel bad for eating dinner in my room. I have lots to do before hitting the sack."

He seems disappointed, but my eyes don't linger on his face long enough to be sure that's the case. Besides, why would he want to hang around me when there's a Victoria's Secret model standing in front of him?

Ugh, I sound like all those loser heroines with too much low self-esteem. When did I become that person?

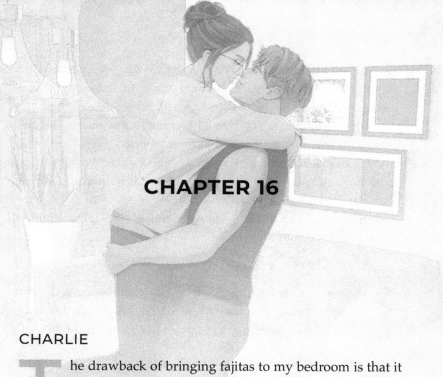

CHAPTER 16

CHARLIE

The drawback of bringing fajitas to my bedroom is that it stunk up the place. Food smells don't belong where you sleep.

It was all for nothing anyway. Troy's comment about our kiss and then seeing him with Brooke stole my appetite. I ended up having to throw the food away because I refused to return to the kitchen while they were still in the living room.

It was hard to concentrate on my work while their voices and laughter carried upstairs. The noise-canceling headphones helped, but then my imagination took over. I kept imagining Brooke smiling and touching Troy in an intimate way, and that kept my mind trapped in an endless torture loop. In the end, I gave up trying to work and called it a night.

I snuck out of the house pretty early, all in the hopes of avoiding Troy. My plan was a success, but that meant I was a zombie, and staying awake during classes could only be accomplished with copious amounts of coffee.

The good thing about today is that I'll escape a Troy ambush again. There's a game night at Fred's, and those usually run late.

Funny how yesterday I wanted Troy to answer my question, but today my bravado is gone. I don't want to know if he was serious or not because if he was, I have no idea what I'll do. Even if Troy is no longer acting like an asshole to me, he and I don't mesh well together. We're from different worlds. He's a jock who enjoys extreme sports; I'm a nerd who gets excited by pretending to be a magical being on the weekends. There's nothing wrong with our life choices, but we have nothing in common.

I'm on my way home to shower and get ready for tonight when Fred texts me.

Hey, it seems my place is double-booked. My roommate planned a special evening with his lady, and he's begging me to postpone game night.

Crap on toast. I call him right away. "Hey, so what are you thinking? I was looking forward to tonight."

"Me too. Do you think we can go to your house instead? It's big enough."

I groan. "I don't know. I was hoping to avoid my roommate."

"Oh shit. Is he still super mad about the chicken incident?"

"Yeah, something like that," I lie.

I can't tell Fred the reason I'm avoiding Troy is because we kissed. Fred has a big mouth, and he'd tell everyone he knows.

"Ah, don't worry, Charlie. We'll be there to defend you in case he decides to be a prick."

"I don't think he will. Let me check with him first, and then I'll get back to you."

"Okeydokey."

Damn it. There goes my plan to avoid Troy for one more day.

I wait until I get to the house to text him. His reply comes a minute later. He doesn't mind. I didn't think he would even though I was kind of hoping for a negative answer.

An hour later, Fred and Blake are at my door, carrying all the food for tonight's sustenance. It's only Tuesday, and while the board games we play usually run for hours, none of us have classes in the morning, so it works perfectly. It's the only day of the week we can make it happen since we're usually too busy on the weekends.

We're just about to start when someone rings the doorbell.

"Are you expecting anyone else?" Blake asks.

"Nope."

I hope it's not Brooke paying another surprise visit. When I open the door, I do find a girl standing in front of it, holding a box with a pie if I were to guess, but it's not Brooke.

Great, another member of Troy's fan club.

"Can I help you?"

"Hi, you must be Charlie. I'm Jane, Troy's sister. Is he home?"

My ill attitude changes in an instant and shame takes over. I was already consumed by ugly thoughts. Jealousy is a monster.

"Not yet. Come on in. I'm sure he'll be here soon."

I open the door wider and let her pass. She freezes for a second when she notices Blake and Fred on the couch.

"Oh, I didn't know you had guests."

I chuckle. "I wouldn't call them guests. Those are Blake and Fred, my partners in crime."

"Hello." Blake waves.

Fred jumps from the couch and reaches the poor girl in three long strides. "Hi, I'm Fred."

"Nice to meet you, Fred." Jane smiles shyly while he stares at her with a goofy grin.

I watch them, waiting for her eyes to either focus on his spiky green hair or the vintage Scooby-Doo T-shirt he's wearing. She doesn't do either.

Instead, she turns to me. "I brought cherry pie. It's Troy's favorite."

"I'm sure he'll love it. Let me make room in the fridge for it."

"We're about to play Betrayal at House on the Hill if you want to join us," Fred tells Jane.

"I've never played that before. What's the learning curve like?"

"Steep," Blake replies from the couch.

I'm not surprised by his grumpy reply. He hates explaining game rules to newcomers.

"Be nice," I say. "Besides, it's not that complicated."

"If you don't mind, I'd like to join. I've always wanted to play board games, but none of my friends are into them."

"Awesome. The more, the merrier." Fred steps closer to Jane and, as if they were old friends, throws his arm over her shoulders. "Don't worry. I'll be your guide this evening. By the time it's over, you'll be a pro."

I expect the girl to shove him off her, but she simply laughs.

My eyes meet Blake's. He gives me a what-the-hell look before shaking his head. I respond with a what-can-you-do shrug and join everyone on the couch. For a brief moment, all thoughts of Troy recede to the back of my mind.

TROY

My shoulder is bothering me again, but I keep the discomfort to myself. I got a ride with Andreas, and I don't need him to get angry all over again over my accident. He hasn't brought up Charlie at all today, but despite his easygoing personality, he also has a mean streak. Mess with him or his friends, and he's out to get you.

We stopped by Zuko's Diner to grab dinner, and during the entire time, Andreas blabbered about a set of twins he'd been screwing—not at the same time, he made sure to point that out. In fact, it seems they don't know he's been tapping them both.

He plans to propose a ménage soon, but I told him it would backfire royally. In his usual fashion, he wasn't worried about it.

We're ten minutes from the house when I receive a text from Charlie. A surge of excitement runs through me just seeing her name pop up on my screen. We're no longer fighting like cats and dogs, which means my previous assessment that I enjoyed my fights with her because of the rush was false. It's her that gives me the high. And I have no clue what to do about it. If it's only a physical thing, then it should go away as soon as we bang. If it doesn't, then that's a problem.

"Who texted you?" Andreas asks.

"Charlie."

"What does she want?" His tone turns dark. Yeah, he's still not over Charlie's part in my accident.

"She wants to know if she can host a game night at our place."

"And what did you say?"

"I haven't texted her back yet."

"Say no just out of spite."

"How old are you? I'm not going to say no."

I text her back with a **No problem**, then look out the window, thinking about the conversation Brooke interrupted. Where was I going with it?

"Fine. I'm curious to see who her friends are. It'll probably be fun crashing her party."

"You're not coming in unless you promise to behave."

"Don't worry. I won't treat Charlie bad or anything. In fact, I'll be so sweet to her, she'll get a toothache."

I glance at him, narrowing my eyes. "Yeah, that's what I'm afraid of."

He doesn't offer another comment during the rest of the drive, and when we park in front of the house, his grin makes me suspect he's up to no good. I get out and head to the front, not bothering to wait for him. He doesn't follow me right away, but when he catches up with me, he's whistling. I notice the backpack strap hoisted over his shoulder.

"What are you doing with that?"

"I missed my gym session this morning. I figured I could lift some weights."

"I thought you said you wanted to crash Charlie's party."

"That too."

I'm not sure what he's planning, but he'd better not pull some crap tonight. I throw him a meaningful glance before opening the front door.

The scene I walk in on makes my steps falter. I see Charlie with two guys I've never met, plus my sister, Jane, animatedly speaking at the same time. They're so into their conversation that they don't notice we just walked through the door.

"Jane?" Andreas says.

The conversation ceases in an instant.

She looks at us, smiling broadly. "Hey, you're home. Hi, Andy."

"What's going on here?" he asks as if he lives here and not me.

"Dude, chill out," I tell him.

"I came by to see how Troy was doing, and then Charlie invited me to play a game while I waited," Jane explains.

"Oh, cool. What are you playing?" I ask.

"Betrayal at House on the Hill," she replies.

"I didn't know you were into board games." I walk closer, not glancing at Charlie on purpose. I'm afraid if I do, it'll show on my face what she's doing to me.

"I've always wanted to play, but no one in my circle cares for them."

"It's because your friends are all lame." The dude with spiked green hair bumps my sister's arm with his elbow, making me frown. A bit too familiar there.

"Who are you?" Andreas asks, not hiding the aggression in his tone.

I whip my face to his, hoping he can see the warning in my eyes, but he's not paying any attention to me. He's staring at Charlie's friend.

Shit. His beast mode is activated.

"You just got here. Shouldn't you be introducing yourself first?" the guy sitting next to Charlie retorts.

Andreas snorts. "Like you don't know who I am."

"Why should they? You're not a celebrity," Jane replies, making my jaw slacken. Ten minutes of hanging out with Charlie has put sass in my sister. I'll be damned.

Andreas seems to be at a loss for words as well. He simply stares at Jane, bug-eyed.

Charlie points at her green-haired friend. "That's Fred, and this is Blake."

I don't miss when she touches the dude's arm. She's standing way too fucking close to him, and I don't like it.

"How do you know Charlie?" I ask.

"I met Charlie through LARPing," Fred replies. "But she and Blake have known each other for like forever."

Crossing my arms, I look at her. "Is that so?"

"Yeah, I've known Blake since we were in kindergarten."

I sense the guy staring a hole through my face, so I move my attention to him. Looking closely, I realize he seems familiar. "I've met you before."

"Sure have. Ludwig dragged me to one of your games. He introduced us." I try to rescue the memory from the depths of my brain, but before I can, he continues, "I'm the editor of the *Rushmore Gazette*. Let me tell you, I loved getting censored by the school administration because of you."

Ah fuck. That explains why he's shooting daggers at me.

"You shouldn't publish garbage then," Andreas pipes up.

Charlie whips her head around so fast, her ponytail slashes across the air. "My article wasn't garbage."

"What's going on?" Jane asks, confused.

"Nothing is going on," I butt in before things get out of hand.

"Charlie and I have settled our differences. Let's just keep the past in the past."

My remark seems to mollify Charlie.

When she looks at me, her eyes aren't crackling fire anymore. "Right. We're no longer archenemies, unless Troy decides to join us for game night. Then all bets are off."

Her lips curl into a mischievous smile that sets my body ablaze. I'm lusting for this girl badly.

"That's an unfair challenge. I've never played that before."

"And you're not going to. I'm not about to waste another twenty minutes explaining the rules," Blake grumbles.

"Hey. It didn't take me twenty minutes to learn," Jane complains.

"I know, but I'm going out on a limb here and guessing your brother will be a more challenging case."

"Blake! Stop it." Charlie hits him on the chest with the back of her hand.

I wave her off. "Nah, it's okay, roomie. Cheap insults like that don't bother me. But if you want to beat me in a game, I have Monopoly lying around somewhere."

Blake makes a face of disgust, but his friend perks up in his seat. "Oh, I haven't played Monopoly in ages. Let's do it."

I glance at Charlie. "What do you say?"

She smirks. "Oh, it's on. And so you know, you're going down."

CHAPTER 17

TROY

Andreas corners me as soon as I enter my bedroom. "What the hell are you doing?"

"I'm looking for my Monopoly game, in case you haven't noticed," I reply, annoyed. He's pissing me off with his attitude.

"Right. I'm talking about the little foreplay between you and Charlie. When did you flip, man?"

"Foreplay? Are you crazy?"

"I know what I saw."

"Uh-huh. Yeah, only your depraved mind would think anything dirty from a polite conversation."

"Whatever. Well, while you look for your game, I'm going to work out." He disappears through the door.

I don't stop him. It's better if Andreas doesn't join us downstairs. He's in an antagonizing mood and needs to chill out on his own.

It takes me five minutes to find the old board game. The box is falling apart, held together by tape. It belonged to Dad. I found it in a donation bin in his garage, though I'm not sure what prompted me to rescue it. I don't think we've ever played it as a family before my parents split up when I was fairly young, soon after Robbie died.

I run my hand over the top, getting sentimental over nothing.

Screw this. I'd better get back to the living room before I fall into a dark hole of memories and can't get out.

When I pass in front of the gym room, I glance inside. Andreas isn't there.

Where the hell did he go?

I get my answer right away when I hear his booming voice coming from downstairs. *Son of a bitch.* He must have changed his mind about working out. I wish Danny were here to serve as a buffer. Usually, the two of us can keep Andreas's mercurial mood in check much easier.

"I found the game," I announce from the top of the stairs.

"Oh goodie," Blake replies sardonically.

His rude comments are beginning to get to me. I can't fall for his goading though. I'm trying to stay on Charlie's good side. Fighting with her no longer appeals to me—unless we're sparring in the bedroom.

Jesus. I think Andreas's way of thinking has rubbed off on me.

We get ready to play the game. The L-shaped couch can't fit all of us, so I grab a folding chair from the closet beneath the stairs and set it right across from Charlie. I want to look at her all night. I hope my cock behaves. She's not even all dolled up tonight. Her clothes are casual and cover most of her body. Her hair is in a ponytail, and she's wearing her big glasses. Still sexy as hell.

The first few rounds of the game are fairly uneventful, everyone busy trying to acquire as many properties as possible. It's only when a few of us start to build houses and hotels that things get interesting. Andreas is currently spending time in jail. It's Charlie's turn now, and she's about to pass through my side of the board. I have three properties, all with hotels, and a mode of transport. Basically, it's a minefield.

I lean back in my chair, grinning like an idiot.

"Come on, roomie. Daddy needs more money for his empire," I say.

"Daddy?" She quirks an eyebrow.

I shrug a shoulder.

Charlie rolls the dice, then lifts her fist in the air when she gets double sixes. "Yes! Take that, sucker."

She blows past my properties, not landing on any of them, to my utter disappointment.

"I'll get you next time."

"I'm happy in jail. I never want to get out." Andreas chuckles, looking pointedly at Jane. He almost went bankrupt after he landed on one of her properties with two hotels.

"Sorry." She chuckles.

He holds her gaze for a moment, almost as if he's in a trance.

Ah shit. My worst fear is happening before my eyes. Jane is totally on his radar now.

I toss a handful of peanuts at him. "It's your turn."

"Hey, I'm not cleaning that mess." Charlie points at me, furrowing her eyebrows as if she were mad. But her eyes dance with glee.

Something has definitely changed between us since that kiss. I wouldn't call our banter foreplay, but it's definitely toeing the line of flirtation territory. I hate to concede that Andreas was right. I should stop, erect a barrier between us, but I don't want to. Deep down, I know if anything happens between Charlie and me, it won't end well. But I'm a fucking glutton for punishment.

"Sorry, darling. I can't do any housework." I point at my arm in the sling.

"But you sure can make a mess." Jane shakes her head. "Typical."

"I know, right?" Charlie piles on.

I snort. "That's rich coming from you. Have you already

forgotten that time I came home and it looked like a Halloween truck had exploded in my living room?"

She rolls her eyes. "Please, I was in the middle of moving. You can't use that as an example."

"Yeah, yeah. Whose turn is it now?" Blake asks, glowering at the board.

"Oopsie. It's mine," Fred pipes up. He reaches for the dice, then leans closer to Jane. "Blow on them for good luck?"

I sit straighter in my chair, ready to put the green-haired idiot back in his place, but Andreas beats me to the punch. "What the hell, dude? She's in high school. Stop putting the moves on her."

Jane's eyes turn as round as saucers. Her cheeks flush.

"Why? So *you* can take his place?" Blake retorts.

"Excuse me?" Andreas stands up, body coiled tight with tension.

I do the same, ready to get in between him and Charlie's friend.

"I should go. It's getting late," Jane announces, looking embarrassed as hell.

I turn to her. "Good idea. I'll walk you out."

"Hold on. I'm coming too." Andreas follows us. Of course he would.

I'm almost certain he only decided to stick around because of Jane.

"Finally," Blake mumbles.

"Blake, stop being such an ass," Charlie replies.

It's an effort to bite my tongue, but I do so because I'm not in the mood to start another argument. My shoulder is suddenly throbbing. I need to stop obsessing about Charlie and worry about my recovery.

"There's cherry pie in the fridge," Jane tells me outside.

"Thanks. I'm sorry the evening turned out sour." I glare at Andreas.

He scoffs. "What's with the look? I didn't do anything wrong.

That punk with green hair, on the other hand, is a fucking perv. Jane is barely eighteen."

"Fred is not a perv." She crosses her arms. "I don't need another big brother protecting me, Andy. Troy is plenty."

Andreas opens and shuts his mouth without making a sound, like a fish out of water.

Ha! It seems I don't need to worry about Jane after all. Thank fuck.

I pull her into a side hug. "Thanks for coming. We'll do something fun this weekend."

"We have Dad's barbeque on Saturday. Now that you can't play, you're coming."

"Ah hell. I forgot about that. Do we need to go?"

"Yes. I already said we would. I'm not going alone."

"That sounds like a lot of fun," Andreas pipes up. "I wish I were off. Maybe I could get the twins to come."

Jane wrinkles her nose. "Ew."

The consternated look on his face makes me chuckle.

He rolls his eyes at me. "Ha-ha. Laugh all you want. At least I'm getting booty. Meanwhile, you're pining for a girl who hates your guts."

His comment kills my amusement in a flash. "Get the hell out of here before I punch you in the throat, jackass."

He flips me off, then strides to his car.

"What's up with him?" Jane asks. "He used to be nicer."

"No, he's always been an ass. He just hid it from you."

"Hmm." She keeps her gaze trained on him until he gets in his Bronco. Then, as if she just finished processing Andreas's comment, she glances at me. "You have a thing for Charlie?"

Thanks a lot, Andy.

"No. That's all in Andy's dirty imagination."

Jane narrows her eyes. "I'm not sure if he's making stuff up. You guys were pretty flirtatious tonight."

I step away from her. "Not you too, Jane."

"What's the big deal if you like her?"

"For starters, we live together. Have you ever heard the saying, *Don't shit where you eat*?"

She rolls her eyes, followed by a sigh. "Okay, fine. I'm not going to bug you about it. But if you want to explore the possibility, I'd say the path is clear."

"What's that supposed to mean?"

"I'm saying Charlie is into you too."

I keep my expression neutral, but I can't ignore how Jane's comment sends a thrill down my spine.

CHAPTER 18

CHARLIE

With Troy unable to play football, we're constantly home at the same time. However, I go out of my way to not spend too much time in his company. It's not only that I'm afraid to explore whatever is going on between us, but I also legit have a ton of work to do.

It's Friday night, and I don't foresee going to bed until the early hours of the morning. I have to finish my editing job. It's a romance novel, and to be fair, I've been procrastinating finishing the assignment. Romance is not something I read for fun, but that's not the issue. The hero reminds me too much of Troy, even down to his description. That leads my mind to wander to him instead of focusing on correcting the grammar in the book. But I'm determined to finish it tonight.

I don't see Troy when I arrive home from class, so I quickly make a sandwich, grab a couple cans of Red Bull, and head to my room. To really keep my mind on the task at hand, I put on noise-canceling headphones and get to work. I'm making good progress until I notice a pattern in the manuscript that begins to irritate me. The author has a crutch phrase that she's already repeated a dozen times throughout the story, and I've only read half of it. Curious, I do a quick document search and get the exact number of offenses. She's used the same phrase twenty-two times. Worst of all, it's not even a good one.

"Oh my God. *My eyelids pressed together*? It's called closing your fucking eyes, damn it!" I yell at my computer screen.

Shit, I'm tired.

"Is everything okay in here?" Troy's voice sounds from the door, making me jump in my seat.

Pressing a hand against my chest, I swivel the chair around. "What the hell, Troy? Don't you knock?"

"I did. You didn't reply." He smirks. "What's making you so angry?"

"Ugh, nothing. It's just this book I'm editing. Bad writing gives me hives."

"Can't you make it better?"

"No. That's not my job. I was hired to fix grammar mistakes and point out glaring plot issues. If I mess with the manuscript too much, I'd be changing the author's voice."

"Gotcha. Anyway, I was going to watch a movie if you're interested in joining me."

My heart skips a beat, and my mouth turns suddenly dry. "What movie?" I ask when, instead, I should have told him I have work to do.

"*It.*"

"Oh, the horror movie?"

"Yeah."

"No, thanks. I don't do horror."

He curls his lips into a grin. "Why not? Are you scared?"

"Fuck yeah. I'm not ashamed to admit it. I once tried to watch *The Exorcist* on a dare, and I couldn't sleep for weeks unless the lights were on."

He chuckles. "We can pick something else. What's your favorite movie?"

Why is he being so nice to me? Immediately, suspicion sneaks into my brain. *"Lord of the Rings*. More specifically, *The Two Towers*. Why?"

"We could watch that. I confess I've never seen the whole trilogy."

"What? Are you serious?" My voice rises to a pitch.

"I might have fallen asleep during the first movie." He rubs the back of his neck, looking sheepish.

"Oh my God, Troy. Take that back. It's sacrilege."

He laughs. "Come on and help me atone for my sins then. Maybe you can turn me into a fan."

A fuzzy feeling spreads through my chest. I've never seen him so open, unguarded. Damn it, I don't know why girls prefer bad boys. Troy's nice version is much more irresistible.

I'm about to cave when a text message catches my attention. It's from the author of the book, asking when I'll be done.

I let out a heavy sigh. "As much as I'd love to indoctrinate you in the ways of Tolkien, I'm afraid I have to finish this job. Rain check?"

"Sure thing. I can't wait to be indoctrinated by you."

I don't know if it's the way he replies that sounds like a sex proposition or how his eyes turn to molten lava, but I'm most definitely hot and bothered now.

t goes without saying that after my convo with Troy, it took forever to get my groove back. I kept staring at the computer screen, seeing nothing, as my mind kept replaying his visit. But I had to push through, which resulted in burning the midnight oil and acquiring a bad kink in my back.

The pain doesn't improve after roughly four hours of sleep. My alarm blares at 8:00 a.m. like a banshee from hell. I'm tempted to shut it off, but unfortunately, I have Mom's work thing, and I'd like to drop by Golden Oaks first.

Resigned, I drag my ass out of bed, bleary-eyed and annoyed. I have to learn not to overcommit to things. I can't remember the last time I wasn't juggling a million balls in the air.

As I brush my teeth, I eye the bathtub. I won't be able to survive the long day if I can't alleviate my back pain. I think I can spare thirty minutes to soak my sore muscles in a bubble bath. I turn on the water, and when the tub is half-full, I toss in one of my bath bombs.

A moan escapes my lips when I sink into the water. This is exactly what I need. Using a folded towel as a pillow, I lean my head back and close my eyes.

Immediately, Troy's image pops in my head. The memory of our kiss comes to the forefront of my mind, making my lips and other parts of my body tingle. My nipples turn into pebbles, and there's a new ache between my legs. *Ah hell.* This need won't go away until I get some relief.

I glide my hand down my belly, then flick my clit with my fingers. A zing of pleasure unfurls in my core, making me arch my back. Damn, I'm so horny, this won't take long. I imagine it's Troy's fingers playing with my sex, probing and teasing. I slide two fingers inside while I apply pressure on my bundle of nerves with my thumb.

"Fuck," I whisper.

I pump my fingers in and out, imagining it's Troy's cock pushing in, filling and stretching me. The pressure keeps building and building, but I don't want to climax just yet. My toes curl, my legs tense as I fight the wave of pleasure that's on the horizon and fast approaching. I slow my movements, but I've already passed the point of no return. There's no stopping this from happening now.

A strangled moan escapes my lips when the orgasm hits me. My hips buckle from the intensity of it. I'm not a fool to give credit to my hand for this; it's all Troy's fault for invading my thoughts, for making me crave him as if he were a drug I was addicted to after one single taste.

I'm uber relaxed now, and if I keep my eyes closed, I run the serious risk of falling asleep.

Fuck it. I guess I'm skipping my visit to Golden Oaks today. I'm too tired to even feel guilty about it.

'm not sure how long I've napped in the tub, but when I blink my eyes open, the water is no longer warm. It's nippy actually. With a groan, I brace against the edge and stand up. Then I notice something alarming. *Oh my God. I've turned into a Smurf.*

"What the hell!"

I jump out of the tub and look at the mirror. My skin is blue from the neck down. I glance at the bathwater, which looks like raspberry Kool-Aid. I didn't notice before thanks to the bubbles. How is that possible? I grab a towel and begin to scrub. The white fabric quickly becomes blue too, but the stain doesn't vanish from my skin.

Realization hits me then. This was a fucking prank.

A roar comes from deep in my throat. I can't believe I was that stupid. Troy played me. He let me believe all was fine between us when in fact he was plotting his revenge. And I fell for it.

Propelled by anger, I wrap myself in a towel and march out of the bathroom. I don't stop until I barge into his room. I find him coming out of his closet, wearing nothing but boxer shorts. Of course he has to be half-naked.

"You ass! I can't believe I fell for your good-guy act."

His eyebrows shoot to the heavens as his eyes widen. "Charlie, what the hell are you talking about?"

"Quit the act already. You won. Look at me!" I open my arms wide, not caring if the towel stays in place or not.

"Why do you look like Smurfette?"

I breach the distance between us, then poke his chest with my finger. "I'm like this because you exchanged one of my bath bombs for something with blue dye in it. Don't even try to deny it."

He shakes his head, still keeping the innocent façade in place. "I swear, Charlie, I didn't do this."

My nostrils flare, a sign that I'm about to go savage on his ass. But what would kicking him in the nuts or punching him in the face accomplish? Nothing. He got me, just like I'd gotten him with the chickens. Now we're even.

I step back. "I should have known you wouldn't simply forget everything. Congratulations, Troy. You really got me."

My eyes prickle, surprising me. I haven't cried in anger since I was a kid. Not wanting him to see me bawl my eyes out, I whirl around and leave his room as fast as I can. By the time I slam my door shut, the first tears have already rolled down my cheeks.

The big hole in my chest tells me these aren't angry tears. They're the broken kind.

When the fuck did Troy get hold of my heart in order to stomp all over it?

CHAPTER 19

CHARLIE

No amount of soap or scrubbing gets rid of the blue tinge from my skin. Running late, I give up on trying to find a solution to my problem. The alternative is to wear a long-sleeved turtleneck and jeans. There's nothing I can do about my hands. I can't wear gloves to a barbecue. It's not that cold.

And to think I masturbated to Troy's image while marinating in blue dye. That added insult to injury. He made me cry, something no boy has ever been able to claim until him. That's what I get for lowering my defenses. Lust played keep-away with my intelligence. It made me forget what type of person Troy is—an egomaniacal asshole.

I don't have time to stop by Golden Oaks. It's the second weekend in a row that I haven't gone. I miss Ophelia and the rest of the gang, but I have to drive to Littleton first because Mom wants to go together as a family. Never mind that the party is halfway between where I live and Littleton.

When I arrive, the garage door is open, but only Mom's car is in it. Shit, did Dad have to work on a weekend again?

When I walk in, I get my answer right away. Mom is in a bad mood, sporting a glower as she finishes getting ready. Ben is on the couch, playing a video game, while Bailey naps by his feet.

"About time you showed up, Charlie. We're already running late."

"Sorry. I had a late night."

She stops in her tracks and takes in my clothes. "What are you wearing? It's going to be a lovely day today. You'll get hot."

I glance at Ben and debate if I should tell Mom about Troy's latest prank. In the end, I decide against it. She's already acting like a dragon; I don't need to give her more reason to be aggravated.

I plop on the couch next to Ben and bend over to rub Bailey's head. She doesn't even stir. Poor thing must be tired.

"What's up with Mom?" I ask softly so she doesn't hear.

"Dad said he couldn't make it to the barbecue. They had a big argument last night."

"Really? Ah, man. I'm sorry, Ben."

He shrugs, keeping his eyes on the game. "It's okay. I had my noise-canceling headphones on."

"Why didn't you call me?"

"I didn't want to bother you. I know how busy you are with school and your side jobs."

"What are you two doing, sitting around?" Mom stands at the edge of the living room with her hands braced on her hips. "Come on. Let's go!"

I jump off the couch, walking fast to meet Mom in the garage. She already has the car on.

The drive to her boss's party is tense as hell. I try to put on a radio station, but Mom barks that she isn't in the mood for music. Considering the shitty beginning of my day, it's fitting that I have to endure a party with Mom in a hellish disposition. I hope Ben and I can escape at the party and not interact with her at all.

Her boss's house is in Malibu, not a usual spot for a technology mogul. He's a genius who built a company out of nothing, and he's now one of the wealthiest businessmen in the country. Mom has been working for his company for over six years, and this is the first time he's hosted a barbecue for his employees and their families. Any company event has been only for the employees and their significant others in the past.

Several cars are parked outside the beachfront mansion, but if we're indeed late, that's another story. Mom asked me to drop by the house at a certain time, and I was only ten minutes late. We didn't encounter a lot of traffic coming here, so it's possible she blew the situation out of proportion because she's in a funk.

Well, that makes two of us, but you don't see me acting out on it.

An attractive man in his fifties greets us when we come in. A beer bottle is in his hand. He's wearing a casual linen button-down shirt and pants. I can tell with only a cursory glance that he likes to work out.

"Tara, welcome! I'm so glad you could come." He gives Mom a casual hug that lasts a second. "Where's Jason?"

Her expression darkens for a moment, but she's quick to put on a phony smile. "He couldn't come. He feels awful, but he had an emergency at the warehouse."

"That's too bad." He switches his attention to us. "And who do we have here?"

"This is my daughter, Charlie, and my son, Ben."

"Hi." I smile feebly, keeping my hands hidden behind my back.

"I'm Jonathan. Nice to meet you, Charlie." He extends his hand, which I was afraid of. I have no choice but to shake it.

"Nice to meet you too."

Mercifully, he's one of those people who maintains eye contact—probably something to do with being a successful CEO —and he never glances at my blue hand. He shakes hands with Ben next and then returns his attention to Mom.

They're talking shop now, which allows me to observe him

more. His dark blond hair is peppered with gray, and expression marks deepen when he smiles, but other than that, he looks quite young. There's no wedding ring on his finger. I remember Mom saying he was divorced, but a guy who looks like him and with all this money must have a young-looking girlfriend.

Charlie, you're being judgmental. He could be single or dating someone his age.

I realize that with Mom distracted by her boss, this is the best opportunity for Ben and me to escape. I pull on his sleeve and point at the outdoor area where several people are mingling near the pool. He nods silently, and together, we slink away from Mom.

Most of the female guests are wearing summer dresses, which makes me stick out like a sore thumb. My turtleneck has to be black to boot. It's not like I don't own brighter colored sweaters. Maybe I was going for something that represented my mood, but now I'm regretting it.

"Let's get something to drink," Ben says.

I follow him to the bar, where a lanky ginger is prepping drinks like a pro. He moves so fast, I'm afraid he's going to drop one of the bottles he's handling.

When it's our turn, I ask him, "Are you training for something?"

"What do you mean?"

"I've never seen someone move that fast behind a bar, not even at a nightclub."

He laughs. "I *am* actually practicing. I'm auditioning for the lead role in the remake of *Cocktail* next week."

I raise an eyebrow. "Is *Cocktail* that eighties movie with Tom Cruise?"

"Yep." He bobs his head up and down. "So, what can I get you?"

"I'll have a dry martini, please." Ben casually leans his forearm against the bar, acting like he's a leery thirty-year-old man, not sixteen.

The bartender chuckles. "Sure, pal. How about a Sprite?"

Ben steps away from the bar, returning to his old self. "Nah. I'll have root beer if you have it."

"Sure thing. And how about you, sugar?"

"Sugar?" I laugh.

"She'll have a Blue Lagoon cocktail," a hateful and familiar voice answers for me. "I think it'll match her… *suit*."

The bartender gives me a quizzical look, but I'm no longer interested in him.

Curling my hands into fists, I turn around. "What the hell are you doing here?"

Troy crosses his left arm over the sling and stares at me with eyes that are cold and ruthless. Gone is the good-guy persona. "I could ask you the same thing."

"Charlie!" Jane walks over. "What are you doing here? Did Troy invite you?"

Oh my God. One of their parents must work for the same company Mom does. This is like a nightmare that will never end.

"No. I'm here with my mother. She works for Slate Corp."

Troy's eyebrows almost meet his hairline. "Your mother works for our father?"

"Wait. Jonathan is your dad?"

"Yeah," Jane replies. "What a small world."

"You don't say," I mumble.

"Hi, I'm Ben, Charlie's brother." He waves in Troy and Jane's direction. "This is a really nice house."

"Yeah, it's cool." She shrugs while Troy keeps glaring at me. "I'm Jane, by the way, Troy's sister."

"Are you in high school?"

"Yeah, it's my senior year."

"Uh, miss? Do you still want a drink?" the bartender asks.

I glance over my shoulder. "Just some water, please."

"Right away."

When I turn around, Troy is already going back to the house.

He goes out of his way to not come near the pool, glancing at it as if some danger lurks in the crystalline water.

"What's the deal with your brother and pools?" I ask, interrupting Ben and Jane's chatter.

"Oh, Troy can't handle pools. Not since the accident."

"What accident?"

Jane's expression clouds. Her mouth tenses, giving me a clue that it's not a subject she likes to talk about.

"It's okay. You don't need to tell me."

"It's fine. Our family doesn't really speak much about it, so it's weird to do so. But I guess since you're Troy's roommate, you should know. It would help you understand my brother."

I'm sensing it's something that irrevocably changed Troy. My heart clenches a little in expectation. Despite my animosity toward him, I'm already suffering in sympathy without even knowing what his trauma is.

"What happened?" Ben asks.

"Our younger brother drowned in a pool when he was three. Troy was eight when it happened."

"I'm so sorry," I say.

"Yeah, it was rough. I don't remember much about it. I was only four then, but Troy took it really hard. He doesn't do pools now."

As angry as I am with Troy, I can't help the guilt that sneaks into my heart. The sentiment is strange and not exactly logical. There's no correlation to Troy's prank and his early childhood ordeal.

"Well, I'm afraid of heights," Ben shares. "Probably because I fell from the neighbor's tree house when I was younger."

"Oh, I was the same way until Troy took me bungee jumping. You should try it."

Ben scrunches his eyebrows together. "Eh, I don't know."

"I'm sure if you ask Troy, he'll take you too."

I'm ready to put the kibosh on that idea, but Ben is quicker in replying, "I don't think so. He's mean."

Mental facepalm. Ben can be so blunt sometimes.

Jane furrows her eyebrows together. "Troy is mean? That's news to me. He can be a pain in the butt, especially when he enters protective mode, but I've never seen him act mean on purpose."

Ben opens his mouth to offer a retort, but I cut in before he says too much. "I never got a chance to ask the last time we hung out. Do you already know where you're going next year?"

"Ugh, don't even get me started on that. I want to stay here and go to Rushmore, but my father is pushing Stanford."

"Stanford is a great school," Ben pipes up.

"I know, but that's not my dream, you know?"

I turn my gaze to the house once more. Jane and Ben continue the conversation, but my thoughts are not in the here and now. They're with Troy.

Was he telling the truth when he said he didn't prank me? My head is telling me he's full of shit. Who else would have done it? But my heart is torn.

Shit. I'm a mess. That's a plot twist I didn't see coming.

CHAPTER 20

TROY

I left the party as soon as I realized I couldn't hang out with Charlie and pretend I wasn't furious with her for accusing me of something I didn't do. That prank had Andreas's hands all over it, and he had plenty of time to plant a fake bath bomb when he came over on game night. He didn't pick up the phone when I called earlier, but as I drive without direction back from the party, I try the jerkface again.

"Troy? What's up?" he shouts over the phone. There's a lot of noise in the background. Considering the time, he's most likely in the locker room, getting ready for the game.

"Did you put a fake bath bomb in Charlie's stuff?" I ask.

"Oh yeah." I can hear the smile in his voice. "Why? Did Charlie take a bath?"

"Yes, asshole. And now she thinks I'm responsible for it."

He laughs, making me grind my teeth. "Please tell me you snapped some pictures for me. I'd love to see the look on her face."

"No, I didn't. I didn't call to congratulate you. I told you I was done fighting with her. Why the fuck did you have to take matters into your own hands?"

"Ah, quit the whining, man. It was just a harmless prank. Get over it."

"I'll get over it when you stop being a fucking meddler."

"Yeah, yeah. You sound like a whipped pussy. Just fuck the girl already and move on. This beta shit you have going on doesn't suit you. I want my friend back."

Coach Clarkson's booming voice echoes in the background. It's time for the pregame talk.

"I have to go," Andreas tells me. "I'll call you later."

He ends the call, which means I have to swallow all my angry retorts as if they were a bitter pill.

In hindsight, it's better this way. I don't want to get into a fight with Andreas over Charlie. We've been friends for years, whereas Charlie is just an annoying brat I have to put up with.

Do you, Troy? Really?

I've given her a chance, and if the last month has proven anything, it's that we're too different to get along. Grandma can't say I didn't try. However, I can't live with a person who doesn't trust me. Who's to say Charlie isn't plotting another bit of revenge right now? Fuck that. I don't want to be looking over my shoulder in my own house.

I make the decision to ask Charlie to move out, but I don't return home until hours later. Instead, I head to the private beach club where Dad has a membership for all of us and chill by the beach. I can't handle pools, but the sea has always captivated me. I love surfing, and if it weren't for football, I might have dedicated more time to it. The idea of traveling the world, chasing the perfect wave, sounds epic.

But as much as the ocean usually calms me, it isn't having the desired effect today. My chest feels unbearably heavy. I thought that after I made up my mind, I'd feel better. Not the case.

There's no sense in postponing what I have to do. It's time to go home.

🐓 🐓 🐓

CHARLIE

I didn't see Troy at the party again. Not that I was looking. *Yeah, right.*

We didn't stay long. No surprise there, considering Mom's mood. On the way back to my parents', I wonder why Mom wanted Ben and me to come. To put on a show? I just know this is the first and last time I agree to a company family event. I'm in college, for crying out loud. There should be a rule that exempts me from bore-fest gatherings like those.

All I know is I can't wait to go back home and try to get rid of the blue dye. I also want to speak with Troy. Jane's comment that her brother isn't mean made me second-guess myself. If I intend to keep sharing a roof with him, I should give him the benefit of the doubt at least. The other times he retaliated, he didn't hide. Why would he lie about this one?

I'm surprised that when we arrive, my dad's car is in the garage. Maybe he didn't really have to work; he simply didn't feel like going to the party. I can tell by Mom's face that she's gearing up for another major fight. I have to get Ben out of the house. Maybe he can stay over. But I erase that idea right away. I don't want Ben around when I have my talk with Troy, and I certainly don't want to avoid that conversation. *Crap.*

Mom is pulling into the driveway when Dad bursts through the garage door, holding Bailey in his arms. Something is wrong.

Mom presses on the brakes, and a second later, I'm out of the car.

"Dad! What happened?"

"Bailey is unresponsive. We need to get her to the vet immediately."

Mom lowers her window and shouts, "Get in here!"

Dad slides into the back seat, and I get back in the front. I'm not even done putting my seat belt on when Mom puts the car in Reverse and burns rubber. All our problems become irrelevant. Bailey is our girl; we can't let her die.

There's a huge lump in my throat, and my eyes are beginning to burn. I turn in my seat to look at her.

"What happened?" I ask through a choke.

"I don't know. I came home and found her passed out in the kitchen next to a vomit puddle."

"She hasn't been herself since yesterday. We should have taken her to the vet, damn it!" Mom hits the steering wheel hard, right before she takes a sharp curve without slowing down.

I don't comment that they probably would have done that if they hadn't been busy fighting. But it's a petty remark and it would help no one. I can guess they must have come to the same conclusion because neither of them speaks again.

We arrive at the vet in five minutes—a drive that usually takes ten. Dad jumps out of the car and takes off to the entrance with me close on his heels. The vet's assistant immediately tells Dad to bring Bailey to the examination room but forbids the rest of us from going after him. Dejected, I sit in the waiting room with Ben while Mom fills out the forms.

Ben rests his head on my shoulder, and with a tearful voice, he asks, "Do you think Bailey will be okay?"

The "Yes" gets stuck in my throat. I can't bring myself to lie to him. Bailey is old, and even if the vet is able to treat her today, it's only a matter of time before she leaves us forever.

"I don't know, Ben. We should prepare for the worst." Fat tears roll down my cheeks. I wipe them away with the back of my blue hand. My fight with Troy becomes small, unimportant in the grand scheme of things.

"I don't want Bailey to die," Ben whines right before his body starts to shake.

I lace my hand with his. "I don't want to lose her either."

The wait is torturous but not long. Fifteen minutes later, Dad joins us in the waiting room. His slumped shoulders and teary eyes say it all.

"Dad?" I jump to my feet.

He shakes his head. "I'm sorry, honey. Our girl is gone. There was nothing Dr. Harper could have done."

Mom stands too and gives Dad a hug. Ben breaks into an ugly cry, so for his sake, I keep my tears at bay, even though I was crying before. There's a big hole in my chest now. I don't want to think what it'll be like to walk into my parents' house and not see that golden fur ball run to greet me. Bailey was a staple of my childhood. There are so many wonderful memories, it's impossible to count them all.

We wait a bit longer for Dad to fill out more paperwork. When we finally get back to the house, Mom wants me to spend the night. But I can't face the house knowing Bailey won't be there. I have to get out of here. It's selfish of me when I think of Ben, but at the same time, that's what my parents are for. Maybe what happened will finally force them to make up.

"I can't stay. I have to study for a test tomorrow," I lie.

"How can you think about tests when Bailey is dead?" Ben cries out.

I open my mouth to defend myself, even though I'm not being truthful, but Dad speaks first, "We all deal with grief differently, buddy. Your sister's way is losing herself in books."

His defense feels backhanded, but I won't complain. He's giving me a free pass.

"Thanks, Dad."

"Please drive safely, Charlie," Mom says.

"I will."

Despite my promise, I barely notice the road on the way back to my house. Everything is a blur. I thought that by putting distance between myself and my parents' house, the pain would diminish, but it works the other way around. By the time I park in front of my place, the choke in my throat is so immense, it's making it impossible to breathe. With quick steps, I approach the front porch. My hands are shaking as I try to unlock the door. I veer for the kitchen in desperate need of something strong to alleviate my pain.

I search each cabinet for the bottle of tequila I saw the other day. It isn't mine, but considering what I'm going through, I don't think Troy will mind. I finally find it pushed all the way back behind some tortilla chips bags. It's almost empty, maybe one shot left in it. I'm about to throw it back when Troy comes down the stairs.

His face is solemn when he says, "Charlie, we need to talk."

CHAPTER 21

TROY

The moment Charlie whirls around, I see something is terribly wrong. Her eyes are bloodshot, her face tearstained. She's clutching an almost empty bottle of tequila as if it were her lifeline.

"What's wrong?" I breach the distance between us in three long strides.

"What do you want to talk about?" she asks in a small voice.

"It's not important right now." I take the bottle from her and set it on the counter. "Tell me what happened."

She can't hold my gaze. Her lips quiver as she lowers her eyes to my chest. "It's…. My dog died today." She tries to hide a sob by covering her mouth with her hand.

I pull her to me without a second thought, crushing her body to mine in an awkward hug. The sling is in the way. "I'm so sorry, Charlie."

"I knew she was old, but it was still a shock. She wasn't sick or anything."

Charlie steps back, easing out of my embrace. I want to hold on to her longer but catch myself in time.

"How old was she?" I ask.

"Fourteen. I can't imagine life without her. Bailey was the sweetest dog." She wipes a tear away, but more keep falling.

I take her hand in mine, then kiss her fingers. She gasps loudly, widening her eyes in surprise. I let go of her, just so I can cup her cheek, rubbing away another tear with my thumb. We don't speak for a moment, but our eyes remain locked. I'm keenly aware of how fast my heart is beating, how shallow my breathing is.

Before I can stop myself, I lean down and capture her lips with mine. There's no trace of tequila on them; she didn't drink a single drop. The kiss is soft, tentative, but when she doesn't resist, I tease at the seam, prying her lips open with my tongue. I can taste her tears, the saltiness on her lips, but also her effervescent passion that seems to grow at the speed of light.

I step closer, sliding my hand behind her head so she can't escape. Her hands find my T-shirt, her fingers curling around the fabric while a moan escapes her mouth. The sound sends a shot of desire straight to my cock. With a groan, I spin her around, pressing her ass to the counter.

"Troy," she murmurs.

"Yes, Charlie?"

"What are we doing?"

I ease off just a little so I can look into her eyes. "I don't know. Is this not okay?"

She doesn't answer right away, which tells me everything I need to know. I try to take a step back, but Charlie holds on to my T-shirt.

"This is more than okay."

She invades my space this time, rising on the tips of her toes to crash her lips to mine. There's nothing slow or easy about this kiss. It's fervid, urgent, and sexy as hell. It sets my body ablaze, it melts my bones, and it vanquishes any doubt I had that this was only a matter of physical attraction. I don't want only her body. I want everything.

If I wasn't injured, I'd take her in my arms and make a beeline to my room because the things I want to do to her require a bed. Cursing my recovering shoulder, I say between kisses, "Let's head upstairs."

"The couch is closer." She steps back, releasing my shirt to take my hand.

I let her steer me to the living room, and then we're on the couch, making out like two horny teenagers. There's only so much I can do with one hand though, but I'm glad Charlie is as eager to explore as I am.

She kisses my neck, sending goose bumps down my spine. "How is your shoulder?" she whispers in my ear.

"It's fine."

"Is it okay if I remove the sling?"

"Yeah."

While she's busy helping me out of it, my hand disappears under her sweater. Her skin is taut and warm to the touch, and I can't wait to taste it. Her lips return to mine when the sling is off. I always feel a tension when I move my shoulder, but I'm too busy exploring Charlie's body to notice. When I brush the underside of her breast, she slides onto my lap, sitting astride me.

"Take off your top," I tell her.

She pouts. "But I'm blue."

"So what? I've always had a thing for Smurfette."

She watches me through slits. "Was that the reason you put blue dye in my bath bomb?"

"No, that wasn't me. Andreas is the culprit. I'm sorry I have stupid friends." She doesn't seem angry anymore, so I press. "I'll take a bath in blue dye to make things even if you want."

"Do you mean, there are more booby traps in my bathroom?" Her eyebrows arch.

"To be honest, I don't know. To be safe, I'd get rid of all your bath supplies."

"Would you really turn blue for me?" She bites her lower lip, driving me further insane with need.

I kiss her again, unable to resist the temptation, while I slide my hand up, cupping her breast over her bra. She doesn't stop me, so I push the fabric aside to play with her nipple. It's as hard as a pebble and begging for attention.

"Damn it, Troy. You're really working your case."

I chuckle. "I'm very motivated. You smell so good, Charlie." I trace her jawline with my tongue, moving along to the side of her neck.

She grabs my arms, digging her fingers in while arching her back.

"Fine. You win," she breathes out.

I lean back and search her eyes. There's redness in them, which makes me feel guilty for a second. Charlie is dealing with grief, and here I am, taking advantage of her.

"As much as I want you, maybe we shouldn't continue."

She frowns. "Why not?"

I trace her hairline with the tips of my fingers, then tuck a loose strand of hair behind her ear. "You've been through a lot today, sweetheart."

Regret immediately takes hold of me when her eyes well with tears. *Fuck.* I shouldn't have said anything.

"Is that the only reason you want to stop? Because you believe I'm not thinking straight?"

I nod, afraid if I open my mouth, I'll say another stupid thing.

She captures my face between her hands. "I've never been more certain about anything, Troy. I'm tired of fighting my feelings. If anything, what happened today has made things clearer to me."

I see nothing but determination and sincerity in her gaze.

"Then fucking kiss me like there's no tomorrow. Don't hold back."

She heeds my words, covering my mouth with hers. I tangle my fingers in her hair, pulling her even closer to me. Risking pain, I reach for her waist with my right arm. I want her pinned to my body until she's molded to me. I'm about to combust on the spot, but when Charlie begins to grind her pelvis against mine, I lose my mind completely.

"These clothes need to go," she says before I can.

"Fuck yeah."

Thanks to my injured shoulder, the process of getting rid of our clothes takes longer than I'd like. She helps me first, pulling my T-shirt off carefully and then lobbing it aside. She stops for a moment to take in my naked chest, staring with hunger in her eyes.

"You can touch if you want," I tease.

"Oh, I will." She traces her fingers over my pecs, then leans down to run her warm tongue over them, making me hiss.

I grab a handful of her hair to bring her devious mouth to mine. I don't kiss her; I brand her with my tongue and teeth before pulling back. "You're not playing fair. I thought you wanted our clothes gone."

"What's the hurry? I'm not going anywhere."

"*What's the hurry*, she asks. Woman, I'm dying here. I need to see you. All I had to hold me over for these past weeks was a little sneak peek of your pussy."

She gasps as if she were offended, then hits my shoulder— my *injured* shoulder.

"Ouch!"

"Oops. Sorry, I forgot," she apologizes sheepishly.

"Let me see your tits and I'll forgive you." I smirk.

"Patience is a virtue, you know?"

"Never had any, ain't gonna start now."

With a shake of her head, she helps me take off my jeans but keeps my boxer shorts on. Her eyes linger on my erection straining against the fabric, and I can guess what she has in mind.

"I do want your mouth on my cock, sweetheart, but let's level the playing field first. Clothes be gone."

She pouts. "You're no fun."

My lips curl into a grin. "Oh, I'm loads of fun. You'll see."

She reaches for the edge of her turtleneck, but before she takes it off, she says, "If you laugh, it's game over."

I'd believe her if she could keep a straight face, but I indulge her. "I won't laugh. Promise."

She finally pulls her sweater off, sitting in front of me in her panties and bra only. Even blue, there's nothing laughable about her appearance.

"Damn, you're breathtaking."

"Really? You dig the *Avatar* look?"

I don't reply right away, too busy thinking of the ways I plan to worship her body.

"Troy?" she asks.

I bring my eyes to her face. "Sorry. What was the question?"

She shakes her head. "Never mind. I got my answer."

I snake my left arm around her back, and with deft fingers, I unhook her bra. Her glorious tits spill free from their restraint, and before the scrap of fabric drops to Charlie's lap, my mouth and hands are on her. I circle one of her nipples with my tongue, teasing the nub mercilessly while I knead her other breast. I don't care about the pain in my shoulder—this is an all-hands-on-deck situation.

Charlie's fingers thread through my hair, and then she yanks at the strands while arching her back. I let go of her breast for a second to pull her onto my lap again. A deep groan escapes from deep in my throat when her pussy rubs against my shaft. She's already soaking wet, and her heat combined with the friction of our underwear grinding together, is sending me careening to the edge faster than I want. *Shit.* I can't pull a quick-draw move on her.

I let go of her nipple with a soft pop, then kiss her lips again, fast and deep. "I'm going to eat your pussy now, darling," I murmur against her lips.

"I want a taste of you too."

I grow harder at the idea of a sixty-nine, but I stomp on it for now. There's a real danger here that the moment Charlie's lips touch my cock, I'll explode in her mouth.

"In good time. Patience is a virtue, remember? Your words." I push her off my lap. "Now lie down and let me feast on you for a bit."

Her cheeks turn an adorable pink shade. I don't comment on it, not when she does what I asked without a fight. She's not as blue as before, but it'll take several washes to get rid of the dye. It doesn't bother me in the least. She's beautiful no matter what.

I peel her panties off with eagerness, almost tearing them in the process.

Charlie chuckles. "Are you that hungry?"

"For you? I'm starving." I sprawl my fingers across her hips, taking a moment to admire her pussy. My mouth waters at the sight.

"What's wrong?" she asks, a hint of insecurity in her tone.

"Babe, there's nothing wrong."

Then I dive in, going straight for the kill. My tongue sweeps over her clit, eliciting a cry from Charlie. Her hips buck toward me, but I keep her in place as I eat her like candy. She tastes like peaches, velvety on my tongue, sweet in the back of my throat. I've never had anything better.

"Oh my God," she moans.

I pull back to insert two fingers inside her while pressing my thumb against her bundle of nerves. I've barely started finger-fucking her when she cries out, and her pussy clenches around me. I increase the tempo, trying to prolong her climax and not think about the tightness in my balls.

"That's it, babe. Come for me."

Her tremors cease, and then she goes utterly still save for the rise and fall of her chest. "Holy fuck," she breathes.

I laugh, then jump off the couch.

She leans on her elbows. "Where are you going?"

"I need something." I run back to the kitchen and look for the extra box of condoms I keep there. It takes me a few seconds to find it and then run back to Charlie.

"You keep condoms in the kitchen?" She raises an eyebrow.

"I lived alone before. Any room in the house was fair game."

I only realize my error when Charlie's gaze darkens. "I see."

"Fuck. That made me sound like a horndog, didn't it? I swear that wasn't the case."

She sits up and takes the box from my hand. "I don't care." Without breaking eye contact, she retrieves a foil packet from the box. "As long as you fuck me like one now."

"Yes, ma'am."

My boxer shorts disappear in the blink of an eye, and the condom goes in place just as fast. Charlie then pulls the same move I did before, making me lie down and then straddling me.

"You've already abused your shoulder too much. Let me take over now."

I reach for her hips, guiding her pussy to my erection. "I can't make any promises."

Bracing one hand on my chest and the other against the back of the couch, Charlie slowly impales herself on me. I clench my jaw, fighting my body. A desperate groan escapes my lips.

"You were saying?" she asks.

"Damn. You're tight."

She begins to move, slowly at first, which works for me. But instinct takes over, and then I'm moving in sync with her hips. We don't speak, and the only sounds in the room are of our labored breathing and the slapping of flesh against flesh.

Getting closer to climax, I sit up to claim Charlie's mouth again. Our tongues mingle in the same rhythm as our bodies. She's getting tighter around me, or maybe I'm growing larger. All train of thought shatters when the release hits me like a cannonball. Charlie lets go of my mouth to bite my left shoulder. The sharp pain only serves to amplify my pleasure. Her body is shaking too, but her whimpers are muffled now that her face is hidden in the crook of my neck.

Eventually, our movements slow down. I relax against the couch, keeping my arms wrapped around Charlie. She rests her face against my chest with a content sigh.

"Are you okay?" I ask.

"More than okay."

"Good."

We don't speak for another minute, but I'm the one who breaks the silence again. "Can I ask you something?"

"Sure."

"Is your character in LARP a vampire by any chance?"

She becomes tense in my arms, then pulls back. Her eyes dart to my shoulder, which no doubt has her teeth mark now.

"Oh my God, Troy. I'm so sorry."

I chuckle. "Why? I can't say I was ever bitten before, but damn, it was hot."

Her face is bright red now. "You must think I'm a psycho."

"Not at all. And, sweetheart, you can make a snack out of me anytime you want."

CHAPTER 22

CHARLIE

I stare at Troy's beautiful, sexed-up face without blinking. Did I hear him right? He wants to keep doing this? My heart and my lady parts shout in excitement, but my head has to come in and ruin everything. I don't regret hooking up with him, but I'm not sure how to progress from here.

"Charlie? Why are you staring at me like that?" he asks through an amused smile.

"Like what?"

"With that deep V between your brows as if you were trying to solve an algebra equation."

"Not algebra, but—"

"Ah, the *but*. Is this when we have the talk? Can't we bask a little longer in the post-sex bliss?"

"I can't. I'm sorry. My mind is already spinning like a top. I don't know what will happen next."

He runs his fingers up and down my arm, giving me goose bumps. "What do you want to happen?"

Oh fuck. He did not just put me on the spot. "That's an unfair question."

"Why?"

"Fine. You tell me what you want to happen."

He leans forward and kisses me tenderly. My toes curl, and tingles run down my spine. My body ignites again, pushing my worrisome thoughts out of the way for now.

"I want to keep doing this," he whispers, then kisses me again right under my ear. "And this."

I swallow hard, hating how his answer has wreaked havoc on my body already. Reluctantly, I push him back. "So you want to keep hooking up casually."

He frowns. "Not casually. I've done that for the longest time. But it's different with you, Charlie. I could never be casual with you."

Sweet baby llamas. I'm about to turn into flames while my heart goes to a hundred. "What do we do then? You understand we live together, right? Talk about adding pressure to things."

He leans against the couch, narrowing his eyes. "How about this? We keep acting like roommates in the common areas and save the fun parts to the bedroom."

"Well, we kind of already ruined that." I pointedly glance at the couch.

"True, but that didn't count."

I nibble on my lower lip, still doubting Troy's proposal will work.

"Of course, if you keep doing that to your lip, I might have no choice but to ravish you where you stand."

My face feels hot. I'm not used to being on the receiving end of such raw sexual energy. And that's what Troy is—sex on a stick.

"Let's take things slow," he continues. "We won't have sex until we go on at least three dates."

I cross my arms, covering my breasts from his view. "Really? You want to go without sex until we've had three dates?"

"What are you saying, Charlie? You can't be in the same room with me without trying to jump my bones?" He chuckles, a sound that's quickly becoming one of my favorite things about him.

Who would have thought that I'd actually find positive traits in Troy to appreciate besides his looks? Is this the same guy who's pushed my buttons and made me see red on multiple occasions?

"I can resist your charms. The question is, can you resist me?" I reply.

He watches me through slits. "Are you challenging me?"

I shrug. "Maybe."

He keeps watching me with his smoldering gaze while the corners of his lips twitch upward. "Roomie, you don't know what you're doing. I never lose a bet."

Feeling sassy, I lean forward until my boobs press gently against his chest. "Me neither. Let's make it more interesting, shall we?"

"What do you have in mind?" he asks in a tight voice.

"How about we don't stipulate a set number of dates before we have sex again? Whoever caves first must pay a price."

"What kind of price?"

"That's to be decided by the winner."

"And what are the terms of the challenge? Is doing this allowed?" He licks my neck, making my eyes flutter closed.

"Yes," I hiss.

"How about this?" He reaches for my breast and pinches my nipple, sending a zing of pleasure down to my core.

"That's… gray area. It depends on the situation."

"What kind of situation, Charlie?" He flicks my nipple again while peppering my neck with open kisses.

"I don't know."

He chuckles against my ear, then tangles his fingers in my hair and turns my mouth to his. The kiss is deep, long, and so fucking delicious. I don't even know what we're talking about anymore.

"When do we start the challenge, babe?" he whispers against my mouth.

"Tomorrow. We'll begin tomorrow."

"Thank fuck." He pushes me down on the couch and then covers his body with mine.

When his erection teases at my entrance, I know I made the right call by postponing the start of our ridiculous bet. Why in the world would I suggest that? I hate losing, and Troy seems to suffer from the same malady. But I won't worry about that now. I have to take my fill of him and hope I manage to curb my sexual hunger later.

Troy finds a new condom and then slams into me without preamble. I cry out, loving the feel of him inside me, stretching me, completing me. We keep our mouths fused together while he thrusts in and out as if he's trying to bottle up every drop of pleasure. He tried to give me some control before, but now he's one hundred percent in charge. He grunts, then leans back to hoist my leg over his good shoulder. My hips rise off the couch, and in this new angle, he can get much deeper. I close my eyes, moaning like a cat in heat as he hits my G-spot.

"Open your eyes, Charlie," he commands.

I look at his flushed face, at the veins bulging in his neck, and I can't help but feel a little nudge in my heart. But the pressure inside keeps building, making it harder to think straight.

Good, I don't need to overanalyze my crazy feelings right now.

When Troy presses his thumb over my clit, I surrender to the wave of pleasure that sends me tumbling into an ocean of oblivion.

"Damn it, babe. You feel too fucking good," he says before he tosses his head back and shouts a string of curses.

He doesn't slow down during his climax, almost as if he wants to stretch the moment for as long as possible. Another mini orgasm hits me then, not as intense as the first one but a surprise nonetheless. I've never climaxed twice during sex before.

Son of a bitch. How am I going to deny myself this much fun?

TROY

I collapse on top of Charlie, spent. In any other circumstance, I'd hit the sack to recover. But since we're starting our ridiculous bet tomorrow, I have no intention of resting. A sex marathon tonight it is.

"Troy, you're crushing me."

"Oops, sorry."

I get off her, standing up to get rid of the condom. When I return, Charlie is already sitting down and, to my disappointment, putting her sweater back on.

"What do you think you're doing?"

"Getting dressed."

"Wait. Do you think I'm done with you?"

She arches her eyebrows and makes an O with her mouth. "Are you serious? How about your shoulder?"

I rotate it backward, wincing as pain flares up. It's not as bad as before, but I'm definitely not recovered. "It's okay. Maybe I can take a bath to relax my muscles. Do you want to join?"

She wrinkles her nose. "Uh, no. I won't be taking a bath until I buy new products. I don't trust that Andreas didn't leave us more surprises."

"Nah, he wouldn't prank me. But I think we should retaliate."

Charlie perks up in her seat. "Really? You want to prank that bastard with me?"

The way her voice rises in excitement is cute as hell. If I'm not careful, I might fall for her.

"Damn straight. I told him I was done fighting with you, but he didn't listen."

Charlie taps her lips with her index finger as her eyes become unfocused. I'm witnessing firsthand her devious mind at work.

"I might have an idea, but I need to check with my sources first."

"Wait. You're not going to tell me?"

"Not yet. Let me find out first if it's possible. I don't want to disappoint you if it doesn't work out."

"He's throwing a Halloween party at his place in two weeks. That would be the best time to prank his ass."

"Really? You want to do it at his party?" She laughs. "That's ruthless, Troy. And Jane said you weren't mean."

"Oh, she did, huh? What else did she say about me?" A grin tugs at the corners of my mouth.

The smile on Charlie's face wilts a little, and her gaze seems troubled. The change is fleeting, making me wonder if I imagined it.

"She mentioned you helped her with her fear of heights."

"Yeah, that was fun. We should do it sometime." I put my boxer shorts on, then my jeans.

"What are you doing?" she asks.

"If I can't ogle your hot bod, you can't ogle mine." I wink at her.

"Fine. I guess that's fair."

"Are you hungry? I could… eat." My eyes linger on Charlie's long legs as she pulls her panties up.

"Will you quit for a second?" She laughs. "I already know who's going to cave first."

"Ha-ha. We still have to establish the ground rules. And one of them is not parading naked in front of me."

"Fine. But that goes both ways, which means no walking shirtless in the house."

Damn it. I was totally banking on my six-pack to win me this bet. But it's okay, I have other ways to make myself irresistible.

"All right. So, food?"

"Yeah. Should we order in?"

"I think we have to. Unless you can whip up a miracle dinner with whatever is in the fridge."

"There's nothing there. I didn't have a chance to go grocery shopping."

"We'll go tomorrow."

She chuckles. "Look at us, planning to hit the store together."

"What? Roommates do that." I smile, knowing very well that we're way past being just roommates with benefits.

The crazy way my heart is beating now is proof of that.

CHAPTER 23

CHARLIE

Can women get blue balls? I feel like that's what I have. After the sex marathon of Saturday night, followed by the exact opposite on Sunday, I'm going through withdrawals. My pussy is in pain and missing Troy's magical wand. He might have ruined me for other men, and at the same time turned me into a nymphomaniac.

I haven't seen him this morning. He did say he had an early appointment with the team's physio. To be honest, I'm glad I missed him. I'm not used to the idea yet that I'm dating Troy. The situation is too surreal. But I can't keep obsessing about him. It's Monday, and I have to focus on the myriad of projects and tasks I've lined up for this week. I'm glad I finished my last editing job. The last thing I need is to read about a fictional character's sex life when I'm purposely denying myself the best sex I've ever had.

I spent an hour talking to Ben yesterday. He was still pretty sad about Bailey, just like me. But thankfully, his girlfriend was there to support him when I couldn't. I still feel guilty as hell for ditching him last weekend. I have to make it up to him.

My first class on Monday is two hours of Italian, which to everyone else seems like a curse. It never bothered me until today. My concentration is shot no matter how hard I try to pay attention to Professor Mantuano. I should be thankful he didn't give us a quiz today. But two hours later, I have a headache that could bring down an elephant. I would have taken painkillers when it started, but I had no water with me, and I'm not one of those people who can swallow pills dry. I'd probably end up throwing up.

As soon as the class is over, I make a beeline for the nearest cafeteria. I get distracted at the checkout line and hardly pay attention to the noise surrounding me. It's not until the girl in front of me mentions the name Troy to her friend that my attention piques. I follow their line of sight and see that the ruckus was caused by the football team, who is taking up three tables in the middle of the room.

My eyes immediately find Troy in the group, still wearing the sling. Andreas is sitting next to him, laughing at something someone said. Danny, the freshman who's temporarily replaced Troy as the quarterback, is on Troy's other side. He doesn't seem to be into whatever it is that sent the entire table into a fit of roaring laughter.

I can't keep my eyes off Troy. He's so fucking beautiful and sexy, more so now that I know what he's capable of in the sack. Suddenly, he turns his head in my direction, and our gazes connect. The amusement vanishes from his face, replaced by pure heat.

Fuck me. Even with the distance, I'm falling prey to his come-hither look.

Someone taps me on the shoulder. "Hello? Do you mind moving along?"

I realize then that the line has moved, and I've just been standing there like a moron, drooling over the quarterback like a football groupie.

"Sorry," I mumble.

It's my turn to pay, so I do so as quickly as possible, then hurry out of the cafeteria. I purposely avoid looking in Troy's direction even if it's hard. I'm glad he didn't come talk to me. We haven't discussed how we should behave in public. We agreed to date, but is he my boyfriend? *Shit*. Why didn't we talk about that beforehand?

I stop under a tree to finally take the painkillers, hoping they'll start to work right away before I have to suffer through the next class. After that, I have to stop by the newspaper and then ho—

A strong arm wraps around my waist, interrupting my train of thought and scaring the crap out of me. I shout, but a second later, Troy's aftershave scent reaches my nose.

"Troy, what the hell!"

He laughs but doesn't let go. "Sorry. I couldn't resist. You looked pretty distracted."

"I was." I turn in his hold so I can properly glare at him. "What are you doing?"

"You left the cafeteria so quickly. You didn't even give me the chance to say hi."

"I have class in five minutes."

His eyes take on a mischievous gleam. "Good. Plenty of time for a proper greeting."

He pins me against the tree and then kisses me long and deep, melting me on the spot. His entire body presses against mine as his right leg nudges mine apart. We would be melded together if the sling wasn't in the way. I should put a stop to it. We're pretty much engaging in foreplay in front of everyone, and my panties are already soaked through. But I'm too weak to stop. I want more. I'm not sure if I'll be able to win our bet after all.

"Get a room!" a random guy yells.

Troy chuckles against my lips and then steps back, leaving me breathless. At least my headache is gone, and I don't think it was the painkillers' doing.

"Why are you laughing?" I ask, caught between arousal and embarrassment.

"Because your face is redder than a tomato."

"Of course it is. You were dry-humping me against a tree!"

He places a hand over his heart and makes a phony expression of indignation. "I was not. My, my, Charlie. You have one dirty mind. I guess you should declare defeat now because it's clear to me who is going to lose the challenge."

I narrow my eyes to slits. "Aha! I see what you're doing. You might have gotten me hot and bothered, Troy, but I'm not the one who has to return to my friends sporting a major boner."

The mirth vanishes from his face in an instant. He glances down, then puts his hand on his hip. "Shit. I guess I didn't really think things through." He looks up again. "That's what I get for having such a sexy girlfriend." He rewards me with a toothy grin. "You'd better hurry up or you'll be late for your next class."

Crap. I lost track of time.

I run across the quad, forgetting to give Troy a smartass retort for making me late. It's okay. I can give him grief later at home. Maybe. Right now, I'm still processing the fact that he called me his girlfriend like it was the most obvious thing. Never mind that I had been agonizing about it not too long ago. How can he make everything so easy?

Because he's not overthinking everything like you, Charlie.

A necessity because I'm traveling in uncharted territory. I like adventure and quests in fiction. In real life, I'm content to remain in my safe zone. And Troy is the opposite of that. In fact, I should probably program "Danger Zone" by Kenny Loggins as the ringtone for him.

Troy is my boyfriend.

A smile blossoms on my lips despite the fact that I hate being late.

When I finally arrive to class—breathless and sporting a sheen of sweat on my forehead thanks to running here—I don't care. Not even when Professor Ross glowers at me and calls me out for my tardiness in front of the entire lecture hall. I quickly take my usual seat and pretend to give a damn about the class, but I've already accepted the fact that I'm getting nothing done today.

t was easy to blow off my classes, but newspaper time is a different matter. Blake will never allow me to skate by and not do actual work.

On my way to the office, Fred finds me, which is good because I do need to ask him for a favor.

"Hey, Charlie. What's the crack?"

I snort. *"What's the crack?* Are you Irish now?"

"Ha, sorry. We have a new hire at the shop straight from Ireland. I've picked up a few things from him."

"That explains it. What did he have to say about your green hair? I bet he dug it, huh?"

Fred quirks a brow. "Why? Because he's Irish? Gee, Charlie, that was weak. You're losing your mojo. That doesn't have anything to do with a certain jock you were spotted sucking face with earlier, does it?"

I stop in my tracks. "What? Where did you hear that?"

"Through the grapevine. You're trending on Twitter. Someone shot a video. Wanna see?"

"No, I don't want to see."

I turn around and continue toward the office. My face is in flames now. Curse Troy for kissing me like that in public.

"So, you and Troy, huh? When did that happen? I thought you hated his guts."

"I never hated his guts. I had an intense dislike for the guy."

"You have clearly moved on from that." He chuckles.

"Clearly."

The newspaper office finally looms closer. I was hoping Fred would just go on his way and leave me alone, but the pest follows me in. I should have known. He's a dog with a bone and he won't stop teasing me until something else catches his attention.

Blake is already at his desk, typing away with determination, but he stops to glance at us. I can't tell if he knows about my *faux pas* or not. He's pretty good at keeping his expression guarded.

"Are you two dating now?" Fred asks loudly in front of him.

Great.

"Who is Charlie dating?" Blake asks.

I groan, rolling my eyes as I take my seat. "Why are you two being such busybodies today?"

"If you didn't want anyone butting in your business, you should have kept your affairs private," Fred retorts with a smirk.

The last thing I want is to tell Blake I'm dating Troy, but keeping it secret will be impossible considering the biggest gossiper in our group already knows. Besides, if it's on Twitter, it's only a matter of time until Blake stumbles across that.

I open my mouth to give him the news when Angelica comes into the office and blurts, "You're dating Troy Alexander?" Her voice is high-pitched, and she has manic eyes, like a small dog that just spotted a ball.

I rest my head in my hand, sighing loudly. "Fantastic."

"What the hell are you talking about?" Blake asks her.

"Oh my God. What kind of newspaper editor are you? Charlie's make-out session with Troy in front of the cafeteria building is trending like crazy on Twitter."

"That doesn't make any sense," he replies.

I glance at him. "It's true. Troy and I are together."

Blake's eyebrows shoot to the heavens. "Since when?"

"Since this weekend."

"But he's an asshole. You hate him."

"Why do you guys keep saying I hate him? That's not true. I had a deep dislike for him. It's different."

"Not really," Fred pipes up. "But what made you change your mind?"

"Several things. I don't want to get into it now."

Blake shakes his head, then returns to his computer screen. "I could tell you that dating Troy is a big mistake, but you're a smart woman. You know that already."

His snide remark does what he intended. It pisses me off. Not because he thinks I'm making a mistake, but because he knows I do believe that. That's what happens when your friend knows you inside and out.

"Why is she making a mistake?" Angelica asks. "Troy is hot as hell. Any girl on campus would die to go out with him."

"And yet he's a senior and has never dated anyone," Blake points out.

"Are you implying he's a player? If so, you're dead wrong. That's his best friend, Andreas Rossi," Angelica replies.

"Oh yeah, that Neanderthal who almost punched Fred for just talking to Troy's sister. You can tell a lot about a person simply by the company they keep."

For fuck's sake. I'm done with Blake's bad attitude. "Really? So what does that say about me? Because you're being a real jerk right now," I snap.

"He must be jealous," Angelica chimes in.

"Oh, that's not it," Blake refutes.

"Ignore him, Charlie." Fred sits on the edge of my desk. "I don't think Troy is that bad. He was pretty friendly at game night. His hothead friend was the one who kind of ruined the evening."

I nod. "Yeah, Andreas can be a prick. Speaking of which, I need your help with putting him in his place."

His eyes widen. "Oh? I'm all ears."

"I was wondering if I could get a custom prop from you."

"You mean a freebie?" He smirks knowingly.

I've hit him up before for free stuff for our LARP events. He's usually pretty chill about it since he also benefits from it.

"Yeah, you know I can't afford to pay. I wouldn't want to spend hundreds of dollars only to prank Andreas either. He's not worth that much trouble."

"It really depends on what kind of prop you have in mind."

"Nothing major. I just need a head."

"A head?"

"Yeah, a severed head." I smile wickedly.

"Oh my God. You want to pull the severed head in the fridge stunt on him. Awesome!"

"Yep. So, can you help?"

"You bet I can, girlie. But on one condition."

"Name it."

"You have to record the whole thing."

I lean back in my chair, smiling from ear to ear. "That goes without saying. If it's not caught on film, it didn't happen. We're pulling the prank at his Halloween party."

"Awesome! Man, I wish I could come, but I already have plans."

"You can't possibly mean that after that douche Andreas almost punched you in the face for talking to Jane." Blake glowers at Fred.

He scoffs. "I'm not afraid of him."

"Oh, I want to come. Andy is such a dreamboat." Angelica makes googly eyes.

Oh crap. I forgot she was in the room. I shouldn't have talked about the prank in front of her.

"Sure, you can come, but on the condition that you won't say a word to anyone about the prank."

"Yeah, Angie. Don't be a party pooper," Fred adds.

She widens her innocent eyes. "I won't say a word. Promise."

CHAPTER 24

TROY

"**Y**ou have gone fucking mad." Andreas shakes his head. "You literally have dozens of hot girls throwing themselves at your feet and you pick Charlie to date? Madness."

I narrow my eyes at him. "Why the hell do you care who I do or don't date? I like her. She's different."

"Why? Because she wants to castrate you when you're sleeping?"

"What's with the drama? You've been watching too many daytime soap operas."

"More like those dark series with serial killers," Danny pipes up from the back seat. "Charlie seems cool."

"She called you Pringles Boy," Andreas retorts.

"Well, I *was* destroying that tube of Pringles." He laughs.

"Trust me, guys. Charlie is awesome."

"Oh my God. Please don't tell me you've gone and fallen in love with her. That's not you, bro." The indignation in Andreas's tone rubs me the wrong way.

"Don't be ridiculous. I'm not in love with her. Like I said,

she's different than any of the hot chicks you mentioned. She's...
exciting."

And that's what I crave the most in anything I do. Excitement, adrenaline. I can't do calm, quiet, boring. I can't let my
mind have time to think about the shit I've done, the lives I've
destroyed.

"Who are you, and what did you do with my friend? Are you
sure you didn't hit your head when you had your accident?"
Andreas peels his eyes off the road for a second to look at me.

"I can't believe she didn't seek revenge after the blue-dye
incident," Danny chimes in.

"Oh, she was livid about it. But now she knows who the
responsible party is." I glower at Andreas.

"Great. Now she's going to turn her psycho act on me.
Fantastic."

"Hey, you brought that on yourself." I glance out the
window, trying to hide my half-smile.

Charlie sent me a message earlier saying her prank idea was
on. She's going to tell me in person tonight.

"Enough about the sexy nerd. You're coming to the next
game, right? Coach wasn't happy that you didn't come last
Saturday."

"I had a family function I couldn't escape from. But yeah, I'll
be there this weekend. I miss the field too much. I can't wait to
get rid of this damn sling."

"What did the physio say?" Danny asks.

"That I could potentially return in three weeks instead of
four. Coach wants me back to training next week already."

"That's awesome news. Well, not for Danny boy though.
Sorry, buddy. Your time will come." Andreas glances at him
through the rearview mirror.

"No worries. It's Troy's senior year. It'd be a shame if he
didn't finish the season."

"We're doing well. We have a chance at winning the champi-
onship," Andreas continues.

"As long as none of us gets injured during winter break," I joke even though I know it's a possibility with us.

"Before I forget, we're going to a party after the game. Your fans miss you."

And by fans, he means the football groupies who are only concerned with screwing one of us. Andreas is more than happy to oblige, but I value quality over quantity.

"I can't wait." I roll my eyes.

"Sarcasm? Really? Come on, man. It's your senior year." He turns onto my street, and I've never been happier for a ride to end. Maybe I can get Charlie to drive me instead from now on.

"I didn't say I wasn't coming."

"Good. For a second, I thought that was your train of thought."

"Are you bringing Charlie?" Danny asks.

"I don't know. I'll ask her."

Andreas parks the car right behind mine and then turns to me. "Are you serious about dating this chick? I mean, I understand fucking around. Psycho or not, she's a hot piece of ass."

I glare at him through slits. "Tread carefully, buddy."

He gives me a droll stare. "Please. Like I'd ever go after a girl you were seeing. I have plenty at my beck and call. I don't need to go through your leftovers."

"I was wondering when the food reference would come up." Danny laughs.

"Whatever. I'm serious, Troy," Andreas presses.

"I'm serious too, Andy. You'd better drop the Charlie subject. You're starting to piss me off. I don't fucking meddle in your affairs, so stay out of mine."

"Fine. I won't say another word about her. But don't come crying to me when she rips your nut sack off and feeds it to the sharks."

"I'm telling you, he's been watching too many serial killer shows," Danny chimes in.

"Thanks for the ride. I'll see you later," I say, annoyed.

I get out of the car as fast as I can. Andreas managed to put me in a foul mood during the short drive from campus to here. Maybe I should walk from now on if Charlie can't give me rides. Andreas has always been a pain in the ass, but as long as he annoyed other people and not me, I was fine with it.

I'm almost at my door when someone calls my name. I turn around and find Charlie's obnoxious friend Blake Ford coming my way.

Gee, what does he want?

"What's up?" I ask cautiously.

"Can I have a word with you?"

"Sure. Do you want to come in?"

"No. What I have to say won't take long."

His attitude immediately puts me in defense mode. "Okay?"

"I don't know what games you think you're playing with Charlie, but she's a nice girl and doesn't need a cocky jock to break her heart."

"Whoa. Hold on. Who the fuck do you think you are to come here and assume I'm going to hurt her?"

"I know your type. Charlie does too. But I guess she must have fallen prey to her physical needs."

I stare at the guy without blinking. *Is he for real?*

Shaking my head, I laugh without humor. "Dude, you know nothing about me, and clearly you know nothing about Charlie either."

He scoffs. "I know nothing about her? I've been friends with her since kindergarten. We dated for a year. Don't tell me I don't know her. I know her better than she knows herself."

A spear of jealousy pierces my chest and then quickly morphs into anger. *Charlie dated this tool? No wonder he's here playing the concerned friend to hide the fact that he's fucking envious. Why the hell didn't she tell me?*

I don't want to let him know his revelation bothers me, so, making a Herculean effort to control my rage, I reply, "If you know her so well, what do you think her reaction will be when she finds out you came here to warn me away from her?"

His condescending expression changes into one of worry, but it only lasts a moment before a cold mask takes its place.

"I don't care how angry she'll be. I did what I had to. If you hurt one single hair on Charlie's head, I'll destroy you, pretty boy. The dean won't be able to help you then."

Fuck. Why would he think I'd hurt Charlie? He doesn't know me, but he's quick to assume the worst because I play football.

What a load of crap.

My nostrils flare as I curl my hands into fists. This asshole is cruising for a bruising, but if I punch him in the face, Charlie will probably take his side.

He turns on his self-righteous heels and strides away with shoulders squared and chin high. I stay rooted to the spot, still pissed at his words. I don't know why I let him get to me like that. I've been judged my whole life; what's one more asshole doing it?

I was right, dating Charlie is definitely something new, and it even comes with knights in shining armor, ready to defend her honor. I wonder what Blake would do if he knew all the kinky stuff I've done to her already. The thought helps me shake off my irritation.

I try to forget the encounter when I get into the house, but his pesky comments are still in the back of my head, tormenting me. Why are my friends and hers all of a sudden shitting on our parade? Andreas thinks Charlie is responsible for my busted shoulder, and even though he acts like a dick, I know he has good intentions. But Blake is an asshole through and through who seems to still have feelings for Charlie. He'd better forget about her. I'm not letting her go.

Jesus, where is this possessiveness coming from?

I have a ton of work to do for school, but I can't concentrate to save my life. My relationship with Charlie has barely begun, yet it's already turning sour all thanks to outside forces. That's not what I intended when I cornered her in front of the cafeteria building earlier. I was only thinking with my dick, and that's my punishment. I should have kept things private a while longer.

It's getting late, and I keep anxiously looking at the clock and wondering when Charlie will get home. I have to stop myself from sending her a message. I don't want her to think I'm needy or controlling her. I wouldn't text her if she were only my roommate, and that's what we agreed to be.

At a little past six o'clock, the sound of her key in the lock has me perking up in my seat. I look over my shoulder and try to keep a straight face. I don't want to look too eager, but hell if a smile doesn't break through anyway.

"Hey," I say.

"Hi. Have you been home long?" She shuts the door with her foot since her hands are occupied with two huge bags.

I jump up from the couch and run to help her out. "I got home a couple hours ago." I take the bags from her hands, frowning at their weight. "What do you have here?"

"Fabric and other materials to make props."

"Oh, is there another LARP event coming soon?"

"Yeah, in a few weeks."

I set the bags down and then pull her to me for a kiss. She melts into my embrace, clutching my left arm as if she needs help keeping upright. Quicker than wildfire, our breathing becomes heavy, and I want nothing more than to peel her clothes off and lose the bet.

She breaks the kiss before I succumb and steps back. "Is this how you usually greet all your roommates?"

"Only the ones who drive me crazy with need. Besides, you're the only roommate I've ever had."

"Really?" She arches her eyebrows.

"Grandma was adamant when she let me stay here that I wouldn't have roommates, so I was surprised when she told me she'd be renting a room to you. You made quite an impression on her. She doesn't like a lot of people."

"Well, I'm very likeable. Only you thought otherwise." She smirks.

"Because you had a bad attitude when we met."

She puts her hands on her hips and glares at me. "And whose fault was that? You made me wait forty minutes and never apologized."

Guilt takes over me. She's not lying.

I rub the back of my neck. "I was a jerk to you. I shouldn't have agreed to the interview that day knowing I'd have to meet my mother right before. She has the ability to suck the joy out of everyone."

"I'm sorry. Your parents are divorced, right?"

"Yeah, for a while."

A shadow crosses Charlie's eyes, but she turns away and veers for the kitchen, almost as if she's hoping I didn't notice her change in demeanor.

"Is there something wrong?"

"No, nothing is wrong. I'm just sad about Bailey."

"I'm sorry. I never had a pet, so I don't know what you must be feeling," I lie.

I know exactly how painful the grip of grief is. But I don't tell her that. I have no intention of ever telling Charlie about Robbie. That's my biggest shame, and I'll take it to the grave.

When she looks at me, I have the feeling she knows I'm lying. She doesn't make a comment, only smiles sadly before looking away again.

"Are you hungry? I can make dinner."

"Yeah, I'm hungry." I hug her from behind as she peruses inside the fridge.

She leans against me, pressing her sweet ass against my cock. Instant erection. "Hmm. You know all you have to do is admit defeat."

"Tempting," I whisper before biting her earlobe. "But I definitely do not want to be at your mercy if I lose."

"You might like what I have in mind."

I dig my fingers in her hip, pulling her closer to me. "Maybe, but I don't want to risk it. Besides, I want to see you beg for me."

She frees herself from my grasp and pushes me off. "You'd better sit and wait. That's not likely to happen."

Since I'm not going to make her cave tonight, I might as well change the subject before I end up begging *her*. "Guess who came by earlier to have a chat with me?"

She looks over her shoulder. "I haven't the faintest idea."

"Your buddy Blake, or should I say, ex-boyfriend?" I try my best to keep the venom from my tongue. I don't think I succeeded.

She whirls around, shutting the fridge door hard. "Blake came here? I can't believe him. What did he say?"

"Basically, he came to warn me that if I broke your heart, he would make me pay." I shrug to hide that I'm jealous as fuck. "The usual empty threat stuff."

"Those aren't empty threats. When Blake says shit like that, he means it." Charlie pulls her hair back. "I can't believe him. He's never pulled a stunt like that before."

"Maybe because he was never threatened by another guy before." I lean against the counter, trying to convey a relaxed stance, when in fact I'm anything but.

"Blake isn't threatened by you. Why would he be?" She pulls a tray of chicken wings out of the fridge.

"He's your ex-boyfriend, isn't he? Maybe he's still harboring feelings for you."

"Please. There are no lingering feelings there. Trust me."

"I don't know. The way he was acting sure sounded like he was jealous."

Charlie narrows her eyes. "Where are you going with this? Do you want Blake to have a thing for me?"

I stand straighter. "No. I just want you to be aware of the possibility. You guys do spend a lot of time together."

The frown disappears from her forehead while the faint hint of a smile appears on her lips. She steps closer to me, wrapping her arms around my waist. "Well, Troy, it sounds like *you* are jealous."

"What if I am?" I grab her ass, squeezing it.

"I'd say you have nothing to worry about." She rises on her tiptoes and presses her lips to mine.

She meant it to be a quick peck, but I keep her in place and devour her mouth. My body turns into a furnace immediately, and my rock-hard erection presses against her belly. She moans against my lips, making me forget dinner, the bet, everything. I just want to rip her clothes off and fuck her on the counter.

I'm breaking all the rules, and I don't care. We're supposed to keep things strictly platonic in the common areas, roommate stuff only. But it seems whenever she's near me, I can't resist having a taste of her sweet lips, of feeling her body against mine.

I'm about to say to hell with the challenge when my phone rings. I'd be tempted to let it go to voice mail if it wasn't Grandma's ringtone.

Reluctantly, I end the kiss and go look for the device.

"Saved by the bell," Charlie murmurs.

"Too bad I didn't want to be saved."

I finally locate the phone under one of the couch cushions. "Hello?"

"Wolfie, I thought I was going to miss you."

"Is everything okay, Grandma?"

"Oh yeah. I'm fine. I'm just calling to see how everything is going."

"Everything is going great." I glance at Charlie.

"How are you and Charlie getting along? I haven't seen her in ages."

"Fine. She's nice." I wink at her.

Charlie smirks.

"Oh good. I was afraid you'd be mad at me for imposing her on you when I forbade you to have any roommates."

"It's your house. I'm lucky you let me live here rent free."

"Yeah, yeah. When can I expect to see you?"

"Uh, I don't know." I love Grandma, but I confess that seeing her with her two boyfriends freaks me out. That's why I prefer to take her out somewhere without them. "Grandma is asking when we're coming by."

"Oh, she is, huh?" Charlie shakes her head. "I heard what she said. I think she meant you specifically."

Fine. She caught me. "Well, you haven't shown your face in a while either. So, when?"

"We can come on Sunday."

I think of the party Andreas wants to drag me to on Saturday. If I manage to convince Charlie to come with me, we might actually stay late.

"How early are we talking?"

"Why? Do you have any late-night plans for Saturday?"

I cover the phone with my hand and smile. "No, sweetheart. *We* do."

CHAPTER 25

CHARLIE

I call Sylvana the next day because she's the only close girlfriend I have. It's not because I have a dislike for my gender; it's just one of those things that happened. I need some advice, and since my best friend is being an idiot about Troy, and Fred can't be trusted to give a sound opinion about anything, she's all I've got.

Troy wants me to go to a football party with him. I reminded him that, not too long ago, I trashed him in the paper and all his teammates must hate me. But besides being the sexiest man alive, Troy also has killer persuasion skills. In the end, he got me to agree, and now I'm panicking. Going to a party with him is definitely something out of my comfort zone.

After I pour out all my worries over the phone, Sylvana asks, "Do you know what you're going to wear?"

"No. I have a cute dress that I wore to the last date I went on, but I don't want to wear that again."

"You can't go wrong with some tight jeans and a sexy top. Don't overthink it. And definitely leave the glasses at home. It's not like you need to wear them all the time."

"Sure, sure. The problem is, I don't think I own any sexy tops. You know if I'm in jeans, I'm wearing a T-shirt."

"Get your act together, girlie. I can't go shopping with you this week, but I can send you links of stuff I think will look good on you."

"But the party is Saturday. If I order online, will it get here in time?"

"Heck yeah. Don't worry. I'm sending some links now. Let me know which one you decide to buy."

"Okay."

"I gotta go. Late for my spinning class."

Before I open any of the links she sent, I finish getting ready, then head downstairs to grab breakfast. Troy is catching a ride to school with me today. He got into an argument with Andreas, but he didn't tell me the details, which means their fight was about me. It seems our closest friends have zero faith that what we're doing is going to work, which is really a kick in the shin. I already have enough doubt; I don't need people piling it on.

It's tempting to go check on Troy, but I fight the urge. If he's still in bed or in the shower, I'll probably want to join him. Hell, we might not even manage to go on a single date before one of us puts their hands up and surrenders.

I begin obsessing about the party. Does that count as a first date? I hope not.

While I wait for the coffee to brew, I check the links Sylvana sent me. Some of the tops are uber tight and with a deep plunge in the front that are a Janet Jackson accident waiting to happen. I don't like any of them, to be honest. They're not me.

Engrossed in my online shopping, I don't notice Troy's approach until he hugs me from behind and rests his chin on my shoulder.

"What are you looking at?"

"Clothes. It seems I need to update my wardrobe."

"Oh, I like that one." He points at a black cropped style that's closer to a bra than a top.

"Of course you do."

"I'm teasing. But why do you think you need new clothes?"

"Uh, in case you haven't noticed, my social activities require different types of ensembles."

"I can't wait to see you in cosplay." He kisses my cheek, waking the butterflies in my belly.

"Only because you think I dress slutty."

He circles around the counter and then glances at me with an eyebrow raised. "Do you?"

I clamp my jaw because unfortunately, Raven the Sorceress likes provocative attire. "Maybe."

His jaw drops. "Are you serious? Damn. I was only joking. When is your next LARP event? Because I'm coming."

"You want to come to LARP?" I fight the smirk blossoming on my lips.

"Well, I don't want to participate."

And the smile wilts before it can bloom.

"Sorry, buddy. LARP is not a show. You can't come and not be a part of it."

Troy wrinkles his nose as if the idea smelled funky. "I'm not sure. I was in a play once and I sucked."

I shrug, trying to downplay my disappointment. Troy doesn't need to love everything I do. I wish he'd be more open-minded though.

"You can create your own character. I can help you with that."

"Hmm, what would be a cool character?" His gaze seems to go inward.

Please don't say something cliché, like a knight.

"Oh, I know. Do you have trolls in your game?" he asks.

"You want to be a troll?" I arch my eyebrows, not expecting that answer.

"Yeah. A cool one, like Shrek."

"Technically, Shrek was an ogre. But I suppose we could use a troll who's not evil. Ben's character is a troll hunter. I'm sure he would get a kick out of hunting you. But I have to check with the other writers first."

"All right."

Well, that's something. He might not be super enthusiastic about LARP, but at least he agreed to try.

He gets distracted by the coffee machine, and I return to my search. Unfortunately, it seems all the clothes on this particular website are on the super slutty side. Not my style at all.

"What's with the frown, babe?"

I sit straighter. "I was frowning?"

"Big time. Does this sudden need to buy new clothes have anything to do with the party on Saturday?"

I twist my face into a scowl. "Yeah. Don't laugh, but I've never been to one of those infamous football parties."

"You have nothing to worry about. Just wear whatever you're most comfortable in. It's not like there's a dress code or anything."

"I'm most comfortable in my pajamas. Should I wear them?" I laugh.

"That depends. Are they the sexy kind?" His lips curl into a wolfish grin.

I throw my hands up in the air. "Oh my God. What's with you and sexy outfits?"

"I'm a guy."

My eyes drop to his crotch. Troy is wearing a snug shirt and sweatpants, which means there's no hiding his erection. My mouth suddenly goes dry while a wisp of desire curls around the base of my spine.

He snaps his fingers, getting me out of my trance. "Hey, eyes up here, Charlie."

Heat creeps up my cheeks. "You're breaking the rules."

"Am I now?"

"Those pants cover nothing."

"I'm dressed. Those are the rules. We never specified clothes that weren't allowed."

I watch him through slits, already concocting payback. "Fine. But you're not going out like that, are you?"

"What's wrong with my clothes?"

"For starters, you're not wearing any underwear."

That devilish grin appears once again. "My, my, Charlie. Aren't you observant?"

I ignore his quip. "So unless your plan is to make every single female on campus stare at your package, then I suggest you change."

"And what if I don't? Are you going to make me?" His eyes gleam with mischief. I hear the challenge loud and clear.

"No. But I can't be held responsible for gouging their eyes out if they dare to stare."

Troy doesn't move a muscle for a couple seconds. Then he throws his head back and laughs out loud.

"I'm serious!" I say, exasperated.

"Sure you are."

"In case you haven't noticed, I'm short-tempered with revenge tendencies." I cross my arms over my chest, aggravated that he's laughing at me.

He walks around the counter and then pulls me into a hug. "You're so darn cute when you're angry, babe."

"How cute are we talking?"

"Cute enough to make me want to do this." He kisses my neck, drawing his hot tongue up to my ear.

My reaction is immediate. My nipples become hard, my breathing turns shallow, and my clit throbs in anticipation even if my head is telling it to cool off. Not willing to simply stand there and take Troy's torture, I turn my face so I can kiss him hard and deep. He responds in kind, grunting like a savage and grinding his pelvis against mine.

I bet I could make him cave right now, but we don't have a lot of time, and there's no quickie with Troy. Reluctantly, I step back. His half-hooded eyes drop to my lips, and he would have followed them if I hadn't pressed my palm against his chest.

"If you want to catch a ride with me, then you have to finish getting ready. And before you complain, underwear is mandatory."

"You're so bossy."

"When it comes to punctuality, yes I am."

Grumbling, he veers toward the stairs. "Fine. I'll put decent clothes on. Don't want you gouging anyone's eyes out on my account."

I shake my head, then go grab a cup of coffee.

"Charlie?" he calls from the middle of the stairs.

"Yeah?"

"Are you free on Friday?"

"I think so. Why?"

"Would you like to have dinner with me?"

The butterflies in my stomach explode in a crazy fluttering while my heart takes off. "Are you asking me out on a date?"

"Yes I am."

The thumping inside my chest becomes louder. *Settle down, damn muscle!*

"That's so sweet." I smirk, trying to hide my excitement.

"Is that a yes?"

I shrug. "Sure. Why not?"

Troy watches me through narrowed eyes for a second, probably catching on to my false casualness, before he says, "It's a date then."

CHAPTER 26

TROY

Keeping my hands off Charlie for the rest of the week is the hardest thing I've had to do. If I could go back in time and stop myself from making the stupid bet, I would. Too late now. The only thing I can do is make Charlie lose, and I plan to do that tonight.

I haven't gone out on a date since I was seeing Brooke, which means it's been ages and I'm rusty. However, I know that to impress Charlie, I can't simply do the usual. She's into LARPing, for crying out loud. Creativity is in her blood. I've agonized about it since Tuesday when I asked her out. I considered taking her to an experimental cuisine restaurant, but Jane convinced me to stick to a place I was familiar with. The last thing I want is to ruin the evening by giving Charlie food poisoning.

I decide on Le Gone, one of my favorite restaurants. You can't go wrong with French food unless you're lactose intolerant, which isn't the case with Charlie. She goes through gallons of milk a week. I also suspect she was a mouse in her previous life, judging by the amount of cheese she eats. My secret weapon to break through her defenses will come later when we get back to the house.

I haven't really spoken to Andreas since our argument, even though I've seen him during practice. I can't throw balls, but I can do everything else that doesn't require the use of my arms. Saturday's game is against our rival school, and it'll be a pain to warm the bench. At least I can give Danny pointers. I'd be lying if I said I wasn't disappointed that I'm not playing. I do miss football. But for now, the game with Charlie is keeping my excitement level high, which means I don't have time to deal with my inner demons.

As I'm heading to the locker room, Andreas stops me.

"Hey, Troy. Got a minute?"

"Yeah."

"Listen, I want to apologize about Charlie. It was an asshole move to interfere."

"Yeah, it was. But no worries, man. Apology accepted."

My statement is true. I won't hold a grudge against him, especially now that he realizes his error in judgment. But that doesn't mean I'm not pranking him later. Charlie told me about her idea, and it's genius. I can't wait to pull that one on him.

"What's the deal with you two? Is it serious?"

"I don't know if it's serious, but we're having fun."

He smirks. "Having fun, huh? I knew you wouldn't be able to resist the sexy nerd. Have you talked to Brooke since you and Charlie got together?"

Andreas, being my best friend, knows I got a weird vibe from Brooke when she got back to LA.

"Not yet. I haven't really talked to her at all in weeks. The last time was when she came by after my accident."

"She's probably nursing a broken heart." He chuckles.

"I hope not."

I know people say it's impossible to stay friends with your ex, but I'd like to believe it's possible with Brooke. She's into high-adrenaline sports like me, and she's fun to hang out with.

In a different scenario, we would be perfect for each other, but because we're so much alike, we were boring together.

"Hey, I'm going to meet the guys later for a quick beer. Do you wanna come?" Andreas asks.

"Ah sorry. Can't. I have a date." I smile even though I didn't mean to.

"Holy fuck. Look at your face. Dude! You got it bad for the sexy nerd."

I school my face into a neutral expression, but I'm not fooling anyone, especially not Andreas. "As usual, you're blowing things way out of proportion."

"Yeah, yeah." He shakes his head, then continues on into the locker room.

Damn him. He knows me too well.

I do have it bad for Charlie, and if I'm honest with myself, it's terrifying, and probably the reason going out with her is a thrill.

'm pacing in the living room as I wait for Charlie. She's not late, I just got ready too early. I let Jane get into my head, and now I'm feeling like a fool. I have a bottle of champagne chilling in the ice bucket, and I bought a rose bouquet. Jesus, it looks like I'm going to propose, not going on a first date. *Hell.* I can't get rid of the flowers because Charlie will see them in the trash can and think I'm nuts. But I can put the champagne away.

As the world would have it, she catches me in the act. "You got me bubbles?"

I turn around and freeze. Charlie is wearing the same snug-fit burgundy dress she wore when she went out with whatever his name was. That was the first time I realized I was in deep trouble. I fucking love that dress on her, and she must be aware of it, because she's sporting a smug smile now.

"What do you think?" She twirls when she reaches the bottom of the stairs.

"Stunning."

With a bounce to her step, she comes to my side. "You look good enough to eat." She gives me a quick peck on the cheek and then takes a whiff of my neck. "Hmm, I love the way you smell."

"Thanks, babe. Remember, you can have the whole thing; all you have to do is ask."

"Tempting." She steps back. "But I'd rather you ask me."

I watch her for a moment, drinking her in. "We'll see."

She turns her attention to the ice bucket I'm still holding. "Are we having some or what?"

"I guess."

I feel my face getting warmer, so I quickly turn around to hide it from Charlie.

"And those flowers?"

Ah shit. What's wrong with me? I'm acting like an idiot.

I grab the bouquet and give it to her. "For you, sweetheart."

She brings the roses to her nose and takes a deep breath. "They smell lovely. Not as good as you though. Thank you."

"You're welcome."

"Why don't you pop that bottle while I go put these in a vase?"

"All right."

"How are we on time? How long until we need to be at the restaurant?"

"Half an hour. It's not that far from here." I open the champagne bottle with a loud pop—at least I didn't screw this part up.

"We probably should call an Uber soon. You never know how long it'll take to find a ride."

I smile to myself, remembering her comment about punctuality. "I have one request for tonight." I turn around, holding two flutes of champagne.

"And what is it?" She takes one.

"That you don't stress about anything. Cheers."

We clink our glasses together, and then, with our gazes locked, we take a sip of the champagne. I'm not particularly fond of it, but Jane said it was a must.

"Okay, I'll try." She takes another sip and then sets the glass down.

"You don't like it?"

"I do. It's not something I drink often though."

Shit, Jane. I shouldn't have listened to you.

I must have shown my disappointment on my face, as she's quick to add. "I love that you thought about it though. Super romantic. You're definitely trying to get lucky tonight."

"Yep. But you know how men live in hope—"

"And die in despair," she finishes for me.

We don't speak for several beats, and I'm highly aware of the stupid smile I'm sporting now. The air between us crackles with electricity and sexual tension. It won't take long until one of us caves to the pressure. My cock stirs in my pants, and I know it might be me tonight.

"So, where are we going?" she asks, breaking the silence.

"It's a surprise."

Her eyes twinkle with excitement. "I can't wait."

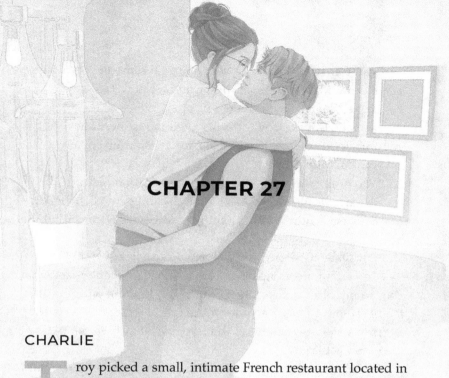

CHAPTER 27

CHARLIE

Troy picked a small, intimate French restaurant located in an unpretentious open mall just twenty minutes from the house. The décor is rustic with a whimsical touch thanks to the exposed brick walls and twinkling lights hanging from them.

There's no hostess; we're greeted by the chef himself as we come through the door. He ushers us to our table in a flurry of excited comments.

"*Monsieur* Alexander. It's so good to see you. Oh, and you brought a lovely *mademoiselle* tonight."

"Yes. This is our first date."

"Is that so? Oh, then you need our very best table. Come this way."

Not long after we're seated at a cozy table in the corner, our waiter comes with the menu. "Can I interest you in something to drink?" he asks.

"Would you like a cocktail first, or straight to wine?" Troy asks me.

I can't answer. I'm too awestruck at the moment. "Hmm, I don't know. Maybe just sparkling water for now."

"Same," he tells the waiter.

When he leaves, Troy turns his attention to me. "I have to ask you this because I feel like I've already messed up royally. What are your favorite drinks?"

"You didn't mess up. The champagne was a nice touch."

He narrows his eyes. "Was it though? You barely touched it."

"Because I didn't want to get wasted before we even left the house."

"Oh. Okay then. Are you saying you're a lightweight?"

"To certain alcoholic beverages, yes. Champagne is one that goes to my head quicker than others. But I'm fine with drinking tequila shots or Duck Farts, for instance."

Troy's eyebrows shoot to the heavens. "Duck Farts? What in the world is that?"

"It's a combination of Kahlúa, Irish cream, and whiskey. But I prefer it without the Kahlúa. It's delicious."

"Noted. Would you like to have that instead of wine? I'm sure they can make it for you."

"Oh no. I don't think it goes with French cuisine. Wine is fine."

"Does it also go to your head faster?" His lips curl into a mischievous smile.

I watch him through slits. "Why do you want to know, Troy? Are you planning on getting me drunk so I can lose the bet?"

He widens his eyes innocently. "Me? Of course not. Are you implying you turn into a nympho under the influence?"

My face bursts into flames. *No, you've turned me into one, Troy.*

"I'm not saying that at all," I lie.

I'm already hanging on by a thread. Sitting across from him in his suit jacket that makes him look like he just sprang from a fashion magazine, plus being under the allure of his intoxicating scent, is already doing crazy things to my body. I really don't need to add alcohol to my system; it'll shut my brain down, and then my body will take control.

"Okay. Just checking." He opens the wine list and does a quick perusal of the menu. "Do you have any preference in mind?"

"Oh please. I know nothing about wine. You go ahead and pick."

He looks up. "What gives you the idea that I know about wine?"

"Aren't you a regular here?"

"Kind of. This is Grandma's favorite restaurant. I always come with her, and she chooses the wine."

"I guess we'll just have to gamble then." I wink at him.

He scrunches his nose. "Maybe we'll let the waiter suggest something."

"Sounds like a plan."

The server returns with our water, and after we tell him we have no clue about wine, he's more than happy to suggest a bottle. We turn our attention to the dinner menu, and I'm faced with the impossible choice of selecting what I want. Everything looks delicious.

"Besides your unusual reaction to alcohol, anything else I should know beforehand?" Troy asks.

I chuckle. "What do you mean by unusual?"

"I've never met someone before who would get drunk from a glass of champagne but could handle copious amounts of tequila and whiskey with no problem."

"What can I say? I'm special."

"Oh, I know that." He smirks.

I watch him through slitted eyes. "Somehow I feel your statement has a double meaning."

"Maybe, but nothing bad. I promise."

I open my mouth to ask him to elaborate, but the waiter returns to take our orders, and when he leaves, I decide to let the subject drop.

"How long have we been living together?" Troy leans back, obviously comfortable. Even though I pegged him to be a rowdy jock when we met, he fits perfectly in this sophisticated environment. He's like a rogue prince from a fairy tale.

"I don't know. Almost two months?"

"Right. And yet I only know that you're into LARP and board games, and you want to be a journalist. Is that correct?"

"Partially. I don't want to be a journalist. I want to write fiction."

"Oh, that's cool. Are we talking books or maybe a screenplay?"

No one has ever asked me that before. Whenever I mention I want to write fiction, all I get is a pitiful glance. I get it, making a living as a fiction writer isn't the easiest career path. Even with the growth of indie publishing, it takes dedication and long working hours to succeed. And even so, many people never do.

"Both? I don't know." I reach for my water.

"Have you written anything that I can read?"

I take a sip and then answer, "Yes and no. I have written plenty of stuff, but it's not ready for the public eye yet."

"Oh come on. Why not?"

"Because... I don't think I'm ready to open myself to criticism."

"You write for the newspaper. Aren't people reading that?"

"Yeah, but it's different."

"Different how?"

"I don't know."

I sense my barriers going up. My muscles are tense, and I can't wait to change the subject. As different as Troy and I are, he's the only one who seems to know exactly where my weak points are.

"I'm sorry. I didn't mean to push you into a corner," he says. "How about you ask me the tough questions?"

I'm not sure if his comment was meant to remind me of when

we first met, but his eyes are devoid of mirth, so maybe it was just a coincidence.

The waiter comes with our wine, and I'm thankful for the interruption.

Wine is poured and tasted. Not surprising, it's amazing.

After I take a couple of sips, I glance at Troy. "Where were we? Oh, it was my turn to grill you."

"Oh boy." He smiles casually, unaware of what it does to me. He's so beautiful that it makes my heart ache with the need to be close to him.

"What do you want to do when you graduate?"

Troy hangs his head low. "Ugh. You had to go there."

"Come on. It's not a hard question. You're a senior!" I say, trying to suppress my laughter, knowing Troy is being dramatic on purpose.

"I know. I'm a business major, but while most of my class-mates are all set with internships or actively looking for a job, I haven't done any of that."

"You can always work for your father."

"Are you suggesting nepotism, Charlie?" He grins.

I shrug. "I mean, it makes sense."

"Nah. It's bad enough that he pushed me into that direction. I have no desire of actually working for him. I'm thinking about taking a year off to go travel, see the world."

"With all expenses paid by your parents," I note and then regret it immediately. That was a judgmental comment. "I'm sorry. I shouldn't have said that."

"No, I get it. Easy assumption, but no, they wouldn't pay for it. It's actually a job opportunity of sorts."

"Oh, how so?"

"I was approached by a digital media company a few months back. They have a YouTube channel, and they're looking for athletes to create content for them. The pay is minimum—it'd only cover basic traveling expenses—but the experience would be priceless."

I can see the excitement shining in his eyes. He's eager to do it, and that brings a sudden pang to my chest. It's ridiculous. We've only known each other for a couple months, and I'm not even sure the status of our relationship yet. It's definitely too new for me to be feeling sad about the possibility of Troy leaving.

"It sounds like you've already made up your mind."

"Not yet. I have time. Besides, many things can happen between now and then." He pierces me with one of his intense stares, completely messing with my ability to breathe properly.

"True." I take another sip of wine, trying to hide the effect he has on me. "A while back, I looked into the possibility of participating in an exchange program."

"You mean, studying abroad for a semester?"

"Yeah. I was looking into partner schools in Europe."

"I take it you didn't apply?"

Sadness takes over me, and I regret opening my big mouth. "No, I didn't." I glance at my plate.

"Why not?"

With a sigh, I look at Troy again. "You're going to think it's stupid."

"No I won't."

"I didn't want to leave Ben for that long. I know he has my parents, but... I don't know. Told you it was a stupid reason." I reach for the glass of water.

"It's not stupid. You're very protective of him. I get it. I'm also like that with Jane."

"But you're not letting that keep you from going places."

Damn it, Charlie. This conversation is getting too heavy and depressing. It's time to change the subject.

"Can we talk about something else?"

"Sure, like what?"

"Tell me your thoughts on Ophelia having two boyfriends."

Troy scrunches his face up as if he's in pain and groans. "God, I try my best to pretend they're just friends."

The appetizers arrive, and we take a break from the ten-thousand-questions game. I don't know how our conversation got deep so quickly. Maybe because we're not really complete strangers. I worry for a bit that we'll end up messing up, such as saying something thoughtless and going back to bickering and arguing. But once the food arrives, we keep our chitchat light.

The evening goes by in a flash, and before I know it, the Uber driver is dropping us off in front of the house. I was a little apprehensive about going out with Troy, but in the end, my worries were unjustified. Dinner was lovely. Troy was attentive, funny, and uber sexy—a dangerous combination to me. A cynic would think that was his master plan—to be charming and irresistible so he could win the bet. But he was too nervous in the beginning for that to be true. Poor thing even forgot to give me the flowers he'd bought.

As we walk side by side toward the front door, my stomach is suddenly tied in knots, as if this were indeed a first date and I didn't know what was going to happen. *Is he going to kiss me? Should I invite him in for a nightcap?*

Those thoughts are ridiculous, of course. We've already fucked like bunnies, and we live together.

Instead of unlocking the door, Troy turns to me and links his hand with mine. "So, here we are." He smiles at me, revealing the twinkle in his eyes that I've quickly come to love.

"Here we are." I smile back.

"I had a wonderful evening."

"Me too."

He doesn't say another word, just stares at me. Blush is slowly spreading through my cheeks. The intensity in his gaze is making me a little uncomfortable. I don't know what to say or do. The sexual tension between us is palpable. There seems to be a magnetic field pulling me to him. I have to fight the urge to jump into his arms and have my way with him right here on our front porch.

"Well, would you like to come in?" I ask to break the silence.

He chuckles. "I thought you'd never ask."

It seems we're keeping up with the charade that this is really a first date. If that's the case, who's going to make the first move? My hand is shaking a bit as I try to find the keyhole.

Gee, Charlie. Take it easy.

"Need some help there?" Troy asks, clearly amused.

Finally, I manage to unlock the door. "No. I got it."

I let Troy walk in first, and then I close the door behind me. My idea is to head to the kitchen to grab a drink, but he turns around fast and pins me against the wall, covering my body with his. His lips find mine, branding me with an urgent kiss. I melt against him, drowning in his scent, his presence. I clutch his arms, pulling him closer to me, needing to feel every inch of his frame pressed against mine. I've never felt this need, this ice-cold fever for anyone before. It gives me chills and burns me up at the same time.

When I think he's going to take things further, he stops, stepping back and leaving me feeling bereft.

"What?" I ask, a little dazed.

"I'm sorry. I couldn't resist. I've been dying to kiss you like that all night long."

"Why did you stop?" I pout.

He shakes his head. "Because I haven't crossed the point of no return yet. Why? Do you want me to continue, babe? Are you waving your white flag?" he says with a smirk.

"No." I walk around him—almost running really—to the kitchen. I need something cold to soothe the ache in my loins.

Loins? Oh God. Who am I? Amy Farrah Fowler?

I don't want to drink more alcohol because I think I've had plenty. If I'm to survive the rest of the evening without succumbing to Troy's charm, I have to be clearheaded. The only thing I see in the fridge is a can of Coke and Troy's sparkling water. If I drink soda now, I won't be able to sleep, so water it is. I press the cool bottle against my forehead.

"Poor babe. Are you hurting that bad?" He chuckles.

I whirl around, mortified to be caught in the act. "Shut up. I bet you need an ice pack to place over your groin."

His eyes take on a dangerous glint as they narrow. "Woman, do not remind me of the worst case of blue balls I've ever had."

"If it's that bad, why don't you use your hand?" I quirk an eyebrow.

He points at me. "You'd better stop that right now. I'm onto you, Charlie Alice Fontaine."

"Wait. How do you know my middle name? I never told you."

"I have a copy of your rent contract and ID." He gives me a toothy, victorious grin.

"Fine, *Wolfie*. I'll stop."

"If I could hate Grandma for telling you that odious nickname, I would."

"Well, I'd better go to be—"

"Oh no. You're not going to sleep yet. Our date is not over."

I put a hand on my hip. "Is that so? What else do you have planned?"

"If you'll follow me to the living room, I've prepared an evening of excellent entertainment."

"Oh, are we doing a Lord of the Rings marathon?"

"No. We can do that when *you* invite me on a date."

I tilt my head with a pitying frown. "Aww, and you were doing so well."

I sit down on the couch, pulling the blanket to me so I can create a barrier against Troy. It's a pathetic effort, but valid. "What are we watching?"

"One of my favorite TV shows of all times. You're probably a fan, actually."

"Oh? What is it?"

"*Supernatural.*"

"What? Are you crazy? I'm not watching that."

Troy's expression falls. "Why not?"

"Because it's fucking scary. I told you I don't do horror."

"You're joking, right?"

"Do you think this is the face of someone who's joking?" I draw a circle in the air to emphasize my point.

"Charlie, *Supernatural* is not a horror series. Where did you get that idea?"

"From watching the first episode. I was freaked out."

"Okay, fine. I concede that the first season is a little spooky, but it gets better after that. Trust me, you'll love it."

"I don't know." I nibble on my lower lip.

Everyone I know has been bugging me to watch the damn series for years. Maybe I should try again. Besides, if it gets too scary, I can always jump in Troy's arms and hide my face against his chest. Maybe that's what he's banking on. But I can't refuse him when he's giving me those puppy eyes.

"Fine. But if I have nightmares, it's on you."

"If you have nightmares, you're more than welcome to sleep with me." He laughs.

"Oh, I bet that's exactly what you want."

"Charlie, you really have the worst ideas about me."

"Yeah, yeah. Put it on already before I change my mind."

He chuckles. "That's what she said."

"I said put it on, not in."

"Sure, sure."

CHAPTER 28

TROY

can't believe how close I came to screwing up the evening.
Why did I think watching *Supernatural* would be a good
idea? Even if Charlie wasn't scared, there's the little issue
that the TV show features two attractive dudes.

We're about to start episode five, and the wine is finally
catching up with me. My eyelids are getting heavy, but Charlie
doesn't seem tired in the least. She's tense, however, clutching
the blanket in a tight grip.

"Charlie?"

"Yeah?" She turns to me.

"You know, it's okay if you want to scooch closer."

She hesitates, not moving for a couple beats, and I'm sure
she's going to say no. To my surprise, she does shorten the
distance between us, and when I throw my arm over her shoulders, she leans against my chest and lets me cradle her.

Unable to resist, I run lazy circles over her exposed skin with
the tips of my fingers. She doesn't stop me; if anything, she gets
nearer, making my blood pump faster. I don't want to make a
move too soon, so I force my attention to the screen. The first two

minutes of the episodes are always intense and scary, and this one is no different. Sam and Dean are facing Bloody Mary.

Charlie is rigid against me, and when the scary part comes, she hides her face against my chest, making me laugh.

"Stop laughing. I hate horror shit."

"I'm sorry, but you're too funny."

She eases out of my embrace, lifting her chin to glare at me. "I'm not too funny."

Her eyebrows are furrowed into a scowl, and her plump lips are set in a severe line. Right now, she's not funny at all. She's a sexy, pissed-off vixen.

"You're right. You're not funny." My voice comes out strained. "You're Venus personified."

I kiss her before she looks away, pulling her flush against my body once more. Her lips taste like chocolate, a trace of the lava cake she had for dessert. It awakens the hunger in me that was already hovering just below the surface. I try to move us to a horizontal position, but my right arm is trapped by the sling.

I pull back. "This thing has got to go."

Quickly, I release the clasp behind my neck, freeing my arm so I can better appreciate Charlie.

"Are you sure you should be doing this?" she asks.

"I'm okay." I push her back on the couch and then yank the blanket from her grasp.

Her dark hair fans around her lovely face. Her lips are partly open, her cheeks are flushed, and her blue eyes are laced with desire. *Fuck.* I'm going to lose this bet in an epic fashion, and I don't care. All my blood has converged in my cock, leaving my brain at its mercy.

"Do you have something to say, Troy?" she asks in a dangerous, husky tone.

Her velvety voice is like a caress, a prelude of what's to come. She knows she has me exactly where she wants me.

"I do. I—"

The shrill ringtone of her phone interrupts my speech of

defeat. I expect her to ignore it, but her hazy eyes become lucid in a flash. She jerks to a sitting position and then jumps off the couch to get to her purse on the kitchen counter.

"Hello?" she answers.

I watch her, keenly aware of the sudden tension in her body. Her eyebrows furrow as she listens.

"Slow down, Ben," she says.

I get off the couch too, any trace of my erection gone. I don't need to hear what her brother is saying to know things aren't okay.

"Okay, I'm coming," she replies before she ends the call, promptly shoving her phone back in her purse. "I have to go to Littleton," she tells me.

"What happened?"

"My parents had a huge fight. Ben said my father packed an overnight bag and left. Mom is locked in her room, crying. Ben is freaking out."

I don't know much about people with Down syndrome, but my guess is they're more sensitive than most. Even if that wasn't the case, he's only a teenager. He shouldn't be alone to deal with his parents' marriage problems. I was young when my parents divorced, but I remember their fights as if they happened yesterday.

When Charlie reaches for her car keys, I say, "You can't drive."

"You don't understand. I have to go now."

I touch her arm, needing to show my support through actions. "I do understand, but doing something reckless won't help anyone. It's a long drive to Littleton, and we've been drinking. Let's call an Uber."

She looks into my eyes for a moment, torn, but finally she relents. "Okay."

I order a ride. "I'm coming with you."

Her eyes become rounder, surprise shining in them, but then her expression turns into relief. "Thank you. I can't believe this.

My parents should know better than to fight when Ben is around. He can't handle shouting and arguments. It really gets to him."

"Can he call someone to stay with him until we get there?"

"The only person he could call is his girlfriend, but it's late, and she's like him. I'm not sure if she would be much help."

I don't understand Charlie's remark about her brother's girlfriend, but it's unimportant right now.

"Okay. How about we call him back when we're on our way? We can keep him on the phone; it might help with his anxiety."

"Good idea."

The Uber driver won't arrive for ten minutes, and while we wait, Charlie almost digs a hole in the floor with the way she's pacing. Nothing I could tell her would make her feel better, so I just let her be.

In all honesty, if it weren't for my busted shoulder, I could probably drive. I didn't drink as much, and I'm as sober as a rock now. But after the speech I gave her, it would be hypocritical to suggest I get behind the wheel.

Charlie calls her brother again as soon as we slide in the back seat of our ride. Judging by the conversation, I get the gist that Ben is somewhat calmer. I don't know what his mother is doing though.

The ride to Littleton seems to take longer than an hour even though there isn't much traffic at this time of night. When the driver stops in front of her parents' house, she almost jumps out and runs to the front door.

I follow her, feeling a little bit awkward for being here. I'm a stranger to them, and I'm about to witness some major family drama. Charlie makes a beeline for what I guess is Ben's room. I'm correct, so I hang back by the door, not wanting to intrude. The teen is on his bed, clutching a pillow. His tear-streaked face and red eyes tell me he's been crying a lot.

Shit. This is bad.

I hover by the door while Charlie sits on the edge of his bed and engulfs him in a bear hug.

"What happened, Ben?" she asks.

"I don't know. I was playing a video game with my headset on when their shouting made it through. I didn't want to hear them, but it was impossible."

"I'm so sorry. Is Mom still in her room?"

"I think so."

"I'm gonna talk to her."

"Okay."

On her way out, she stops next to me and whispers, "Do you mind keeping him company?"

"Not at all."

She squeezes my arm and then heads down the corridor.

I finally dare to walk into Ben's room, unsure about what to say or do.

"What game were you playing before?" I ask, feeling stupid the moment the question comes out of my mouth.

"The Witcher."

"Oh, cool. It's one of my favorites."

"Yeah, mine too."

I glance around his room, noticing Ben shares Charlie's enthusiasm for fantasy realms, board games, and comics.

"Charlie tells me you also participate in LARP. She's convinced me to come next time."

Ben's eyes widen. "Really? That's cool. What character are you going to play?"

"A troll."

A smile appears on his flushed face. "That's awesome. I'm a troll hunter. You're going to need a costume."

I make a face, which results in Ben laughing. "What?"

"Your expression of horror was priceless. I wish Charlie had seen it."

I rub the back of my neck. "She's seen it already."

"What's the deal between you and her? Are you dating now?"

I'm taken aback by his question, which is stupid. I told Jane about Charlie and me, so why wouldn't she have told her brother?

"Yes we are."

Ben's expression becomes serious. "If you're Charlie's boyfriend now, then I have to come clean about something."

Gee, what could he possibly want to tell me?

"Okay."

"The prank with the chickens was my idea. My girlfriend's parents own a farm."

I stare at him without blinking for a moment, trying to keep my laughter bottled in, but it bubbles up my throat anyway. Charlie returns, finding me in such a state of amusement that I have tears in my eyes.

"What's going on?" she asks.

"I told Troy the chickens were my idea. I think he lost it," Ben deadpans.

Swallowing my laughter, I wipe the moisture from underneath my eyes. "I'm sorry. Your brother gave me the giggles."

With a half-smile that doesn't reach her eyes, Charlie shakes her head. Her reaction sobers me up. They're dealing with a shitty family situation, and here I am, laughing like an idiot.

She turns to her brother. "I talked to Mom briefly. She's a mess, so you're coming home with me." As an afterthought, she glances my way. "That's okay, right?"

Why would she think I wouldn't be okay with that?

"Of course, babe."

"That might mean I won't be able to come to the party with you."

I'm disappointed by this turn of events—I was looking forward to introducing Charlie to my friends—but I keep my face neutral. "Hey, there are parties every weekend. It's no big deal if we miss this one."

I'd go and wait in the living room while Charlie helps Ben pack a bag for the weekend, but I'm afraid to bump into her mother. To avoid a possible awkward encounter, I stand in a corner and start looking for troll costumes on my phone.

This is definitely not how I envisioned my first date with Charlie would end.

CHAPTER 29

CHARLIE

I wake up before sunrise, feeling wretched about what happened last night. My back is sore from sleeping on the air mattress, but stiffness is the least of my worries. I couldn't get Mom to talk to me, which means I still don't know exactly what prompted my parents' fight, only what Ben told me he overheard.

Mom accused Dad of having an affair.

The idea brings bile to my mouth. I always believed my parents had a happy marriage. Growing up, it was rare for me to see them argue, and even when it happened, they made up quickly. I'm devastated by the possibility that Mom is correct in her suspicions.

Ben is still sound asleep in my bed. I tiptoe to the bathroom, and after I take care of my morning business, I head downstairs. My heart is heavy as I prepare coffee like a robot. Tears gather in my eyes, burning them. A few rogue ones manage to escape, rolling down my cheeks. I hastily wipe them dry, refusing to succumb to the sadness. Ben might be mistaken, or Mom could be wrong. It's too soon for me to fall into despair.

The wooden boards on the stairs creak, alerting me that my solitude is over. Troy is the one who woke early, like me. His hair is a mess, sticking out at odd angles, and he seems to be half asleep as he trudges to the kitchen, rubbing his eyes. He's also breaking our rules by only wearing sweatpants that hide nothing and no T-shirt. His pants hang low, emphasizing his delicious V that immediately turns me on. I'd complain, but he's offering me distraction on a platter, and I desperately need that.

"Morning, babe." He pulls me to him and kisses me softly on the lips.

Hmm, minty toothpaste flavor.

"Good morning," I whisper against his mouth, glad I brushed my teeth before coming down.

"Why are you up so early?" we both ask at the same time.

"Jinx," I say, making him chuckle.

"I couldn't sleep. And you?"

"Same." I step back, looking away.

"How are you feeling?"

I take a deep breath before answering, "Awful. I can't say I'm surprised about my parents' fight. They've been arguing for a while."

The coffee has finished brewing, so to keep me from going too deep into my grief, I focus on pouring Troy and me some. I know he's a caffeine addict like me.

"I'm really sorry, Charlie," he says, and I know he means it wholeheartedly.

"Thanks."

He understands better than anyone. His parents divorced, so I can imagine there was a lot of fighting as well before they finally called it quits. I hate to think my parents are going in that direction, but if there's no saving their marriage, then it's better for everyone if they go their separate ways.

I prepare our drinks, putting enough hazelnut creamer in mine that you could call it dessert and not coffee. Troy drinks his with just a splash of milk.

I offer him a mug. "Here."

He takes a whiff of the coffee, making a humming sound. "Thank you, babe."

We don't speak for a while, getting lost in our drinks and thoughts.

Troy is the one who breaks the silence first. "Do you know what you're going to do today?"

"No clue. I have to keep Ben distracted."

"Come to the game with me. It'll be fun."

"It's too late to get tickets."

Troy gives me a droll stare. "Charlie, I'm on the team. I have season tickets for family. They're pretty good seats."

I'm not a sports person, but I'm sure going to a game would be fun, even if Ben and I don't know much about football. "All right. What time does the game start?"

"At two. We have time to do other stuff, like find me a troll costume."

I give him a small smile. "Oh yeah. We have to do that. I totally forgot about it."

"If I don't have a costume, then I can't participate. Works for me." He shrugs.

Narrowing my eyes, I reply, "I'll get you a costume. Don't worry. And it's too late now. I've already signed you up."

He sets his mug on the counter and approaches me, caging me in against the fridge. His right arm is sling free, and he circles it around my waist while he cups my cheek with his left hand. "Fine. Now I want to make your knees go weak and set your body ablaze."

Good on his word, he kisses me hard, plunging his tongue into my mouth in a deliciously possessive way. I reach for his biceps, needing the support since he has turned my legs into jelly. The temperature in the kitchen goes up, creating a little inferno where clothes aren't mandatory. He parts my legs with his muscled thigh, creating a crazy good friction between them. His erection presses against my belly, and I want to free his cock and wrap my mouth around his girth, bet be damned.

I'm about to beg Troy to take me right here on the kitchen counter when a throat clearing douses the fire faster than having an ice bucket poured over my head. Troy jumps back, covering his crotch with both hands. He doesn't turn, just pretends to look for something on the shelf above the counter.

"Ben, you're up," I state the obvious.

"Yeah. The smell of coffee was like a beacon to me."

"Would you like a cup?" I ask, pretending my face isn't burning up.

I should have known better than to make out with Troy out in the open when Ben could walk in on us anytime.

"Sure, I'll have some." He pulls up a stool and then leans his elbows on the counter. "What's for breakfast? I'm starving."

I give him a cup of coffee, then go investigate our food situation. Peering inside the fridge tells me what I already guessed—we're low on food. "We have eggs, but we're out of bread."

"Do you have any cereal?" he asks.

"No, I finished the last box yesterday," Troy replies. "Let's go out for breakfast. My treat."

"Oh, we could go to Zuko's Diner," I suggest.

Troy cuts me a glance, and I don't understand his peculiar look until I remember what happened in front of the restaurant. The splash that ignited our feud. It feels like eons ago.

"It'll be good to reminisce," I add.

"For the record, I felt awful immediately after I did that."

"It's okay, Troy. I'm not mad about it anymore. And I have my share of regrettable acts when it comes to you."

His eyebrows scrunch together. "I hope not recent acts."

My lady parts clench, reminding me of those past performances. I glance at Ben, but he doesn't seem to be following the conversation. Thank heavens.

"No. I have zero regrets about those," I tell Troy honestly.

His eyes turn to molten lava in a split second, and a small

tent appears in the front of his pants. I'd laugh if Ben wasn't around.

No, Charlie, you wouldn't laugh. You would be down on your knees, having a different kind of breakfast.

Oh my God. My conscience can be such a whore.

"Can you please stop with the sexual innuendos? It was bad enough to witness you in an act of foreplay a minute ago."

My eyes turn as round as saucers. "Ben! What the hell?"

"What? It's true." He shrugs.

"You can be such a brat sometimes." I storm out of the kitchen, running to the stairs.

"Charlie, where are you going?" Troy asks me.

"To change." And that's all I say before I disappear into my room.

I'm so fucking embarrassed, it's not even funny. And there I was, naively thinking Ben wasn't aware of the context of my conversation with Troy. Stupid me.

CHAPTER 30

TROY

Besides getting caught by Ben in the kitchen, I'd say the rest of the morning went smoothly. I wasn't able to find a troll costume that I liked though, so that's something I'll need to sort in the coming week. It's bad enough that my curiosity got me roped into participating; I'm not going to wear something embarrassing.

We're now just outside the stadium in line to get in. It's surreal to be with the fans and not in the locker room with my teammates. Technically, I have to head there and get ready with them, even if I'm sitting on the bench, but I want to make sure Charlie and Ben are situated before I have to leave them.

We missed tailgating, but I'm not sure if Charlie would have enjoyed it anyway. I still have hopes I can persuade her to come to the party tonight, and I didn't want her turned off to the idea beforehand. The issue is Ben. He's a teen, so technically, he could stay home alone, but I'm sure Charlie wouldn't want that. And we can't bring him with us since he's a minor and it would be bad form to bring a kid to a party where booze was running freely.

As we stand in line, I'm recognized by some people, including fans of the opposing team. They're our rival school after all; they know my face and hate my guts. The assholes attempt to get me riled up, but their taunts can't find their mark. They're on my turf, and soon the Rushmore crowd drowns out their stupid shit. Charlie becomes tense next to me, and with just a glance, I can tell she's gearing up to defend my honor.

"Relax, babe. It's okay. They're gone now."

"They were awful and so rude." She seethes.

"I'm used to that. It's no big deal."

"Yeah, sis. If Troy cared about what others thought of him, he wouldn't be dating you." Ben laughs.

She hits him upside the head. "Quit being a brat."

"Ouch." He massages his head, glaring at Charlie. "I definitely shouldn't have interrupted you two this morning. Now you're in a mood."

I chuckle, but when I catch her glowering at me, I try to cover my slipup with a cough.

We're finally inside, and I make sure Charlie and Ben have everything they want from the concession stand before I escort them to their seats.

On our way down to the front row, I hear my name being called by someone in the crowd. I search the seats until I see Brooke waving animatedly at me. I wave back, but I don't stop or change course. I can't talk to her right now, nor do I want to.

"Was that your friend who came by the house when you got hurt?" Charlie asks.

"Yeah."

"I'm surprised she hasn't come by again," Charlie adds.

"We're not that close." I almost add "anymore" but that would no doubt result in a string of questions, and now is not the time to go down memory lane.

Eventually, I'll have to tell Charlie that Brooke is my ex. It was a punch to the gut to find out Blake was her ex from the douche canoe himself. I don't want that to happen to her.

"Here we are," I say when we reach our row.

Ben continues along until he finds his seat, but Charlie hangs back. "I wish you could stay with us. We're bound to not understand a thing and cheer at the wrong times."

"I highly doubt that's going to happen."

I reach for a strand of her hair and tuck it behind her ear. Almost immediately, her cheeks become pinker. I love how Charlie blushes when she's embarrassed or excited.

"Well, you'd better make sure your teammates don't lose to those assholes."

"They won't. Andreas knows that if they mess up, they won't hear the end of it from me."

"Good."

I swing my arm around Charlie's shoulders, pulling her to me for another scorching kiss. I swear I try to do sweet and easy, but I can't when it comes to her. She's a spark that always ignites me. I'm aware that we're putting on quite a show for all the cameras surrounding us. In less than a minute, our kiss will be all over social media. It's for that reason alone that I pull away faster than I want.

"Okay, I really have to go before I kidnap you," I say.

"Oh, we wouldn't want that," she says with a smirk, but then it turns into a frown. "I'm sorry you can't play today."

"It's okay. I needed a break. Besides, Danny is kicking ass. It'll be good for the team next year to know their new quarterback can handle the pressure."

"Tell them to break some bones."

"What?" I laugh.

"Not the right thing to say? In performing arts, we say break a leg, but I didn't think it would apply here, and 'good luck' felt lame."

I shake my head, fighting the urge to kiss her again. "I love how your mind works."

Immediately, I realize that was the wrong thing to say. Charlie is now staring at me like a deer caught in headlights, and her lips are making a little O.

To downplay my slip of the tongue, I continue on like nothing is amiss. "I'll see you later, babe. Have fun."

My head is whirling as I dissect why I said that. I didn't say I loved her, but it was pretty close. Regardless, I used the damn L-word in a sentence, and that always gets girls in a tizzy. I hope it doesn't change anything between us. I like Charlie, but we're just beginning to get to know each other. There's no way in hell I've fallen in love with her already. I'm not one to get swept up by feelings.

I force those worries to the corner of my mind, and when I enter the locker room and hear the ruckus my teammates are making, my relationship doubts are so far back, they might as well not exist anymore.

"My, my. Look what we got here. Troy fucking Alexander is in the house," Puck, our giant linebacker, announces.

He walks over and pats me on my back so hard that it jostles my shoulder, making me wince.

"Gee, careful there. I do want to come back sooner rather than later."

Puck cringes. "Oops. Sorry."

Andreas comes over, watching me with a thousand questions in his eyes. He wants to know how my date went, and knowing the perv, he'll ask for all the details.

"So?" he starts.

"I have nothing to report."

"Come on, man. Maybe if you paint me a good picture, I'll consider sticking to one girl for a while."

Puck scoffs. "Yeah, right. When hell freezes over." He turns to me. "Is your girl watching the game?"

"Yeah. She brought her brother too."

"Cool, man. Nice to see Andy's heathen ways haven't rubbed off on you."

Puck comes from a super religious family and has been with the same girl since high school. He loves to pick on Andreas's amoral ways.

"Shut your piehole, altar boy," he rebuffs.

"Make me." Puck seems to grow in size, towering over Andreas.

Their banter is harmless, so I just head to my locker to put my uniform on.

A few minutes later, Coach Clarkson's booming voice cuts through the room, commanding everyone's attention.

His determined gaze finds mine, but all he does to acknowledge my presence is nod slightly. He proceeds to give the team a pep talk, and I usually hang on his every word, but I'm having a hard time getting focused since I'm not playing. I spot Danny next to Andreas, and a pang hits my chest that he's going in my place. I told Charlie I was fine with not playing, but being here with my teammates makes it harder to pretend that's true.

I hear my phone's text tone inside my duffel bag. Since I'm not invested in the coach's speech, I fish the device out. It's a message from Brooke.

When were you going to tell me you had a new girlfriend?

What the hell? Is she mad at me? It sure as shit sounds like it. *Damn it.* She picked the wrong time to annoy me with her bullshit.

I didn't think I had to.

I click Send, even knowing my reply is harsh. Her reply comes through a few seconds later.

Wow. Just wow.

It's pointless to continue the convo, so I just shove my phone back in the duffel bag and try to forget my ex is acting like we just broke up yesterday and not two years ago.

CHAPTER 31

CHARLIE

I take back everything I've ever said about football. Being in the stadium, feeling the contagious energy of the crowd, made me understand why people love it so much. I still don't know most of the rules, but in the end, it didn't matter.

There was also the added bonus that I wanted the opposing team to lose badly all thanks to the encounter with those bullies earlier, and the Rushmore Rebels delivered. It was a hard game, and the score remained tight throughout the entire three and a half hours, but in the end, the Rebels won. My voice is hoarse from screaming.

Troy texts me that he might not be able to sneak out to ride with us. I totally understand. This victory was amazing, and I'm sure the celebration in the locker room is crazy right now. I tell him not to worry. His reply is to let him know when we're in the food court and he'll try to make it.

The crowd is slow to leave, and since we're all the way down, it takes at least ten minutes for our row to move. Ben and I file out, and then we trudge along with the rest of the people. It feels like an eternity before we finally reach the top of the stairs. I get out of the traffic headed for the exit and look for a quieter spot to text Troy back.

He'll be here in a few minutes, so I wait, keeping my eyes peeled and searching for him in the crowd. But I find someone else first, and I wish I'd missed her altogether. Brooke, Troy's beautiful friend, is coming in my direction. It's too late now to pretend I didn't see her, and it's clear she's making a beeline in my direction. She's with a friend, a brunette just as tall as she is but not as pretty.

"Hey. Charlie, right?" Brooke asks me with a phony smile plastered on her face.

"Yep. How's it going?"

"Oh, pretty good. So, you and Troy, huh?"

I knew she had ulterior motives for coming to speak to me. Thanks to my snooping of Troy's Instagram profile before my interview with him, I know they're close, probably dated at some point. But he's never mentioned her, so I wasn't going to ask. Judging by Brooke's fake friendliness, my assumption was correct. If they didn't date, then she has a major crush on him.

Too fucking bad.

"Yeah."

"I don't get it," the friend says. "Weren't you the girl who wrote that nasty article about him? Why would he date *you*?"

I narrow my eyes for a second, but when I reply, it's with a saccharine smile. "You know what they say: there's a fine line between love and hate. I guess we were just bound to cross it."

"Oh, so now you think Troy is in love with you?" She scoffs. "In your dreams."

"Tammy, please." Brooke touches her friend's arm as her face twists into an expression of discomfort.

Yeah, I'm not buying it.

The ugly brunette takes a sip of her soda first before replying, "What? I was just saying what everyone knows. Troy doesn't love anyone but himself."

Whoa. Maybe we have more than one scorned woman here, not only Brooke.

"I'm pretty sure his only problem is that he has high standards," Ben says before I can.

"Oh my God. The retarded boy speaks." The bitch looks at Ben with disdain, an expression I know too well. What she doesn't know is that every bully who has taunted my brother because of his Down syndrome has paid the price.

Brooke gasps, looking genuinely shocked by her friend's comment. It doesn't matter. My vision has already turned red, and before anyone can stop me, I pull my arm back and punch the bitch in the nose.

Her head jerks back right before she screeches, creating a commotion. "What the hell! You broke my nose."

Unlikely, since I didn't hear anything crack.

My pulse is pumping in my ears when I reply through clenched teeth, "Be glad that's all I broke."

Troy appears suddenly, breaking through the crowd to get to us. "What happened?"

"That filthy whore broke my nose." The girl points at me.

"You called her brother the R-word," a lady I hadn't noticed until then cuts in. "It's because of disgusting, prejudiced people like you that there's still a stigma today if people are different."

Wow. I didn't expect anyone to stand up for me. Her defense brings tears to my eyes.

She glances at me and smiles as a way to say she has my back.

Troy turns to Brooke. "That's the company you keep nowadays?"

"They were both out of line," she retorts, crossing her arms.

"I want to go. Can we go, Charlie?" Ben asks, clutching the sleeve of my jacket. His small voice breaks me.

I pull him into a side hug, ignoring the throbbing in my hand. "Yeah, let's go."

I'm too angry to check if Troy is following me. I just want to get out of here. The onlookers are smothering me.

A second later, he places his hand on my lower back and, using his body, makes way for us to pass. I never considered myself a damsel in need of a savior, but Troy's protectiveness feels nice.

We continue in silence until we get to my car. When I grab the door handle, I realize I'm still shaking and in no condition to drive.

Troy circles my wrist, keeping me from opening the door. "I'll drive."

"Don't be ridiculous. You can't drive with your shoulder like that."

"You're still reeling from what happened." He frowns. "Your arm is shaking."

"I can drive," Ben pipes up.

I glance at him with a refusal on the tip of my tongue. He can drive in Littleton, which is much quieter than here.

"I can do it, Charlie. Trust me," he insists.

"You have your driver's license?" Troy asks.

"Yes. I've had it for four months already." Ben puffs his chest out proudly.

Troy turns back to me, concern in his eyes. "Let him drive, babe."

I want to argue, but if I say anything, it might do more harm than good. I know my brother—he's putting up a tough front, but he's a mess inside. Growing up, he fought depression among other things because of assholes who treated him badly.

"Okay," I say. "But I'm sitting shotgun." I walk around the car, leaving Troy no choice but to slide across the back seat.

During the drive, I expect him to ask for details about what happened, but he keeps quiet. The silence becomes a heavy blanket of discomfort, and I eventually can't take it anymore.

"The game was amazing," I pipe up, turning to face Troy in the back seat.

He nods. "It was, but hell, I was a wreck the whole time. I thought I was going to lose my voice with the way I was shouting."

"I kind of lost mine," I say.

Troy smirks. "Hmm, I did notice a new sexiness to it."

"Dude, I'm right here," Ben complains.

"Oops. Sorry."

I laugh despite the horrible way the day ended.

"Is there any chance you would consider going to the party with me tonight?" Troy asks softly. "It's going to be epic."

I bite my lower lip, torn between a straight "No" and a "Maybe". After the altercation with Brooke's friend, and the way the blonde was acting all shady, I do want to show up at the party as Troy's date. Call it vanity or whatever with a pinch of possessiveness. But there's Ben to consider.

"I don't know. Are there going to be more people like that airless bimbo who name-called Ben?"

Troy winces. "Honestly, I don't know."

"You should go, Charlie," Ben says. "I think I'm ready to go home if Mom is feeling better."

My stomach bottoms out, and my chest, which was already tight as hell, constricts further. Ben staying with me was a way to distract him from the turmoil back at my folks'. I feel guilty, even though it's irrational. I can't control what ignorant people say or do.

"If that's what you want."

Ben nods. "Yeah, it is. I had fun today though."

I watch his profile, trying to sniff out the lie. His expression is serene, but Ben's always had a better poker face than me.

If he spirals down a dark tunnel again because of that bitch, I will break her nose for real the next time I see her.

CHAPTER 32

TROY

I confess that knowing Charlie went *Million Dollar Baby* on Brooke's friend made my admiration for her grow. I'd already known she was fearless and short-tempered, but her fierce protection of her brother moved me more than she could have known.

It also opened up old wounds that have never fully healed. I failed Robbie by not paying attention, and he drowned a few feet from me. Erroneously, I thought that was my parents' job, but they made it abundantly clear that I should have kept an eye on him. I was his big brother, after all. They weren't wrong, and the guilt has consumed me ever since.

Their mother came by to pick up Ben earlier, and with that, Charlie had no valid excuse not to come to the party with me. Regardless, I thought I'd have to use my convincing skills, but she surprised me by agreeing to come without me having to ask twice.

We had an early dinner, and now I'm waiting for her to get ready. I never asked if she'd bought any of those sexy tops she was looking at. They were nice, but I'd prefer if she wore a dress again. I love her legs; plus, a dress would give me easier access. I'm already over our bet. Life is too short, and I'm not going to keep punishing myself over nothing. God knows I already do that plenty with reason.

I'm nursing a beer while I wait. The only good thing about not being able to drive until the sling is off is that I don't have to worry about my alcohol intake.

I turn when I hear Charlie come down the stairs. Those old wooden boards creak so loudly that even the neighbors must hear when one of us goes up and down.

My jaw drops as I drink her in. She's not wearing jeans— thank fuck—but a short black pleated skirt with a spiked belt looped around her hips. Her top is a vintage *Highlander* T-shirt with the movie's catch phrase "There can be only one" typed across it. There are a bunch of headless dude icons and one with his head still attached, holding a sword. Man, I need to get me one. It's awesome. But what really completes the look and causes a stir in my jeans is the leather jacket and the over-the-knee fuck-me boots she's wearing. I won't be able to leave her alone tonight, or jackasses will be all over her.

"Hi. What do you think?" she asks with a cheeky smile. She knows perfectly well she looks hot as sin.

"Okay, I changed my mind. Let's stay home so I can get you out of those clothes stat."

She chuckles, shaking her head. "No way, Jose. I didn't spend an hour getting ready for you to destroy my look with your caveman urges."

I cross the distance between us in two long strides and pull Charlie flush to my body. "Oh, babe. You'll know how caveman I can be when I bend you over that couch and fuck you until you can't remember your own name."

"What are you saying, Troy? Is that your declaration of defeat?"

The "Yes" is on the tip of my tongue, but when I do say it out loud, I'm going to make good on my promise and pound her into oblivion. *Damn it.* Thinking about it is making my cock rock hard in a painful way.

"Hmm, no. This is my declaration of victory when you come to your senses and admit you can't resist this sexy machine."

A bubble of laughter escapes her throat, dousing the furnace inside me.

"Okay, Mr. Sexy Machine. We'll see how the evening goes."

I step back and then hold up her right hand for inspection. It's still a bit red, but the swelling has gone down. "Does it hurt?"

"Not so much. It was a good call putting ice on it when we got back."

"I can't believe I missed the punch. I would have loved to have seen that."

She pulls her hand back as her face twists into a scowl. "It felt good punching her in the moment, but it doesn't erase the ugliness that came out of her mouth. Words can't be unsaid."

"I know. I'm so fucking mad about what happened. I can't believe Brooke would be friends with someone like that."

Charlie tilts her head to the side as if she's scrutinizing me. This is the moment when I should tell her about my past with Brooke, but I really don't want to get into it right now.

"She's your ex, isn't she?"

Well, damn. So much for not talking about it. "Yeah. We dated in high school and through my first year of college."

"Why did you break up?"

"She went to school in New York, and the relationship fizzled with the distance."

"She's back now."

"Charlie, Brooke and I broke up over two years ago. There's nothing going on between us. We remained friends while she was away, but since she came back, we haven't really talked."

"Besides when she came over to check on you." She quirks an eyebrow.

"Yeah, and that was the last time. Why are you asking me all these questions? Please tell me you're not jealous." I smirk, guessing she is.

She snorts. "No. But if I'm asking all these questions, it's because you haven't provided the information yourself."

"Didn't think it mattered. I mean, I don't hang out with her all the time, unlike you and your ex Blake."

She throws her hands up in the air. "Oh God. Please don't be one of those possessive boyfriends who doesn't tolerate their girlfriends being friends with guys."

"Let me make myself clear. I'm only a caveman in the bedroom, and trust me, you'll like it."

She narrows her eyes. "I'm beginning to suspect you're referring to the tweet I wrote."

"Oh, when you called me a Neanderthal?"

"Yeah."

"I swear that wasn't the case." And I'm not lying. I had forgotten about that stupid tweet. "Grab a drink before I call an Uber. We're supposed to be celebrating tonight."

She sighs. "Okay. You're right. Let's leave the past in the past."

"Cheers to that."

CHARLIE

I don't know why I decided to ask about Brooke right before we left the house. I'd sworn to myself that I wouldn't broach the subject, and then bang, my tongue got the better of me.

He asked if I'm jealous. Of course I am. Any girl would be if Brooke had dated their boyfriend in the past. She's a freaking cover model.

I hate that I'm feeling so insecure about myself. I'm not blind. I clean up cute. And Troy has shown me time and time again that he likes what he sees. But it still manages to get to me.

Damn it, Charlie. Shake it off. You're Raven, the hottest sorceress in all the land.

"Our ride is here," Troy tells me, bringing me back to the here and now.

I glance at the beer in my hand, then chug it, taking several large gulps in one go before setting the bottle back on the counter.

"Thirsty?" Troy smirks.

"Not anymore."

The ride is short, only ten minutes. The party is being held at a frat house. Troy told me which one, but I already forgot. I texted Blake earlier to ask if he wanted to join us as a joke. His reply came swiftly—a string of angry and barfing emojis. I also extended the invite to Fred and Sylvana, but both already had plans. It would have been nice to see familiar faces here, but on the other hand, venturing out of my comfort zone is something I have to do from time to time.

The party is already in full swing when we get there. Everyone we pass greets Troy as if he were a celebrity. It's all high fives and shouting. People don't seem to care that he had no part in the game's outcome today since he didn't play.

Despite all the attention on him, he doesn't let go of my hand for a second, and when he stops to chat with some people, he introduces me as his girlfriend. Not a single person mentions I'm the girl who wrote the nasty article about him. I'm guessing no one knows or cares except Brooke and her nasty friend.

We finally reach the core of the party, the open kitchen where most of the team is gathered. Andreas is on top of the counter with red Solo cups in both hands. He tilts one of the cups back and then the next before he glances in our direction. Even from where I stand, I can see his eyes are glassy. He must have started drinking as soon as he left the stadium.

"Hallelujah, Troy Alexander is finally here. Someone give him a fucking drink already."

Danny, the young quarterback, gets to us first. Instead of speaking to Troy, his attention is on me. "Hey, Charlie. I'm glad you could come. What do you want to drink?"

"I'll have a beer, thanks."

Bending over, he fishes a bottle from the cooler on the floor next to the counter. He twists the cap off before passing the bottle to me. "Here, you'd better drink the good stuff. I can't vouch for what's in those plastic cups."

"I'll have a beer too. Thanks for asking," Troy pipes up.

"Get one yourself," Danny replies with a good-humored laugh.

Troy shakes his head and then glances at me. "See the shit I get from this rookie here?"

Before I can reply, Troy slings his arm around Danny's neck and brings him to the level of his right hand so he can mess with the guy's curly hair.

"Hey, cut it out," Danny complains.

Two of Troy's teammates see the scene and join in the wrestling or whatever this is. I step back, not wanting to get my beer knocked out of my hand. I only stop when my back presses against the wall.

It doesn't take long for Troy to be engulfed by his teammates, out of my reach. He hasn't hung out with them in a while, and this is an important evening for the team. I'm fine with just watching and hoping no one bothers me.

But of course, my solitude doesn't last long. Wherever those guys are, a flock of giggling girls follows. It's easy to spot what kind of clique they belong to. The sorority girls are all dressed to the nines as if they were going to a wedding reception instead of a football party. They're all wearing cocktail dresses, and their hair's styled to perfection. Then there are the cheerleaders, wearing jeans and sexy tops like the ones Sylvana wanted me to wear. And finally, I see some girls who are clearly athletes judging by the confident way they move and talk. Their attire is less sexual, and they make me look puny next to their top-notch physiques.

One of them catches me staring and walks over. She looks familiar. "Hey, I haven't seen you at any of these parties before. I'm Vanessa."

"Hi, Vanessa. I'm Charlie. Yeah, it's my first time here."

"Are you a freshman?"

"Oh no, I'm a junior. And you?"

"Sophomore. Did you go to the game?"

"Which one?"

She smiles. "The football game, obviously. No one here would ever go to one of our games."

Finally, it dawns on me where I know her from. Ludwig has a major crush on her and keeps her picture by his desk. "You're on the soccer team."

"Yeah."

Someone shrieks, drawing our attention to the noise. It's one of the cheerleaders losing her shit over a spilled drink.

"Oh crap. Better see what my evil twin is crying about now."

"That's your sister?" The question slips from my mouth before I can stop it.

Vanessa gives me a pitiful smile. "Yep. Heather Castro, the Ice Queen of Rushmore, is my twin. There are worse fates; we could be identical."

She pushes her way through the crowd to get to her sister.

I search for Troy and see he's still busy socializing with his friends. It'd be fine to wait for him, but my bladder has other ideas. I shouldn't have guzzled down all that beer before coming here. I go in search of a bathroom, but the house is so crowded, it's impossible to get to anything. Finally, I ask a girl next to me.

"Oh, you don't want to use the bathroom downstairs," she tells me. "It's disgusting." She staggers forward, tripping over nothing.

Great. Drunk as a skunk.

"Use the one upstairs," a different girl chimes in. She looks more lucid, so I follow her advice.

I head for the stairs, and I'm actually surprised it's not off-limits. In fact, traffic is pretty heavy going up and down. Soon I find out that there's a second party going on in some of the rooms. Yeah, this is definitely party central. I'm about to ask again where the damn bathroom is when I see two girls stumble out of a room. They leave the door ajar, and with a quick peek inside, I spot the door to a bathroom. This is someone's bedroom, but my bladder is about to fail.

Fuck it. If they wanted to keep people out, they should have kept it locked.

I walk in, closing the door behind me, and then hurry to the bathroom. I try not to look at anything too closely; this is a guy's bathroom, after all, and it's also been turned into a Grand Central Station restroom. I pee standing up, even though it takes me ages to get it going in this position. Guys are so fucking lucky. In moments like this, I have serious penis envy. After a minute in a squat position that has my thighs burning, relief comes, but also the knowledge that after this first piss, I'll need to go every fifteen minutes. *Oh joy.* I should have gone straight to tequila.

I'm washing my hands when I hear a noise outside the bath-room—a drunk girl, judging by her slurred speech, and someone else. My hand is on the door handle when I hear Troy's voice.

What the fucking hell?

CHAPTER 33

TROY

lose track of time goofing around with the guys, and when I look for Charlie, she's no longer chatting with Vanessa Castro, the midfielder of the girls' soccer team. Afraid she got upset that I ignored her and left the party, I text her. When she doesn't answer, I go looking for her.

There seems to be more people now than fifteen minutes ago, and getting anywhere in the house takes a lot of shoving and pushing. I stretch my neck, trying to find her on the makeshift dance floor. I do find Vanessa with her teammates, but no sign of Charlie. I decide to talk to Vanessa and ask if she knows where Charlie went when I'm intercepted by Brooke, who pretty much throws herself into my arms.

Her makeup is smeared, and her eyes are bloodshot. Even if those weren't clues enough, she's wasted; her breath smells like tequila.

"Troy, the person I've been looking for the whole night." She hiccups.

I straighten her and then push her back. "What's the matter with you?"

"What's the matter with me? I'll tell you what's the matter with me. I shouldn't have ever let my parents convince me to go to New York. If I had stayed, we'd still be together."

Fuck me. I knew it. She came back because of me. I wasn't crazy when I got that vibe from her at the diner.

"Come on, Brooke. Don't do this now. You're drunk."

"I know I'm drunk. I had to. It's the only way I can tell you the truth. Liquid courage, right?"

I sense the crowd around us is staring. Not everyone is shit-faced out of their minds yet, and I'm sure some are hanging on to every word we say. I have to get Brooke out of here.

"Come on. Let's talk somewhere in private."

As much as I'm pissed that she's causing a scene, I can't leave her alone in this current state. For starters, it's not safe. There are a lot of weirdos on campus. Plus, I do owe it to our shared past to hear her out and explain that I'm with Charlie, and that's not going to change. There isn't any chance Brooke and I will ever get back together.

I steer her toward the stairs. There must be a quiet room where we can talk. In the back of my mind, I know this will look bad. I hope Charlie doesn't believe the gossip when she hears about it. Once on the second floor, I try every door until I find an unoccupied room.

"I'm such an idiot. I hate New York. Always have. Why did I go?" she whines.

"Come on, Brooke. Sit down." I push her onto the bed, stepping back quickly before she drags me with her.

I don't want this situation to get more awkward than it already is.

"You were right, Troy. I did come back because of you. Seeing you during the holidays made me realize I missed you terribly. Every single guy I dated after you didn't compare."

I listen to Brooke pour her heart out, but the only feeling she can summon from me is pity. There isn't a single spark left of what we had before.

"Aren't you going to say anything?" she asks.

"What do you want me to say?"

Her shoulders sag forward as she laughs without humor. "That you feel the same way."

"I can't do that."

"Why? Because of Charlie?"

"No. She has nothing to do with this."

Brooke sits up straighter, and a new glimmer of hope shines in her bloodshot eyes. "So you're not in love with her?"

"I didn't say that."

"Fuck, Troy. You're not making any sense."

I run a hand over my hair. "I don't want you to think that if Charlie wasn't in the picture, then I'd be with you. That's what I'm getting at. I care about you, Brooke, as a friend. Nothing more."

Her face twists in agony, and more tears gather in her eyes. "It would have been kinder if you told me we couldn't be together because you were madly in love with your roommate."

"That wouldn't be fair. I can't compare what we had with what Charlie and I have."

"What do you mean?" She wipes her face with the back of her hand.

"You were my first girlfriend, Brooke, and that's something no one can take away. You'll always be a cherished memory. Well, besides this one."

She snorts. "Gee, thanks."

"But Charlie is...." I struggle to put into words what she means to me. She drives me insane, whether with desire or grievance. She pushes my buttons like no other, but she also makes me feel alive. She's a high I never want to come down from.

"She's what?" Brooke asks.

"She's endgame," I say, not knowing it to be true until the words come out of my mouth.

Brooke's eyes turn rounder. "Oh my God. You *are* in love with her."

Maybe she's right, but I don't want to admit that out loud.

Like saying Charlie is endgame wasn't a big enough declaration of love, Troy.

I pass a hand over my face, giving my back to Brooke. "I have to find her. Do you need me to call you an Uber?"

"No, Troy. I can find my own way home. I'm not as hopeless as you think I am." She walks around me and out of the bedroom with her chin raised high.

Fuck. This conversation could have gone a million times better.

I pull my cell phone out of my pocket, and seeing Charlie hasn't texted me back, I call her. A second later, I hear her ringtone coming from nearby.

I whirl on the spot, noticing then that the light in the bathroom is on. When Charlie pushes the door open, holding her phone in her hand, I'm slammed by a wave of anger and disappointment.

"You've been there the whole time?" My question is rhetorical. Obviously, she didn't fly into the bathroom through the window.

"I'm so sorry. I didn't mean to eavesdrop."

"Really? Could have fooled me. You had plenty of time to make yourself known. Why didn't you, Charlie?" I raise my voice, expecting her to get riled up immediately. She's a firecracker, after all. But instead, she winces and stares at me with guilt-ridden eyes.

"I don't know. As soon as I heard you, I panicked and froze. Then she started spilling her guts out, and I had to see where it was going."

"You mean, you had to find out what I would do," I retort, still angry as hell, but at least I didn't shout.

She nods, crossing her arms over her chest. I've never seen

her so subdued and small. I'm filled with the impulse to engulf her into a hug and tell her everything will be fine, but I'm still riding on the anger. I don't know what I resent the most, the fact that she felt the need to spy on me or that she overheard my heartfelt confession.

Fuck!

"I don't expect you to forgive me. What I did was pretty shitty."

"Yeah, it was."

I catch a quiver of her lips, but she clamps her jaw tight, then lowers her gaze to her phone and begins to type.

"What are you doing?" I ask.

"Ordering an Uber. I don't expect you to come home with me. You should stay and party with your friends."

"The hell I'm going to let you go home alone," I shout again, but this time, I'm frustrated with myself and I don't know why.

"It's fine, Troy." She won't meet my gaze.

Ah hell. I walk over and cave, bringing her close. "It's not fine. We came together, and we'll go home together." I kiss her forehead before I step back, lacing my hand with hers. "Come on. We have to brave a sea of drunk people to get to the front door."

CHARLIE

I've never felt more wretched in my entire life, not even when I accidentally set Blake's five-hundred-dollar costume on fire two years ago. I knew eavesdropping on Troy's conversation was wrong, but jealousy and insecurity clouded my judgment for a moment. I had to know what he would do upon hearing his ex's confession. I had no idea he would say what he did in the end. And now I don't know what I'm going to do with that information.

He said I'm endgame. How does he know? It hasn't been that long since we were at each other's throats. It's too soon for him to be making those types of declarations—at least that's what my mind is telling me. My heart, on the other hand, skipped a beat when he said that.

The ride back home is quiet. Troy is sitting as far away from me as possible. The distance feels like a chasm. We both thank the driver when he drops us off, but no words are exchanged between us as we walk side by side to the front door.

The urge to cry returns. I messed up royally, and my heart is now twisted in agony. I don't want him to see me like this. I'm too full of pride for that, so as soon as he opens the door, I say good night and make a beeline for the stairs without looking back.

I'm two steps shy from it when Troy circles his free arm around my waist and pins my back to his chiseled chest. "Don't go," he whispers in my ear.

Butterflies flutter in my stomach as I melt against his body. I close my eyes for a second and allow myself to get lost in the feel of his arm keeping me in place, on the way his warm breath turns my already overheated skin into molten lava.

"I don't want to go, but...."

He turns me around, keeping me trapped against him. "I didn't mean to get so angry."

"You had every right to. I broke your trust."

"You didn't break my trust, not exactly. You didn't hide in that bathroom on purpose with the intent of spying on me."

"No. It was a matter of too many beers and a too small bladder."

He chuckles. "I can't stay mad at you when you say stuff like that, babe."

His eyes drop to my lips and stay there. He doesn't make a move, maybe because he's still gung ho on not losing the bet. I couldn't care less about that anymore.

"You win," I breathe.

He brings his eyes back to mine. "What?"

Oh for fuck's sake. Lack of sex has clearly addled his brain.

I rise on my tiptoes and kiss him hard and deep, leaving no room for doubt.

This is my surrender.

CHAPTER 34

CHARLIE

Troy responds in kind, matching my passionate tempo stroke for stroke. I don't know what to do with my hands; I want to touch him everywhere, but I also want him to touch *me* everywhere.

The arm in a sling is a hindrance. I reach behind his neck and open the clasp. His response is a deep groan that I can feel all the way down to my core. He makes quick use of both hands; they disappear underneath my skirt to grab my ass. I'd jump in his arms if it weren't for his injured shoulder. I'm sure he could lift me, but I won't be responsible for prolonging his recovery.

I hold his face between my hands and tilt my head to the side, trying to deepen the kiss. His tongue darts into my mouth, fiery, possessive, and then he does what I wanted him to do all along—he picks me up, lifting me off the floor. I wrap my legs around his hips, hooking them at the ankles and trying my best to be as light as a feather—if that's even possible. I half expect Troy to bring me to the couch. He did say he was going to bend me over it and fuck me into oblivion. But instead, he veers for the stairs, going up two at a time.

Our mouths stay fused together, trying to compensate for all the days we denied ourselves the taste of the other. We did make out, but always with restraint, never with this mind-numbing abandon.

Troy takes me to his room, even though my bedroom is closer to the stairs. The door is semi shut, so he kicks it open with a bang before almost running across the room, aiming for his king-size bed.

He tries to break the kiss to put me down at the edge of the mattress, but I'm not having any of it. We fall together on the bed, and our limbs quickly twist together. We stay in that lovers' embrace for a while, exploring each other with our tongues and hands. With each passing second, my body burns for him brighter, and the overwhelming yearning is agony, but the sweetest kind. I don't know how long we stay like that, but eventually, he slides off me, keeping one leg firmly between mine.

"What's wrong?" I ask against his mouth.

"Tired of getting poked by your belt."

Oh shit. The spikes. I completely forgot about them.

"Sorry."

I have to move away from his mouth to rotate the belt until I find the clasp, but Troy is intent on distracting me. His mouth strays to my neck, peppering my skin with delicious open-mouthed kisses that leave me panting like I've just run a marathon.

I finally locate the damn clasp and manage to pull my belt off just in time before Troy rolls over me again and nestles between my legs. His erection pushes against me through our layers of clothing, and now I want nothing more than to see them gone. I reach for the back of his shirt and yank the fabric until he finally decides to cooperate. He leans back, sitting on the balls of his feet, and finishes the job, pulling the T-shirt off fast like a ninja and mussing his hair in the process. The sexy look combined with the lust in his eyes makes my clit throb so hard that if he wasn't blocking access, I'd take care of the problem myself.

"Fuck, you're so beautiful," he says.

I know I should say thank you, or at least return the compliment, but I'm suddenly consumed with a voracious need that can only be satiated by Troy on top of me, fulfilling the promise he made earlier before we left for the party. I want him inside me, pounding into me so hard that I leave an imprint on the mattress.

"Yeah, yeah, clothes off." I reach for his jeans' button and then the zipper. But I can't do more while he's sitting in that position, watching me with a Cheshire cat smile. "Troy, help here."

"What's the matter, babe? Are you in a hurry?"

"Yes," I hiss. "Don't tell me you aren't. These past few days have been torture."

"Oh, but the torture is only about to begin, sweetheart."

He jumps off me—*finally*—and removes his jeans and boxers. I forget about his ominous comment in an instant at the sight of all his naked glory. Damn it, he looks like a golden Greek god. *Every. Single. Part. Of. Him.* I could spend all eternity staring at him and never get my fill.

He returns to the mattress and runs his fingers over one of my boots. "You know, I think we should keep these on." He continues his exploration, and now his fingers are running over my skin, leaving a trail of goose bumps in their wake.

I open my mouth to protest, but he silences me by pressing his index finger over my lips. Undeterred, I grab his wrist and suck that offending finger into my mouth. Troy hisses, narrowing his eyes. If he wants to torture me, well, two can play that game.

With his free hand, he lifts my skirt and pauses, his eyes widening a fraction.

That's right, babe. I dressed to kill tonight. I knew he would try to get a peek under my skirt, and I was hoping the little black lingerie number would bring him to his knees. I couldn't have foreseen that I'd be the one gladly losing the battle.

I'm his endgame.

Those were the words that obliterated the barriers I had erected around my heart. The memory of his confession makes my chest warm. My heart seems to overflow with emotion. Is Troy my endgame? As I take him in, I'm blasted with a mix of pure joy and euphoria that makes my entire body tingle. When I look into his eyes, something clicks into place. I feel light and whole, and I never want this feeling to go away.

I let go of his finger with a soft pop, and that seems to unfreeze him from his lustful daze. He rubs a rough thumb over my swollen lips, then reaches for both sides of my panties, curling his fingers around the fabric. He rolls them painfully slow down my legs, and now I get his meaning that the torture is just beginning. How can he stand this when I know he's about to blow?

I lower my eyes to his erection, and it's almost like it's daring me to touch it. I move toward it, but Troy captures my arm and lifts it above my head, then does the same with my other one, and finally, the meaning of his words penetrates my brain. He uses my panties to bind my wrists together and secure them to the headboard.

"Troy, what are you doing?"

His lips curl up. "You surrendered. Now I must make you pay."

There goes my clit, throbbing again in anticipation. I have no idea what Troy plans to do now that I'm immobile, but whatever it is, I know it's going to be earth-shattering.

His eyes drop to my exposed sex, and he licks his lower lip. "As much as I want to taste you, I'm hanging by a thread here."

He reaches over to the nightstand and pulls a condom packet from the drawer. I follow his every move while I try to break my hands free.

"Don't even try, babe. You lost the war. Now you're at my mercy."

"Is that so?" My voice is husky.

Troy doesn't reply as he finishes rolling the condom down his length. Still silent, he spreads my legs farther apart and then lifts one of them over his good shoulder before lowering his body to mine. The tip of his erection rubs against my entrance, making both of us moan.

He rests his forehead against mine and lets out a shaky breath. "Hell, whose idea was it to go without sex for so long?"

"Probably yours." I laugh, but in fact, I don't know anymore.

And when he pushes inside, sheathing himself in me, there's no chance I can remember. My brain takes a vacation, and all I can process is the intense pleasure that's making my body go haywire.

I forget that I'm bound and jerk my arms forward, needing to touch Troy as well. Frustration seeps into me when I can't. "Ugh, this is so un—"

Troy crushes his mouth over mine, cutting off my tirade at the same time that he plunges into me fully. He swallows my moans, taking control of the kiss, of the pace, of everything. Pulling back slowly he then slams into me again. He tries to keep the rhythm steady, but after a few more pumps, his movements become frantic, out of control. I can feel the pleasure building below, and I want to do something—grab on to his shoulders, sink my nails in his back. I'm miserable that I can't do any of those things, and yet I can't deny that being bound while Troy fucks me is the most erotic thing I've ever done.

He abandons my lips for a moment to kiss my neck and my shoulders.

I arch my back and beg, "Troy, please. Let me touch you."

"No," he replies gruffly.

As I near climax, I bring my legs closer together, even though one is secured over Troy's shoulder. He grunts again, louder, and then, taking a cue from my playbook, he bites me. Pain and pleasure mix, sending me spiraling over the edge. I cry out, uncaring how loud I am. He pumps into me faster, almost in a frenzy. It's not much longer until he finds his release. His body shudders on top of me, slowing down. Breathing hard, he hides his face in the crook of my neck, blowing hot air against my already burning skin.

I move my leg, sliding it off his shoulder. It falls numb on the mattress, but everything else in my body is alive.

CHAPTER 35

TROY

can't move. My right shoulder is burning, but fuck it, it was totally worth it. This was the hottest sex move I've ever pulled with anyone. Beneath me, Charlie's breathing is out of whack, just like mine.

"Troy?"

"Hmm?"

"Are you still alive?"

"Barely."

"Thank God. I thought I was going to live through *Gerald's Game*."

Laughter ripples through me. Only Charlie would make such a comment. I roll off her but keep her cocooned within my embrace. "Are you telling me you couldn't rip those panties?"

She pouts. "I could, but I'd hate to ruin them. They're so pretty."

I bring my lips to hers, unable to resist the temptation she dangled in front of me. Anything she does that brings my attention to her mouth makes me want to kiss her.

I'd keep savoring her, but Charlie turns her face away.

"You're not starting this again while I'm still bound. I can't feel my hands."

Remorse pierces my chest. I didn't stop to consider what staying in this position for too long would do to her. "Does it hurt?" I ask as I untie her from the headboard.

"A little." She rubs her wrists, then opens and shuts her hands. "The bite on my shoulder hurt more."

Shit. I glance at the mark, feeling really bad about it. "I'm so sorry. I got carried away." I shake my head. "Ah hell. I'm an idiot."

Charlie laughs as she reaches for my face. "Relax, babe. I was just teasing you. It only hurt a little."

Relief washes over me. "Thank God. I really liked when you bit me, so I wanted to return the favor."

Her eyebrows pinch together as she narrows her eyes. "What are we now, a couple of vampires?"

"Hey, you started it." I kiss her nose and then jump out of bed to get rid of the condom.

I could toss it in the trash bin in my room, but I need something from the bathroom—painkillers. Now that the heat of the moment has passed, I can feel the consequence of my reckless decision. The pain isn't as sharp as when I returned from the hospital, but it's not great either. I hope I didn't buy myself another week on the bench.

"I knew I shouldn't have removed the sling," Charlie says from the door.

She's leaning against the frame with her arms crossed, still fully naked save for the boots. My cock stirs awake again at the sight.

"If you hadn't, I would have done it myself." I turn around, ready to go for round two.

Charlie's gaze slowly travels down my body until she sees I'm locked and loaded once more. Her lips curl into a satisfied grin. Wordlessly, she unfolds her arms and walks over. I swallow hard, my pulse already accelerating at the promise of more good times. She stops in front of me, not breaking eye contact.

"What do you have in store for me now, my dear lord conqueror?"

"What?" I try not to laugh, but how can I when my crazy girl keeps saying stuff like that?

"I'm on the losing side. I'm at your mercy, remember?"

"Oh, that. Hmm. I have a few ideas." I kiss her shoulder where the love bite is still red.

She shivers beneath my caress.

"Are you going to share them?" she whispers.

"Yes, dear, I will. Let's get back to bed. The night is young, and we have a lot of catching up to do."

An annoying blaring sound wakes me from a pleasant dream. Still refusing to acknowledge the noise, I drag a pillow over my head. Charlie moves next to me, and a moment later, the noise ceases. I sense a shift on the mattress, so I blindly reach for her, curling my arm over her stomach.

She snuggles against me, and I begin to drift once more into dreamland.

"Troy," she whispers.

"Hmm?"

"We have to get up." She traces circles over my chest, pebbling my skin.

"No we don't. It's Sunday."

"Exactly. Your grandma is expecting us."

Ah hell. I had completely forgotten about it. We did promise to visit, and I can't say I'm not coming now. Charlie will go without me, and that will earn me the title of the shittiest grandson alive.

"Ten more minutes."

She makes a tsking sound and then frees herself from my hold. I'm too tired to fight to keep her in bed with me. I expect her to get up right away, but instead, I feel her body slinking lower on the mattress. The hand that was playing with my chest also moves down until it wraps around my cock. I hadn't even noticed I was already sporting morning wood.

"Charlie," I moan against the pillow.

She doesn't answer with words; she licks me from base to tip before her mouth covers my shaft.

"Fuck." My hips buck ever so slightly, but then I relax against the mattress and let Charlie do her thing.

My God, my girl has an expert tongue. I swear it feels like I'm inside her pussy and not her mouth. But she has a mean streak too. She keeps bringing me close to the edge and then slowing down right before I'm about to come. I'm close to flipping her over and taking control of the situation.

"Babe, you're killing me. Also, we're going to be late."

She lets go of my erection with a wet pop but keeps her hand wrapped around the base. "No we're not. Watch me."

I pull the pillow off my face and place it under my head so I can better do as she commanded. "I'm watching."

She smiles wickedly at me before resuming her task. It doesn't take long for her to bring me to the point of no return. Her ministrations combined with the visual of the most beautiful girl in the world sucking me into oblivion do the trick. I throw my head back and let out a guttural sound as I come into her mouth. Charlie keeps sucking me while pumping me with her hand until I have nothing left to give. With a shudder, I sink back into the mattress utterly spent. Honestly, I didn't think I had it in me to have an orgasm this morning after the all-nighter we pulled.

"All right. That was your ten minutes," she says.

I open my eyes to glare at her. "There's no chance those ten minutes are gone."

"It doesn't matter. You're awake now."

I sit up, grabbing her by the waist to drag her back to me. "Yes, but I'm hungry."

"Fine. Let's get breakfast, then."

She still doesn't get what I have in mind. "I have all the sustenance I need right here. Come on, babe. Sit on my face."

Her cheeks go from pink to tomato red in a split second. "Really?"

"Yeah. Don't make me beg."

She grins. "Like I would."

Twenty minutes later—we showered first, it didn't take me twenty fucking minutes to make my girl come—we head down to the kitchen for a quick breakfast. I sit on the stool and watch Charlie work her way around the kitchen like she's racing.

"What's the hurry, sweetheart? It's not like we told Grandma a specific time."

"I want to beat traffic."

"There's no traffic on Sunday."

She pauses to give me a droll look. "You've clearly never visited Ophelia on a Sunday. It's prime visitation day. The place will be packed, and we might not even find a parking space if we arrive there late."

"Wow, I didn't realize families visited the residents that often."

"They don't, only on Sundays. I'm not sure why."

"Maybe they go after Sunday mass because they feel hella guilty."

She chuckles. "Maybe."

"Do you think Grandma knows about us?" I ask.

"How could she? Unless your sister told her."

"I doubt it. Jane is discreet. She wouldn't blabber about my love life to anyone."

"We should invite her to come to LARP next weekend. I'm sure Fred would love the surprise." She smirks.

"Yeah, I'm sure he would." Suddenly, my good mood turns sour.

"You don't have to worry about Fred. He's harmless," she assures me.

"No guy is harmless unless he has no dick."

Charlie rolls her eyes and resumes making coffee. A minute later, she sets a cup in front of me and then leans against the counter with a mug of her own.

We don't speak for a moment as we blow into our hot beverages. I bring the cup to my lips and take a tentative sip.

"You know Andreas has a thing for your sister, right?"

I choke on my drink and also manage to spill some on my jeans. Shit, it's hot. Charlie laughs at my clumsiness.

"How do you know?" I ask, not hiding my annoyance.

"It was obvious. At game night, he couldn't take his eyes off her. And let's not forget that he almost beat Fred up for asking her to blow on the dice for luck."

I run a hand through my hair. I was hoping I had misread the signs. "Fuck. I was afraid that would happen."

"She's eighteen, right? You can't keep all the guys away from her. She's gorgeous."

"Watch me," I retort angrily.

She shakes her head and takes another sip of her coffee.

"You think I'm being ridiculous." I square my shoulders, too tense for someone who just had the best blow job ever.

"Only a little. I mean, I get it. You're protective of your sister, especially considering what hap—" She stops abruptly, her face going ashen as she realizes she said too much.

Edgier than before, I ask, "Considering what, Charlie? What were you going to say?"

I can't mistake the sudden tension on her face or the guilt shining in her pretty blue eyes.

"Jane told me about your brother."

A bucket of ice-cold water pours over my head. I can't breathe. I can't move. I can only stare at Charlie while my heart gasps for air.

"Troy?" She sets the mug down and moves closer.

I put my coffee down with a jerky movement, spilling it all over the counter, and then stand up. "She had no right to tell you that."

"I'm sorry."

"Why are you apologizing? You weren't the one who gossiped." I look at the ceiling, laughing without humor. "I can't believe I just said Jane was discreet a minute ago. I guess I don't know my own sister."

"She didn't mean to gossip. She was trying to make me understand you." Charlie walks around the counter and stops in front of me.

"Why?" I frown, crossing my arm over the sling.

"So I wouldn't smother you to death in your sleep." She gives me a tentative smile, and damn it, it almost works. *Almost.*

"I don't know why she would tell you that. I never speak about Robbie. Not even Andreas and Danny know."

"Why is that?"

I look away, unable to hold her stare when the guilt of my fuckup comes back with a vengeance. I don't want Charlie to see the monster rearing its ugly head.

"Can we drop the subject? Please?"

She touches my lower back and then rests her forehead between my shoulder blades. "Okay. But know that I'll be here for you when you're ready to talk. Always."

The "always" gets to me. It makes me so thankful and yet undeserving of her. I let my brother die. What would she think if she learned that? I swallow the lump in my throat, vowing to never let her know.

"We should go. It's getting late."

I step forward and away from Charlie's touch, missing the contact at once.

CHAPTER 36

CHARLIE

can't believe I let it slip that Jane had told me about their brother's death. It's obviously a forbidden subject, yet I went and blurted it out. *Fuck me.*

Now Troy is acting cagey and moody. His sullen disposition is not only ruining what I was hoping would be an awesome day, but it's also making me feel horrible.

My chest is tight as I imagine what it must have been like for him to lose his brother at such a young age. My thoughts predictably wander to Ben and how I spent my entire life terrified something would happen to him. My concerns haven't lessened as we've grown older—if anything, they've increased—but I'm better at hiding my protectiveness for Ben's benefit. What I confessed to Troy on our date—my crippling fear that prevented me from applying for the exchange program—is something I've never told anyone, not even Blake.

When the sign for Golden Oaks comes into view, I let out a breath of relief. Hopefully, Ophelia, with her quirky sense of humor and no-bullshit attitude, will be able to get Troy out of his funk.

As I predicted, the place is full, but we're not so late that we can't find a parking space. I snag a spot as far away as possible from the main entrance. It's tight, and if my car were any bigger, it wouldn't fit. I turn off the engine and glance at Troy with a small smile on my lips.

"Ready?"

He looks at me, his expression unreadable. My grin wilts as I'm blasted by his cold stare. I begin to turn, but he swings his arm around my shoulders, pulling me to him. His mouth slams over mine, rough and desperate. Wow, the boy is intense. I'm swept away by the passion of his kiss, melting against him. When it seems I'm about to combust on the spot, he pulls back suddenly, leaving me bereft and also so aroused.

Ah shit.

"Okay, now I'm ready." He smirks and then opens the passenger door.

Sweet baby llamas. I can barely think straight after that kiss, and he expects me to get out of the car and walk? I don't even know if I can move my legs.

I pull the vanity mirror down and check my reflection. My lips are swollen, and my light pink lipstick is smeared. I can't go in like this. I search for tissues in the glove compartment, but before I can actually fix my makeup, Troy opens my door.

"What are you doing, babe?"

I whip my face to his. "Fixing this." I point at my mouth.

He chuckles, and immediately, my irritation dissipates. I love when he laughs. My heart does a cartwheel, and a fuzziness in my tummy makes me feel strange. All because I used "love" in a thought about Troy. Does that mean I'm in love with him? My heart skips another beat as an answer. My brain freezes, and a gasp escapes my lips.

"What's wrong?" he asks, his tone filled with concern.

Like a moron, I shake my head. "It's nothing."

Troy keeps staring intensely at me. It doesn't help that my face feels warm, which means my cheeks are giving away my embarrassment. I quickly wipe off the lipstick and slide out of the car. He immediately places his hand on my lower back, sending ripples of heat up my spine and through the rest of my body.

Charlie, control yourself. You spent the night and morning fucking his brains out.

My inner pep talk does little to help me. It actually makes me even more hot and bothered. It won't do to walk into Golden Oaks like this. I have to start thinking of something completely unsexy to rescue my mind from the gutter.

I can't think of anything.

"I forgot to ask, what's going on with the prank we're going to pull on Andy? You didn't forget, did you?" Troy asks, saving me from myself.

"Shit. I kinda did. Let me text Fred real quick." I fish my phone out of my purse and send him a message.

I don't expect him to reply right away—it's too early for him—so when my phone pings with a reply, I'm shocked.

"What did he say?" Troy leans closer, peering at my screen.

"Hey! Stop peeking at my private messages." I push him off, pretending to be offended.

"Do you want me to start developing jealous boyfriend tendencies? Because I will if you start sending private messages to your buddies."

I glance at him, dreading to read truth in his statement. But Troy's eyes are dancing with amusement, and his lips are upturned.

"I like some possessiveness… in the bedroom."

Ah hell. I had to open my big mouth and put me right back into crazy nympho mode.

Troy groans. "Why did you have to say that? Now you've woken Junior." He points at his crotch. There's definitely a bulge there.

"Junior?" I snort. "I didn't know you named it."

"Babe, all guys name their dicks."

"Oh yeah? What do Andreas and Danny call theirs?"

"Excuse me?" He arches his eyebrows. "I'm not going to discuss my friends' penises with you."

This moment is too surreal. I can't believe we're talking about male anatomy when we're a minute away from meeting his grandmother.

We're right in front of the entrance, so I have to school my features. "Okay, okay. Let's try to behave."

"You're the one who started it," he replies tartly.

"You're the one who had to kiss me like you wanted to bang me right there in the car." I poke his chest.

"Keep up with the sassy attitude and that's exactly what I'm going to do."

Heat rushes through my face, especially when I belatedly notice a family right behind us. They must have heard the tail end of our conversation, judging by the wife's horrified expression and the husband's smirk. I let them go in first and won't budge from my spot until I can't see them in the lobby anymore.

Troy seems to have guessed why I'm stalling and doesn't rush me. I take the lead when I'm ready, saying hello to the receptionist working today.

She smiles and then tells us that Ophelia is waiting for us in the gardens. We continue down the corridor in silence. Troy refrains from touching me. I'm glad he's keeping his distance, but I can't help but wonder if he's acting nonchalant now because he doesn't want his grandma to know about us. Not willing to have a repeat of this morning and say what I shouldn't, I stop in my tracks right before we're about to walk out the back door.

"Do you want your grandma to know about us?"

He gives me a quizzical look. "Of course. Unless you don't want her to know."

"I have no reason to hide from her that we're dating."

"Good. Me neither." His eyes seem to twinkle with mischief.

"What?" I ask, immediately suspicious that he's up to no good.

"What if we don't tell her right away, just pretend we're nothing but friends until I sweep you off your feet and kiss you senseless in front of her?"

I stare at him without blinking for several beats until I finally say, "No."

His expression falls. "Why not?"

"Because I don't want to make out in front of your grand-mother," I whisper-shout.

He sticks his tongue out. "You're no fun."

Heavens above, why do guys have to act like toddlers sometimes?

We find Ophelia chilling in a lounge chair, sipping a drink that could be regular iced tea or a Long Island. Hard to tell. Her boyfriends aren't around, which surprises me. She smiles when she notices our approach and sits up straighter, pushing her oversize sunglasses over her now pink head.

"Charlie, Wolfie. I was afraid you weren't going to make it."

I give her a hug and then Troy follows me, kissing Ophelia on her cheeks.

"Well, we almost didn't make it," he says.

"Why is that? Partied all night long?"

He gives me a naughty glance. "Something like that."

Ophelia, who is the sharpest lady I've ever known, doesn't miss the gesture. "Oh my. Have I inadvertently played Cupid?"

Hell. I'm blushing so hard now that it's a miracle steam isn't coming out of my ears.

"Gram, you're making Charlie uncomfortable." Troy sits on the lounge chair next to her, leaving me standing there to suffer my humiliation alone.

Jerk.

"What did I say? You're young and attractive. You should be going at each other like ferocious bunnies. I know I would with my boys if my joints allowed."

Kill me now.

Troy makes a face that clearly tells me he's regretting putting me on the spot. *Ha!*

I pull up a chair on the other side of Ophelia.

"Speaking of which, where are Jack and Louis?" I ask.

"Oh, they're out, running errands. I had to send them away because—"

"Jane? What are you doing here?" Troy sits straighter in his seat.

"You didn't know I was coming?" She glances at Ophelia.

"Must have slipped my mind to mention it."

Troy's gaze travels over his sister's shoulder, and he becomes visibly tense. "Oh great."

Curious, I turn around, and see the source of his irritation is an attractive, middle-aged woman who is sashaying in our direction. Her hair is bleached white-blonde, and her sunglasses are even bigger than Ophelia's. She's way too overdressed for a visit at Golden Oaks. She must be Troy's mother.

My spine goes taut, and sudden nervousness takes hold of me. I'm usually not bad with parents—Blake's folks adore me—but I sense it's going to take more than a sincere smile to win this lady over.

"Good morning. I see you beat me here, son," she deadpans.

"Yeah, Charlie got me out of bed early."

Gee, thanks, Troy, for throwing me at the shark without a warning.

She turns to me, and even behind the sunglasses, I can sense her eyes assessing me. I try not to squirm in my chair. If I had known I'd be meeting her, I'd have picked something nicer to wear instead of my faded jeans, Chucks, and a vintage T-shirt. At least my hair isn't in a messy bun, and I put makeup on to hide the dark circles.

"Oh, is that your new roommate?" she asks him as if I wasn't sitting right there.

I jump from my seat and extend a hand to her. "Yes, I'm the roommate."

"Actually, she's no longer my roommate. She's my girl-friend," Troy pipes up.

I swear the woman's handshake tightens when she learns that, and then she drops my hand as if touching me burned her. I wonder if anyone noticed that or if it was just my imagination.

"Is that so? Does that mean you moved out?"

"Uh, no," I say, looking at Troy for help.

Finally, he notices I'm floundering and jumps off his chair to come stand next to me. "Why would she move out?"

"Do you think it's a good idea to live with a girl you just started dating? Living together is a commitment, not a whim." She turns to me. "No offense, darling."

Yikes. Tell us how you really feel, why don't you?

"Oh, sit down, Elaine, and stop raining on everyone's parade," Ophelia butts in. "Just because you couldn't make your marriage work doesn't mean your son can't live with his girl-friend without causing the Rapture."

She twists her face into a scowl. "I'm sorry. I felt it was my duty to point out the obvious. But you're right; it's not my place to comment. Kids are so independent nowadays." She glances at Jane. "But don't you get any ideas. You're not going to move in with any boy while you're still living on my dime."

"Gee, Mother, double standards much?" Troy retorts angrily.

"Oh, honey, society is full of double standards. I'm merely protecting my daughter."

The small hairs on the back of my neck stand on end. Did she just insinuate that my parents don't care about me because they didn't say I couldn't live with Troy? To be fair, they don't know I'm dating him, and I doubt they would bat an eye, considering their marriage is hanging by a thread.

Immediately, my anger dissipates, and it's replaced by an overwhelming sadness.

If I knew how this day would toy with my emotions, I wouldn't have left the bed.

CHAPTER 37

TROY

Charlie is morose after we leave Golden Oaks. I don't need to be a genius to guess meeting my mother put her in that state. Curse the woman and her evil ways. I wish Grandma had told me Mom would be paying a visit today. I'd have canceled ours.

The drive back home is quiet, and not even the radio manages to fill the void.

"Hey, don't let my mother get to you," I tell her once she parks in front of the house. "She's a witch, and she will suck the joy out of you if you let her."

Charlie gives me a pitiful smile. "I'm not upset about what she said exactly. She did remind me about my parents' fight though."

"Do you want to drive to Littleton today? I'll come with you."

She shakes her head, staring straight ahead. "No. Only if Ben needs me. I'm not sure I'm ready to deal with what's coming."

She means if her parents get a divorce. I hate seeing the sadness in her eyes. When my parents split up, I had already been in a dark place, so one more bad thing didn't impact me as much.

"I have an idea. Why don't we invite your friends for another board game party?"

She turns to me, and this time, the smile seems more genuine. She cups my cheek, and because I can't help myself, I take her hand and place a kiss on her open palm.

"Thanks for suggesting it, but everyone is busy today. But I know what can make me feel better."

A sly grin unfurls on my lips as my mind wanders off to Hanky-Panky Town. "What?"

"A Lord of the Rings marathon. It's high time I introduce you to my favorite series ever."

My smile wanes a little as a smidgen of disappointment comes through, but I hide it from Charlie. It's not like we haven't had plenty of sexy times in the past twenty-four hours.

"Sounds good, babe," I reply.

"I promise you'll love it."

"And if I don't and end up falling asleep, I know you have a special way to wake me up." I wiggle my eyebrows up and down.

Her cheeks become bright pink, and suddenly, the air between us is charged with electricity.

"Let's head inside before you get any ideas," she says.

I follow her out of the car, rearranging my cock in a more comfortable position. "Too late; they're already in my head."

When we come to the front door, we find a box waiting for us. It has Charlie's name written on top in block letters.

"What is it?"

She lets out a squeak. "This must be from Fred."

I open the door and let Charlie walk in ahead with box in hand. She sets it on the kitchen counter and peels off the note attached to it.

"What's in the box?" she reads out loud. "Oh my God. No way." She laughs, but I don't get it.

"What's so funny?" I ask.

She widens her eyes. "Come on, Troy. *Seven*? The epic final scene where Brad Pitt loses his mind over the box?"

It finally dawns on me. "Oh shit. Don't tell me Gwyneth Paltrow's head is inside that."

"No, silly. Actually, I have no idea whose head is inside."

Charlie grabs a pair of scissors from the drawer and cuts the tape. The first thing I see when she lifts the flaps is blonde hair and fake blood. Carefully, Charlie pulls the prop from the box. She lets out a yelp and then drops the prop back in the box.

Damn. If she got spooked even knowing what it was, I can only imagine Andreas's reaction.

"Hey, I want to see."

She closes the box again, keeping both hands on top. "Better if you don't."

"Charlie, what the hell? What's in the box?" I know I sound exactly like Brad Pitt now.

She grimaces, keeping her hands in place. "Before I let you see it, you have to understand that Fred has a dark sense of humor, and I'm sure he didn't mean to upset you."

I bristle. "What's that supposed to mean?"

Charlie lets out a heavy sigh. "The head in the box is a fake of your sister."

"What?" I shout, making Charlie wince. "Let me see this."

I pry the package from her and reopen it. Bile pools in my mouth when I remove Jane's fake severed head from the box. It's so lifelike that it feels like I'm holding her actual head.

"This is so fucking wrong," I say. "Why would he pick Jane as his model? Is he a fucking psycho?"

"Oh my God, no. I'm pretty sure it's because he also noticed Andreas's interest in your sister. Like I said, twisted sense of humor."

"We can't use this." I put the head back, wishing now that I had listened to Charlie and not peeked.

"Are you sure? It would be epic."

"Imagine if it were Ben's head."

Charlie's eyebrows furrow, and her eyes become hard, but the moment only lasts a few seconds before she relaxes once more. "Disturbing, but Ben would probably love it."

Now that the shock has passed, I can see the appeal of using the prop. "I guess we could use it if Jane agrees."

"Yeah, and we should totally invite her to come to the party."

"No, absolutely not," I object vehemently. My visceral reaction to the idea surprises even me. I'm protective of Jane, but not to this level. Maybe it's the certainty that Andreas has a thing for her that triggered it.

"Don't get mad at me for saying it, but Jane will start dating soon—guys you don't even know. How terrible would it be if she dated Andreas, your best friend?"

"It's because Andy *is* my best friend that I know he's the last guy on earth I want dating my sister. He's a player, Charlie. The worst kind."

She holds up her hands. "Okay, okay. I'm not going to broach the subject again. What about Fred? Would you *allow* her to date him?" She quirks an eyebrow.

"He just made a fake severed head of her likeness. The answer is a million times no. She's too young to be dating anyone."

Putting her hands on her hips, Charlie stares at me hard. "Troy Wolfgang Alexander, I won't tolerate that kind of Victorian mentality from you. She's eighteen, for crying out loud. I'm sure she's already dated plenty of guys, and you don't even know."

"I seriously doubt it. My mother is stricter than me. And Victorian mentality?" I chuckle. "At least you didn't call me a caveman this time."

"I don't think Neanderthals cared much about who their sisters shacked up with."

"Shouldn't it be *caved* up?"

She throws her hands up in the air. "Ugh! You're impossible.

Just because of that, you're on popcorn duty—and none of that microwave crap. I want the real deal."

I don't move right away, too busy staring at my gorgeous girl. My sexy nerd turns even more irresistible when she's mad and bossy like that. I love it.

I love *her*.

The realization sets in my chest, but instead of becoming terrified, I'm centered, whole. My easygoing smile vanishes when I stride in her direction and slam my lips to hers, claiming her mouth in a possessive way. Her surprise only lasts a moment before she surrenders to the assault.

I'm taken over by a frenzy. I have to connect to Charlie skin to skin right now, or I'll go mad. I yank at her clothes with only one hand since my arm is back in the sling. Mercifully, Charlie is caught in the same urgency as me and shrugs off her jacket and T-shirt on her own. We only break apart when it's necessary to remove a piece of clothing. In less than a minute, I have her bent over on the couch, and I'm fucking her into oblivion.

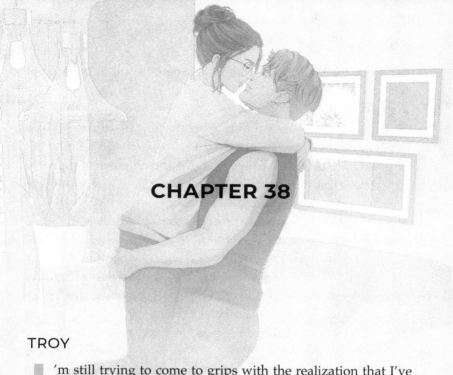

CHAPTER 38

TROY

'm still trying to come to grips with the realization that I've
fallen in love with Charlie fast and hard. I was friends with
Brooke first before we went out, and it felt like a natural
progression of our relationship. Everything with Charlie is
brand-new, and I find myself way out of my depth. I'm only
certain of one thing: there's no chance in hell that I'm confessing
my feelings to Charlie anytime soon. I don't want to scare her
away.

It's no surprise that my protective nature has extended to Ben
though. I can imagine pretty well what he must be going
through because I also lived through it. Of course, it's worse for
him since he's stuck in his parents' house and can't really escape
the fights. If his school wasn't in Littleton, I'd suggest he stay
with us for a while.

He friended me on social media after we met, so I shoot him
a message to ask how he's doing. I was expecting a generic
answer, so when he pours his heart out to me, I know I did the
right thing by reaching out.

As the week progresses and Charlie doesn't mention any of

the things Ben told me, I suspect he doesn't want to burden her with his problems. I've done that countless times before in order to protect Jane too.

On Thursday, I have a light schedule, but Charlie is stressed about some deadline for the paper. I know I've been keeping her busy, so I decide to make myself scarce and help Ben at the same time. I head to Littleton so we can hang out. The plan is for me to pick him up at school, and then we'll go from there.

I'm a little early, so I park the car and head for the entrance to wait for him. It's easier than trying to tell him where I parked. My head is down, eyes glued to my phone, when the sound of girls giggling catches my attention. I look up and find a cluster of them not too far from me, staring in my direction and whispering to each other. Ah, teenagers making me feel like I'm part of some boy band. I shake my head and return my attention to my phone.

"Hey! Quit staring at my sister's boyfriend like he's a piece of meat," Ben shouts. "Shoo!"

I glance up just in time to see him motion the girls away with a wide gesture of his arms as if they were little birds. The sight is comical. His face is flushed red when he walks over, holding the straps of his backpack.

"I'm sorry about that," he says. "Sometimes I wonder if there's something in the water here that affects the female population of the school. They're more boy crazy than normal."

I chuckle. "It's okay. They weren't bothering me for long. I just got here."

"Good."

We walk back to the car, and I ask, "What do you want to do today?"

"There's something I've been meaning to do for a while, but I've been too afraid to go by myself."

I quirk an eyebrow, curiosity piqued. "What is that?"

"Jane told me you helped her with her fear of heights by taking her bungee jumping. I'd like to try that."

Shit. He's a minor. No operator will allow him to jump without one of his parents present. I'd hate to disappoint him though.

I stop next to my car and wait for Ben to reach the passenger side to break the bad news. "You need parental consent for that since you're under eighteen."

"Got it."

I frown. "You did?"

"Yep. It's all square with the place we're going."

"Okay then. Let's go."

A s Ben's turn to jump approaches, I can tell he's getting visibly tenser. It doesn't help that quite a few people had the same idea to jump today. There's a group of guys—probably seniors in high school, judging by their letterman jackets—making a ruckus as they wait in line behind us.

"It's okay, Ben. Try not to think about how high you are. And before you jump, don't look down."

"Okay."

A few minutes later, Ben is all strapped up and ready to go. Right before he steps on the platform, he glances over his shoulder, eyes wide with panic. "I-I don't think I can do this."

"Nonsense. You got this, buddy. Remember, don't look down and let go."

He nods and steps forward. The operator gives him more encouraging words, and after a few more steadying breaths, he jumps with his arms wide open as if he's really letting go of his fear and fully embracing the experience. He shouts in excitement as he drops and doesn't stop hollering when the cord recoils, sending him flying upward again. I take the stairs to wait for him at the bottom. He keeps bouncing up and down for another minute until he eventually loses momentum and swings to a stop.

There's a group of ten kids waiting there as well, and after hearing pieces of their conversation, I realize they're from the same high school as those guys waiting in line with us. This is a senior year dare.

Ben finally comes down, and as the operator helps him out of the harness, I notice a dark stain on the front of his khaki pants.

"Oh my God. Dude! Did you piss yourself?" a guy shouts, pointing at Ben.

Laughter follows and I get ready to step in, but Ben looks down at the mess and, to my surprise, bursts out laughing too.

What the hell?

"I did! I peed in my pants. But it was so awesome!"

A few guys break from the group to high-five Ben, making me relax a fraction. I still eyeball the rest to make sure they aren't talking smack about Ben.

"Hey, Troy. Can you take a picture of me?" he asks.

"Sure."

I snap a few photos, even a few with the guys who high-fived him. We move on when someone else jumps.

"Hey, I have a pair of sweatpants you can borrow," I tell him.

"Okay. Cool. I didn't want to soil your car seat."

"Are you sure you're okay?"

"Yeah. Normally, I would be so embarrassed, but maybe I'm still riding on adrenaline. It's my fault for not going to the restroom beforehand. I usually have to pee when I'm nervous."

"I think everyone does." I laugh.

"Do you ever get nervous before you have to do something?"

I grin. "Heck yeah. I get jitters before every game. But it's also such a rush."

"I get that now."

Back at my car, I open the trunk and pull out the sweatpants from my duffel bag. "Can I be honest with you?"

"Sure," Ben says as he takes the pants from me.

"I'm terrified of going to LARP."

"Really? Why?"

"I had a really embarrassing moment during a school play when I forgot all my lines. I've avoided anything remotely related to theatrical performances ever since."

"That's the beauty of LARP. There aren't any lines to memorize. It's all improv. All you need to know is who your character is, what he can do—such as special powers—and then react to the situation given. It's super fun."

I nod. "All right. If you say so."

Ben heads back inside the building to change. While I wait, I snoop on Charlie's social media profile to check her pictures of past LARP events. It backfires royally when I find way too many images of her with that stuck-up ex-boyfriend. I should put the phone away, but I'm a glutton for punishment and keep scrolling down until I finally come across a few photos of when they were still a couple.

Fuck. Why hasn't she deleted these?

My pulse accelerates as possessiveness takes over. I know it's ridiculous to suffer from retroactive jealousy, but it seems when it comes to Charlie, logic has taken a vacation.

CHAPTER 39

CHARLIE

Can someone overdose on too much sex? Since I raised the white flag and declared defeat, Troy and I have been doing it whenever we're together. I can't get my fill of him. Even when I manage to carve out time to study or work, thoughts of him invade my brain. It's no surprise that after a week into this sex marathon, I have dark circles under my eyes, and I have to triple my intake of caffeine. I haven't had much sleep.

I'm not complaining. Far from it. Besides all the mind-blowing orgasms I've had, being consumed by Troy keeps my mind from thinking about my parents too much. Dad hasn't returned home, and after a short and painful conversation with my mother, it doesn't sound like he will anytime soon. She mentioned going to couples therapy, but judging by the defeat in her voice, it didn't sound like she believed it would help.

If it weren't for Troy keeping me busy, I would have for sure succumbed to a depressive state. I *am* gutted that my parents might get a divorce, but my main concern in this mess is Ben. I've spoken to him every day. He sounds okay; the upcoming

LARP weekend in a few weeks is keeping his mind occupied. He's helping Tammara with some of the writing too, which is awesome.

It's Friday after lunch, and I'm at the newspaper. I'm behind on an article I have to deliver, and Blake is on my case. He didn't say anything when I came in half an hour ago, but I've been sensing him eyeballing me ever since. Ludwig and Angelica are out, and Blake's constant staring is getting on my nerves. It's already hard enough to concentrate when my eyes want to shut and I can't stop yawning.

Finally, I can't take it anymore and whip my head in his direction. "What?"

"I should be asking you the same question. What's going on with you? I know Halloween is just around the corner, but it's a little early to dress up as a zombie."

"Bite me, Blake."

"See? What's with the attitude?"

"I'm tired, if you haven't noticed, and I have a deadline."

"I'm quite aware of your deadline. I'm the one waiting for it."

I grumble, returning to my laptop. I have to squint my eyes behind my glasses to make the words stop dancing on the screen. It's like I ate magic mushrooms before coming here.

Blake scoffs. "I knew you dating that jock would affect your work ethic."

I jerk my head up to look at him. "Excuse me? How is my work ethic affected?"

"You're late in delivering the article, and Sylvana said you haven't sent your boyfriend's character sheet yet."

"The event is in three weeks. I have time."

"Really? You're just going to deliver that last minute so the other writers have to scramble to fit him in the storyline? Besides, doesn't he want to study the character before he has to play it?"

I rest my head in my hand, letting out a groan. *Crap on toast.* Blake is right. "Shit."

"You forgot you had to do it, didn't you?"

Blake knows me too well.

"I totally did. Troy is going to kill me."

From the corner of my eye, I catch Blake's condescending shake of his head, which turns my irritation into ire. "You don't know what's going on, so keep your judgmental opinions to yourself."

He glowers at me. "No, Charlie, I don't know what's going on with you, and whose fault is that? It's like you've become a different person since you started dating that playboy. You ignore my texts; you don't call back."

"Maybe I'm still annoyed that you stopped by the house to warn him off. That was messed up, Blake."

He sits stiffer in his chair. "It was warranted. Look me straight in the eye and tell me you wouldn't do the same thing for me if the situation were reversed."

I want to keep holding on to my anger, but the truth is, if Blake started dating a girl who had been mean to him beforehand, I'd probably do worse than what he did.

Breaking eye contact, I reply, "You also kept badgering me about this stupid deadline. I wasn't in the mood to deal with Blake the editor."

"I'm sorry if you felt I was only contacting you because of the article." His voice softens. "I've been under a lot of stress too."

Guilt takes away the rest of my annoyance. I've been neglecting my friends since before I started dating Troy. It all began when I moved in with him. "Why are you under a lot of stress?"

He pushes his dark hair back, mussing it a little. "I've applied to a bunch of internships, and so far, I was only called to one interview, and I don't even know if I did well or not."

"I'm sure you aced it."

He shakes his head. "I doubt it. It was last week, and I haven't received a call back asking to come in for a second interview. I'm pretty sure I blew it."

"Where was the internship at?"

"Matrix Media Group."

That's one of the biggest media companies in the country. I'm not surprised Blake managed to snag an interview. He's extremely talented and qualified.

"Wow, that's amazing, Blake."

"It would be amazing if I got the internship. I hate being in this limbo." He dips his chin, threading his fingers through his hair.

"They *will* call you back, and if they don't, fuck them."

"Fuck them?" He chuckles. "It's my dream company."

"So?" I shrug. "If they can't see what an amazing asset you would be to them, then they don't deserve you."

With a smile still on his lips, he glances at his laptop screen. "Only you could make me laugh in my current state."

I lift my cup of coffee in a salute. "Well, at least I'm still good at something. I can't promise I remember how to write though."

Blake's expression becomes serious again. "Writer's block?"

"If only that were the case."

"What's the problem?"

"It's my parents. I think they're going to get a divorce."

Blake glances at me again, his eyes as round as saucers. "Shit, Charlie. I'm so sorry. What happened?"

There's a burning in my eyes and a knot in my throat that I try to swallow. Speaking about my family issues with Blake might not be the best idea. Troy never broaches the subject, and I'm grateful he doesn't. But with Blake, it's a different story. He's almost part of the family, so of course he wants to know what the problem is.

"I don't know. My mother has been complaining he's working too hard, coming home late, and even working on weekends. She accused him of cheating. I think the situation has reached the boiling point." My vision becomes blurry; the threat of a tear spill is very real. But I can't stop now. I have to tell Blake everything. "My father has moved out of the house. I don't know if he'll come back."

A sob escapes my lips just as hot moisture rolls down my cheeks, the first set of tears finally breaking free. I cover my face with my hands, ashamed that I couldn't hold it together in front of Blake. I hate crying in public; it doesn't matter that Blake is my oldest friend and he's seen me at my worst.

I hear the scrape of his chair and then sense his approach. He swivels my seat, then lifts my hands off my face.

"You don't need to hide your sorrow from me, Charlie."

He pulls me up, making me stand so we're almost at the same eye level. I still have to crane my neck a little to stare into his eyes since he's a head taller than me.

"You know I hate crying. I feel so pathetic."

He wipes my cheeks with the pads of his thumbs. "You're not pathetic. This whole situation sucks. It's okay to be sad. I wish you had confided in me sooner. I wouldn't have bothered you about a stupid deadline."

"I was in avoidance mode. If I didn't talk about it, didn't think about it, then I could pretend nothing was going on."

"That's just plain stupid."

I hit his chest playfully. "I'm not stupid."

"I know. But you sure act like it sometimes."

I narrow my eyes. "I thought you were supposed to be consoling me, not making me feel worse."

"You know me. That's how I roll, babe."

He chuckles, and I can't help it, I laugh too.

Then I hug him, pressing the side of my face against his chest. I can't remember the last time Blake and I had a moment like this. I guess since we broke up. That decision was mutual, and there were no lingering romantic feelings on either side. But I think we never wanted to cross the line and give the impression of the contrary. His hand goes to my head, and the soft strokes make me remember the time when we were five and I fell from my bike and scraped my knee. Blake did the same thing then too.

"Unbelievable." Troy's tight voice sounds in the room, making my blood run cold.

I jump back and turn toward the door. Blake makes an annoyed sound in the back of his throat; I make no sound at all.

Troy is standing there, eyes blazing with fury as he holds a tray with two cups of coffee and a brown bag. He came to surprise me with goodies and found me in an intimate embrace with my ex. No wonder he's glowering, his jaw locked tight.

"Troy, what are you doing here? I thought you had class." I take a step forward, wiping away the remnants of my tears.

He doesn't miss the gesture, which makes his angry expression soften a little. "Class was canceled. The teacher got the flu. I thought I'd surprise you. Funny how things worked out."

His quip feels like a dagger piercing my chest. Even though his expression is no longer murderous, he's still angry.

"Don't get your panties twisted in a bunch, buddy. I was just consoling a friend in need," Blake pipes up.

Troy narrows his eyes. "Right. And I was born yesterday."

Shit. He's not going to let this one go. It's all Blake's fault. If he hadn't shown up at the house to have a talk with Troy, he probably wouldn't be as furious as he is now.

"Oh, what's in the bag?" I ask to change the subject.

He glances at it with a frown, almost as if he forgot he was holding it. "Uh, chocolate-filled croissants."

My favorite. I only mentioned it once in passing, and he remembered. I feel guilty and moved at the same time.

Blake returns to his desk without saying another word to Troy.

Since Troy doesn't seem inclined to move, I walk over and kiss him on the lips. It's like kissing a wooden door. *Damn it.* I feel horrible even though I didn't do anything wrong.

"Thank you," I say.

"Why were you crying?"

"Because her parents are probably getting a divorce," Blake replies bluntly.

"I was updating Blake on the drama, and I kind of lost it. He was just being supportive," I explain.

"Hmm." That's all he says while he glowers at Blake.

What is he thinking?

"Come sit with me." I tug his arm.

"I think I'll go. Don't want to take up more of your time." He heads for the door, and then he's gone. He didn't even kiss me goodbye.

My heavy heart constricts further. In my current weakened state, the tears return to my eyes easily. It's an effort to keep them from falling. I go back to my desk without glancing at Blake.

After a minute, he says, "I knew your boyfriend was an ass."

"Shut up, Blake. Just shut up."

CHAPTER 40

CHARLIE

Troy doesn't come home for dinner. I begin to worry and call him. It goes to voice mail. I don't trust my voice at the moment, so I text him instead. My stomach is tied in knots as I wait for his reply. I get that he's angry, but why can't he just talk to me instead of giving me the silent treatment? That's fucking mean.

The pasta Bolognese I cooked is now cold and unappealing. If I ate a couple bites, that was a lot. This situation with Troy has taken away my appetite. My heart is too heavy, and my head is too full.

While I wait for Troy to come home, I put on *The Big Bang Theory* in the background and work on his character sheet. He told me he wanted to be a fun troll like Shrek. To me that translates as sarcasm and dark humor. I base the character off Fred, hoping he doesn't notice that Troy will be pretty much acting like him—that is, if Troy still wants to come with me to LARP.

A pang flares in my chest, followed by insecurity. Did I ruin things between Troy and me already? I hate feeling like this, caught in a whirlpool in the middle of the ocean and not knowing which way is up or down.

I have to force the words out, glad it's just a character sheet and not an entire story line. Another five hundred words and I'm done. It's getting late. I check my phone again for the thousandth time. Still no word from him. Maybe he's out with his friends, but he told me he might be playing tomorrow. He wouldn't party the night before a game, would he?

My heart jumps to my throat at the sound of any car that drives by. This is crazy.

I wish Troy had let me explain the scene he walked in on earlier. My fingers hover over his name. I want to ask him when he'll be home, but I don't want to come across as a clingy girlfriend.

Annoyed, I toss the phone aside and stare at the TV screen. It's the scavenger hunt episode, one of my favorites, and yet all the jokes are falling flat.

Tiredness begins to claim me. My eyes are droopy, and several yawns sneak up on me.

I lie down, pulling the blanket over me. My glasses get crooked, so I remove them and set them on the coffee table. Penny just told Raj to run back to India. I want to stay up to catch the final scene of Amy and Howard singing Neil Diamond at The Cheesecake Factory, but I don't.

I wake with a slight shake of my shoulder.

"Charlie, wake up."

I blink my eyes open, and my vision remains blurry for a few more seconds. Finally, Troy's image sharpens. His hair is damp, and I smell fresh soap and toothpaste wafting from him.

Did he just shower?

I sit up, rubbing the sleep from my eyes. "What time is it?"

"It's past eight."

"Past eight? How is that possible? When I lay down, it was already ten."

"It's past eight in the morning."

"What?" I glance at the window, noticing then the light pouring through the blinds. "I slept on the couch? Why didn't you wake me when you got home?"

"It was late, and you looked too peaceful. I didn't want to disturb you."

I get up in a huff, annoyed that Troy let me sleep on the couch even if his explanation makes sense. I would have done the same thing for him. Truth be told, my irritation has a different source. He probably thinks I fell asleep on the couch, waiting for him, which is so not the case.

Liar, liar, pants on fire.

He's already wearing a jacket, and his duffel bag is by the front door. "Are you leaving?"

"Yeah, I have to be at the stadium early." He shoves his hands in his pockets. His sling is gone.

"So you *are* playing today."

"Yeah. Probably not for the entire game though."

The atmosphere surrounding us is thick and uncomfortable with the weight of words unspoken. I can't let him go without talking first.

"Are we okay?" I blurt out, not beating around the bush.

He doesn't speak for several moments, but his hard eyes remain locked on my face. "I want us to be."

I breach the distance between us, even though there's nothing welcoming about his stance. "What you saw yesterday was a friend consoling me. Nothing more."

"And I believe you, Charlie. But there isn't a single guy on this planet who would be okay with their girlfriend being best friends with their ex."

"Are you saying you don't trust me?"

"I don't trust *him*." His eyebrows pinch together.

"Well, then trusting me has to be enough," I retort angrily. "Please don't ask me to pick between you and Blake, or any of my other guy friends for that matter."

A muscle in Troy's jaw twitches. "I have no issue with you being friends with guys, Charlie. That's not the problem. How would you feel if I started hanging out with Brooke?"

My heart bleeds at the thought. "That's not the same thing. She wants you back!"

Troy takes a step back, pinching the bridge of his nose. "I can't have this conversation with you right now. I'm already running late."

He bends over and grabs the strap of his duffel bag.

"What about tonight? Do you still want me to come to Andreas's Halloween party?"

God, why do I sound so pathetic?

He gives me a quizzical look, and then, forgetting his duffel bag, he steps into my space. He reaches for the back of my head right before he crushes his lips to mine. He kisses me hard and fast, and then, leaning his forehead against mine, he whispers against my lips, "I want you to come. Very much so."

I curl my fingers around his T-shirt, afraid he'll move away. "Good."

I kiss him again, not satisfied with the first one. Troy doesn't end it abruptly like before; he takes his time, savoring my mouth like I'm savoring his. When we finally break apart, we're both a little breathless.

"Was this our first fight as a couple?" I ask.

He chuckles and rubs my cheek with his thumb. "I guess so. Too bad we don't have time for makeup sex."

"I guess we'll have to save that for later." I wink at him, feeling a million times better.

His eyes become hooded and locked on my lips. "Yeah."

I'm not stupid to think this issue is over. I have no plans to cut Blake out of my life, but maybe I need to establish new boundaries. I understand Troy's point of view, and if the situation were reversed, I'd probably be more consumed by jealousy than him.

"By the way, what are you wearing tonight?" I ask.

"Oh, Andy, Danny, Paris, and I are going as the Horsemen of the Apocalypse."

"Who is Paris?"

"A guy on the team. You haven't met him yet."

"And what does your costume entail?"

"An all-black ensemble and skull-painted faces."

"That's cool. I didn't know you knew how to put makeup on." I smirk.

Troy flashes me a toothy grin. "I was hoping you would do it. Of course, if you're busy with your own costume, I'm sure Andy can find another volunteer."

"Hell to the no! I mean, he can get whoever he wants to do his makeup, but no one touches you but me."

Troy's smile grows wider. "That's my girl." He pulls his phone from his pocket and curses. "Shit. I *am* late. Coach will have my balls."

He heads for the door, then stops before walking out to look over his shoulder. "I'd kiss you goodbye, but that would probably make me even later."

"It's okay, babe. My kisses don't expire."

A different emotion crosses his eyes, and I get the impression he wants to tell me something, but all he does is smile before he walks out.

The moment he leaves, my chest becomes heavy again. I rub the spot, trying to soothe the phantom pain away. We parted ways on a positive note, so why the hell do I still feel like the worst of the storm is yet to come?

CHAPTER 41

CHARLIE

I watch Troy's game on TV and try not to think about the fact that he didn't ask me to come this time. Was it because he knows I'm not a sports fan, or maybe he secretly regrets me coming the last time? I know my thoughts are irrational and have no merit, but when the camera shows Brooke's face in the crowd, jealousy makes me see red. Her being there might not be because she's still trying to win Troy back. She might enjoy football for real. But that doesn't comfort me. Maybe I should have been a better girlfriend and asked for tickets.

I turn off the TV and stomp to my room. I never asked Troy if Brooke had been invited to Andreas's party, but I'm going to assume she was. I didn't have the chance to put her in her place when I caught her with Troy the last time, but if I see her tonight, all bets are off. What she did was fucked up. Getting drunk and coming on to Troy while I was somewhere in that party. Never mind her cunt of a friend who called Ben names.

This year was the first that I didn't think of a creative Halloween costume. My parents' issue and Troy have kept my mind distracted. It isn't a real problem when half my closet is filled with cosplay outfits, though most of them aren't sexy enough for tonight's party. I only have one that will do. I pull the zipper of the garment bag down and run my hand over the smooth red velvet fabric of Raven the Sorceress's dress. It hugs my curves in all the right places and has a plunging neckline that's made to make men go crazy. She's the master of seduction in our game, a reformed bad girl, per se.

I take my time in getting ready, knowing Troy won't be home for hours. I have a towel wrapped over my head and my body snuggled in my fuzzy robe when I hear the doorbell ring.

Ah crap. Who can it be?

I decide to ignore it, but it rings again.

Shit. I'd better see who it is.

I make sure to tiptoe down the stairs, just in case whoever is outside isn't someone I want to make aware I'm home. I look through the peephole and see Jane standing there.

Doesn't she know Troy has a game?

I open the door a fraction, hiding half my body behind it. "Hi, Jane. What are you doing here?"

"Oh, did I catch you at a bad time?"

"I just got out of the shower. You know Troy is at the game, right?"

"Yeah, but I actually came to see you. Can I come in?"

"Sure." I step away and let her through. This is the first time I've been alone with her, and I'm feeling a little self-conscious to be standing naked under my robe. I pull the lapels closer.

"You must think my visit is super strange, but I have two reasons for being here."

"All right. What are they?"

"I want to see the prop Fred made of me." She sounds eager.

"He didn't make it. His father owns a company that does that for movies."

"Gotcha. So, can I see it?"

"Of course, but let me warn you, it's pretty disturbing." I walk to the closet under the stairs where we stored the box.

"Oh, I'm a horror movie enthusiast. Didn't Troy tell you?"

I wrinkle my nose. "He didn't mention it, but maybe it's because I'm the opposite. I'm slowly going through the first season of *Supernatural*, which, according to him, is the scariest of them all."

Jane laughs. "Oh my God. *Supernatural* is not scary."

"It is to me." I lift the box and then bring it to the kitchen counter. "Here. Have fun."

Jane opens the box like a kid opening a Christmas present. She carefully pulls the head out, then smiles from ear to ear at the sight. "Oh my God. This is awesome."

"Why did Troy think you would have a problem with it?"

She scowls. "Because my brother still thinks I'm a little kid."

"It's because of what happened to your brother, huh?"

"Yeah." Jane's voice grows sadder. My clue to change the subject.

"What was the second thing you wanted from me?"

Her grim expression vanishes, and there's now the hint of a smile on her face. "Oh, I wanted to ask if you could do my makeup for Halloween. Troy mentioned you were doing his."

When did Troy have time to tell her that? I just volunteered for the job this morning. I don't voice my question though. I don't want her to think I don't want to help her.

"Sure. But I warn you, I'm not a professional by any means."

"As long as you're better than me."

"What's your costume?"

"Harley Quinn in the classic black-and-red jumpsuit. I was thinking you could paint my face white and black around the eyes. I want to be unrecognizable."

"That sounds simple enough. Do you have a big party at your high school?"

"Something like that. It's not at my high school. Someone is throwing a party. Don't let my brother know or he might tell my mother."

I don't like that Jane is asking me to keep stuff from Troy, but in this case, I have to agree with her. He's a little too medieval when it comes to her.

"I won't tell. I promise."

"Awesome." She grins. "Oh, one more thing. Can you take a picture of me with the head?"

I laugh. "Sure."

If Fred were here to witness this, he might fall in love with Jane on the spot. But I won't tell him this happened. The last thing I need is one of my friends getting involved with Jane.

Jane is long gone by the time Troy comes home from the game. I'm still wearing my robe, but my makeup and hair are done. He comes straight to my room and sweeps me off my feet while crashing his mouth to mine.

"Troy! You're going to ruin my makeup."

"Fine. I won't kiss you on the mouth, then." He starts to fumble with my robe, pulling the lapels apart while the sash is still in a knot. "Please tell me you're naked under this."

"Yes. Oh my God, what's with you? Is this a postgame shot of libido thing?"

His rough hands cover my breasts, kneading them while he flicks my nipples with his thumbs. "Don't you know sports make men hornier?"

"I never dated a jock before, so the answer is no, I didn't know."

"Well, babe, you're soon going to find out there are more perks to dating a jock than a hot bod." He unties the sash but doesn't bother to remove the robe before he drops to his knees and parts my folds with his hand.

"Troy…." My voice comes out strangled.

Our eyes meet, and I swear I melt under his heated gaze. I run my fingers through his hair, needing some type of anchor.

He kisses each side of my thighs, and then he licks my clit, drawing a loud moan from me. With each sweep of his tongue and playful bite, he drives me crazy. My legs can barely support my weight. Troy must have sensed that because he keeps a firm hold on them.

My head is getting dizzy, and suddenly, the room begins to spin. I close my eyes while I try to cling to the sweet moment just before an orgasm, but Troy's caresses are merciless, and when he sucks my clit into his mouth, I lose the battle against my body. I yank his hair and cry out as I attempt to ride the wave of pleasure without collapsing to the floor.

My body is still shaking when Troy unfurls from his kneeling position, picks me up, and almost runs to my bed. A moment later, he's inside me, fucking me so hard that I begin to see stars again in a matter of minutes.

CHAPTER 42

TROY

I t was almost impossible to leave the house. When Charlie walked down the stairs, wearing her LARP costume, I couldn't control myself. I dragged her to the couch and begged her to ride me. Now I'm about to park in front of Andreas's building and I'm sporting another boner. All it took was a glimpse of Charlie's golden leg peeking out from the slit in her skirt.

"Ready?" I ask in a gruff voice.

"Yeah." Her eyes drop to my crotch. "Oh, babe. Again? Did you accidentally take Viagra?"

"No, that's all you, darling, and that dress."

She glances outside where a few people wearing costumes are walking in and out of the building. The whole campus is one big Halloween party.

"I could help you out." She reaches for my zipper.

"Oh my God, Charlie. I love you."

Her hand stops, her eyes rounding as she stares at me. Neither of us speaks for a moment. I don't dare to breathe.

What the hell did I just do?

"You love me?" she asks, breaking the silence.

"Hmm." I rub the back of my neck, tongue-tied all of a sudden. How fucking ironic.

"Troy?"

I look away, leaning my head against the car seat. "Fuck. I swore I wouldn't open my big mouth. Please don't get weird on me."

She reaches for my hand. "Why would I do that? I mean, my hands are magical. They get guys to tell me they love me all the time."

There's humor in her tone, but even so, her comment triggers my jealousy. Frowning, I turn to her. "Please don't say that, not even as a joke."

She leans across the gap and kisses me softly on the lips.

"You're going to ruin your makeup," I whisper.

"I don't care." She eases off and stares into my eyes. "Were you scared to confess your feelings to me?"

"Afraid I would freak you out? Yeah." I run a hand through my hair. "This is all new to me. I've never felt this way before. Unsteady, unraveled."

"I feel the same way," she murmurs.

"You do?"

She nods. "I think I've spent the past few weeks equal parts terrified and ecstatic. When I look at you, it almost hurts, like a sweet agony. You rob me of air, Troy."

My heart skips a beat. She might not have said "I love you", but fuck if that doesn't come close enough.

I reach behind her head, tangling my fingers in her hair. Then I lean closer but stop short of kissing her, remembering the reason I can't. "Damn it. Curse my stupid idea to wear skull paint on my face tonight."

A loud knock on Charlie's window makes her jump back and shriek. Paris is outside, grinning like a maniac.

"Holy shit." She places a hand on her chest.

"Come on, Troy. Save sex in the car for the way back home," the idiot shouts.

She rolls her eyes at me. "Let me guess. That's Paris."

"Yep, that's him." I pat her thigh. "Come on. We'd better go before more people start to think we're doing what he said we were."

I get out of the car first, sprinting to circle around it and help Charlie out. Paris and his date are waiting for us by the curb. After introductions are made, we walk together to Andreas and Danny's apartment. Even before we reach the front door, we can hear the loud music echoing in the hallway. This isn't a dorm building, but because it's on campus property, most of the residents are students at Rushmore.

Paris and his date enter the party first, but just as Charlie and I are about to cross the threshold, she grabs my arm. "Oh no. We forgot the head."

"No we didn't, babe. While you were getting ready, I dropped it off. Danny is in the know. He'll place the head in the fridge and signal us."

"I wish Fred were here to see this."

"I'd have invited him if Andy didn't have an issue with your friend," I say.

"I know."

She takes my hand, and we head inside.

Twenty minutes after we arrive at the party, Danny gives us the two-thumbs-up signal. The place is full but not completely packed to the gills. But most importantly, Andreas isn't drunk out of his mind yet. We want him lucid for this.

"Hey, Andy, we're out of Perrier," I say.

"There's more in the fridge," Danny pipes up from the other side of the counter.

Charlie gets her camera ready.

Andreas turns to the fridge. "You and your fucking Perrier, Troy. I swear to Go—" He jumps back, almost falling on his ass. "Motherfucker. Jane!"

I move closer, getting a prime view of Andreas's panicked face. I bet he looks ashen under his makeup.

"What's Andy freaking out about?" Paris pushes him out of the way. "Holy crap. That's freaky." He pulls the prop from the fridge. "Dude, is this your sister?"

I flatten my lips, trying not to laugh. Now that I got used to the sight of Jane's severed head, it doesn't bother me as much anymore.

"It sure is," Charlie replies for me. "Hey, Andreas. Say cheese." She points the camera at him and takes several pictures.

Still stunned, he doesn't lash out at Charlie like I thought he might. Instead, he turns to me, wide-eyed. "What the hell, Troy? That was a sick joke. I'll have nightmares for days. I need a drink." Fumbling through the kitchen, he opens several cabinets until he finds a bottle of Patrón, something he usually hides at parties. He might come from money, but he's stingy as fuck.

Charlie walks over to me, giggling. "Oh my God. That was so epic."

"Did you get everything, babe?"

"Oh yeah. I got the moment on video and then several pictures. Man, Jane is going to love this."

I watch Charlie text my sister, keeping a goofy smile on my face. The crazy feeling in my chest seems to expand. The words Charlie told me in the car make total sense. It's a sweet agony to stare at her and keep my hands to myself when all I want to do is kiss and love her.

Man, I have it bad.

Unable to resist the temptation any longer, I wrap my arms around her waist and bring her back flush to my chest. Leaning close to her ear, I whisper, "I wouldn't mind going home now and having my wicked way with you."

"Troy, we just got here," she replies feebly.

I bite her earlobe. "So? We pranked Andy. That was the high-light of the party."

"When you put it that way," she whispers, leaning against me. "I have to use the restroom first."

Reluctantly, I let her go. While she's away, I step into a conversation with Paris and Puck about today's game. It's easy to lose track of time with those guys. I'm laughing about a joke Paris told us when suddenly, someone yanks my arm, turning me around.

"Charlie?" I frown, noticing her furious expression. "What's going on?"

"What the hell, Troy! I can't believe you would take Ben bungee jumping behind my back!"

"Calm down. Why are you yelling at me? He had a great time."

"Really? You call this a great time?" She shoves her phone in my face. I have to step back and pry the device from her hand to see what she's trying to show me.

It's a video of Ben jumping. Someone caught the whole thing, including when he lost control of his bladder. And then later, there's a shot of him in wet pants. I can't hear what the person who shot the video is saying, but the name of the video makes it clear that it's nothing kind: **Watch this idiot pee in his pants while bungee jumping. HILARIOUS.** If the headline wasn't bad enough, the comments that follow are vile and disgusting. It makes me see red.

Charlie yanks the phone from my hand and strides away.

"Where are you going?" I follow her.

"Leave me alone, Troy."

She bumps into someone coming in and bounces back. Fate would have it that Brooke is the one who collided with Charlie.

"Hey, where's the fire?" she asks with an uncomfortable smile on her face.

Charlie glances at her and, before I can do anything, shoves Brooke so hard that she trips on her high heels and falls down.

"What the hell!"

I'd stop to help her up, but Charlie is already out in the hallway. I can't let her leave in that berserk state.

"Sorry, Brooke," I yell as I run after Charlie.

Charlie took the stairs down and is already one floor below when I catch up with her. I grab her arm, making her stop.

"Babe, please. Don't be like that."

She yanks free from my hold. "Don't be like that? Troy, do you have any idea what this video will do to Ben when he sees it?"

"You don't know if he will."

"Oh my God, Troy. Wake up. Of course he will. Do you know how I came across this disgusting footage? Some guys were watching it and laughing like hyenas." Angry tears roll down her cheeks, making me feel even worse than I already do.

"I'm sorry, okay? Ben was the one who suggested bungee jumping. We couldn't have known that would happen."

"I could have! It's not the first time. Damn it, Troy! And how did you even get the operators to let him jump? He's a minor."

"He said he got your parents' permission."

"That's bullshit. They wouldn't have done that." She throws her hands up in the air. "Ugh! I can't talk to you right now. I have to go home."

"I'll take you."

She raises her hand, halting me. "No. I'm too angry. It's better if you leave me alone."

I get into her personal space. "No, I'm not going to back down, Charlie. You're acting completely irrational. You don't need to talk to me, but I'm taking you home, and that's final."

She shoots daggers from her eyes, and from the way she's clamping her jaw hard and flaring her nostrils, I know she wants to lash out again. But thankfully, she simply whirls around and continues her trajectory down the stairs.

The five-minute drive feels like an eternity. We're seething in silence, and that will only make the resentment fester. I can't believe she lost it like that because of the video. Yeah, it's bad, but she could have talked to me without causing Armageddon.

She's out of the car as soon as it stops. I stay put and let her march up to the front door and disappear inside without following. I'm too fucking angry, and if I go in, God knows what's going to happen. I don't want to make things worse.

I need to cool off, but sitting in the car alone won't do, so I turn the engine on again and take off.

As I drive without direction, I wonder how you can love someone so much and hate the things they do.

CHAPTER 43

CHARLIE

'm shaking with fury as I take the steps two at a time. I wanted to punch all those guys who were laughing, watching Ben's video. But when I saw Troy in the footage, all my ire was redirected at him. How could he put Ben in that situation and not tell me about it? I'm so mad, I could scream.

He doesn't follow me in the house. *Smart.* I can't talk to him while I'm so consumed with rage. I hear his car peel away from the curb as soon as I bang the door shut. Once in my room, I pack an overnight bag. I can't stay here. I have to make sure Ben is okay. And when did he and Troy become friends who hang out? Ben never told me about it, and I talk to him every day.

I should change, but I'm afraid Troy will come back, so I just hurry down the stairs and then out the door. Behind the steering wheel, I have to take a couple deep breaths to calm down. I'm glad I didn't have time to drink more than beer at the party, and the anger has burned off all the alcohol from my system.

Traffic is madness. It usually is on Saturday, made worse thanks to Halloween. It takes me forty-five minutes to finally reach the highway to Littleton. My phone rings, and the car dashboard shows it's Troy calling. I guess he's home. Guilt pierces my chest. Now that I'm a bit calmer, I can see that I never gave him a chance to explain. My short-fused temper got the best of me. *Shit.* I even shoved Brooke, unprovoked. *What a mess.*

I let the call go to voice mail. I'm not ready to talk to him yet, and I probably shouldn't while I'm driving. A new song comes on the radio, "Stay the Night" by Zedd and Hayley Williams. It hits me right in the feels. Are Troy and I meant to break?

Tears gather in my eyes, turning my vision blurry. I lean sideways, reaching for the glove compartment. I feel around for the tissue package I have in there somewhere, not daring to take my eyes off the road.

"For fuck's sake, where is it?"

A blaring horn makes me straighten in my seat, and the last thing I see is blinding lights fast approaching.

TROY

Charlie didn't answer the phone. That was hours ago. I've parked my ass on the couch and have been pounding one beer after another. *Where the hell is she?* I would have called Ben if it wasn't so late. Most likely, she went to Littleton.

I still can't believe her reaction. I get she's protective of Ben. I'm protective of Jane too. But she didn't give me the chance to explain. She went total psycho in the blink of an eye. I'd already known she was short-tempered—our beginning is proof of that —but hell, I hadn't expected her to do a one-eighty on me like that.

I'm about to call it a night when my phone rings. My heart skips a beat. Despite the fact that I'm mad at Charlie, the yearning hasn't gone away. I dive for the phone, afraid the call will go to voice mail.

"Charlie, babe, ar—"

"Troy, it's Blake."

My blood runs cold. *What the hell?*

"Where's Charlie?" I jump from the couch, more on edge than before.

"There's been an acci—"

"Where is she?" I'm already veering for the door.

"At Saint James."

"How is she? Is she conscious?"

"She's in surgery. Broke her leg."

"I'll be there as soon as I can. Thanks for calling me."

"Don't thank me. Thank Ben." The line goes silent.

"Asshole."

I slide behind the wheel and gun the engine. The damn beeping sound reminds me to put my seat belt on.

"Yeah, I hear ya, motherfucker."

I click the belt in place right before I take a sharp curve, burning rubber. My heart is pumping like a factory, and my hands are already sweaty from holding the steering wheel too tight. I should be mindful of the speed limit, especially since I've been drinking tonight, but my need to get to Charlie as fast as I can trumps everything.

A traffic jam makes me lose my mind. *No, no, no. I can't get stuck here.* I know if Charlie's in surgery, it'll be hours before she's out, but that doesn't make me less frantic.

Finally, the line of cars begins to move. I decide to take the next exit and get to the hospital via another route. The highway is usually fast, but apparently not tonight.

Another twenty maddening minutes later, I park my car in the first spot I find and then run like a madman through the parking lot. When I burst through the sliding doors of the hospital, I must be quite the sight since I'm still in full skull makeup.

"I'm looking for Charlie Fontaine," I tell the receptionist. "She was brought in earlier an—"

"Troy?" Ben calls out.

I turn toward the sound of his voice.

He walks over and, without hesitation, gives me a hug. "I'm glad you came."

"Thanks for letting me know. Do you know what happened?"

He steps back and wipes the tears from his cheeks. "No. We got the call and rushed here. Mom and Dad talked to the doctors away from me."

We return to the waiting area, and I find Blake, Fred, and a curly haired brunette I haven't met yet. Blake glowers at me but keeps his piehole shut. Fred gives me a sympathetic nod, and the girl simply stares at me blankly. I could be a ghost for all she cares. A middle-aged blonde woman with red-rimmed eyes that are filled with anguish walks over. Charlie's mother, I guess.

"You must be Charlie's boyfriend," she says. "Do you know why she was driving to Littleton so late in the night?"

Her tone is accusatory, and I don't blame her for it. But I can't tell her why without coming across as the biggest asshole in the world. If I had followed her into the house, I wouldn't have let her get behind the wheel.

"She was worried about Ben," I say without elaborating why.

"Why would she be worried about him?"

"Mom, please. It's not Troy's fault Charlie got hurt." Ben jumps to my defense.

Does he already know about the video?

"Is everything okay here?" a male voice asks behind me.

I turn around and lose my ground for the second time tonight. Staring at me is none other than Bill, my mom's boyfriend.

"Dad, this is Charlie's boyfriend," Ben introduces us.

Anger surges within me with the confirmation that Charlie's father has been unfaithful. I can't fucking believe it. There's no trace of recognition in his eyes, and it takes me a second to understand it's because of my makeup.

"Hi, sir. My name is Troy Alexander," I reply coldly, wondering if my answer will trigger his memory. I get nothing.

"Oh. Well, I wish I could say it's nice to meet you, but under these circumstances, I can't. Do you have any idea what Charlie was doing on the road?" His question doesn't have an edge like Charlie's mother's did. Too bad. If it had, I could have given him an answer with a bark.

"She wanted to see Ben," I say.

Guilt shines in the man's eyes, and he doesn't even remember who I am.

Asshole. But I can't think about that now.

"How is Charlie?"

"She has a few bruises on her face thanks to the airbag, but the worst injury is her broken leg. Thank heavens," he replies.

"How long until she's out of surgery?"

"Another hour," her mother replies.

"You look familiar. Have we met before?" Charlie's father asks me, narrowing his eyes.

I know I should lie, but I'm too pissed to do so. In the moment, I want him to know who I am, consequences be damned.

"Yes, we have actually. At a restaurant in Manhattan Beach not too long ago."

He stares at me blankly for a moment, as if he's trying to fish out the memory from his brain. Then his eyes go rounder, his face pale. But instead of confirming it, he schools his expression again. "No, it doesn't ring a bell. If you'll excuse me, I'm going to grab some coffee in the cafeteria."

I glower at his retreating back, but after he disappears around the corner, I feel the full impact of my discovery.

Charlie's father is having an affair with my mother. This will destroy Charlie and Ben.

I'm going to lose her.

CHAPTER 44

TROY

I ignore Blake to the best of my ability. I don't even know why he's here. Charlie's condition isn't life-threatening, and she's not his girlfriend. As a matter of fact, why was he even called, and who did it?

Charlie is out of surgery now, and her parents and Ben are with her. I wonder if she'll want to see me. I lean my elbows on my knees, resting my head in my hands. If she tells me to go away, I'm going to lose my mind.

A throat clearing catches my attention.

"Charlie is asking for you," her father tells me.

Wordlessly, I get up from my chair and follow him down the hallway. When we turn a corner, he stops in his tracks and turns to me.

"You can't say anything to Charlie."

"Excuse me?"

"Please. I'm begging you. I've decided to end things with Elaine."

I scoff. "A little too late, don't you think? The damage is done."

"No, it isn't done," he grits out. "Tara doesn't know about the affair, and she doesn't need to."

"Oh trust me, she knows."

His face goes even paler than before. He reaches for my arm, gripping it in a tight hold. "Did you already tell her?"

Annoyed, I pull free from his grasp and reply through clenched teeth, "No, I didn't tell her, but she suspects it. Can we go now? I'd like to see Charlie."

He steps back, passing a hand over his face. "She's in room 307."

It's clear that he doesn't intend to walk with me. Whatever. I'd rather not be in his despicable company either.

I continue on alone, and with each step I take, my heart rate accelerates. It's beating at a staccato rhythm by the time I reach her room. The door is open, and from the threshold, I can see her mother sitting in a chair, looking tired as hell as she rests her head on Ben's shoulder.

I knock on the doorframe. "May I come in?"

She stands abruptly, pinching her lips together. I don't know what I did, but she clearly doesn't like me very much. Either that asshole Blake talked trash about me, or she has premonition powers and suspects my mother is responsible for her unhappiness.

"Of course." She glances to the side. "Come on, Ben. Let's give them some privacy."

I step out of the way to let them through, and then I close the door. I don't want anyone eavesdropping on this conversation. Stepping forward, I steel myself for the image of Charlie in a hospital bed, but it does nothing. When I see her bruised face and her leg in a cast, my chest feels like it's caved in.

"Charlie," I murmur.

She smiles weakly. "Hey."

I move to the side of her bed but refrain from touching her. I'm not sure if she'll let me. "Are you in a lot of pain?"

"No. They gave me super-strong sedatives. They're going to

make me sleepy, but I wanted to see you before the drugs dragged me to dreamland."

"I'm here, babe."

"Troy, I'm so sorry for going total psycho bitch at the party. You didn't deserve how I treated you."

A wave of relief washes over me. She's not mad at me anymore. But the sentiment quickly vanishes when I remember the worst of the storm is yet to come. I push those negative thoughts to a corner of my mind, out of the way but easily accessible. A time will come to deal with them, but not right now.

I take Charlie's hand in mine, squeezing lightly before I lean forward and kiss her forehead. "I'm sorry, darling. I should have come after you, not taken off like a coward."

"No, you were right to give me space." She cups my cheek. "I love you that much more for that."

My breath catches, and then a slow grin unfurls on my lips. "You love me?"

"Very much so."

"It's the first time you've told me that, you know?"

Her brows furrow. "No it's not. I told you yesterday."

"Kind of." I run my hand through her hair, unsurprised to see it tremble a little. "When I got the call about you, I got so scared. It was one of the worst days of my life. If anything worse had happened to you, I...." I shake my head as the guilt of Robbie's death becomes a million times heavier. "I couldn't live with myself."

"Troy, what happened wasn't your fault. Just like Robbie's death wasn't."

I recoil as if she'd struck me. "You don't know what you're saying."

"Not the details, but I can read a guilty heart when I see one. Why do you carry such a burden?"

I walk away, giving my back to her. "It was my fault Robbie died, Charlie. I was supposed to be watching him in the pool. I got distracted, and he drowned."

"You were only eight when it happened. No parent should put that responsibility on a child."

I laugh bitterly. "Oh, my parents were the first ones to put the blame on me."

"That doesn't make it true."

My eyes burn, and the lump in my throat becomes too large. I can barely breathe. "In this case, it does, Charlie."

"Troy, look at me."

Crossing my arms, I look over my shoulder. Charlie's blue eyes are brighter than before, and tears have left streak marks on her cheeks.

I turn fully and stride back to her side. "Babe, don't cry for me. I'm not worth it."

"You're worth these tears and a million more. I'm so sad that your parents let you grow up with that terrible guilt. You're a good person, Troy. Much better than me. Sometimes I think I don't deserve you."

I carefully capture her face between my hands and softly kiss her on the lips. "You've got things twisted around. I'm the one who doesn't deserve you."

The secret that her father asked me to keep comes to the fore-front of my mind, making my statement even truer.

She chuckles against my lips. "Fine. Then we're both unde-serving rascals who are perfect for each other."

A knock on the door makes me straighten up. Charlie's mother is back and still sporting an unfriendly look.

"Charlie needs to rest. You can come back tomorrow."

"When can she go home?" I ask.

"In a few days."

"I can turn the office room downstairs into a temporary bedroom for you," I tell Charlie.

"Oh, she won't be going back with you. She'll be staying with us for a while."

"Mom, I didn't agree with that," Charlie complains.

"Hush now, honey. You need to rest." Her mother fusses over her, adjusting her pillow and then lowering the bed.

"You should stay with your folks for a while, sweetheart," I tell her softly. "It'll be good for you. I'll come visit every day until you're ready to come back home."

Her mother narrows her eyes, but mercifully, she keeps any retort to herself.

Charlie's eyes are already getting droopy when she replies, "Okay."

CHAPTER 45

CHARLIE

I t's been a week since my accident, and Troy has come by every day to see me. I couldn't fight both my parents when they insisted I recover at their place. Dad patched things up with Mom and moved back. Funny how I don't consider their house as home anymore. The house I share with Troy is home. No, that's not right either. *He* is home. He once confessed I was his endgame. Now I know he's mine too.

Blake, Fred, and Sylvana have come to see me as well, but never at the same time as Troy. I told Blake that he needed to learn to coexist with Troy because he wasn't going anywhere. I don't think he approved of my decision, but he also didn't argue with me. I'm sure me recovering from an accident made him go easy on me.

Yesterday, Troy came over straight after the game, and because it was at the end of the day, he spent the night in Ben's room. Not that he didn't sneak into my room after everyone had gone to bed or anything. It was fun to make out in my old bedroom like two teenagers.

The issue now is, it's morning, and he's still in my room.

"Troy." I shake his arm.

Troy is spooning my side. His arm is wrapped around my stomach, one of his legs is covering mine, and his nose is pressed against the crook of my neck.

"Hmm?" he replies.

"You need to go back to Ben's room. It's morning."

"Five more minutes," he murmurs.

"Psst!" Ben's head pops around the now semi open door. "Mom is up. Just thought you should know."

"Told you." I give Troy a light shove.

He rolls over, miscalculates, and ends up on the floor.

"Ouch," he blurts out.

Ben snorts. "Smooth, very smooth."

"Are you okay?" I crane my neck to get a better view. This whole immobility deal is already driving me crazy.

"Yeah, I'm fine. I'm glad your room is carpeted." He jumps back to his feet with the grace of a cat, and my body responds, remembering Troy's fingers between my legs last night.

Damn it. Now I'm horny again.

At least he's wearing a T-shirt with his sweatpants rather than his usual state of undress, but there's an unmistakable bulge in the front that makes my face unbearably hot.

I glance at the door and let out a relieved breath. Ben is already gone.

"You'd better go before my mother catches you here."

"I'm going. Definitely don't want to lose my visiting rights." He leans over and kisses me on the lips. It's too quick for my liking.

Pouting, I say, "I can't wait to move back home."

"Me too, babe. We'll try to convince your folks again today. If they refuse, I'll just have to break you free like the Weasleys did for Harry in book two."

"Oh my God. I can't believe you know Harry Potter. You're just a nerd in disguise, aren't you?"

"Liking HP is hardly a qualification to be a nerd. Who doesn't like it?"

"Charlie?" Mom's voice echoes in the hallway.

"Crap. She's coming and you're still here."

Troy glances at the door and then back at me. Nonchalantly, he pulls up a chair and sits down.

"What are you doing?" I hiss.

"It's too late for me to sneak out now."

A second later, the door opens, and Mom comes in. "Charlie, wh—oh, Troy. I didn't realize you were here."

"Just came in." He flashes her an innocent smile.

Mom's lips become a thin flat line as she watches Troy through slits for a second. She hasn't warmed up to him yet, and I don't know why. True, she knows about our rough beginning, but he's been the perfect boyfriend from the get-go. I, on the other hand, have messed up royally already.

She turns to me. "I just came to ask what you would like for breakfast."

"I was thinking maybe we could eat out today. I'm tired of being cooped up."

Troy snorts, earning a questioning glance from me.

"What?"

"Sorry, you said, 'cooped up,' and it made me think of chickens."

I don't know if I should laugh or groan and end up doing a mix of both. The source of our amusement flies right over Mom's head, naturally.

"I guess we could go to your favorite diner," Mom replies.

"Really? Awesome."

Troy stands up. "I guess I'd better get into the shower, then."

"What, you're not going to help me with mine?" I joke, loving to see Mom's outraged expression and Troy's are-you-crazy look.

"Ha-ha, Charlie. You're hilarious." Mom comes to help me out of bed, and Troy uses that moment to make his escape.

"I was joking, but it's not like he hasn't seen me naked before."

Mom rolls her eyes. "Trust me on this, save your naked moments for sexy times. You don't want to ruin the magic by making him help you bathe."

I wrinkle my nose. She's right.

Since we're talking about relationships, I ask, "How are things with Dad? Is he going to stay for good?"

"We agreed to go to couples therapy. That's something," she replies in a clipped tone.

"Do you still believe he was cheating on you?"

It makes me sick to my stomach to ask, but I have to think about Ben. I don't want my parents to start fighting all over again. And if Dad was having an affair, that's something I don't think anyone can get past, no matter how hard they try. Once the trust is broken, it's gone forever.

"That's not something I'm comfortable discussing with you, Charlie. Now let's get you cleaned up for that boyfriend of yours." She helps me out of bed.

"How come I have the impression you don't like Troy very much?"

"He took Ben bungee jumping without asking us first, for starters."

"Ben already told you that he lied to Troy and bribed the operator to let him jump without parental consent."

I can't believe he'd do something reckless like that, but considering the shitty situation at home, it's not completely surprising. Ben was only trying to forget about the fighting for a while.

"It doesn't matter. He should have confirmed with us."

Gee, when Mom wants to be stubborn, she's worse than me.

"Well, you'd better get used to him. He's not going anywhere."

Mom locks her eyes with mine. "You love him, don't you?"

"Yes I do."

"I hope he's worth it."

It's impossible to miss the bitterness in my mother's tone. It makes me angry that she can't accept my happiness because her marriage is on the rocks.

"He is, Mom. Troy is worth everything."

An hour later, we're finally heading out of the house. My stomach is glued together already, making me regret I ever suggested going out for breakfast. Every little task takes forever with me hopping on one foot. I'm still getting used to my crutches, and Troy doesn't know if he should help or laugh.

"At that pace, we'll get there for lunch," Ben pipes up.

"I don't know, buddy. I think dinner," Troy piles on.

I scowl at them. "Shut up, you two. This is hard."

"Do you want help, honey?" Dad steps closer, but I shrug his outstretched hand off.

"No, I have to practice. I don't plan to sit around the house until the cast is off. I have classes to attend."

"Maybe we should take two cars," Mom says as she joins us outside. "More room for you in the back, Charlie."

I open my mouth to protest, but Troy cuts me off. "I'll take my car."

"Then I'm coming with you," I say, earning a disapproving glance from both my parents.

"Me too," Ben chimes in.

I can see them both gearing up for an argument, but the sound of a car fast approaching draws our attention to the road. This is a residential street; the speed limit is only thirty. Who's driving like this is a Formula One track?

A red sportscar stops in front of our house, burning rubber as it comes to a halt too abruptly.

"Son of a bitch," Troy mutters.

Dad takes a step forward, and a second later, a blonde hurricane exits the vehicle. Troy's mother.

What the hell is she doing here? Looking for him?

"Elaine, what are you doing here?" Dad asks her. He sounds nervous.

She laughs derisively. "Isn't this the picture-perfect image? Jason Fontaine, going out with his precious family." She staggers on her high heels, highly intoxicated, judging by her slurred speech.

"Elaine, you need to leave. Now!" Dad grabs her arm and tries to steer her back to her car.

"No!" She breaks free. "I'm not leaving until I tell everyone what a coward you are."

"I can't believe this," Mom grits out. "Is she the woman you were screwing, Jason?"

My stomach bottoms out. *Troy's mother is my father's mistress?*

I glance at Troy, imagining his shock is the same as mine. But he doesn't look surprised. His gaze is anguished and filled with guilt when our eyes lock.

"I'm sorry, Charlie," he says softly.

"You knew?" I ask, not daring to believe the truth that's right in front of my face.

"Oh yes, Troy's known for a while, right, son?" his odious mother replies. "But instead of standing by me, you betrayed me. You picked his side just so you could keep fucking his daughter."

"Mother! That's enough." Troy grips his mother's arm and drags her to his car. "I'm taking you home."

She doesn't fight him, but even if she did, it wouldn't matter. The damage is done.

I turn around too fast, needing to get away from this scene, and almost fall on my face. Ben reaches for my arm just in time and steadies me. My parents start to argue, but I block them out.

I just want to get out of here. With Ben's help, we make it back to the house.

"I think I'm going to be sick," I say.

There's not a chance I can get to a bathroom in time, so I hop on one foot to the kitchen sink and throw up the little bit of food I had in my stomach. My tears come down in rivulets, and even after I quit dry heaving, they don't stop.

"It'll be okay, Charlie," Ben says.

Damn it. I'm supposed to be offering him comfort, not the other way around.

"He lied to me, Ben."

"No, he omitted the truth."

I whip around to face him, incredulous that Ben is defending Troy. "It's the same thing."

Ben drops his chin to the floor. "I like Troy."

His heartfelt admission makes everything ten thousand times worse. I love Troy with all my heart, but how can I stay with him after this betrayal? And even if I could move past it, there's no erasing the fact that his mother broke up my parents' marriage. How can I pick him over my family?

This is hopeless.

CHAPTER 46

TROY

After I drop off my drunk-ass mother at her house, I call Andreas. I know I won't be able to talk to Charlie anytime soon, and I need to vent all my frustrations to someone. I don't disclose anything over the phone, just ask if he's home. He tells me to come over.

I find him slouching on his couch, watching football with a beer bottle in hand and a bag of chips on his lap.

"Where's Danny?" I make a beeline to the fridge. I can't do this without a drink.

"Went to visit his mom." Andreas glances at me and immediately notices something is up. "What's with the frown? Did something happen?"

I chug the beer down, almost emptying the bottle. "Yeah. My mother was screwing Charlie's dad."

"What? Are you serious?"

"I'd never joke about something like that. A few weeks back, Jane and I caught Mom with a mysterious man at a restaurant in Manhattan Beach. It was Charlie's father, only I didn't discover that until I met him at the hospital."

Andreas passes a hand over his face. "That's brutal, man."

"That's not the worst of the story. The asshole asked me to keep it a secret from Charlie. I mean, how fucked up is that?"

"Shit. And you kept your mouth shut and she found out anyway, right?"

I down the rest of the beer. "Yep. In the most spectacular fashion too. My mother showed up at her parents' house, drunk out of her mind, and spilled the beans. I had to drag her ass out of there before things got worse."

"And what about Charlie?"

I stare at the empty beer bottle while I fight to get air into my lungs. I've never felt such agony like this before. "The way she looked at me, man… so broken, and betrayed." I sigh. "I don't know."

"Dude, it's obvious she cares about you. Sure, she'll be mad as hell for a few days, but after you explain you didn't really have a choice, she'll have to understand."

I shake my head, knowing it won't be easy. "You don't understand, Andy. My mother is the person responsible for breaking up her parents' marriage. Even if she could forgive the fact that I kept that information from her, I'll be a constant reminder of the betrayal."

Andreas gets off the couch and heads over to the kitchen. He has his serious expression on, the one he usually saves for game day. "First of all, your mother wasn't responsible for breaking up anyone's marriage. If Charlie's father had an affair with her, it's because he wasn't happy in his marriage."

"Do you think that's going to matter?" I retort angrily, slamming the bottle down on the counter.

"Fine, maybe it won't matter. But if Charlie is really into you like you're into her, she'll forgive you. Grovel, do everything you can to win her back."

"I thought you didn't like Charlie."

He shrugs. "I didn't like her when she was your enemy. I have nothing against her now."

"We haven't broken up."

Yet. I know it's coming. I saw the certainty in her eyes that she believes we're over.

"Then start working on your recover game right away, Troy. You're the fucking Rushmore Rebels' quarterback. You don't know defeat."

I stand straighter. "You're right. I'm not going to give up Charlie without a fight. She's my endgame."

"That's what I'm talk—wait, what? She's your endgame? For real?" His eyes widen.

"Yeah, for real."

"How do you know?"

"I just do. Hopefully, you'll get that someday."

He twists his face into a scowl. "No, thanks. Hard pass. I like my bachelor life too fucking much to give it up. The only chains I'd be down for are the ones that come with whips."

"Why do you have to make everything so dirty?"

He lifts his shoulders in an it-is-what-it-is gesture. "That's how I roll, man. What are you going to do about Charlie?"

"I can't go back to her folks'. It must be war central right now, and my presence would just make everything worse."

"What about your mom's car?"

"Ah hell. I'd forgotten about that."

Andreas grabs his jacket from the back of the highchair. "Come on. We're going back, and now you have an excuse. I'll drive your mom's car, and you talk to Charlie."

"Shit. That means I have to get her car keys first. Great."

"Perfect. That should give everyone time to chill out back at Charlie's."

He heads for the front door like he's about to step onto the field before a game, his shoulders squared and chin high. He said I don't know defeat, but he's the one who doesn't believe in it.

CHARLIE

I've been lying in bed, crying my eyes out since Troy left with his mother. At least my parents are no longer shouting, but only because Mom kicked Dad out of the house. She asked for a divorce—no, shouted for one. Even the neighbors must have heard her.

Troy has called several times and sent a dozen messages. I've ignored them all. I'm not ready to deal with his betrayal face-to-face. I'm so torn about everything. Maybe Ben is right, and Troy was put in a terrible situation. But it changes nothing.

There's a knock on the door, and then Ben pushes it open. "Charlie, are you feeling better?"

"Not yet." I sit up in bed. "How are you?"

"I'm okay. At least now we know."

"You're handling this better than I am."

"I think I accepted it a long time ago." There's a pause, and Ben seems guilty about something. "Troy is here. He wants to talk to you."

"No." My voice comes out in a desperate plea. "I can't talk to him right now, Ben. You know that."

"A-are you going to break up?"

"I'd like to know that too." Troy comes in after Ben, and I feel like my heart stops beating for a second.

"You shouldn't have come."

"No, I had to, Charlie. I couldn't just stay home because it's killing me not knowing where we stand. So, I'll ask you again. Are we breaking up?"

He pierces me with the saddest, most broken gaze I've ever seen on him, and it destroys me. I want to tell him that we can move past this, but I can't form the words.

"I don't think there's any other way," I reply through a choke.

Tears well up in my eyes. My heart squeezes so tight, I can't breathe.

Troy remains stoic, frozen; the only glimpse of emotion I can see are in his anguished eyes. He clenches his jaw and then says tightly, "I'm not going to try to explain myself, or ask for your forgiveness. I know right now, nothing I say will make you feel better or change your mind. I'll walk away and give you the space you need, but I'll wait for you, Charlie. However long it takes, I *will* wait for you."

"Troy—"

"No, don't say anything. You can't ask me to stop loving you. It won't happen. You don't need to move out. I'm going to stay with Andy until you're ready for me to come home."

I'm witnessing the boy I love with all my heart shatter in front of me, and I can't bring myself to end his suffering. I'm frozen, powerless.

Troy turns to Ben and squeezes his shoulder. "Take care of your sister, buddy."

He's gone before I can get a word out.

It turns out, the song was right. We were meant to break.

CHAPTER 47

CHARLIE

It's been five days since I broke up with Troy, and I'm a complete wreck. Dad didn't move out like I'd expected him to, but the situation at my folks' is tense as hell. It's gotten so bad that Tammara's parents invited Ben to spend the week with them.

My heart is squeezed tight as I step foot into my house. Good on his word, Troy has moved out, and his absence is like a black hole in what used to be paradise to me.

Fred drove me—I couldn't deal with Blake and his I-told-you-so stare. He sets my bags on the floor and asks, "Do you want me to bring your bed downstairs?"

"What's the point? I still have to go to the second floor to shower and change clothes."

"True."

We don't speak for a while, and the silence begins to smother me.

I sense his eyes burning a hole through my face. Without looking at him, I say, "Out with it already, Fred."

"I know it's not my place to mention it, but are you sure you can't fix things with Troy? You look pitiful."

"Gee, thanks, Captain Obvious."

"I'm serious, Charlie. It's not his fault that your dad is an ass —um, that he cheated."

"I know, but it's his fault for not telling me as soon as he found out."

"Honestly, you can't say you wouldn't have kept your mouth shut as well if the situation had been reversed. You're recovering from an accident."

Fred's words feel like a dagger twisting in my chest. He's not wrong, but I can't even think about Troy without remembering that horrible scene with his drunk mother, telling everyone about the affair.

"Can we please stop talking about Troy?"

"Okay. Well, what do you want to do?"

"I think I just want to be alone for now. Work on some school assignments."

"Okay then. I'm off tomorrow if you want to hang out."

I already know I won't, but it will be easier to decline his offer tomorrow over a text message. If I say no now, he's going to bug me until I agree to do something.

"Sounds good."

As soon as Fred walks out the door, I'm swept under a wave of sorrow. My chest is too tight, and I can't get air into my lungs. I try to watch TV, but quickly, I realize it won't work. The only thing showing is Troy's picture. The sanest thing would be to move out, if I had that option. Everything in this house reminds me of him.

I head to my room. Maybe if I surround myself with my things, it will help. But as soon as I reach the landing, my gaze travels down the corridor to his bedroom door. I move toward it, knowing that opening that door will only make things worse. But I'm a glutton for punishment.

My eyes zero on in his bed, and a choke gets lodged in my

throat. I move toward it and then run my fingers over the mattress. My eyes burn as they fill with tears, and yet I don't turn around to walk away. I lie down and bring his pillow to my nose. I'm drowning in his scent, in his presence, but I don't care.

Can someone die of heartbreak? Because it feels like that's what's happening to me. The tears come through a loud choke, and quickly, they drench Troy's pillow. I hold on to it and don't fight the ugly cry that wrecks me to pieces.

wake up, bleary-eyed, not knowing where I am for a moment. But Troy's faint aftershave scent reaches my nose, reminding me that I slept on his bed last night. I sit up, rubbing the sleep from my eyes. I feel weak, hollow, but not completely destroyed as I did yesterday. The sharp pain in my chest is still there, though.

Slowly, I get ready for another bleak day. Thanks to the cast, it takes me an hour to get to the kitchen and fix my caffeine deprivation problem. As I wait for it to brew, the tone of a text message draws my attention to my phone. I left it on the kitchen counter yesterday. I'm surprised the battery didn't die.

The name that pops on my screen makes my stomach clench tight. Ophelia hopes I'm going to visit her today. She wants to talk. There's no need to specify the topic. I'm tempted to blow her off, but she's always been kind to me, and in all honesty, I'm in deep need of her advice.

I reply that I'll be there, and then I text Fred. He offered to spend time with me, so that's what we're doing today. His answer comes swiftly. He's a minute from my place. It seems he wasn't going to let me blow him off today and was already en route to kidnap me.

Exactly a minute later, he's knocking on my door. I hop

toward it to be faster. I'm getting better with the crutches, but it's still a pain to use them.

"Morning, sunshine," he greets me with a broad smile.

"Why are you so cheerful? Isn't it too early for you?"

"Yep, but I need to bring an extra dose of good vibes to counter your foul mood."

"I haven't had coffee yet." I hop back to the kitchen.

"I brought treats." He follows me.

"Good."

"What are we doing today?" He sets the treats bag on the counter.

"I have to visit Ophelia at Golden Oaks." I grab two mugs from the cupboard, purposely giving my back to him. I'm sure he'll have an opinion about it.

"Do you think visiting his grandmother is a good idea?"

I sigh, turning around. "No. But I owe her an explanation. I broke Troy's heart."

"Hmm. Okay."

Fred doesn't press further, allowing me to have breakfast in peace. I have to force the doughnut down, though because my appetite is gone. The knots in my stomach are taking away all the joy of eating.

We keep the conversation light on the way to Golden Oaks. Fred monopolizes most of it. But by the time he parks in front of the building, I'm a ball of nerves.

"Here we are," he says. "Do you want me to go in with you?"

"No, it's better if I talk to her alone."

He covers my hand with his. "It's going to be okay, Charlie."

I nod, and then get out of the car.

Cheyenne is behind the reception desk this morning, and I wish she weren't here. She hasn't seen me since the accident. Plus, she knows me well and immediately notices I'm a hot mess.

"Honey, is everything okay?" she asks.

"No, not really. But hopefully, it will be better after my visit. Is Ophelia in her apartment?"

"Yes, she's expecting you."

"Okay, thanks."

Ophelia's apartment is an efficient unit with a small kitchen, a living room, a balcony facing the gardens, and a master suite. Once, I asked her if she missed her spacious house, but she said she'd rather live in a small place and have good company than live in a mausoleum alone.

The front door is open, so I call her name as I walk in.

"I'm outside, Charlie," she replies.

I cross the living room, finding her sitting on a chair with a blanket over her lap and a mug of tea between her hands.

"Hi," I say.

She turns to me with a tight smile on her face. "Would you like some tea? The water in the kettle is still hot."

"No, I'm good, thanks." I pull up a chair.

There's a moment of silence when Ophelia just stares at me, making me uncomfortable.

"Where are Jack and Louis?" I ask.

"Probably out, pestering someone. How have you been, dear?"

I shrug. "I've been better."

"Dreadful thing, what happened with your folks." She shakes her head. "Elaine's never had much of a moral compass."

"She didn't sin alone," I reply bitterly.

"No, but that showdown was all her. She's always been like that, creating drama and placing the blame on others instead of owning up to her mistakes."

Ophelia's comment makes me think about what Troy told me. "Did she really blame Troy for Robbie's death?"

Her eyes cloud, and her mouth becomes a flat line. "Yes. She and Jonathan both did. I tried to tell Troy it wasn't true. He wasn't supposed to be looking after Robbie. He was a kid, for crying out loud, and Robbie had his floaties on. Elaine and

Jonathan got distracted at the party and didn't notice that he had somehow gotten rid of them. I was the one who found Robbie, drowned in the pool." She closes her eyes and shudders. "It was awful."

"Troy vehemently believes he's guilty."

She shakes her head. "I've lost count of how many times I've told him the truth."

My eyes fill with tears again, and there are too many to keep contained. I wipe off the ones that roll down my cheeks.

"You must think I'm a terrible person to have ended things with him."

Ophelia gives me a pitiful glance. "Oh dear. I don't think that at all. I can read in your eyes how much this separation is costing you."

I drop my gaze to my lap. "I miss him so, so much. But it feels like a betrayal to my mother if I'm together with him. It's stupid."

"No, it's not. You're a good daughter, but remember, you can't keep your happiness on hold because someone close to you is miserable. Life is too short for that kind of nonsense."

Sagging my shoulders forward, I let out a heavy exhale. "I know. I just need more time."

CHAPTER 48

CHARLIE

Six weeks have gone by since the breakup. Blake, Fred, and Sylvana all helped me during the first week until I got used to the crutches, and they also alternated in giving me rides to school.

Good on his word, Troy has given me space. He hasn't called or texted. His absence from my life has been glaring, awful. And living in Ophelia's house without him is the hardest thing I've had to do. I thought that with time, the hole in my chest would hurt less, but the pain is as acute as ever.

My parents decided to stay married and give it another try. They've been seeing a therapist, and I hope they can work things out. I don't know how Mom had it in her to forgive him. I know I couldn't forgive my husband if he had an affair, and to be honest, I haven't forgiven Dad yet.

Glutton for punishment as I am, I've been watching all of Troy's games on TV. Whenever I see him on the screen, it feels like a dagger is piercing my chest. God, I miss him so damn much. Is it fair that I'm putting us through this misery when my parents have already decided to put the past behind them?

Ophelia's words come back to haunt me. I said I needed more time, and I think—no, I *know*—I'm ready.

I pick up my phone and pull up Troy's number. I want to text him, but I don't know what to say. Sorry doesn't seem to cut it. He told me he'd wait for me, but I feel like I'm the bitch in this story. He moved out of his own house so I wouldn't have to look for a place to live. He was the perfect boyfriend, and I'm a fucking shrew.

Instead of calling or texting him, I text Jane instead, asking if she can talk. If I'm going to ask Troy to forgive my idiocy, I have to show him how much he means to me. She replies to my message a minute later and tells me she'll come over.

As I wait, I begin to run through ideas of what I could do for Troy. The time speeds by, and before I know it, she's knocking on my door. I've been leaving it unlocked during the day since it's such a pain to move these days.

"Come in," I tell her.

"Hi, Charlie," she greets me, then closes the door. "You know it's not safe to have the door unlocked, right?"

"I know. I'm just too lazy to get up from the couch. Don't tell your brother, okay?"

She makes a face that I can't interpret. "I haven't mentioned you to him at all."

My heart sinks. Why did I think Jane would be sympathetic to me?

"Oh. You must think I'm awful for breaking up with him."

"I get why you did it, but I hate seeing my brother hurting that bad. Are you sure you can't get past what my mother did?"

"I miss Troy terribly, Jane. But I was too caught up in my own pain to be able to stay with him."

"Was?" she asks. "Does that mean you're not sure about your decision anymore?"

"What I did was awful, I know. I hurt him. So saying 'I'm sorry, can I get you back?' won't do."

She widens her eyes in surprise. "Oh my God. You're getting back together!"

"If he wants me back."

Insecurity takes hold of me. He told me he'd wait, but honestly, I wouldn't blame him if he didn't.

"Charlie, my brother is crazy about you. I've never seen a guy more in love with someone than he's in love with you."

I smile weakly. "I feel the same way about him. You have no idea how agonizing the six weeks have been. Which proves that I'm the stupidest girl alive for ever letting him go."

"I'm not going to say you weren't, but I'm also not going to hold that over your head. I'm guessing you want my help with wooing my brother back?"

"Yes. I want to sweep him off his feet."

Jane laughs. "Sure. It's nice to see a girl making the big, romantic gesture for a change instead of the guy with the boombox outside the girl's window."

"Right? So what should I do?"

She eyes my cast and furrows her brows. "You know Saturday's game is the last one in the season, right?"

"Yeah, I'm aware. I've been following the games on TV."

"I have an idea, but it'll require Andy's assistance and a cheerleader uniform."

My eyes widen. "Oh boy. I'm afraid to ask."

TROY

Six weeks have gone by since I moved out of Grandma's house. I haven't talked to Charlie at all during that time, but I've seen her on campus on a few occasions. Those instances were brutal, and it just made the wound in my chest bleed more. Thank God for football, which has kept me busy. The Rushmore

Rebels are kicking ass and taking names. Today's game is the last one of the season, and it feels monumental. It's the end of an era.

The rush of winning games doesn't compare to being with Charlie though. Nothing will ever compare. Ben has been keeping me updated. He's turned into our biggest supporter and believes I've given Charlie enough time to wallow in her guilt. His words, not mine. Their parents aren't getting a divorce after all, and my mother has moved on as well. She's dating a young Hollywood producer. It probably won't last, but at least her new boyfriend isn't married.

A ping from my phone warns me of an incoming text.

C harlie is going to Golden Oaks this Sunday. That's your chance.

I smile at Ben's message. He's the best spy. I text him back saying I'll be there. Despite our breakup, Charlie continues to visit Grandma. I've increased my visits too, but I've purposely avoided going when I knew Charlie would be there. It was an effort to keep my distance from her, but I didn't want to ruin everything by putting the second part of my plan in motion too soon.

On the day we broke up, I had every intention to beg her not to end things. But on the drive to Littleton, I realized groveling wouldn't work. Charlie's protectiveness would kick in big time. So I retreated and bided my time, waiting to strike when her resolve to stay away had weakened. According to Ben, the time is now.

Coach expects us in the locker room in half an hour. Andreas and Danny are already making noise in the kitchen, preparing breakfast. As usual, they're also chatty and loud, but all I can hear from my bedroom are muffled voices as if they're whispering.

When I walk into the room, they stop talking at once and glance at me.

"What are you girls gossiping about?" I grab a box of cereal and fill a bowl.

"Nothing," Danny replies.

"I can't believe this is your last game of the season," Andreas says. "I'm already so fucking sad."

I watch him through slits. "Right. Because you're a big, emotional guy."

"Hey. There's a heart beating underneath all this muscle, bro." He presses a hand against his chest in an exaggerated gesture.

"Yeah, yeah. Just don't cry in your Cheerios, okay?"

Andreas turns to Danny. "Do you see the shit I have to put up with? You'd better treat me better, bro."

Danny shakes his head. "Sure, Andy." He turns to me. "Is Jane coming to the game?"

I stand straighter. Danny's never asked about Jane before. "I think so. Why?"

He shrugs. "No reason. Just curious."

"She asked for six tickets, actually. I wonder who she's bringing with her."

"Maybe your grandma and her two boyfriends," Andreas pipes up.

I groan. "Fuck. You're probably right. I can't deal with them."

"Why? Because they're sharing her?" Danny laughs.

"That's not the problem. The issue is that they love to talk about their sex life."

Andreas wrinkles his nose. "Ew. Why did you have to say that? Now I'm picturing your grandma doing the Eiffel Tower."

"Thanks for putting that image in my head, jackass," I say.

"You started it." He grabs an apple from the fruit bowl.

"Come on. Let's go. Talking about geriatric sex is not how I envisioned starting my day."

"Like it was mine," I grumble.

I banish that disturbing visual from my mind and think about Charlie. My heart immediately picks up speed. Tomorrow is the day. If I can't convince her to give me another chance, then that will be it for us. Which means I can't fail.

CHAPTER 49

CHARLIE

'm staring at my reflection in the mirror, thinking I must be crazy. I'm in the middle of the cheerleaders' locker room, getting ready to perform in front of thousands of Rushmore Rebel fans. This is the grand gesture Jane came up with. With the help of Andreas and his connections, I'm now an honorary cheerleader.

I pull on my skirt, trying to cover more of my ass. Man, their outfit is skimpy.

Vanessa Castro, the soccer player I met at the party I went to with Troy, comes over and stands next to me. "You're looking good, Charlie. The uniform suits you."

"I can't believe I'm doing this." I run my hand over the microskirt.

"Me neither," Heather, Vanessa's twin and cheerleader captain, pipes up. "I don't know how you're going to perform the routine on crutches."

"Please, Heather. All Charlie has to do is stand still and shake the pom-poms while you dance around her. Simple." Vanessa smirks.

"Why are you even here? Don't you have a game or something?"

Vanessa looks at me, then back at her sister. "I couldn't pass up the chance to see this performance. Besides, my game isn't until much later."

"I think it's very sweet that you're doing this for Troy," Jackie, a petite brunette, tells me. "He's such a dreamboat."

"You think every guy on the team is a dreamboat," Heather points out.

"But they are. Why do you think I became a cheerleader?" She shakes her ass and winks at her friend.

Lots of smartass comments pop in my head, but I bite my tongue and keep my opinions to myself. They're helping me, after all. I lock eyes with Vanessa, and she seems to guess exactly where my thoughts went.

"To be fair, most of the girls on campus are boy crazy," she says.

I nod. "I'm slowly beginning to realize that. I've been in my nerd cave for too long."

"And you still managed to snag the most eligible bachelor on campus." She smiles.

"And to lose him." I frown and look around the locker room. "Oh, I'm so nervous. What if I mess up and embarrass not only myself but him as well?"

"You'll be fine." She squeezes my arm.

"Sure, sure. That's why I feel like I'm going to throw up."

"If you need to hurl, you'd better do it now. We're going out in five minutes," Heather tells me.

Shit. Shit. Shit. Why did I let Jane convince me this was a good idea?

TROY

I'm with my teammates, ready to run onto the field. Outside, the crowd clamors, infusing me with the familiar rush of adrenaline. I'm going to miss this. My only regret is that Charlie isn't here to see me play. Hopefully, she'll come to the playoffs. I just have to bring my A-game tomorrow and convince her that we belong together.

With a roar, we storm the field. The crowd goes wild. The band plays our anthem, but not from their usual spot in the bleachers. They're down on the field too. Maybe they've prepared something special for today's game. We head for the bench, and then I notice the cheerleaders are also with the band.

The music changes to a familiar tune. It's only when the actual song spews from the speakers, mingling with the band, that I recognize it. It's "Hey Mickey," but the lyrics aren't the original. Instead of Mickey, the singer is saying Troy.

The band parts, giving space for the cheerleaders to do their routine. Then I see her. Charlie's in a cheerleader uniform, singing along. She can't dance like the other girls thanks to her crutches, but she's shaking her ass to the beat of the song. Her eyes catch mine, and then she winks at me.

"Dude, is that your girl?" Puck, our linebacker, asks me.

"It sure is."

I can't keep my eyes off Charlie. I'm afraid if I do, she'll disappear, and then I'll realize I'm hallucinating the whole thing. I'm grinning from ear to ear as I watch her perform with the cheerleaders. When the song ends, she heads in my direction. I don't wait for her to reach me. I run to her, meeting her halfway, and crush my lips to hers.

The crowd goes even crazier, shouting and whistling.

She drops her crutches and then throws her arms around my neck. God, I missed her mouth, her smell, the sounds she makes when she kisses me. I'm sporting a raging boner in the middle of the football field in front of thousands of spectators, and I don't care one fucking bit.

Charlie breaks the kiss, but her mouth stays close to mine. "I'm so sorry, Troy. I was an idiot for letting my emotions drive you away. Please say you forgive me."

"Babe, I told you I'd wait for you."

"I was afraid you would realize with time that I wasn't worth it."

"You're worth it, Charlie. Get that into your thick head. I love you so damn much. You're not getting rid of me that easily."

I kiss her again, even though I shouldn't. Coach Clarkson is probably about to have an aneurysm because I'm delaying the game.

Someone taps my shoulder. "Okay, lover boy. You'd better save the make-out session for after the game."

I pull back but keep Charlie firmly in my hold.

Andreas bends over, grabs her crutches from the grass, and then hands them over. "Shit, girl, that uniform fits you like a glove. Maybe you should join the squad."

She shakes her head. "I don't think so. I've never felt more self-conscious in my life."

"When do you have to return it?" I ask.

"I don't know. I was planning on bringing it home to wash it first."

My lips curl into a wicked grin. "Good."

We return to the bench, and sure as shit, Coach is fuming.

"Oh no. Did I get you in trouble?" Charlie asks.

I chuckle. "Nah. That's the coach's normal expression."

"I'd better go find my seat. Go break some bones."

"Says the girl with her leg in a cast," Andreas mutters next to me.

I ignore him, way too fucking happy right now to let his comments get to me. I watch Charlie walk toward the bleachers with Vanessa Castro in tow. I didn't even know they were friends. I don't look away until Charlie vanishes from sight.

"All right, everybody, you've had your fun. Now it's time to focus," Coach begins his pep talk.

Knowing Charlie is here to watch me is better than any motivational speech anyone could give me. I've got my girl back, and now it's time to prove that I'm not the unenthusiastic football player she thought I was when we met.

I'm going to play the best game of my life.

CHARLIE

After the game—which the Rushmore Rebels won, by the way—we all head out to celebrate at a pizzeria recommended by Andreas. And when I say we, I mean, Ophelia, her boyfriends, Jane, Ben, and Danny all join us.

I had the best time watching Troy play. It was thrilling, and also sexy as hell to see him in his element. I lost my voice from shouting so much. I couldn't believe how wrong I had been about Troy not giving a fuck about football anymore. He was on fire on that field, and now I understand why his fans treat him like a god. He *is* one.

It's almost eleven by the time we walk through the door. Troy made me keep my cheerleader outfit on, and now he's watching me with that hungry gaze of his that makes my toes curl in my shoes. I thought he was going to pounce as soon as the door closed, but instead, he's just staring at me.

"What?" I glance down. "Something wrong?"

"No, there's nothing wrong. I just want to drink you in first, memorize every inch of your body."

I smirk at him. "I didn't know you had a thing for cheerleaders."

"I don't have a thing for them. I have a thing for *you*. The uniform is just a bonus."

"This cast makes it uber sexy." I lift my leg jokingly.

He walks over, and like they do in the movies, he takes me in his arms and angles our bodies sideways as he kisses me. It's a deep and fast kiss that leaves me breathless. When he straightens us again, I want to jump in his arms. Too bad it's impossible right now. But Troy seems to be having the same train of thought as me. He sweeps me off my feet and heads for his bedroom, taking the stairs two steps at a time.

We don't speak as he carefully sets me on the edge of the mattress. My body is humming with anticipation, and my fingers tingle with the need to touch him. Wordlessly, he kneels in front of me, opening my legs. His warm hands feel like gasoline over my already burning skin.

"You know, I was ready to ambush you at Golden Oaks tomorrow," he confesses.

"Really?"

"I wouldn't have taken no for an answer."

He runs his fingers up my thighs until they disappear underneath my skirt. My clit throbs, ready for Troy's fiery touch, but he stops at the edge of the cheer briefs. Desire spreads through my body like wildfire, but it's my love for the beautiful man in front of me that overflows my heart and takes over everything.

I cup his face, fighting the tears that are quickly gathering in my eyes. "I wouldn't have said no."

His heartfelt smile is like a caress. "You didn't need to make a big gesture to win me over. I would have come running with just a simple text."

"That wouldn't have been enough. I messed up, Troy. I let my fear and anger drive you away. I couldn't accept your love because I was afraid it would hurt my mother and Ben too much. I was a coward." A rogue tear escapes my eye.

Troy reaches for it and wipes it off with his thumb. "No you weren't. It took courage to put your family first."

I capture his face between both hands and bring my face

closer to his. "Never again, Troy. I'll never take you for granted again. You're it for me. Search over."

Looking deep into my eyes, he says, "Search over indeed."

Then he claims my mouth, and we both silently vow to make up for the lost time.

CHAPTER 50

TROY – THREE MONTHS LATER

oday is Robbie's birthday, a date that always leaves me unbearably sad and consumed with guilt. But it's also the first day of a LARP weekend, and after postponing coming to one of those for a month, I couldn't say no to Charlie anymore. I mean, what's a better way to distract myself from the torment of my past than by pretending to be someone else for two days?

The past three months with Charlie have been incredible, but with my looming graduation on the horizon, I have a decision to make. The offer to be an ambassador for a digital media company and travel the world is still on the table. I haven't accepted it yet because I don't want to leave Charlie. I want all my adventures to be with her.

I eye the brochure I picked up from the school administration on my desk. Charlie mentioned once that she considered applying to an exchange program but didn't because of Ben. I could hear the wistful tone in her voice when she told me that story. Ben is thriving now, and their parents are doing okay, so there isn't really a reason for her not to follow her dreams.

My thinking is also self-serving. We could go to Europe together, using our place there as a home base for our travels. I don't know if she's going to see it that way, but fuck it, I won't know the answer if I don't ask.

I grab the brochure and put it in my backpack with my character sheet. Then I glance around my room to make sure I didn't forget to pack anything. When I make it downstairs, Charlie has breakfast ready—coffee, pancakes, and bacon.

"Good morning, babe," she greets me with a big smile.

"Morning. Wow. Is that all for me?" I set the duffel bag down and circle around the kitchen counter to pull her into a hug.

"Yep. You need your energy for this weekend's quest, my dear Gunther."

I chuckle. Gunther Crook is the name we came up with for my character. We must have been drunk when it happened.

I kiss her deeply and would keep it going, but my stomach has other ideas.

"I guess I *am* hungry after that morning workout." I bite her lower lip and then turn around to grab a piece of bacon.

"Don't talk like you were the only one who had to work." She smacks my ass and then saunters out of my reach.

Charlie's phone breaks our silly moment, and I'm glad. I was close to attacking her mouth again, which would have led to more sex. Not a bad thing, of course, but I want to get on the road early to avoid traffic.

She answers, "Hi, Blake."

I try to suppress a groan and fail. Blake and I have agreed on a truce. We'll never become best friends, but we can now be in the same room without arguing... much. It's hard for me to accept their friendship, but he's important to her, and I have to understand that.

Charlie glances pointedly at me, her silent plea for me to be nice. I shove a piece of pancake in my mouth, then smile.

She listens to what he's saying, furrowing her eyebrows a little. "Hold on," she tells Blake.

She covers her phone's mouthpiece and whispers, "Blake's car broke down, and he needs a ride. Fred and Sylvana already left. Do you mind if he comes with us?"

I sigh in resignation. She knows I'd never say no to that, but I appreciate that she asked. "Fine. But you owe me." I point at her.

She rolls her eyes and tells Blake the good news. To be fair, it must pain him just as much to ride with me, so that's something.

t takes just thirty minutes on the road for Blake to complain about something. I've been listening to Iron Maiden, and he has a problem with that.

"Can you please change the music?" he moans from the back seat.

"I guess we can listen to pop for a while." Charlie reaches for the radio control, but I bat her hand away.

"What do you think you're doing?" I ask her.

"Come on, Troy. It's two against one."

I laugh. "Where did you get the impression this was a democracy? I'm driving, and what did we learn from watching your now new favorite show?"

Charlie's shoulders sag forward. Pouting, she replies, "You drive, you pick the music. I shut my cakehole."

I tap her leg. "Exactly."

"Jerk," Blake mutters from the back seat, earning a glower from me via the rearview mirror.

"What was that, bro?"

"Saying what Charlie should have."

Blake is being an asshole, but I choose to let it slide. To be fair, I'm also not playing nice with the music. But to make a point, I listen to Iron Maiden for five more minutes before I switch to a classic rock station. That's my compromise; I'm not going to listen to pop music.

When "Carry On My Wayward Son" by Kansas comes on, I pump up the volume and sing it at the top of my lungs. Charlie joins me in the singalong, and to my surprise, Blake does too. By the time we arrive at the campgrounds where the event will take place, I'm no longer bothered by Blake's stick-up-his-ass ways.

I'm surprised to see all the cars in the parking lot. I didn't realize it was that big of an event.

"How many people come to these things?" I ask, something I should have done way sooner.

"We usually get ten to fifteen participants, but this is the first spring event, so we probably have double that."

Great, twice as many people to witness my humiliation. I'm glad I'll be almost unrecognizable, wearing my troll costume. It was a good call to not tell the guys I was coming this weekend anyway. Andreas and Danny have been pestering me about it for weeks. If they knew it was today, I wouldn't put it past them to come here to capture my humiliation and post it all over the internet.

I veer for the trunk to grab our stuff, but Blake beats me to it, and not only does he haul out his duffel bag, but also Charlie's.

"I'll take that." I reach for her bag strap.

"Will you relax? I was just being helpful," he says.

"Give it to me. I can carry it," Charlie butts in.

"Nonsense, babe. I'm good." I flash her a smile.

"Fine. Be my guest."

She skips ahead, bouncing her glorious hair. It's longer now, almost to her waist. The movement is hypnotizing, and for a moment, I'm content to just watch her go.

I'm suddenly shoved to the side when someone flings his arm around my shoulders and leans into me. "Troy, my man. I can't believe you actually made it."

Fred, one of Charlie's closest friends, is the one making the fuss. Since he's not a pain in the ass like Blake, and has no past with Charlie, it was easy to warm up to him even after the severed head prank.

"I totally caved. But what can I say? I've seen Charlie's costume, and it's best if I'm here to fend off any jackass who thinks he has a chance with her." I glance at Blake fleetingly.

"For the thousandth time, I do not want Charlie back," he says before storming off ahead.

Fred pats me on the shoulder. "You really don't have to worry about him. He has zero interest in Charlie as a lover. I think he has a new girlfriend, but you didn't hear it from me. Blake is uber private."

"Like I'd gossip about his love life." I scoff.

Fred grins. "Come on. Let's get you registered, and then it's show time."

CHARLIE

Troy is so nervous, it's adorable. He keeps fidgeting where he stands, watching what everyone does with rapt attention. He told me once that he hated anything theatrical thanks to a bad experience where he forgot his lines in a play, but the beauty of LARP is that it's all improv. You just have to go with the flow and stay in character.

After the dark forces cast a curse across the entire land, my character, Raven the Sorceress, suggests a partnership with Gunther Crook. Blake's character, Philippe Di Biase, is a rogue vampire knight who's against it, but he's also against every idea the group suggests. That's his character.

While Blake is busy with his monologue, listing why trusting a troll is a terrible idea, Troy steps closer to me and whispers, "Why am I not surprised this toad is against me?"

"Shh, you have to stay in character." I elbow him lightly in the stomach.

He pinches my butt in retaliation, daring me with his eyes to say something. I watch him through slits, but then Blake asks Gunther a question.

"Come again?" Troy asks.

"I asked what you have to say for yourself, monster."

"Well, for starters, who are you calling a monster, bloodsucker?"

Blake puffs out his chest. "I'm a valuable member of the king's court. You're nothing but a grotesque creature who lives in a filthy swamp."

Troy crosses his arms and leans casually against a tree. "This 'grotesque creature' is the only one who knows the secret path to the Dark Lord's castle. Don't want my help? Too fucking bad."

Okay, I think he's into it now, but probably because of his feud with Blake. I don't care, he's saying exactly what Gunther Crook would, so everyone is happy.

"Oh, pipe down, Philippe," I intervene. "Gunther is our only hope to save the lands from a much worse threat."

"Besides, if he tries anything, he'll meet my blade," Ben adds, holding his fake sword menacingly.

Troy becomes our guide, and we continue playing until the nonplaying characters make an appearance to put a wrench in our plans. A battle ensues, and when I throw a homemade bag filled with rice at a bad guy and call out a spell, the NP character makes a big show of dying and then drops to the ground. That is apparently too much for Troy, and he immediately loses his shit. He leans his hands on his knees and bursts out laughing. His reaction makes everyone else self-conscious. I grab his arm and drag him away from the scene.

"Hey, where are we going?" he asks.

"You were making everyone uncomfortable when you broke character," I hiss, not wanting to be overheard.

"Ah, babe. I'm so sorry. I didn't mean to ruin the fun."

"I know, but I think that's enough LARP for you for the day. You're still too green."

"I'll show you green." He reaches for my waist and then tosses me over his shoulder.

I smack his back. "Troy, put me down."

He laughs and breaks into a jog, only stopping when we reach our cabin. He kicks the door open, and when he sets me back down, he doesn't give me a chance to talk. His mouth is on mine in an instant, hungry, possessive. His hands explore my body in an urgent way, sliding down my sides until they reach the slits of my skirt. Caught up in his fire, I yank at his costume, fighting with the straps that are keeping his armor in place.

"Ugh, why are there so many of them?" I complain.

"Leave them." He pulls my dress over my head, leaving me standing in nothing but my lingerie.

"Not fair. I'm practically naked."

He answers by getting rid of his pants and boxers. "Not the only one anymore."

His lips claim mine again, and then we're tumbling over the mattress. Troy is between my legs, pressing his erection against my center.

"I'm still wearing my panties," I say against his mouth.

He grabs both sides of them and yanks the fabric, ripping it into two pieces. "Not anymore."

"You owe me a new pair." I grab his face, pulling his mouth back to mine.

"Sure, sure." He enters me fast and hard, drawing a loud moan from my lips.

He doesn't stop or slow down; we're both too horny for making love slowly. The bed creaks dangerously, and I'm afraid we're going to break it. But despite the loud noise the furniture is making, Troy keeps pumping harder and faster until both of us are at the edge of a cliff. He grunts when he comes, and I bite his shoulder when I do seconds later.

This is us. Crazy, impulsive, complete.

Minutes later, I'm resting with my head against his chest.

He's still wearing his troll armor, so I make lazy circles with my fingers around his belly button.

"If you're hoping for a second round, I'm going to need a few more minutes," he tells me.

"It's okay. I'm happy just staying like this for a little bit."

We don't speak for another minute, and then I decide to ask something that's been nagging me for a while—what he plans to do after he graduates. We've been avoiding the topic since we got back together, but we can't do that forever.

"Babe, have you decided what you're doing once school is over?"

"I have, actually."

I lean on my elbow so I can see his face, my heart hammering in my chest. "Really?"

"I'm taking that brand ambassador job I told you about."

"The one where you have to travel the world?" I ask through the lump in my throat.

My worst fear is coming to pass. Troy is going to leave me.

"Yeah."

I sit up, putting some distance between us. "It's a great opportunity."

Troy rolls out of bed and then grabs something from his backpack before sitting next to me. "Here."

"What is this?" I grab the brochure from his hand.

"You told me you wanted to study abroad for a semester. There's still time to apply, and the lady at the administration office told me you would be a shoo-in."

"I don't understand."

"I want us to see the world together, Charlie. We'll start with Europe while you're in London. We can travel on weekends. I don't want to go anywhere without you, babe. Those miserable six weeks we were apart were enough."

I'm on the verge of crying, but I keep the tears at bay for the moment. I gave up on the idea because of Ben before, but my brother has proven to me over and over again that he doesn't need me to be his champion. He can fight his own battles.

I want Troy to come to a realization of his own as well. Jane told me what today is, and the haunted glints I caught in his eyes a few times when he thought I wasn't looking killed me. I don't want Troy to keep carrying this immense guilt.

"I will apply under one condition."

"Oh? What is it?"

"I want you to stop blaming yourself for what happened to your brother."

He recoils, closing off his expression in an instant. Facing away from me, he breathes out heavily. "I wish it were that simple, Charlie. My own parents told me it was my fault."

"No offense, babe, but your parents are vile. Ophelia told me what happened. Your parents got distracted, socializing, and didn't see when Robbie removed his water wings. She was the one who raised the alarm when she got near the pool. Do you remember that?"

"No, not really." He presses a closed fist against his chest. "My memories of the pool are blurry at best. My only vivid memory is of my mother shaking me in a rage, screaming it was my fault."

"Oh, Troy." I throw my arm around his shoulders and hug him tight. "I'm so sorry."

He leans into me. "How come Grandma never told me that story?"

"She did, many times over. But I think you just blocked her out."

Troy turns to me. "Thank you for telling me again."

His eyes are so damn sad, but at least the anguish is gone.

"I couldn't let you keep believing that lie. You're a good person, Troy, better than anyone I know. You deserve to be free of that awful guilt."

He cups my cheek. "You're so good to me, Charlie. Sometimes, I think I'm dreaming."

"Not a dream, I promise." I place a featherlight kiss on his lips. "So, do we have a deal?"

"If that means I get to see the world with you by my side, yes, that's a deal."

THE END

Thank you for reading *Heart Stopper*! Curious to know what's the deal between Andreas and Jane? Read their story in *Heart Breaker*.

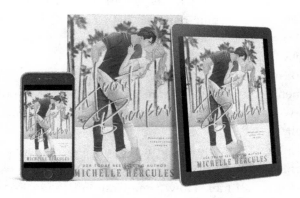

Player.
Casanova.
Heartbreaker.

I've heard it all. But the truth is, I'm the king of wanting what I can't have.

Jane is a beacon of light I didn't expect to find. Her innocence
and joy call to my dark soul.

But she's off-limits, my best friend's kid sister. And I'm a
damaged jerk with enough baggage to fill a jet plane.

All it took was one taste for my resolve to stay away to crumble.
Now I can't get her out of my head, out of my mangled heart.

If her brother finds out about us, he might kill me. If Jane finds
out about my past, she'll never speak to me again.

This love is a disaster waiting to happen, and yet, I can't help
going back for more.

FREE NOVELLA
CATCH YOU

Want to read another enemies-to-lovers sports romance? Then **scan the QR code** to get your free copy of *Catch You.*

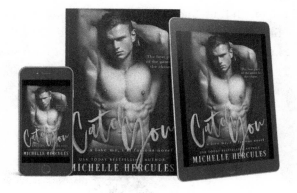

Pride and Prejudice meets Veronica Mars in this enemy-to-lovers romance.

Kimberly
I had always thought Owen Whitfield fit the mold of the

brainless jock perfectly. Group of idiot friends? Check. Vapid girlfriend? Check. Ego bigger than the moon? Check. As long as he stayed out of my way, coexisting with his kind was doable. Until one day our worlds collided, changing everything. He pissed me off so badly that I had no choice but to give him a taste of his own medicine. Little did I know that my act of revenge would come back to bite me in the ass. How was I supposed to know Owen would turn out to be the best partner in crime I could hope for?

Owen

I never paid much attention to Kimberly Dawson, but I knew who she was. Ice Queen was what we called her. She was gorgeous, no one could deny that. But she was also a condescending bitch, which was enough reason for me to stay the hell away from her. She thought I was a dumb jock, and that was okay until she came crashing into my life. Against my better judgment, I let her embroil me in her shenanigans, forcing us to spend too much time together. It was my doom. She got under my skin. She was all I could think about. I never thought I would be the knight in shining armor to anyone, not until she came along.

Scan the QR code to get your FREE copy!

ABOUT THE AUTHOR

USA Today Bestselling Author Michelle Hercules always knew creative arts were her calling but not in a million years did she think she would become an author. With a background in fashion design she thought she would follow that path. But one day, out of the blue, she had an idea for a book. One page turned into ten pages, ten pages turned into a hundred, and before she knew it, her first novel, The Prophecy of Arcadia, was born.

Michelle Hercules resides in Florida with her husband and daughter. She is currently working on the *Blueblood Vampires* series and the *Rebels of Rushmore* series.

Sign-up for Michelle Hercules' Newsletter:

Join Michelle Hercules' Readers Group:
https://www.facebook.com/groups/mhsoars

Connect with Michelle Hercules:
www.michellehercules.com
books@mhsoars.com

facebook.com / michelleherculesauthor
instagram.com / michelleherculesauthor
amazon.com / Michelle-Hercules / e / B075652M8M
bookbub.com / authors / michelle-hercules
tiktok.com / @michelleherculesauthor?
patreon.com / michellehercules